THE HUNTERS
OR THE HUNTED

The largest of the Troopers was not the tallest, but he was built like a stone fence.

"My name is Cobb," he said. "The Tinker told us you were out there last night. What did you see?"

Looking over the man and the other Troopers in turn, Cassidy fixed them all with a taut, grim stare. "You tell me," she said. "You tell me what can gut a horse like it was a rabbit and hang it up off the ground on a tree stump. Tell me what can carve a man up like a rip saw. Tell me what the hell stinks so bad that you almost gag just breathing its rotten smell—just tell me what the hell it is you're hunting . . ."

By Karen Ripley
Published by Ballantine Books:

PRISONER OF DREAMS

THE TENTH CLASS

The Slow World:
Book One: THE PERSISTENCE OF MEMORY
Book Two: THE WARDEN OF HORSES

THE WARDEN OF HORSES

Book Two of *The Slow World*

Karen Ripley

A Del Rey® Book
BALLANTINE BOOKS • NEW YORK

A Del Rey® Book
Published by Ballantine Books

Library of Congress Catalog Card Number: 94-94029

ISBN 0-345-38119-X

Manufactured in the United States of America

First Edition: June 1994

10 9 8 7 6 5 4 3 2 1

To Jaffie, Gypsy, Rosie and Sadie:
my gray mares.

PART ONE ◀▐▐▐

Chapter 1 ◀▥

"Whose stupid idea was this anyway?" Cassidy muttered, ineffectually wiping the back of one wet and sticky forearm across her perspiring forehead.

From her seat in the dirt a few feet away, Rowena looked up sharply at her. The brunette seemed heedless of the steady trickle of ropy slime that dripped from her own dirty elbows. She gestured with the limp object she held in her hand. "You mean *this* 'this'?" she asked. Then she made a grander gesture, encompassing the whole of the muggy little forest glen where both of them sat. "Or do you mean *this* 'this'?"

"Either," Cassidy growled, glaring for a few seconds at the soggy swatch of material that she held in her own hands before she summarily tossed it aside. "Both!"

"Oh," Rowena said. She shrugged agreeably. "Well, either or both, it was *your* stupid idea."

"Thanks for reminding me," Cassidy said.

For a few moments both women were silent, so silent that the ambient sounds of the small clearing became surprisingly amplified. It was already late afternoon, sliding into early evening, although the summer sun was still high on the horizon. Squirrels frolicked across the limbs of the surrounding oaks and beeches, chattering and clucking as they raced from tree to tree. Birds, disturbed from the branches, exploded into flight. From the brush at the edge of the glen, Cassidy's big gray mare, Dragonfly, snorted and grunted softly to herself as she browsed on the tender growth of twigs.

After almost three days of persistent rain, the sky had finally cleared. The sunlight had cranked up the humidity, turning the wooded land into a nearly tropical environment. Every leaf and branch still dripped with water, and a hazy sort of half-mist

3

lurked along the ground beneath the underbrush. The ground upon which she and Rowena sat was barely more than mud, but Cassidy scarcely noticed anymore. Both of the women's clothing had been soaked through for so long that neither one of them had even bothered to make the futile search for somewhere dry to sit.

"Shit!" Cassidy muttered with resignation, leaning forward to again pick up the mushy rabbit skin that she had just tossed aside. "Look at this thing—it's *slimy!* How the hell are you supposed to tan these things?"

Glancing down at the equally disappointing effort that she held in her own hand, Rowena shrugged once more. "How should I know?"

"You worked in a clothing factory, for Pete's sake!" Cassidy snapped, slapping at a mosquito on her arm.

"Yeah, and they kicked me out—jeez, they kicked me out of the whole village because of the mess I made there," Rowena reminded Cassidy needlessly. As Cassidy's scowl softened apologetically, the larger woman went on, "Besides, that was cloth and this is leather." Peering critically at the soggy rabbit hide, she amended, "Well, maybe not *leather*—actually, it looks more like one of those pie crusts I made when they tried to have me work in the kitchens."

Whether or not that had been Rowena's intention, the comment brought a brief and crooked smile to Cassidy's face. With one last rueful look at the gooey and shapeless mass of the wet rabbit skin, she daintily draped the raw hide over a convenient branch and said, "Come on, let's go check our snares; maybe we caught supper."

"Okay," Rowena readily agreed, tossing aside her own limp rabbit skin as she got to her feet.

As they left the clearing and pushed into the dripping brush, Cassidy had to concede that Rowena's candid assessment had been correct on both counts: In both cases it *had* been Cassidy's stupid idea. She was the one who had initiated their hasty flight from the simple farming village where both of them had been living. Not that Cassidy had had much choice; even if she hadn't wanted to leave, to move on and continue her search to solve the mystery of her past, the suspicious fire that had nearly destroyed all of the village's major farm buildings had forced her to go. Cassidy hadn't had anything to do with the fire—indeed, she'd nearly been killed fighting it—but as a newcomer and a Horseman she'd been the obvious target for blame. And it wasn't worth the risk of getting hanged just to stick around and try to correct the misunderstanding.

Cassidy really didn't regret leaving the village; she didn't even regret that Rowena had been compelled to come with her. The indefatigable brown-haired goatherd no more belonged in Double Creek than had Cassidy. The only thing she really regretted was the precipitous nature of their flight. They'd been forced to leave with little more than the clothes on their backs: no food, no bedrolls, no weapons. They'd had nothing but the pocket knife and matches a sympathetic stableman had given Cassidy when he had facilitated their escape.

That dearth of material possessions partially accounted for Cassidy's second stupid idea. Not only had the rainy weather made it increasingly impractical to travel without another change of clothing, but she also realized that the two of them would appear somewhat suspicious unless they were wearing something less obvious than their faded jeans and T-shirts. There was no way they could make cloth or other fabric, but Cassidy remembered the ornamented leather clothing worn by the Troopers she had seen along the river the night of the big fire. She and Rowena weren't likely to be able to kill a deer; Cassidy wasn't even sure if she would have wanted to. But there were rabbits everywhere. So what if they had to lace a few smaller hides together; how hard could it be?

Sighing at the memory of her naïveté, Cassidy ducked under a low-hanging dogwood bough, setting off a shower of droplets that caught her right over the top of her shoulder blades. Since her shirt was already soaked, the drenching didn't even feel welcomingly cool. At least it temporarily brushed off the gnats. Behind her, Rowena deftly caught the branch before it could slap her in the face.

Everything about their trip had been more difficult than Cassidy had realized it would be. She had spent most of her time in this unfamiliar world traveling by horseback, but those first journeys had differed from the most recent one in several important ways. First of all, she had been traveling with people who were well prepared to be on the trail. Both the Horsemen who had initially found her and the Villagers who had rescued her from a flood had the food and equipment for crossing the rough and wooded land. With them both she had never had to worry about what to eat or where to camp. Most important, they had all known where they were going, even if Cassidy hadn't.

Running away from the village with Rowena had been a considerably more haphazard undertaking. Rowena didn't even know how to ride; after two days of traveling bareback behind Cassidy on Dragonfly, the poor woman had saddlesores the size of pancakes on her butt. The wet weather had hardly helped. Cassidy felt sorry for her, but there was no way they could have risked stopping.

Then there was the diarrhea. Because it was late summer, the woods and upland meadows they crossed were a good source of a plentiful supply of edible berries and nuts and wild apples. What neither of the women had anticipated was the rebellious reaction of their digestive systems to a steady diet of that kind of food. By their third day out of the village, Cassidy could have sworn they were spending more time on rest stops than they did actually riding.

Nothing about the journey was turning out the way Cassidy had expected; knowing how little choice she'd had in the matter barely ameliorated her disappointment with the way things had gone. At least the gray mare was sound and strong, and they had been able to cover a lot of ground.

Now if we just knew where the hell we were going, Cassidy thought glumly.

They had already been on the run for eight days—and it seemed as if it had been raining for the last ten of them. For the first few days Cassidy had hardly even given any thought to the direction in which she'd wanted to go; she just wanted to put as much distance as possible between them and any pursuit from Double Creek. Since the barn fire had sent all of the village's horses fleeing out into the far fields, she and Rowena had been granted an obvious immediate advantage. But Cassidy figured it wouldn't take more than a day or two for the village's stablemen to round up at least some of their mounts. And then there was the unpredictable matter of Allen's return.

Slapping at another whining mosquito, Cassidy doggedly tried to put all thought of the big, bearded man out of her mind. The sheriff had not been in the village the night of the fire. Rowena was almost certain that Allen had been sent to the distant village of Silverstone again, and so the only decision the two women had made about direction when they'd first fled was not to head south, toward Silverstone, for fear of meeting up with him.

Cassidy had no idea of how to reach her elusive goal, the

Warden of Horses, leader of all that world's Horsemen. Yolanda, Raphael, and Kevin, the three Horsemen with whom she had first traveled, had deliberately deviated from their course to the Warden in order to pursue the Villagers who were herding horses. And when Yolanda was killed in the flood, and Cassidy was separated from the two younger Horsemen and rescued by Allen and the other Villagers, she had entered a society that seemed to revile the mysterious Warden. Since then Cassidy had only had one brief encounter with anyone who could have helped her reach her goal—an unexpected meeting with several of the Warden's mounted Troopers. The incident had only served to galvanize her determination to find the man.

Her boots slipping on the wet and rotted leaves of the winding little rabbit trail, Cassidy again shook back her sweat-soaked hair. The heat and humidity in the bowerlike run was like a sauna. The physical discomfort helped Cassidy pull her mind away from the vivid memory of Valerie, the calm and warriorlike Trooper she had encountered in the village's river bottom pasture the ill-fated night of the fire. The woman had been sympathetic but unable to take Cassidy with her to the Warden. All she had been able to do was give Cassidy a talisman, a little beaded ornament from her own mare's mane, and to urge Cassidy to present it for admission to the Warden's garrison. The problem was, she had neglected to tell Cassidy how to get to the garrison in the first place.

But the Troopers had given Cassidy one possible clue. When they had melted back into the foggy night, they had ridden east. And so by the third day of their flight, Cassidy and Rowena had turned east, as well.

So far they had seen no signs of pursuit from Double Creek. In fact, until yesterday they hadn't even seen any sign of any other human presence, not even so much as a foot- or hoofprint. But then at midday the day before, riding along in a dismal drizzle, they had crossed a long meadow that had been bisected by the broadly trampled passage of a large group of people. Once her initial alarm and wariness had abated, Cassidy could see that Rowena was right; the tracks were at least a day old, their edges softened and blurred by the rain. Because of the sod there were very few distinct footprints anyway, and no hoofprints that Cassidy could see; but from the width of the path and the amount of trampling that had been done to the ocher-colored grass, it must have been at least a dozen people. There had also been long scored tracks on the

exposed parts of the sandy earth that had looked like the
wheelmarks of carts; from the depth of the marks Cassidy had
deduced the vehicles had been heavily loaded.

She and Rowena had knelt in the wet grass, trying to reconstruct something about the first sign of people they had encountered since they had left the village. Cassidy had run her
fingers along a particularly weird score mark; it had been singular, not part of a pair of wheels, although it had repeated elliptical loops along its course. Noticing what Cassidy had been
studying, Rowena had suddenly given a little hoot of recognition.

"It was Tinkers," she had said with a broad grin.

Cassidy had at least a vague idea of who Tinkers were. She
remembered that Aaron, one of the village stablemen, mentioned them as the source of certain simple manufactured
things, such as the matches he'd given Cassidy, and his cooking pots and pans. But Cassidy had had a problem reconciling
that fuzzy image of kettle-makers with the evidence of a large
traveling troop of people.

"Where are they going?" she'd asked Rowena.

The brunette had laughed again, shaking back the rain from
her frizzled hair. "With the Tinkers, who knows? They trade
stuff, so they're always traveling."

Cassidy had frowned, studying the strange tracks again.
"You mean they don't come from any village?"

"They go to every village," Rowena had corrected her.
"Come and go, that's what they do. They make the stuff they
trade."

That prospect would have been a tempting notion, had they
anything to trade. The two women probably could have gotten
all of the supplies they so sorely lacked from the itinerant peddlers. As it was, though, Cassidy had been far more concerned
with their security.

"We're going to have to be careful that we don't catch up
to them," she had told Rowena.

But Rowena hadn't seemed worried. "That shouldn't be too
hard," she'd said. "A band of Tinkers is pretty hard to miss!
Besides, I don't think they'd give us any trouble; they aren't
loyal to any territory or village."

"I'd still just as soon steer clear of them," Cassidy had said
with finality. They had then veered off at an angle from the
broad trampled path in the meadow and continued eastward.
And although they had seen no further sign of the Tinkers, or

of anyone else, it hadn't been until that next afternoon that Cassidy had felt truly certain they had safely avoided the traveling tradesmen.

Crouching again, Cassidy began to creep along the steamy tunnellike trail of the rabbit run where they'd set their snares. Wiping her sweaty hair back from her face, she realized that her hands still reeked of the semiputrefied rabbit hides. She wondered if she and Rowena smelled that bad all the time and just didn't notice it.

The rabbits had been Rowena's idea. After their less than satisfactory experience with a vegetarian diet, the buxom woman had grown increasingly interested in the multitude of rabbits that crossed their path in an average day.

"You know, people *eat* rabbits," she'd told Cassidy.

"Yeah?" had been Cassidy's reply. "Well, I've got news for you: People have to be able to *catch* rabbits to be able to eat them."

"Rabbits can't be that smart," Rowena had said. "I bet we could catch them."

"In case you haven't noticed, we aren't that smart, either," Cassidy had grumbled. But she had agreed to call a halt to allow her friend to try her skill, even though she suspected Rowena just wanted an excuse to get down off the horse again.

As it turned out, skill didn't have much to do with catching rabbits. They'd managed to snag their first one by way of a comical game of two-man team tag. Rowena had scared up a rabbit and took off running after it. Unimpressed with the plump woman's chances of outrunning even a stupid rabbit, Cassidy had merely waited. A couple of minutes later, much to her amazement, the rabbit reappeared, scurrying back through the brush directly toward her. Cassidy simply tackled it. She'd had no compunctions about snapping the creature's neck, considering how stupid it had been and how hungry she was. By the time Rowena came limping back, Cassidy had used her little knife to skin and gut her catch.

To their wonderment, the two women soon discovered that a rabbit shaken out of its usual habitat almost always circled around again and eventually came back to its hole. They caught several more rabbits using the same strategy. Then Rowena decided it would be more energy-efficient to locate one of the numerous rabbit runs and simply set snares along the heavily traveled pathway. Although they didn't have any rope or wire or string, necessity was proving to be a pretty good teacher. By trial and error, Rowena managed to devise some perfectly functional traps using wild grapevine and snares she fashioned from a thin braid of Dragonfly's long tail hairs.

Suddenly they were assured of a steady supply of rabbits anywhere that they stopped long enough to scout out the local rabbit runs and set snares. It was the first really good piece of luck Cassidy and Rowena had had, and the cooked rabbit meat was such a welcome addition to their previous diet that it hadn't even occurred yet to either one of them to become bored with it.

If only I hadn't come up with that stupid idea about using their hides, Cassidy thought sourly, half sliding down an incline made particularly slick by its covering of wet dead leaves. Although it had seemed like a brilliant idea at the time.

But Rowena had also been enthusiastic at first; she'd even expressed regret that they'd wasted the hides of the first few rabbits they'd caught. That was before they'd both figured out that neither one of them knew a damned thing about how to treat and preserve hides. Obviously just getting the skins off the rabbits and scraping off the hair wasn't enough, although that was hard enough when all you had was a little pocket knife.

"Shit," Cassidy muttered, edging around the first of the snares they had set along the rabbit run. It had not been sprung.

"Keep going," Rowena said from behind her. "We still have three more."

Cassidy just grunted and scooted forward again, dodging another drenching from a wet branch. The problem with rabbit runs, she'd decided, was that rabbits were so *short*. She and Rowena nearly had to travel on their hands and knees just to keep to the trail.

And the problem with their ill-fated attempts to cure rabbit hides was that in the warm humid weather the skins seemed more inclined to rot than to become preserved. Even their best efforts were still nothing more than soggy swatches of slimy leather. Cassidy couldn't imagine putting one of the damned things on any part of her body—and the smell! Somehow their old clothing, no matter how wet and worn, was beginning to look more and more regal.

The second snare was also empty, although it had been sprung. Cassidy crouched aside and let Rowena come up alongside her in the run. The brunette was far more adept at resetting the snares than was Cassidy. That was more a matter of patience than any real skill, Cassidy was forced to admit. Patience was something at which Rowena had always been able to exceed her.

And patience had proven a badly needed quality on their journey. Rowena had endured the hardships and discomforts stoically, more often than not providing Cassidy with the necessary encouragement and sense of humor. Once again Cassidy realized just how much she owed the loyal and uncomplaining woman.

When they started forward again, Rowena assumed the lead along the rabbit path. Scrambling along behind the larger woman, Cassidy reflected further on just how important Rowena had been to her. Since the first moment some several weeks ago when Cassidy had suddenly found herself in that totally alien place, stripped of nearly everything familiar to her—even her own real name—she had striven toward only one goal. In her struggle to regain her memory she had discovered one true and faithful ally in the goatherd. There had been other people before Rowena who had helped Cassidy: the Horsemen who had first found her and the other Villagers who had saved her life and shared her daily work. But none of them shared one essential thing with Cassidy; none of them *remembered* their previous life, their existence before they had come to that weirdly out-of-joint world. Only Rowena could understand and share Cassidy's desperate desire to go home again.

"Hey!" Rowena exclaimed from ahead of her. The word embodied happy surprise.

Cassidy crept forward to see the limp body of a trapped rabbit tethered to the sprung snare. It was a good-size one, plump and still warm. Her pleasure at the thought of fresh meat was only slightly tempered by the reminder of another slimy rabbit skin to strip and attempt to cure.

Rowena delicately pried loose the horsehair noose from the dead rabbit's neck, passing its carcass back to Cassidy. While Rowena reset the snare, Cassidy thoughtfully regarded the furry body. It seemed singularly fitting to her that in that world, of all places, she should be reduced to crawling along rabbit runs, strangling the hapless creatures with something as simple and primitive as a snare braided of horsehair; while at the same time in that same world, things such as guns and cigarette lighters and sunglasses saw fit to appear at capricious intervals. Cassidy almost had to laugh out loud when she imagined the picture she and Rowena must have presented, sweaty, soaked, and dirty, crawling along through the leaves and dirt in search of dead rabbits.

Another mosquito tickled the back of her neck, and Cassidy automatically reached up with her free hand to swat it. A few seconds later the tickle returned. This time Cassidy could feel that it wasn't a mosquito, either; something wet was slipping down from the area of her hairline and slithering across the nape of her neck, into the collar of her T-shirt. Irritated, she wiped at the moisture. *Great—probably bird shit!* she thought as she brought back her hand to inspect her fingers. Then her nostrils flared and she suddenly felt as if her heart had stopped beating.

It was slime, black slime, foul and—

Unwillingly but reflexively, Cassidy's head jerked up and she peered through the trailing curtain of wet green alder leaves that formed the canopy of the rabbit run above her. For a moment she could see nothing but the dizzying verdant sway of the bushes and trees overhead, glittering with moisture and trembling in the breeze. It was green on green, a living, shifting ceiling that defied penetration. Then another stream of slime, a glistening rope of ebony mucus, spun down through the branches and landed on her forearm, and she could at last see where it was coming from.

Almost directly above Cassidy, at least twenty feet up in the boughs of an impressive old-growth beech tree, hung the enormous shape of something dark and loathsome, something with skin like wet leather and a stench like week-old meat, something whose whole oozing bulk pulsed and throbbed like the beat of one great heart.

Something like a *monster*.

The weight of the dead rabbit in Cassidy's hand felt like a rock, like a weapon, and without thinking she threw it, uselessly but noisily up through the branches toward the black monstrosity that was suspended like some hideous fruit in the big tree. Then she found herself shouting incoherently, panicked into a complete frenzy as she pounded on a startled Rowena's back and pushed the astonished woman forward by the sheer force of her own terror.

To Rowena's credit, she ran without hesitation, even though she must have thought that Cassidy had gone berserk. Bursting through the wall of brush and up out of the rabbit run, the two women bounded up a shallow slope and through a thin stand of young birch. Then they were sliding down the other side of the embankment and out into the more open old-growth forest. Wet leaves slipped like ice beneath Cassidy's boots and she had to weave and dodge wildly to avoid running headlong into a tree trunk as the furious gush of adrenaline drove her mercilessly on.

When they were out in the open amid the big trees, Rowena had a chance to look behind them and see that nothing was chasing them. She made a lurching grab for the back of Cassidy's T-shirt. Their momentum kept them stumbling on for a few more yards, despite the strength with which Rowena hauled back on Cassidy; but they both finally fell to their knees in the thick leafy humus.

"Jeez, Cassidy. What the—?" Rowena panted, still gripping the back of Cassidy's shirt.

Eyes wide, her breath coming in rapid gasps, Cassidy just kept looking back the way they had come. It took her a few moments to realize that Rowena had not seen the hanging monster above them.

"Hornets! There was a great big nest of hornets right over us!" she said when she could speak. "Let's get out of here."

"Wait—what about our rabbit?" Rowena looked at Cassidy as if she half expected the smaller woman to just pull it out from under her shirt. "What did you do with our rabbit?"

"The hell with our rabbit!" Cassidy retorted, lurching to her feet again. "I'm not going back there again!" She started forward with such force that she actually began to drag Rowena after her.

"What is going on?" Rowena protested, staggering unwillingly after Cassidy. "What did you do with—"

That was the moment when the earth fell away from under them, the leafy floor of the forest parting like a trapdoor and sending them both tumbling downward in a shower of dirt and twigs and wet leaves.

Chapter 2 ◄▐▐▐▐

Cassidy was not injured, but in her shock and confusion it took her several moments to realize it. She had more or less landed on Rowena, which had cushioned her fall but which probably hadn't done much for the other woman. They both were covered with dirt and leaves; Cassidy had to spit something cold and fungusy-tasting out of her mouth before she could speak.

"Rowena, are you okay?"

The two of them flailed about, untangling themselves.

"I think so. What the hell happened—where are we?"

Cassidy was lying on her back in a couple of inches of cold, debris-strewn water, looking up at an irregular rectangle of leaf-framed light far above their heads.

"Some kind of damned hole," she said, beginning to feel annoyed. As the initial surprise of their unceremonial tumble receded, she found herself growing more angry than frightened.

Rowena pulled herself up into a sitting position, puffing through pursed lips to blow the wet leaves free from her face. "Are you all right?" she asked Cassidy.

Absently rubbing her forearm, Cassidy nodded. "Fine, considering what happened," she said. She sat up unsteadily and the distant rectangle of light shifted and danced. "We could have broken our necks!" she added.

As her vision cleared, Cassidy could see that she and Rowena were sitting at the bottom of some kind of man-made hole that had been dug out of the forest floor. The sticks and other debris with which they'd been showered had apparently formed the hole's covering. The reason the opening above them looked so small was that the walls of the pit were slanted inward, narrowing as they rose. And the reason the opening

14

looked so far away was that it was: At least ten or twelve feet above them.

"What is this?" Rowena repeated, also staring skyward. "Some kind of trap?"

"Looks like it," Cassidy said, "but it sure isn't for catching rabbits!"

The two wet, disheveled women exchanged a significant look.

"For deer, maybe?" Rowena offered.

But Cassidy frowned. "Who would be out here trapping deer?" she said. "We haven't seen another human being in over a week, and there isn't even a path or a trail anywhere near here."

A vague chill ran down Cassidy's spine as Rowena awkwardly gained her feet. "I don't like this," the brunette said anxiously. "Let's get out of here."

"I'm all for that," Cassidy agreed, accepting Rowena's hand and lurching stiffly to her feet. It would be growing dark soon. The idea of spending the night in the pit held absolutely no appeal whatever. Especially if that—that *thing* had dropped down out of the beech tree and followed them.

The two of them quickly inspected their prison's earthen walls. Although the sides of the pit were roughly hewn and contained numerous protruding tree roots, the surface had surprisingly few handholds. Both the walls' height and their inward slant made it impossible to get any real purchase with hands or feet; and the damp soil was so friable that it merely crumbled off when they attempted to climb it.

"Shit," Cassidy muttered, glaring up at the squarish opening far above their heads. "I'd hate to have to *dig* my way out of this thing."

"Yeah, especially with our bare hands," Rowena echoed, "but I'd also hate to be stuck down here. In fact," she added, "I *already* hate being stuck down here."

Cassidy briefly considered Calling Dragonfly. The horse was probably still browsing back in the little glen and would have come at once if Cassidy had exerted the force of that mysterious telepathic connection between them. But she hesitated. She couldn't think of any way the horse could help them get out of the pit; and she was wary of exposing the mare to any unnecessary risks if whoever built the trap was nearby.

Studying the rectangle of light, an aperture green with the overhanging tree boughs and dappled with the shadows of their leaves, Cassidy frowned in concentration. "What if I got up on your shoulders?" she suggested.

Rowena stood with her back against one of the pit's damp earthen walls and made a stirrup for Cassidy with both hands. The smaller woman put one booted foot in the clasped hands and, using Rowena's shoulder to steady herself, pushed up and flung herself against the wall. Cassidy's fingers clutched uselessly at the protruding stubs of several severed tree roots. Dirt tumbled down from her grasping hands, further bombarding both herself and Rowena.

"Can you get up on my shoulders?" Rowena grunted, struggling to keep her footing in the muck on the bottom of the hole.

"I don't know," Cassidy said, still trying to just keep her balance. The inward slant of the pit's walls forced her to lean outward, making it almost impossible for her to remain upright with all of her weight on just one foot. Then a particularly large chunk of dirt broke free under Cassidy's scrabbling hands and landed right on Rowena's upturned face. With a sound of both surprise and disgust, she involuntarily jerked aside, sending Cassidy tumbling back down to the flooded floor of the pit.

Rowena stared down at her with an expression that wavered between sympathetic apology and helpless amusement. Frustrated, Cassidy slapped the surface of the muck with the flat of her hand, sending up a spray of humus and leafy debris.

"This is just *great!*" she snarled, clenching her fists.

Rowena leaned down, offering Cassidy her hand. "Let's try again," she suggested. "And this time I won't look up!"

After getting to her feet, Cassidy carefully inspected the walls of their earthen prison, looking for an area with the most tree roots and the least avalanche potential. Then they tried again. That time she didn't waste time trying to find any handholds until she had managed to scramble all the way up onto Rowena's shoulders.

"Ow!" Rowena grunted as Cassidy's bootheels dug into her collarbones; she swayed, but steadied herself again.

"Sorry," Cassidy said. She had to spit out a mouthful of dirt to speak.

"Can you reach the top?" Rowena asked her, wincing as she struggled to keep her balance.

"I can try," Cassidy replied.

The top of the pit was still at least a yard above the reach of her hands, but at least at that level the tree roots were larger horizontal feeders and not nearly as thin and fragile as those that protruded lower in the hole. Holding her breath, Cassidy leaned slightly to her left, stretching out her arm toward the truncated nub of one of the thicker roots. Her fingers closed around it and locked. Although the root was only the diameter of her wrist, it held when she pulled downward on it.

"Well?" Rowena said anxiously from below her.

"I've got something I can grab on to," Cassidy said, "but I don't know how I'm going to get up any higher."

More dirt, loosened by Cassidy's manipulation of the root stub, tumbled down across her chest and onto Rowena below. Ignoring it, Cassidy searched for another handhold. There weren't any other roots sticking out far enough for her to be able to grasp them; but her exploring fingers brushed the cut end of another large feeder root several inches above the first one. Using the first root for leverage, Cassidy stretched up and began to claw the dirt away from around the second.

"Hey!" Rowena protested, suddenly shifting beneath Cassidy's feet.

"Sorry," Cassidy said. "These roots are buried; I've got to dig them out. Stop wiggling," she added.

Rowena grumbled something Cassidy couldn't make out, but she did stop shifting.

Once Cassidy had two handholds, she could pull herself up off of Rowena's shoulders. She had to dig her knees into the soft earth of the pit walls to anchor herself; trying to use her feet to brace herself just served to dislodge the dirt from beneath her boots. The inward slant of the hole seemed especially pronounced when Cassidy was trying to cling, flylike, to the wall. Hastily she unearthed another root and inched upward. Luckily the upper few feet of soil were more compacted and the tree roots were tough and numerous. Still, Cassidy's whole body was aching by the time she'd reached the lip of the pit, and her arms trembled with fatigue.

"Almost there!" Rowena shouted in encouragement. "You can make it now!"

Worming her torso forward, Cassidy wriggled until she was able to get one of her elbows up over the edge of the hole. She was glad she still had a firm hold on a root with her other hand because the moment she tried to place any weight on her leading arm, loose dirt at the lip of the pit came free, raining down into the hole. Clearing the edge of the opening, with a grunt

Cassidy flung herself farther. Her scrabbling fingers shot out, closing on a half-buried root on the forest floor.

For a few moments, once she knew for certain that she could get the rest of the way out of the pit, Cassidy just lay there panting while muscle tremors shook her arms. She was wet and filthy and sore. The forearm she had bruised in the initial fall into the pit now ached like an old burn. Her sense of triumph at getting out of the trap was sorely tempered by her nagging feeling of generalized disillusionment with the way their whole trip had been going.

Ironically, it took Cassidy's feelings of guilt about having taken Rowena away from the safety of the village to make her remember that her friend was still waiting at the bottom of the pit. She forced herself to move again, pulling herself the rest of the way up onto firm ground. Cassidy sat up and turned around, peering back down into the hole. There at the bottom, she saw Rowena's upturned face, looking up patiently at her with an expression only of expectation and not reproach.

"I'm going to find a big branch or log that you can use as a ladder," she called down to Rowena.

"Find one with lots of side branches on it," Rowena called up. Now that Cassidy was free, the other woman obviously felt no real doubt that she, too, was as good as out.

It didn't take Cassidy long to find a suitable log; the only problem was that it was so heavy she could barely drag it over to the pit trap. The sun was sinking down onto the horizon by the time she had finally wrestled the stout section of dead wood up to the hole's gaping mouth. And by then even Cassidy had lapsed into thinking beyond their immediate problem. As she manhandled the log to get it tilted down into the opening of the pit, she was already pondering such mundane matters as where they should set up camp for the night, and what they were going to have for supper now that she'd thrown away their only rabbit.

"Look out below," she told Rowena, letting the long log slide.

Although Rowena might not have looked particularly athletic, Cassidy had long since learned that she was surprisingly fit. Months of scrambling over hill and gully after the village's herd of goats had given Rowena a good deal of agility and endurance. Within moments after the end of the log had splunked down into the muck on the bottom of the earthen pit, the larger woman was determinedly crawling up the makeshift ramp.

"Jeez, what took you so long?" Rowena demanded in mock complaint as she neared the top of the hole. "I was starting to think you stopped to take a shower!"

It had become a standing joke between the two of them, as they had both decided early on in their journey that the one thing they were going to miss most about the village was its excellent indoor plumbing system. And so for a moment Cassidy just grinned in reply as she took hold of Rowena's arm and helped her climb off the log. She did not immediately notice the sudden strange look on the brunette's face. It was only when Rowena remained uncharacteristically silent, staring slightly slack-jawed off over Cassidy's shoulder, that Cassidy realized something was amiss. She slowly turned to face whatever Rowena saw.

Standing not ten feet from them was a man. Cassidy's initial response—the profound if irrational relief that it was just a man and not a monster—came and went in the space of one heartbeat. Then she just stood and stared at him, not sure if she was more surprised by the fact that he was nearly naked, or that he held a long rapierlike knife at his side, or just that he was even there at all. When she was able to find her voice, she saw no reason to be tactful.

"Who the hell are you?" she demanded still clutching Rowena's arm.

The man was taller than either of them, probably a good six feet, and as wiry as a whip. His skin was darkened, not so much by natural pigmentation as by exposure to the elements, and his hair hung in a long tangle of undistinguished brown. Against the sable color of a full beard and mustache his eyes nearly leapt out of his face, their whites brilliantly clear and their irises a pellucid grayish blue. All he wore was some kind of breechclout that had been formed from the twisted scrap of a worn bit of fabric; it barely covered his pubic hairline.

The man made a little gesture with the glinting blade of his big knife and lifted his upper lip just enough to reveal his teeth. "Come on," he said. "You've done a real good job of getting out of there."

Straightening up so that she could take one step away from the edge of the pit, Rowena peered suspiciously at the man. "How long have you been here?" she asked.

The man said nothing, but Cassidy suddenly understood Rowena's implication. "You've been here all the time, haven't you?" she accused him. "In fact, I bet you're the bastard who dug this damned trap in the first place!" She gestured angrily.

But the man didn't even flinch; he merely repeated blandly, "You've done a real good job getting out."

Ignoring the long-bladed knife that he wielded, Cassidy glared purposefully at the aggravating man. In contrast to his luxurious mane and the fullness of his beard, his body bore very little hair; his skin was as smooth and brown as well-oiled leather.

"Who the hell are you?" she asked again.

But the wiry man infuriatingly ignored the questions, much as if they had never been asked. He just made a minute economical gesture with the tip of his knife, the sinuous muscles in his forearm flexing effortlessly as he beckoned them both forward.

Steadfastly ignoring the summons, Cassidy glanced sideways at Rowena. "Who *is* this oaf?" she asked.

Rowena was frowning. "I'm not sure, but I think he might be a Woodsman," she said hesitantly. "I didn't think they even existed; but if they do, then I guess that must be what he is."

Equally exasperated by both Rowena's tentativeness and the dark man's bland confidence, Cassidy made an irritated snorting sound. "I don't care what he is," she asserted, tugging on Rowena's arm. "As soon as the rest of our Troop catches up, he'll be—"

Rowena barely had time to comprehend what Cassidy had been trying to do when the breechclouted man interrupted her with a loud yip of laughter. "Good!" he said. "Fast thinking—I like that." Then, so swiftly that Cassidy had not even seen it coming, he sprang forward and brandished the gleaming blade of his big knife right before her astonished face. "But there's no Troop; you travel alone." He grinned at her then, his small white teeth baring in a feral display. "I've been watching you two all day."

Cassidy took an involuntary half step backward, a movement partially necessitated by Rowena automatically jerking back. Indignant at being seen through so easily, she countered, "Then you know that we're Horsemen."

Still holding his blade motionless before her, the brown man smiled thinly and said, "Not much help in the forest, is it?"

Rowena had the presence of mind to try another tack with their antagonist before Cassidy managed to get her insolent throat slit. "Are you really a Woodsman?" she asked him.

The man made a casually indifferent gesture, tossing back his long tangled hair. "Call me what you want," he said nonchalantly, his knife still held in an unwavering grip before Cassidy's face.

Studying him more closely, Cassidy could see that he wasn't exactly dirty, just disheveled and sun-browned.

"Why did you dig this trap?" Rowena asked. "For deer?"

But the lean Woodsman had obviously lost interest in the conversation. He was eyeing both of the women with an alarming kind of intensity.

Cassidy glanced briefly at Rowena, trying to judge if their best choice would be to fight or to flee. She could Call her mare if they had to flee, but if they ended up having to fight . . .

"Take off your clothes," the Woodsman said.

The command was so unexpected that for a moment Cassidy was certain that she must have misunderstood him while her attention had been diverted thinking about their dilemma. But when she and Rowena just stood there gaping stupidly at him, the wiry man calmly repeated his demand.

"I said take off your clothes—all of them."

Fear and resolve married in Cassidy to produce a stiffly negative reaction. "Like hell!" she shot back defiantly, instinctively crossing her arms over her chest and taking another half-step backward.

When Cassidy bumped into Rowena, the brunette murmured under her breath, "Cassidy, that's a pretty big knife he's got."

As if on cue, the Woodsman gestured with the weapon, the sharp tip of its thin blade circumscribing a small circle in the air right before Cassidy's face. "Nicely now," he said evenly, with just the slightest show of his teeth, "or I'll have to take them off for you."

Cassidy's shoulders tightened and she felt her hands automatically ball into fists. If they made a run for it, he'd never be able to catch both of them; but whoever he did catch was going to be in big trouble. And if they chose to fight, the only weapon she had was the little pocket knife. She stared directly into the bluish-gray eyes, too outraged to retreat any further.

"No," she said.

"Cassidy!" Rowena hissed at her ear. "Let's just give him the damned clothes!"

Cassidy's head jerked slightly as she shot Rowena an unwilling look of pure surprise. Her reaction to the suggestion was so unshuttered that the brunette immediately understood Cassidy's presumption. That was one of the many disadvantages of being able to remember their old world in the oddly skewed new one: Cassidy was constantly basing her assumptions on values and constants that seemed to have no parallels in that place.

Rowena almost gave in to a sudden burst of inappropriate but helpless laughter. The best she could do was try to stifle the sound as she hissed under her breath, practically into Cassidy's ear, "Cassidy, he doesn't want *that*—jeez! all he wants is our *clothes!*"

Cassidy felt the heat of a blush pouring across her flushed face, the reaction fueled even further by the transparency of her assumption. The Woodsman was regarding both women quizzically. Trying to reclaim the situation as best she could, Cassidy said a bit too loudly, "I don't care what he wants, I'm not taking off my clothes!"

Only Rowena's sense of exasperation at her combative friend kept the goatherd from giggling aloud at the ludicrous exchange. "Cassidy," she reminded her, sotto voce, "*he* doesn't remember sex—and this is *not* the time to remind him!"

Two things brought the extended confrontation to a halt: Cassidy's reluctant concession to the practicality of Rowena's approach, and the sudden touch of the flat of the Woodsman's blade against the tender skin of her neck.

"Now take off your clothes," he repeated mildly.

Spreading her hands in a gesture of acquiescence that persuaded him to back off slightly, Cassidy bent and began to tug off her boots. Because both the boots and her socks were still damp, it took some cursing and hopping about to accomplish the deed. Then she started to shuck off her jeans.

Beside Cassidy, Rowena quickly and uncomplainingly shed her own clothing. Cassidy was increasingly annoyed at the brunette's tractable attitude until she remembered that Rowena had been there a lot longer than she had and had already been fairly well absorbed into the village's nearly genderless society until Cassidy had come along to remind her that anything different was possible.

Until I reminded her about sex, Cassidy told herself ruefully, trying to keep from glancing up at either Rowena's half-clad body or the Woodsman's nearly naked one.

By the time she had to pull her T-shirt over her head, Cassidy found herself almost wishing that she wore a bra. Pausing with the bunched-up shirt held in front of her, she looked pointedly at the bearded man. He couldn't want her panties, too—what the hell use would they be to him? But at her visible hesitation the Woodsman made a gruff little sound, brandishing the knife again. Muttering impotently under her breath, Cassidy stepped out of the last of her clothing.

Fortunately Rowena had been correct about one thing: All the wild-looking man had wanted was their clothes. Gesturing them back with another wave of the long blade, he quickly gathered up all of the discarded garments. He paid absolutely no attention to their nudity, and Cassidy had to fight to keep from calling any undue importance to it by instinctively trying to cover herself with her arms and hands. She tried to stand as Rowena stood, alertly but impatiently, without any visible fear.

When he had all their clothing, the Woodsman bundled it against his chest with a grunt of satisfaction. Then, obviously and deliberately, he moved his gaze from the two women to the edge of the pit trap and then back again, while a humorless smirk pulled at his lips.

Shit—he wouldn't push us back down into that hole again, would he? For some reason that possibility alarmed Cassidy more than had any part of the previous confrontation. Darkness would be falling soon. The image of that hideous thing hanging high in the branches of the ancient beech tree leapt insistently into her mind. Beside her Rowena shifted, taking an involuntary step back from the edge of the pit.

But once he had satisfied himself that he had genuinely frightened the two women, the brown-skinned man laughed dismissively at them. "No need for that then, is there?" he said. He waved his rapier blade in a final little salute, then turned and practically vanished. Cassidy never took her eyes off of him, but she could have sworn that he just melted back into the forest and disappeared, like a drop of water hitting the surface of a pool and fading into nonexistence.

The two of them stood there for a few moments, too surprised to move. Then Rowena let out her breath in a long sigh and said, "Jeez, he had me worried for a minute there. I sure as hell didn't want to have to climb out of that damned hole again!"

Cassidy looked at her in mild astonishment. "Climb out—is

that all you can worry about?" She gestured dramatically. "He took all our clothes—he's got our matches, our knife!"

Rowena shrugged and said, "Well, at least we've still got our rabbit skins."

Yeah, our stinky slimy rabbit skins! Cassidy thought, kicking out in frustration at the nearest scuffed-up pile of dead leaves and nearly stubbing her bare toe on the tree root concealed beneath it. *Great!* "Let's get out of here," she said.

Cassidy forged on ahead of Rowena in grim silence for the several minutes it took her to calm down. When she spoke again, her tone was slightly less hostile.

"Who the hell *was* that guy?" she asked, shaking her head irritably.

"A Woodsman," Rowena said simply.

"But you said you weren't even sure there was such a thing as Woodsmen."

Rowena had caught up to Cassidy by then and walked alongside her. "I've never seen one before," she explained, "but sometimes the guys around the barns would joke about them—you know, the way they do about monsters. So I figured that Woodsmen were just something that they made up, too."

Well, I've got news for you, Cassidy thought grimly, *monsters are real, too.* But she said nothing, and Rowena went on.

"From what I've heard, I guess they're like some kind of hermit or something; you know, people who don't fit in. Except I got the impression that they're maybe a little crazy, too."

Cassidy grunted. "People who are crazy and who don't fit in: Rowena, you've just described *us!*"

Rowena flashed her a quick, ingratiating grin. "No, people who are crazy, don't fit in, and are *naked:* Now, *that* describes us!"

Cassidy grunted again, refusing to yield to the urge to smile. Thinking of the Woodsman's own near nudity, she grumbled, "No wonder he wanted our clothes . . . I hope he enjoys the panties!"

It was nearly dark by the time they had backtracked to the little glen where they had left the gray mare. Walking barefooted in the forest had proven to be a tricky business, and both women's feet were tender, bruised, and scratched by the time they limped into the clearing. Halfway back, Cassidy had actually begun to look forward to retrieving the wretched rabbit hides again; she would have been happy to wrap any-thing, even a putrid pelt, around her sore and aching feet. As her stomach rumbled emptily, she doubly regretted having lost the one fresh rabbit they had snared, even if butchering it without her knife would have been a challenge.

When they stumbled into the shadowy glen they found Dragonfly pretty much where they had last left her. The horse stood quietly beneath one of the big black oaks, her long tail slowly swishing at the first of the evening's more voracious mosquitoes. She nickered when she saw Cassidy, but Cassidy's attention had been diverted.

The damp little clearing where she and Rowena had sat to work with the hides was littered with a confetti of scraps of tattered rabbit skins. All of the hides they had collected had been slashed to pieces and strewn about. Amid the litter of sticky swatches they found the mutilated remains of their vine and horsehair snares, also neatly sliced into tiny and useless bits. Disappointment and discouragement weighted Cassidy's heart like stones as she turned to Rowena.

The brunette looked close to tears, but she managed to summon up a quip. "Well, now we know where he was while we were busy trying to get out of his trap."

"Wonderful—I'm so glad he wasn't bored!" Cassidy snapped. Seeing Rowena wince at her outburst, Cassidy im-mediately tried to temper her anger. "Wonderful," she re-peated, but more quietly, nudging a scrap of rabbit skin with her bare toe. "Now what the hell are we going to do for clothes?"

Rowena spread her hands in an automatic placating gesture. "Well, it's warm enough that we won't really get cold, even at night, and we're already riding bareback, right?"

Reluctantly Cassidy had to grin. "If you think you have a sore butt now, wait until you try riding with no jeans between you and that horse," she warned the brunette. Sighing, she surveyed the scene of the destruction in the darkening glen. Along with her clothing she had lost their matches, pocket knife, and the little horsehair token that the female Trooper had given her the night of the fire. "Shit," she said, "no clothes, no food—not even any stinky rabbit skins! What the hell are we going to do now?"

But Rowena's optimism was indefatigable; she seemed to feel the solution was obvious. "We go find the Tinkers," she said simply.

Chapter 3 ◀︎▥

Cassidy and Rowena had plenty of time to settle on a plan of action the next morning as they scrounged around the woods for enough wild crabapples and berries to eat. They agreed that there'd be little problem deliberately catching up with the Tinkers; after all, they had the gray mare, while the Tinkers' large group moved on foot, further slowed by their heavily laden carts. And it wasn't as if the Tinkers' trail would be hard to pick up or follow. Cassidy's one nagging doubt about the idea was still its safety.

"How do we know these guys won't just turn us back over to Allen or the rest of the Villagers?" she asked Rowena for about the fifth time as they gorged themselves on their somewhat sour breakfast fruit. "If they figure out who we are, we might just as well not even have left Double Creek."

But Rowena was unperturbed. "First of all, they're headed away from Double Creek," she reminded Cassidy, ticking off the points on her fingers. "They sure aren't going to change their whole route just to make trouble for us. Second, I told you the Tinkers aren't loyal to any one village or territory; they travel everywhere. And third, how the heck are they going to know who we are if we don't tell them?" She gave a little snort of laughter and added, "They sure aren't going to recognize us by our clothes!"

Wincing as she bit into a particularly sour berry, Cassidy resisted the joke. She was still uneasy about being naked; not exactly when she was alone with just Rowena, but the idea of meeting new people without having her clothes on still made Cassidy distinctly nervous. Despite Rowena's repeated reassurances that no one they met would find any sexual context in the two women's nudity, Cassidy had to admit that it was the

26

one single thing that bothered her more than any other aspect of the task ahead of them.

Riding Dragonfly bare-butted turned out to be not quite as unpleasant as Cassidy had feared. Rowena even joked that she preferred it. "Less chafing!" she insisted. And Cassidy was glad to be mounted up and under way again, even if it was toward an increasingly uncertain future. The weather cooperated by remaining almost uncomfortably warm; they purposely had to avoid riding out in the sun for too long to avoid burning their newly exposed backs.

It wasn't hard to backtrack to where they had crossed the Tinkers' trail two days earlier. By late afternoon they had reached the stretch of sandy meadow where they had first intersected the broad path. They decided to follow the trail for a few more hours, knowing they would still be camping well behind the traveling band.

Cassidy was depressed to discover how hungry she'd become during the course of the day. They had stopped whenever they'd found any likely-looking bushes or berry canes, but after having become accustomed to eating meat, the diet of fruit was haplessly unsatisfying. At least they could still make a fire, even if starting one was a laborious task without the matches. Early on in their journey the two women had discovered that wrapping the berries and other raw fruit in green leaves and cooking them in the coals greatly improved the taste and seemed to reduce the hazard of diarrhea. And without a knife they had to improvise more than ever.

Picking cautiously at the too-hot slurry of mashed blackberries, Cassidy glanced across the fire to where Rowena sat. It was funny how by the end of the day their mutual nudity no longer seemed especially odd to her anymore. "Just what do you know about these Tinkers?" she asked curiously.

Rowena's chin was already stained from the berries. "Not a whole lot," she admitted. Even naked, Rowena never seemed to have trouble getting comfortable sitting on the ground. Once again Cassidy marveled at the woman's uncomplaining endurance. "They came to Green Lake once when I was there, but I didn't get to see much of them." She grinned at the memory. "I was still on 'probation' for that clothing factory fiasco!"

Cassidy grinned back appreciatively. Rowena had told Cassidy more than once that she didn't know what the Green Lake Villagers would have done with her if Allen hadn't come along and taken her back with him to Double Creek. Cassidy had begun to think the big sorrel-haired man specialized in rescues; except if he was to catch up with them under their current circumstances, he wouldn't be there to rescue them.

"I don't even know if that was the same bunch of Tinkers we're following now," Rowena continued.

Cassidy cocked a quizzical brow at her. That possibility had never occurred to her. "Just how many bands of these Tinkers are there anyway?" she asked.

Rowena shrugged. "You've got me," she said. "I don't know how far each band travels, or even where they all come from, except that it's not any of the villages."

"Great." Cassidy sighed, tossing aside her empty, berry-stained leaves. "I'm glad we're not going into this half-cocked!"

By the next morning the sky had clouded over again, which made it somewhat cooler, but Cassidy was more anxious about the possibility of rain. She wasn't especially worried about losing the Tinkers' trail; it would have taken a major gullywasher to have obliterated the tracks of so many people and carts. She was more concerned with the mundane matter of having to ride naked in a soaking rain. On top of the continuing indignity of insect bites, sunburn, and bramble scratches, it would have been the final insult.

She and Rowena had agreed that their best plan of action would be to try to find one or two of the Tinkers who were separated from the main group before they showed themselves. That way, in case the encounter went badly, the two women could still easily escape on Dragonfly if they had to. If they caught up to the Tinkers in time, the group's midday stop might give them the opportunity they needed. Some of the Tinkers would have to go get water, wash up utensils, or—if nothing else—go off into the bushes to relieve themselves. And if they didn't catch up by midday, then by evening they should have been able to create an encounter.

As the morning progressed, Cassidy found herself feeling increasingly irritated and hungry again. She realized that part of her irritability was anxiety; she still had real reservations about their whole scheme. But she and Rowena had rehearsed the story they would give the Tinkers so often that she had almost begun to believe it herself. Cassidy tried to reassure herself with thoughts of food and clothing, two things the Tinkers were sure to have that the women sorely needed. And they always had the gray mare, Cassidy reminded herself; any time if they really needed to get away, at least they had a horse.

Not that she was very helpful with that damned Woodsman! Cassidy could not keep from reminding herself.

By midday it had begun to rain, a surprisingly chilly drizzle that streamed down from the leaden skies in a misty curtain of droplets. The gray's steaming back had never felt quite so welcomingly warm between Cassidy's bare thighs. Shortly after the rain had begun, they caught up to the band of Tinkers.

The terrain was wooded and hilly, but the slopes were long and gentle and the trees were mostly old growth with plenty of clearance beneath them. Once they knew they were getting close, the women on the horse had been cautious about cresting each hill. As the dreary afternoon wore on, they finally could actually hear the Tinkers moving through the forest ahead of them: the creak of cart wheels, the clink and jingle of metal, even the occasional sound of voices. They slipped down off the mare and crept up the last slope on hands and knees, inching carefully over a carpet of wet leaves in the gray pall of mist that hung beneath the big trees.

Peering carefully over the top of the crest, Cassidy was amazed by the sight below them. Across the little valley wound a remarkable little procession of over a dozen people and all of their possessions. Against the dim gray and green of the rainy forest hills, the bright clothing and richly painted carts of the Tinkers stood out like brilliant splashes of color, and their voices rang like music in the damp drizzly air. Cassidy had not seen anything even remotely like them anywhere in that world.

It was difficult to pick out details from that distance, but Cassidy could see that the group seemed to be almost evenly divided between men and women, with a wide range of ages, shapes, and sizes. The common denominator they all appeared to share was a penchant for unique and festive clothing. Not only were none of their garments like anything else Cassidy had ever seen there, no two outfits were even similar to each other. After the drab uniformity of the Villagers' clothes, the diversity of fabric and color and design was delightful. *Looks like we came to the right people for clothes!* she thought wryly.

The Tinkers had several large wooden pushcarts, all of them intricately carved and painted. Two of the carts looked like traveling forges, capped with sheet-metal hoods and little jointed chimneys. The others were loaded to capacity with an impressive variety of things, from bolts of cloth to pots to boots to barrels, all sheltered from the drizzle by colorful canvas awnings. But there were three carts in particular that made Cassidy gape in surprise. Instead of being pushed along, these carts were being pulled by their long wooden shafts. But they weren't being pulled by horses or even by people; they were being pulled by Tinkers riding on—

"Bicycles!" Cassidy exclaimed softly.

Beside her, Rowena wriggled a little closer, staring in fascination. "Yeah, neat!" she said.

That suddenly explained the funny single-wheel tracks they had seen in the meadow; they had been from the bicycles' wheels. The spindly two-wheeled vehicles looked so exotic and yet so achingly prosaic that Cassidy felt a sudden wave of longing go through her at the sight. Bicycles were one of the *missing* things. Her flood of nostalgia rapidly bloomed into a full-blown throb of hope: If the Tinkers had one missing thing, might they have more of them? Could they possibly *know* things—things that could help Cassidy and Rowena find their way home?

A poke from Rowena's elbow in her bare side broke Cassidy's runaway train of thought. "Look," Rowena hissed at her, "they've even got dogs!"

Cassidy hadn't even noticed the dogs at first, but there were three of them frolicking along among the carts. Two of the animals were little more than animated balls of fur, yipping at each other and everything else as they scooted along. The third dog was a larger lop-eared mutt the color of ripe wheat that seemed to tolerate the others with a certain resigned dignity.

Reluctantly Cassidy pulled back and slid a little way down the wet hillside. "We'd better stay back a bit yet," she said, "unless we want those dogs to spot us." Seeing Rowena's expression change from wonderment to disappointment, Cassidy added, "Besides, if we drop back far enough we can ride again."

The idea of riding again rather than walking definitely appealed to Rowena. "Okay," she said, then offered hopefully, "Maybe they'll stop early for the day because of the rain."

Cassidy wouldn't have been willing to bet on it, but she just agreed. "Yeah, maybe they will."

And much to Cassidy's surprise, the Tinkers did call an early halt. The rain had not worsened as the afternoon went on; it never became any heavier than a persistent drizzle, and even that finally subsided to a damp foggy stream of droplets. Cassidy had become accustomed to the Horsemen's and the Villagers' sense of priorities, where the comfort of the travelers ranked a distant second to expediency. Apparently the Tinkers subscribed to the theory that the quality of a journey was as important as its speed.

When the group of men and women called a halt for the day, they selected a relatively sheltered slope near the bottom of a wide valley for their camp. The site was upland enough to be well drained, but clear and level enough to allow a spacious camp. There was a small creek at the base of the valley, and enough old-growth trees to assure a good supply of dead wood for fires. The Tinkers really didn't need the trees for shelter because, quite to her surprise, Cassidy saw that they had come well equipped with a variety of tents and canvas awnings.

Cassidy and Rowena dismounted and left Dragonfly behind to creep up closer when the Tinkers first set up camp. It was not too hard for them to get as close as the top of the preceding hill without being seen; even had it not been for the cover of the gray skies and foggy mist, the slope was well forested. In addition, the Tinkers seemed to be singularly unconcerned about guarding their rear. They probably had no reason to assume anyone would be following them.

As the group began to unload and set up their tents, unpacking food and bedding, several people broke away to gather firewood. One woman, a stout blond who looked gargantuan in a voluminous purple dress, carried two metal buckets down to the creek for water. But there wasn't much good cover around the stream and it would have been difficult to approach her without first being seen by the entire camp. Rowena and Cassidy waited until they saw two people, a man and a woman, cut off into the surrounding trees carrying small wicker baskets before they decided to risk contact.

Mounted on Dragonfly, Cassidy felt slightly less vulnerable, although she still could not completely shake off her sense of uneasiness at being naked. *Naked and dirty and wet,* she reminded herself glumly as she guided the big horse obliquely across the wooded hillside to intersect the area where the two Tinkers had disappeared only minutes earlier. The warmth and bulk of Rowena's equally naked, dirty, and wet body behind Cassidy was her only source of moral support. Once again Cassidy wondered if they were doing the right thing by revealing themselves to the Tinkers. The most compelling argument she could think of for doing it was also the simplest: She honestly didn't know how she and Rowena would be able to continue without help.

The gray mare stepped almost silently through the foggy, smoke-colored mist, her broad body slicing gracefully between the dripping bushes and around rocks and trees. Cassidy knew the horse could find the two Tinkers even if she couldn't; she merely sat back and let the mare set their course. And when the gray's long, scimitar-shaped ears suddenly pointed forward, Cassidy tensed, preparing herself for the encounter with the strangers.

As Dragonfly stepped out from behind a wide hedge of wild loganberry, the brightly clad pair looked up at them in surprise. The man—a boy, really, for he looked to be scarcely Kevin's age—and the older woman who was with him had been picking berries. When the horse and her riders suddenly appeared from out of the mist, they let their partially filled baskets dangle forgotten at their sides. Neither of them appeared frightened, but the boy's dark eyes widened in surprise.

"Who are you?" he asked immediately.

Inordinately pleased to for once be on the receiving end of that particular question, Cassidy tried to keep in mind the effect of her and Rowena's somewhat unorthodox appearance, and to resist the impulse to be flip or sarcastic now that the tables were finally turned in her favor. Instead she just gazed down steadily at the pair for a moment, taking their measure.

The dark-eyed boy appeared to be about sixteen or seventeen, although he was nearly as tall and lanky as the Woodsman had been. The pleated gray pants and loosely cut rose-colored shirt he wore tended to conceal his teenage boniness, but his long-fingered hands and his protruding Adam's apple betrayed his adolescence. He had a curly head of hair the color of fresh wood shavings, partially contained under a broad-brimmed gray felt hat that was rakishly decorated with pheasant feathers.

His female companion was almost his exact opposite in physical type, short and plump where he was tall and thin, clad in brightly patterned striped pants and blouse. She had wide-set brown eyes and long straight brown hair, damp from the drizzle and held back in a tail at the nape of her neck with an ornamental metal clip. Big round golden hoops hung from both her earlobes.

Just when the woman appeared about to speak, Cassidy did. "I'm a Horseman," she said.

The boy's lips parted silently, rejoined, and then suddenly split again into an infectious grin. "Then you're the first naked Horseman I've ever seen!" he told her. Raising his berry basket, he gestured toward Rowena. "And who's she?"

Cassidy had to keep reminding herself that the boy's natural reaction to their nudity was curiosity, even amusement; nothing more. But she was beginning to wish that she herself had never remembered about sex.

"She's my friend." Continuing, she plunged gamely into the little speech she and Rowena had planned. "We're really glad we came across your group. We've been traveling and we need to get some food and other supplies."

The short brown-haired woman looked up at them with unconcealed amusement. "Like some clothes?" she said.

"Yeah, like some clothes," Cassidy admitted. She was all ready to launch into their prepared explanation for the circumstances that had led to their current state of undress, but that didn't prove necessary.

"Okay," the lanky boy agreed immediately, "but you'll have to talk to Click." He grinned again, an entirely amiable expression that seemed to suggest that perhaps the idea of naked Horsemen would be a welcomed novelty in their camp. "Come on, I'll take you to him."

"Hey, what about these berries?" the plump woman reminded him.

The boy offered her his basket. "You can finish, Wanda—please? I have to take them to camp."

Giving him a playful, indulgent swat on his bony backside, the older woman complained unconvincingly, "Jimmy, you're the laziest boy I ever met! You'd do anything to get out of work."

"Next time I'll do your job, too," Jimmy promised her, already starting to step away from the berry bushes.

Wanda merely snorted her disbelief as, with a shake of her head, she turned back to her picking.

"Come on," the boy said to Cassidy and Rowena, waving for them to follow him back down the hillside. "I'll take you to Click."

Twisting slightly so that she could look back over her shoulder, Cassidy exchanged a dubious look with Rowena. It couldn't just be that easy, could it? They had been prepared to do anything—lie, plead, threaten, bargain—to gain a hearing with the Tinkers. Could it be that all they had to do was ask? The boy hadn't even asked them for their names!

As he led them back down the slope to the Tinkers' campsite, Jimmy stepped briskly along, his lanky stride nearly as long as the gray mare's. He seemed as unperturbed by the gloomy afternoon and the wet mist as he had by their request; he was actually whistling tunelessly under his breath as he approached the camp. He never even looked back to make sure that they were still following him.

Several people in the camp looked up from their tasks as the odd trio approached. Jimmy acted as if he were the parade marshal of an extremely important little procession; he was nearly strutting the last hundred feet, his rose-colored shirt fluttering like a red flag. Men and women bent over cook fires, busy with pots and pans and jars, looked up with smiles or laughter. Other Tinkers, unfurling canvas or setting tent pegs, offered waves or whistles.

Cassidy noted that although their arrival had attracted quite a bit of attention, none of the Tinkers looked alarmed or unfriendly. The most volatile reaction they provoked came from the two smallest camp dogs, the shaggy little creatures the size and shape of floor mops, who darted out to dance, yipping excitedly, around Dragonfly's legs.

The dogs' high-pitched greeting prompted a response from one of the women watching. Cassidy recognized the huge purple-clad woman who had earlier gone down to the creek for water. At the dogs' insistent yapping she rose from her seat before a large cook fire and turned to bellow at the miscreant canines. Still barking in an exuberant frenzy, the two raggy little creatures wove one last zigzag course between the mare's legs before turning to run back to the big woman. As she bent to catch them they launched themselves right up the front of her purple dress and then up into her arms, where they sat cradled on the pillowlike shelf of her huge bosom like the two cups of some bizarre fur brassiere.

Looking down over Jimmy's shoulders, Cassidy saw that the young man was leading them directly to the edge of the camp, where three men were working to erect one of the larger tents, a green and white striped structure that required at least a half-dozen poles to support it. Two of the men were brawny, one of them dressed like a blacksmith in a leather apron with short split legs that fastened over his beefy thighs like chaps. He was completely bald, his bare head gleaming with moisture; on each massive bicep was a tattoo of an eagle. The other burly fellow was pounding in tent pegs, wielding a heavy mallet as if it were nothing more than a tack hammer. He wore brown bib overalls and a sleeveless blue shirt that was tightly stretched over his powerful muscles. The third man, much leaner and far more graceful than the other two, was unfurling canvas. All three of them turned in attention as Jimmy and the two riders approached.

"Well, Jimmy," the blacksmith called out, "what have you found now?"

"A beautiful horse," the big man with the mallet said heartily, with an intensely appreciative scrutiny for the mare that Cassidy was not sure she trusted. She put her hands possessively on the gray's withers as the horse came to a halt.

But it was the third man who Jimmy addressed as he pulled off his broad-brimmed hat with a flutter of wet feathers and made a respectful little bow. "I have two ladies, Click," he said earnestly, "and one a Horseman. They—" Then Jimmy broke off, suddenly blushing.

For one brief adrenaline-hyped moment, Cassidy thought the boy's embarrassed hesitation was due to her and Rowena's nudity, and she could feel the heat flushing across her own face. But before she could remind herself that, as usual, sex had nothing to do with it, Jimmy explained himself. Turning back to the two women on the big gray horse, he stammered awkwardly, "I'm—I'm sorry—I never even asked you your names."

Still fighting her ingrained disbelief that such an omission could be a greater breach of etiquette among the Tinkers than was stark nakedness when meeting strangers, Cassidy almost stumbled over her own name. "Uh, my name is Cassidy," she blurted out. "And this is Rowena."

To Cassidy's continued surprise the third man, whom Jimmy had addressed as Click, gave them both a quick but dignified little bow in greeting. He was, Cassidy noticed, oddly handsome in an unconventional sort of way. His shaggy brown hair was so dark it was nearly black. He had deep umber-brown eyes, the same color as the thick mustache that spread below a nose just long enough and imperfect enough to prevent him from being standardly attractive. He was not a young man; his eyes were deeply bracketed by sunrays of lines and there were twin streaks of gray in the tips of his mustache. But he wore his maturity well. He indicated the blacksmith and the other brawny man with a wave. "This is Tad, and Willie; I am Click."

Polite greetings were murmured all around, but Cassidy continued to study the Tinkers' leader surreptitiously. Click was as tall as Jimmy, which was a few inches taller than the other two more stoutly built men, but his body had a supple, well-muscled look that was only accentuated by his choice of clothing. Instead of loose pleated pants his fawn-colored trousers were fitted, hugging his long calves and thighs. He wore a green pullover shirt with a deep V neck, which revealed a worn leather thong knotted around the tanned skin of his throat. Over the shirt he wore a loose leather vest fronted with pockets and ornamented with metal rings and conchas. Rather than riding boots he wore a low type of boot that was laced up the front. Cassidy had noticed that it seemed to be the preferred footgear among the Tinkers.

Having recovered from his initial embarrassment, Jimmy quickly delivered the rest of his announcement. "They've come looking for food and supplies—oh, and clothes."

Click regarded Cassidy and Rowena with a calm and overtly appraising look; after just thirty seconds of it, Cassidy found herself becoming distinctly uncomfortable. Not that there was anything even remotely threatening in the directness of his gaze; in fact, quite the opposite was true. If anything, Cassidy thought that the dark-haired man had a surprisingly inoffensive stare. It was just that there was something barely hidden in those umber eyes, some spark of knowledge and perceptiveness whose seductive appeal she found nearly more dangerous than outright hostility would have been. She thought that like Allen, Click was a man who *knew* things.

"Food and supplies, yes," Click finally said, his tone softly neutral, "but what clothes they have I find well worn."

Behind him, Tad the blacksmith and Willie both guffawed softly. Only Jimmy seemed confused by Click's comment. Cassidy shifted uncomfortably on Dragonfly's back, prompting Click to give her a pleasant enough little nod.

Then, when it had finally become their turn to present their case to the Tinkers, Cassidy found herself momentarily tongue-tied. Luckily, Rowena was seldom at a loss for words and when Cassidy didn't immediately speak, the brunette sharply poked her in the small of her bare back and hissed, "Come on—tell them why we're here!"

"Uh, I'm a Horseman," Cassidy said. She cleared her throat. "Rowena is my friend. We've been on the trail for several weeks."

Click was still looking directly at them with that same unnerving calm. Cassidy found herself helplessly racing forward through the story she and Rowena had fabricated, blurting out the last of it with artless haste.

"All the rainy weather soaked our packs, and we lost most of our equipment trying to cross a flooded river. We tried to spread everything out—our clothes, I mean—overnight to dry them. But something came along and ate them." She paused for breath, then suddenly stumbled onward again to explain, "Leather! Our clothes were made of leather—that's why something ate them." Wincing inwardly, she tried to school her expression to polite nonchalance as she met Click's imperturbable gaze. "We think it was foxes," she concluded lamely.

That time the two burly men did not laugh aloud; but Cassidy could see from their faces that it was costing them very dearly just to contain themselves. Yet once again Click just regarded them in thoughtful silence, his handsome face as pleasant as a cream-fed cat's.

"I can see you've had a bad piece of luck," he said at last. There was a twinkle in those deep brown eyes, a silent laughter that did not touch his mouth and yet at the same time was openly appealing. "When did you say this . . . misfortune happened?"

"Uh, yesterday," Cassidy fumbled, the fabrication now as clumsy as it was obvious.

"A bad piece," Click repeated, the crinkly lines around his eyes deepening, "and yet it could have been worse."

When Cassidy couldn't find her tongue, Rowena promptly spoke up. "What do you mean, worse?" she asked him.

Spreading his hands with a half shrug, the Tinker replied, "Why, there're Woodsmen in these parts. If it hadn't been for the foxes, one of the wild ones could just as easily have relieved you of everything you owned."

Unable to convincingly stifle their mirth any longer, Tad and Willie had to turn back to their task raising the tent to keep from laughing right out loud at the two women. But Click seemed to possess remarkable self-control in that respect. He didn't even crack a smile as he gestured and called out to the big purple-clad woman with the two yappy little dogs still cradled on her bosom.

"Bonnie," Click said, "get some soap, please, and take these ladies down to the creek to wash. Then find something agreeable for them to wear." He looked back to Cassidy and Rowena, giving them a slight nod while his bright eyes crackled with wordless humor. "And then they can join us for supper, if they wish, and we'll discuss the rest of their needs."

Relieved to be released from the head Tinker's presence, Cassidy guided the gray mare away from his partially erected striped tent. The woman he had called Bonnie set down her two hyperkinetic little dogs again so that she could search through one of the bundles by her cook fire. The dogs pranced around Bonnie, throwing out random yips in the mare's direction. Apparently they were less impressed with the horse in particular than they were with any unexpected activity in general. To them Bonnie's search for the soap was equally as exciting as having strangers in the camp.

None of the other Tinkers seemed to be paying much attention to their visitors, however. As she and Rowena waited on the mare's back, Cassidy noticed that the other men and women were all busy with their tasks, setting up tents and preparing food. Already several fires were blazing around the campsite and the pungent tang of woodsmoke scented the air.

When the big blond woman had found what she wanted from among her supplies, she looked up at Cassidy and Rowena. She was so huge that she made the buxom Rowena look almost petite by comparison; in the gaudy purple dress she resembled an ambulatory version of one of the Tinkers' brightly colored tents. She had a chain of redundant chins like white rolls of pastry. But her eyes, regarding them then with amused expectancy, were shrewd and kindly.

"You might as well get down now," she said wryly, "unless you intend to bathe the horse, as well?"

Rowena and Cassidy hastily slid down off Dragonfly's back. As they followed Bonnie down to the creek, her two little ragmop dogs frisked along with them, quickly drenching their fur in the wet grass and weeds. The horse dropped back a bit and then began casually to graze, cropping the turf with her customary enthusiasm. And although Cassidy threw several less-than-surreptitious glances back over her bare shoulder, none of the other Tinkers seemed to be paying any inordinate attention to either the gray horse or the two naked women who walked ahead of her. All of them were pretty well engrossed in their camp preparations; even Jimmy had disappeared among the carts. It was difficult for her to accept, but Cassidy finally realized that the only reason she and Rowena had drawn any interest had been because they were strangers, and not particularly because they were naked strangers. Once the initial introductions were over, everyone was content to wait for further socializing. Even Bonnie left them once they had reached the bank of the creek.

The soap Bonnie had provided was soft and sweet-smelling and lathered impressively even in the cold creek water. Cassidy temporarily laid aside her misgivings about the Tinkers to luxuriate in the pure pleasure of just getting clean again. She realized she hadn't had a decent bath since the night of the fire in Double Creek; she never thought one could feel so good.

After Cassidy and Rowena had rinsed themselves off, Bonnie reappeared with soft, fluffy towels. While they dried themselves and fluffed out their wet hair, the immense blond woman proffered a selection of clothing. Cassidy was a little overwhelmed by the diversity of what was being offered to them, but it was simple to make her choice; she picked what looked the most comfortable, durable, and practical. She found a pair of tan breeches very similar to what Click wore, sewn with tailored panels so that there was no inseam on the inner thighs, and a loosely cut cream shirt with long sleeves that could be rolled up and secured at the shoulders in warm weather. Much as she would miss her good old jeans and T-shirt, Cassidy had to admit that these clothes were a lot cleaner and just as comfortable. She also selected boots, tall suede leather ones very much like her old riding boots, but with a softer sole and a low heel for walking.

Rowena was no Horseman and her taste in clothing was unexpectedly revealing about her personality. Obviously seeking to escape the Villagers' universally drab and formless attire, the brunette unabashedly enjoyed indulging herself in a pair of long pleated pants made of something stretchy and subtly spangled with metallic threads. She topped them with an oversized shirt of plum-colored cloth with leather insets across the chest. She didn't much care for high boots, either, being far happier with a pair of the Tinker-style low laced boots. Twirling around for Cassidy's approval, Rowena grinned at the picture she presented.

"I'm glad we lost those rabbit skins," she whispered loudly to Cassidy.

As Bonnie gathered up the extra clothing, she smiled indulgently at the two women. "Later you can pick out some extra things," she said. "But first I'm sure you'd rather have something to eat."

While Cassidy still felt a niggling uneasiness about returning to the camp and Click's company, Rowena's eagerness to have a real meal again was transparently obvious. Cassidy wished the two of them could have had a little time alone first to discuss their strategy, but she couldn't think of any way to arrange it that wouldn't have appeared suspicious and awkward. She would just have to trust that Rowena would stick to their original plans and would let her take the lead in any negotiations that might be necessary with the leader of the Tinker band.

Shaking back her freshly washed hair, Cassidy nodded politely to Bonnie and said, "We'd be very grateful."

Dragonfly still grazed contentedly along the edge of the camp. In many ways the horse's priorities were strikingly similar to Rowena's; neither of them seemed to be burdened with Cassidy's paranoia. As they came back into the camp she saw that most of the people were then sitting around the cook fires. The tents and awnings all were set up and the tantalizing odors of cooked meat and fresh bread hung in the damp air. Bonnie's two little dogs scurried along ahead of them, weaving around fires, seated people, and parked carts. The larger dog, lying beneath one of the carts, barked playfully at the smaller ones. Unintelligible murmurs of conversation and some laughter could be heard floating over the camp. The fading light brought the pooling of deep purple shadows, but the glow from the cook fires and the oil lanterns that hung from the tent poles was cheery and persistent. The scene was unfamiliar to Cassidy and yet so intrinsically welcoming that she felt some of her trepidation ease as they followed Bonnie back into the camp.

At Click's big striped tent several people had gathered around a large firepit. The aromas of their cooking perfumed the air, and Cassidy felt her mouth begin to water even before she could identify any of the specific foods being prepared there. Tad the blacksmith and Willie, the big man in the overalls, looked up from their seats on the grass with good-natured greetings for her and Rowena.

"Ladies, welcome back," Tad called out. He was manning a big iron skillet that rested on a metal grill over the fire, deftly manipulating the pan so that its contents swirled about, sending up a savory cloud of steam.

"Come on, sit with us," Willie said. He gestured with his big beefy hands, even though they both were filled with plates and mugs. "You both know Wanda, right?"

As she and Rowena drew up to the fire, Cassidy recognized the short brunette who had been picking loganberries with Jimmy. Wanda was smoothly stirring a large bowl full of some dark concoction that appeared to be made from those same berries, but she spared a moment to look up and give them a pleasant smile.

"I see Bonnie found something suitable for you to wear."

This comment came from another woman at the fire. She was not someone they had seen before, but her tone, too, was friendly. From what Cassidy could see in the firelight, the woman was a fairly attractive redhead with a fine-boned aristocratic-looking face and a facile smile. She was wearing loose trousers and a sleeveless shirt that was partially unbuttoned; but she was so flat-chested that there seemed nothing calculated about the style. The woman was pouring what smelled like coffee from a big ceramic pot, and she held out a mug to Cassidy with an inquiring lift of her brows.

The fragrance of the freshly brewed coffee tempted Cassidy and she nodded vigorously, just about to thank the red-headed woman when another voice smoothly cut in.

"Why, Moira—are you saying that the ladies' original outfits weren't completely suitable?"

There could be no mistaking the owner of that soft, gently mocking voice, yet Cassidy found herself starting. She quickly looked down to see that she and Rowena had been standing right behind Click, who was seated at the fire with his back to them. The discovery almost made her take an involuntary step backward, but when she jerked her gaze back up again she saw that Moira was still holding out the steaming cup of coffee to her. Reaching for the mug, Cassidy stepped aside so that Rowena could also be served.

"Boy, whatever you're cooking sure smells terrific!" Rowena said to Tad as she took a cup of coffee from Moira.

With her natural gregariousness, Rowena had immediately found a common chord with the burly bald man. Tad, obviously fond of food and cooking, visibly puffed with pleasure at the praise. "I hope you'll enjoy it," he said, ducking his shining head modestly.

Maybe they don't remember sex, but there's nothing wrong with their grasp of food! Cassidy thought.

"And we'll be having loganberry shortcake for dessert," Wanda added, giving her bowl one final stir.

Sinking down cross-legged on the grass, Cassidy glanced over to see Click's dark eyes studying her and Rowena. There was nothing secretive about his surveillance, and when he caught Cassidy's eye he nodded slightly to her with a pleasant expression. Deliberately looking away, Cassidy concentrated on her coffee cup.

"Start passing me those plates, Willie," Tad said then, tugging the big skillet across the grill toward himself. "Everything's ready to eat."

While the food was being dished up conversation was limited to relayed requests and polite murmurs of thanks. When Cassidy glanced around the rest of the camp she could see that the same mealtime ritual was being repeated at the other cook fires. Darkness had nearly fallen then, and in the foggy gloom of the encroaching night the small groups of Tinkers clustered around their fires and lanterns seemed wreathed in little clouds of golden haze. Even the dogs were finally quiet, probably collapsed somewhere within begging distance.

"Anything else, Cassidy?"

Tad's gruff but friendly inquiry startled Cassidy out of her reverie and she quickly shook her head at the blacksmith. "This is great," she assured him, digging into her heaped plate of steaming meat and vegetables with determined heartiness. Once she had taken a bite, however, there was no need for her to fabricate enthusiasm; the stew *was* delicious, hot and hearty and perfectly seasoned. After a diet of berries, crabapples, and rabbit meat—even after the Villagers' bland but nourishing fare—the food seemed incredibly good. Cassidy didn't think she'd eaten anything like it since she'd found herself in that godforsaken place.

During the meal the conversation was casual and varied, but no one even mentioned Cassidy and Rowena's sudden and awkward arrival in their midst. The topics were simple and mundane things: a loose wheel on a cart that would need attention; how many kegs of nails they had left in their stores; what they thought the weather might do. Rowena occupied herself with eating, earning Tad's continuing approval by asking not only for seconds but also for thirds. Cassidy was a little more circumspect, partly because she was trying to inconspicuously analyze the Tinkers' conversation for useful information and partly because she was still vaguely nervous about even being there in their camp at all.

Throughout the meal she was aware that Click was watching her and Rowena. Again there was nothing secretive or sinister about the dark-haired man's observation; his appraisal was frank and ongoing. But Cassidy found herself purposely looking away from him, concentrating on Tad and Willie's affectionately insulting banter or on Wanda's dry humor as she dished out generous portions of shortcake. As dessert was served, Moira offered them all more coffee. As Cassidy held out her mug, it seemed to her that the red-haired woman flashed her a quick and knowing wink over its rim.

Cassidy didn't know what to make of Click's attention, and that uncertainty troubled her more than any obvious threat would have. She felt uneasy about what the Tinker's terms might be for the help he was offering them, especially if he found out that she and Rowena were actually fugitives from Double Creek. It was like having to wait for the other boot to drop to sit there sharing a meal with those sociable people, not knowing how they might react once she and Rowena were forced to come up with some sort of plausible explanation of why they were out on the road alone.

And something else about Click himself as man, not just as the head of the Tinker band, disturbed Cassidy. She had convinced herself it was not a sexual thing; that was simply not a part of that world. But she thought to herself as she covertly studied the tall man's lean and finely planed profile in the flicker of the firelight that if anyone there was ever going to remember sex, Click would have gotten her vote as the most likely candidate for the distinction.

Rowena had just finished devouring seconds of the shortcake when Cassidy glanced down and realized that she still had half of her initial helping left. Anxiety was dulling her appetite, but she forced herself to finish the dessert so as not to appear conspicuous. When Willie began gathering up dishes, she impulsively blurted out, "Rowena and I can wash the dishes—it's the least we can do."

"Yeah, we'd be glad to," Rowena echoed. "That was the best meal I've ever eaten!"

But even as Willie automatically demurred, Click intervened.

"No, Willie and Moira will take care of that tonight," he

said, gracefully gaining his feet. He gestured expansively at Cassidy and Rowena. "You ladies are our guests, and now I would be happy to have you join me in my tent."

It was not phrased as a command, yet his tone did not exactly suggest a request either. Cassidy stiffened, torn between simple panic and a fatalistic desire to just get the inevitable confrontation over with. She did not even realize how long their awkward silence had stretched until Rowena sharply elbowed her in the back.

"Sure—thank you," Cassidy said quickly. As Click gestured again and stepped forward to lead the way across the few yards of trampled grass to the striped tent, she found herself almost wishing that sex *was* a factor. At that point she would rather have had to stave off seduction than interrogation.

They had to duck to enter the tent's flap, but inside the canvas structure was just tall enough for a man of Click's height to stand upright. Glancing around in the warm yellow light of the two lanterns that were hung from the top of the main poles, Cassidy was surprised to find that the floor of the tent was piled with the bedding and other personal possessions of at least four or five people. Somehow she had just assumed that as the head man Click would rate his own tent; it was obvious he shared that one with several of the other Tinkers.

Cassidy looked up right into Click's face, meeting the dark eyes that were alight with contained amusement. From the perceptive spark in those eyes she knew that he had surmised what she had been thinking, and she was suddenly embarrassed by the presumption she had made.

Rowena had been looking around the tent, too, but the cheerful brunette had come to a totally different perspective. "This is really nice," she said to Click. "It must be great when you're traveling to be able to sleep under a roof, especially with all the rain we've been having."

Click gave her an agreeable nod, the silvered wings of his mustache lifting slightly. "Helps to keep away the foxes, as well," he remarked casually. He waved toward the piles of bedrolls. "Please sit if you like."

Like it or not, Cassidy didn't feel that they had much choice. Still keeping one eye on Click, she sank down onto one of the thick rolls of blankets. Rowena dropped down beside her, but where Cassidy was tense the brunette seemed completely comfortable.

Click folded his long legs and perched on the lid of a small wooden chest, sitting right across from them. "You've made a lifelong friend in Tad, Rowena," he said, casually cupping his palms over his bent knees. "I'm afraid all of us are far too spoiled by his good cooking to properly appreciate it."

"Well, if he always cooks like that," Rowena replied, "he'll always have a friend in me."

Glancing them both up and down again, the dark-haired man nodded thoughtfully and said, "Moira was right; the clothes really are quite suitable."

The unexpected small talk only grated on Cassidy's taut nerves; rather than calming her, it served to heighten her anxiety. She found herself wishing that Click would just get on with it and ask them what he must want to know about their circumstances. But Rowena didn't seem at all put out by the delay; if anything she seemed to be enjoying the little chat.

The brunette fingered the bloused sleeve of her splashy new shirt. "Do you make all of this stuff yourselves?" she asked Click.

"Some of it," he replied. "Some we take in trade." He looked directly at Cassidy, catching her with a vague unconscious frown on her face, which she quickly tried to erase and replace with the semblance of polite interest. "The boots and shoes are all made by Sheila; she's our cobbler." He looked back to Rowena. "She's also done most of the leatherwork you see on the clothing."

"It's beautiful stuff," Rowena said, touching the insets on her own shirt. Cassidy had no doubt that the brunette was recalling the coarse and bland clothing worn by all the Villagers. "Do you make the tents, too?"

Growing increasingly annoyed at Rowena for prolonging their ordeal, Cassidy only half listened to Click's response. She was more concerned about how well their fabricated story would hold up to his questioning than she was interested in the Tinkers' professional work.

"Willie does our canvas work. Moira is a potter; Jimmy is her apprentice. We also have a cooper, a cartwright, and several metalworkers and seamstresses." Cassidy glanced up just in time to catch one of Click's soft almost smiles. "You see, we do a lot more than just make pots and pans."

"I think it's great," Rowena said. "When you know how to work with your hands like that, you can always come up with anything you need."

"Almost anything," Click said. He pulled up one fawn-clad

leg, crossing that ankle over his other knee. "I'm sure that we can come up with whatever you ladies will need for the rest of your journey."

Realizing that she had left Rowena to do all of the talking thus far for both of them, Cassidy finally found her voice. "We really won't need a lot of stuff; just a few basic things like bedrolls and some food."

"Yeah, especially food," Rowena said.

Cassidy threw her a quick disapproving glance, but Click only seemed amused by the buxom woman's enthusiasm. "All of that can be arranged easily enough," he said. He casually flexed his arms, lacing his fingers around the booted ankle that rested over his knee. "After all, providing goods is what we're here for."

There was a moment of silence, a brief hiatus in the conversation during which Cassidy first glanced down into her lap and then looked up at him again, blinking. She had just realized, much to her chagrin, that the matter of payment had not yet been broached. It was a knotty problem, one that she and Rowena had not been able to resolve on their own, and one that she could see that Click would not bring up first.

"We, ah, don't exactly have anything to trade for the supplies," Cassidy said reluctantly, forcing herself to keep looking steadily into that dark lean face. "When we lost our clothes and equipment, we lost everything we owned."

"Of course," Click agreed almost sympathetically. "A bad piece of luck for sure."

Cassidy warily studied that placid face, trying to determine if Click was laughing at them behind that affable manner. Beside her, Rowena shifted slightly on the bedroll on which she sat. Cassidy was grateful that the brunette was keeping silent then and letting her do the actual bargaining.

"But we'd be willing to work in exchange for the supplies we need," Cassidy told Click, projecting a forced sense of confidence.

The tall man tipped his head back, the yellow lantern light washing over the clean planes of his aquiline face. Cassidy thought he was going to laugh, but he didn't. Stroking the edge of his mustache with one forefinger, he merely looked thoughtful. "I'm sure that something mutually agreeable can be arranged," he said.

Was he mocking her? It was so difficult to tell. He was as smooth as butter with his deep brown eyes and his gentle irony. For not the first time in recent hours, Cassidy found herself wishing that she and Rowena had just kept riding and had never come into the Tinkers' camp at all. But then her resolve stiffened and she looked directly at Click, challenging his comment with perfect seriousness.

"We may not have all of your special skills," she said tersely, "but neither one of us is afraid of hard work."

Spreading his hands palms up, Click quickly said, "I have no doubt of that." The lines around his umber eyes deepened and his mouth quirked again in that near smile. "After all, you've already offered to wash dishes."

He *was* mocking them, Cassidy thought furiously . . . or was he? In the next moment she was less certain again as Click's hands relaced themselves over his knees and he calmly went on.

"In about a week's time we'll reach the Long River. If you wish to travel along with us until then, we would be happy to provide you both with food and shelter during the journey." Anticipating Cassidy's dissent from the expression on her face, Click again spread his hands and intercepted any possible protest by adding "That is merely hospitality." His eyes sparkled. "We'll even throw in the clothing. And if you have helped us with our business along the way, then once we reach the Long River we would be glad to stock you with additional food and supplies, if you choose to leave our band then."

If and not *when*—Click's smooth audacity rankled Cassidy so much that for a few moments she didn't even realize that he had just made them a very generous offer. Luckily Rowena had not been wasting her time gnawing over every imagined insult, and she spoke up before Cassidy's lapse became overly obvious.

"That'd be great," she said. "That's very nice of you. We'll do anything we can to help pay our way."

"Good," Click said, rising gracefully to his feet again, "then that's settled. Now let's have Wanda get you some bedding and help get you settled for tonight."

Surprised, outmaneuvered, and still feeling impotently irritated at Click, Cassidy suddenly found herself being ushered along with Rowena out of the big green and white tent. Outside around the campsite the cook fires had burned low, and most of the light came from a few strategically placed oil lanterns and a thin coating of moonlight. Most of the other tents were dark, and only a few Tinkers still sat around their firepits or moved in the shadowy pools of darkness around the parked carts. At the edge of the camp, like a ghostly white blur, Dragonfly stood calmly hip-shot in the darkness.

Wanda sat by Click's cook fire, softly humming to herself as she combed out her long straight hair. As the woman looked up at the three of them, Cassidy realized that she was probably one of the people who slept in the big striped tent.

"Wanda, these ladies will be traveling with us," Click said. Cassidy suspected the brown-haired woman already knew that, since she could easily have heard everything that had been said inside the tent. "Would you help them get settled for the night, please?"

Nodding pleasantly, Wanda stood and beckoned for Cassidy and Rowena to follow her. A few yards from the cook fire Cassidy glanced back toward the tent; but Click had vanished, just as swiftly as had the Woodsman.

"This is very nice of you," Rowena said as Wanda began to unfasten the tarp covering one of the big wooden handcarts.

"Well, we like having guests," Wanda replied, as she rummaged around inside the cart's bed.

There was nothing sinister about the woman, nothing inherently sinister about the whole situation, and yet Cassidy could not fight down her continuing suspicion. As Wanda pulled out the canvas and poles for a small, pup-style tent and then began to sort out bedrolls and towels, Cassidy was forced to consider that her hesitancy to accept the Tinkers' help was just paranoia of the worst stripe: She was suspicious of them precisely because they were so kind and friendly to her and Rowena. She tried to remind herself of the sour weather they'd endured on the trail, the meager food, and the Woodsman's piracy. They were due some good luck; why couldn't she just let go as Rowena seemed to have and accept that?

With a little guidance from Wanda, Cassidy and Rowena were able to erect their simple tent at the edge of the encampment, on a site near the gray mare and, for Cassidy, deliberately removed from Click's vicinity. Just having bedrolls again was sheer luxury after all those nights they had spent on the bare ground; the little tent seemed the ultimate in extravagance. By the time they had settled down under the small sheltering walls of canvas, the rest of the Tinker camp was nearly dark and silent. All that remained of the evening's events was the faint odor of cooked meat and smoke in the damp night air.

Rowena yawned hugely and snuggled contentedly into the

padding of her bedroll. Cassidy knew she shouldn't begrudge the woman her comfort, yet in some vague and illogical way she resented Rowena's simple acceptance of their fate. If she couldn't share the brunette's calm satisfaction with the way things were progressing, then she wanted Rowena to feel some of the same niggling suspicions that she did. It wasn't fair that the damned woman was so trusting—why should Cassidy be the only one to suffer?

"You still awake?" Cassidy whispered loudly.

"Yeah," Rowena said, but Cassidy could tell that she was stifling another yawn.

"Well, what do you think?" Cassidy persisted.

"What, about this?" Rowena asked. "I think we should say the hell with the Warden and just stay with these guys—the food is terrific!"

It only took a few moments of stiff silence before Rowena realized that Cassidy had entirely missed the humor in her response. "Cassidy, I was just *kidding!*" she said.

But Cassidy just grunted, barely mollified.

"Listen, they're going in the same general direction as we were anyway," Rowena went on. "And it's a lot safer to travel with a big group like this than it would be on our own."

Cassidy could hardly have argued either point. The only objection she could have raised would have been that they hadn't even known if they'd been traveling in the right direction in the first place; and it didn't seem very productive to bring up that possibility right then. And Rowena was more on target than she ever could have known when it came to the subject of their safety. Cassidy could not entirely keep from her mind the frightening image of those foul and monstrous hanging creatures.

But she didn't have to *like* the fact that Rowena was right. And once the soft snores began to rise from the larger woman's bedroll, Cassidy slid out from under her own cover and silently pulled on her boots. Navigating by moonlight, she crept out across the wet grass to where Dragonfly grazed.

The horse's equanimity didn't rankle Cassidy; rather, she found it soothing. She leaned against the mare's warm and familiar flank, gently rocked by the horse's breathing. The gray grunted tolerantly and exhaled softly as her upper lip deftly searched through the turf for the choicest blades of grass.

Perhaps Rowena was right, Cassidy considered reluctantly; perhaps falling in with the Tinkers was going to help them.

But the inherent problem with any circumstances that tended to make their lives easier was Cassidy's unspoken fear that Rowena would decide that whole world wasn't so bad after all, and that she would forget all about the urgency of finding their way home again to the place from which they'd come. Yes, that was the crux of it: Cassidy was afraid that Rowena might go back to just accepting that world—and that if her friend gave up, Cassidy herself might be tempted to do so, as well.

"No, that'll never happen," Cassidy vowed softly to the horse, burying her cheek in the fragrant and silky flank. "No matter what happens, you and I are going home again."

Chapter 4 ◄▥

During the night the wind had shifted, and by morning the sullen humidity of the past few days had begun to dissipate. Cassidy and Rowena were sitting at a cook fire nursing second cups of coffee with Wanda, Tad, and Willie when one of the women from a nearby group of breakfasters came over to them and introduced herself.

"I'm Carlotta," she said after Wanda had introduced Cassidy and Rowena. "Click told me you two might be looking for work."

Tactfully put, Cassidy thought dryly, quickly studying the woman before them. Carlotta was middle-aged but well maintained, lithe and trim in a one-piece outfit made of suede leather and some type of gauzy yellow material. She was about Cassidy's height and had short ginger-colored hair and hazel eyes. Like Wanda, she also wore earrings, long dangling ones that appeared to be linked chains of tiny rings. And like Tad she had a tattoo, a small rose on her right wrist. She also had numerous rings on her fingers.

"What kind of help do you need?" Cassidy asked her carefully, eyeing all of the jewelry.

Carlotta's hands were long and sinewy with slender fingers; several of her rings were set with stones that winked in the sunlight as she gestured across the camp toward the parked carts. "Usually Teddy helps me with my cart," she said. She threw Tad a look and continued, "But he's been trying to work with Tad—he hopes to apprentice as a blacksmith. And with these hills—whew!" Carlotta puffed melodramatically, fanning herself with one beringed hand. "I could use a relief pedaler or two."

Rowena's eyes lit up. "You have one of the carts with the bicycles?" she asked.

Carlotta nodded, continuing, "I figured if you girls were used to riding a horse then you must have better legs than I do."

Deciding that Carlotta's offer was probably as good as any they would receive, Cassidy quickly said, "Sure, we'd be glad to help you with your cart." After all, she thought, how hard could riding a bicycle be?

"Good," Carlotta said happily. "I'm just getting packed up now; if you want to throw your stuff in my cart, you're welcome. We should be breaking camp pretty soon."

"Well, this won't be so bad," Rowena whispered to Cassidy a few minutes later as the two of them packed up their little tent and their bedrolls. "It'll beat walking—it'll even beat riding a horse."

Cassidy knew Rowena was only joking with her crack about riding the mare; the brunette had actually become a fairly adept rider in the past week or so. But after further consideration, Cassidy began to wonder if Rowena's breezy confidence wasn't a little misplaced. After all, if pedaling the bike cart was so damned easy Carlotta wouldn't have needed any help. She didn't point that out to Rowena, however; she merely said, "Fine—you can take the first turn."

By the time the camp was packed up and ready to roll, Cassidy and Rowena had been introduced to most of the remaining Tinkers they didn't already know by name. Cassidy judged that Jimmy was probably the youngest member of the group, and the oldest appeared to be Paul, their cooper. They even called him "Old Paul"; he was bent and gray-haired and wizened, but he looked as tough as the hickory staves that were piled in his cart and his eyes were as bright and shrewd as a crow's.

Several of the Tinkers had their own carts, filled with the materials of their trade. The remaining carts, like Carlotta's, served double duty carrying not only wares but also the communal stores of tents, bedding, and food. Cassidy also noticed that almost all of the Tinkers who were not directly involved in the pushing or drawing of the carts carried bundles or backpacks to help distribute some of the load. For not the first time she was puzzled that they didn't use horses for draft animals. It would have made sense considering how much material they had to move across the countryside every day. Then again, she reminded herself, the search for sense in that world was likely to be a doomed enterprise.

When they brought their baggage over to Carlotta's cart, both Cassidy and Rowena were amazed at the collection of items the older woman carried. It soon became obvious that Carlotta was a metalworker. But in addition to the usual mundane and practical objects, such as hand tools and hinges and doorknobs, she also made purely ornamental items, such as jewelry and decorations for clothing. She even had an extensive collection of horse-related creations, including engraved copper-port bridle bits and ornate harness brasses.

Seeing their surprise, Carlotta merely smiled. "You like?" she asked, holding up an elaborate silver necklace for their inspection. "It's not all hoes and gate latches, believe me—although I'll tell you, with most of these farmers we deal with, they wouldn't know a gold earring from a copper bullring!" She laughed, her long earrings swinging as she stuffed their bedrolls into the cart on top of her jewelry trays. "So I try to make a little bit of everything."

"Your jewelry is beautiful," Rowena said sincerely, reaching out to touch one of the heavy rings on Carlotta's slender fingers. The largest ring had a milky blue stone the size of a small bird's egg set in it. "Did you make all of these yourself?"

Touched by the honest appreciation, Carlotta spread her hands, displaying the rings for Rowena's inspection. "Most of them," she said. "Some I've traded for with my friends, and some were gifts."

"Wow," Rowena said, inelegant but eloquent praise.

Carlotta was ready to climb up onto the bicycle that was attached to her cart, but Rowena quickly offered to take the first turn pedaling the two-wheeler. "I'd like to give it a try," she said, and the spark of eagerness in her eyes apparently convinced the metalsmith.

Cassidy asked if there was anything she could carry on her horse, but Carlotta just shook her head. "No, why don't you just ride along for a while," she said.

Cassidy didn't notice Click until the Tinkers were just getting under way. If she had expected him to undertake a purely supervisory role on the trail, then she would have been surprised to see that the packframe strapped to his back was one of the most heavily loaded. And he didn't take any kind of command position, either; in fact, he was bent over Sheila's

cobbler's cart, checking a wheel, when the group got under
way. Feeling almost guilty for the luxury, Cassidy hopped up
onto the gray mare's back and studiously avoided looking over
at the dark-haired man as she rode alongside Carlotta's cart.

Because they were essentially a group of people traveling on
foot, and not traveling lightly by any means, the pace the Tinkers set was much slower than the driven pace that Cassidy
and Rowena had maintained since they'd fled the village. Then
again, no one was chasing them, Cassidy reminded herself. But
despite the slower speed, the Tinkers' travel was hardly leisurely. They were moving a great quantity of goods over
wooded and hilly terrain, not an easy job. Rowena was one of
the first people to discover just how difficult it could be. She
had been pedaling Carlotta's bike cart for only a little more
than an hour when she had to concede that her legs were about
to give out on her.

"Jeez, and I thought I was in pretty good shape," the brunette admitted once Carlotta had smilingly replaced her on the
bicycle and Rowena had assumed her more familiar place behind Cassidy on Dragonfly's back. "That cart must weigh a
ton—these people must have thighs like iron!"

Keeping that in mind, Cassidy didn't wait any longer than
the group's midmorning break to offer to take over the pedaling chore from Carlotta. She had already noticed that none of
the Tinkers spent all of their time pushing or pulling the carts;
that job was constantly rotated among several different people
so that each vehicle had a number of attendants. She even saw
Click taking his turn with one of the forge-topped carts.

Pedaling Carlotta's bicycle was fun at first; in some vague
and inchoate way it made Cassidy feel connected to the past
she could not remember. The two-wheeled vehicle had a padded leather saddle and short curved handlebars. The wheels
were metal rimmed but the spokes were made of taut thin
wires; the front wheel was slightly larger than the rear, because
the back wheel had to fit partially under the foreboard of the
big wooden cart. She didn't have to worry about keeping her
balance because the bike's frame was firmly bolted to the
cart's shafts by a crossbar that ran behind the seat.

It didn't take Cassidy long to begin to sympathize with
Rowena about feeling ill-prepared to take on the task of pedaling the cart. After the first long slope the muscles of her
thighs and calves complained sharply. If not for Carlotta and
Rowena helping by pushing on the rear of the cart, she prob-

ably would never have made it up the second hill. She found herself looking longingly at the gray mare, who tagged along at the edge of the procession. But pulling the cart on the level was only mildly taxing, and going downhill was actually fun. And no matter how tired her legs grew, Cassidy was determined that she would keep on pedaling until the midday break was called.

The day grew progressively warmer as the morning went on, although the enervating humidity of the past few days was finally gone. As both the sun and the temperature climbed, many of the Tinkers began to adjust their clothing to accommodate the heat. All of their garments, even the most fanciful looking, had been designed to be quite adaptable and practical. Long-sleeved shirts like the ones Cassidy and Rowena wore were made with loose sleeves that could be opened and pushed back or rolled all the way up to the shoulders and fastened there. Vests, shirts, and other overgarments were fashioned to be opened down the front or sides, and even the most form-fitting pants were made of fabric that was absorbent and cool. Cassidy found herself only mildly disconcerted when she first saw one of the women partially bare her breasts beneath an opened shirt. Redevoting herself to her pedaling, she decided that unless people began to shuck off their pants she was not going to pay any undue attention to something that obviously meant so little to the Tinkers.

As the morning's trek continued, Cassidy was constantly forced to keep revising her opinion of those people. The first casual mention she'd heard of the Tinkers was from Aaron, one of the Villagers who had befriended her. The reference hadn't really made any distinct impression on her. Tinkers were the people who made things, that was all she knew about them. She hadn't even realized that they were itinerant until she and Rowena had crossed their tracks. Before that she guessed she had just hazily assumed that they all lived in some big Tinker village somewhere, banging out pots and pans. That very ignorance was one of the reasons she had resisted the logic of Rowena's conclusion that they should seek out the Tinkers' help when they found themselves literally stripped of all their possessions on the trail. She had been afraid of them.

Meeting Jimmy and Wanda and the others had proved a surprising education. The Tinkers were treating her and Rowena with unfailing kindness and hospitality. They had not even pressed the two women for any realistic explanation of their impoverished circumstances—something Cassidy certainly would have done had the situation been reversed. And so even though she still felt a certain guardedness around them, and even though she still innately distrusted Click, Cassidy had decided she was glad she had let Rowena talk her into coming into the Tinker camp.

As if we had much choice! her little inner voice chided her.

Above and beyond her willingness to admit that she had been wrong about them, Cassidy also found herself beginning to genuinely like the traveling tradesmen. It would have been difficult to not have. In direct contrast to the single-mindedly driven Horsemen and the dour farmers of the village, the Tinkers were a naturally cheerful lot. It wasn't just their good food or their colorful clothing or their fondness for ornamentation. As they traveled along they enjoyed talking and joking. They frequently laughed aloud; a few of them even whistled or sang, sounds so incredibly evocative to Cassidy that the first time she heard them she'd felt an inexplicable pang of longing go through her, even stronger than the sense of nostalgia she had felt when she had first seen their bicycles. That the Tinkers often sang badly was not considered a fault; their spontaneity and enthusiasm more than compensated for their lack of talent. It seemed to Cassidy that the Tinkers possessed the one thing she had felt was so painfully lacking in the other people of that woefully skewed world: personality. They were capable of holding opinions, and actually seemed to take some joy in living.

Several times throughout the morning, especially once she had taken over pedaling Carlotta's bike cart, Cassidy found her eyes seeking out Click. She told herself it was because she mistrusted him and just wanted to keep a watch on his whereabouts; but the truth was that she was still very curious about the Tinkers' leader. And every time she'd looked, she found him in motion, helping to push a cart, readjust a load, or just sharing a laugh with one of his fellows as he strode along with his backpack.

Cassidy had to concede that Click was a dynamic man, but she told herself that a certain amount of presence was necessary to supervise such a divergent group of people. She still wasn't sure how any group in that world, be they Horsemen, Villagers, or Tinkers, chose their leader. Someone like Allen, who was intelligent, fair-minded, and courageous, was a logical choice for sheriff of Double Creek; but Misty, a bitter old woman, was the last person Cassidy would have picked to be the village's mayor. In some ways Click reminded her of Allen; not physically, of course, but in some of the other qualities they both possessed. The only problem with that was Cassidy really didn't want to be reminded of the big sorrel-haired sheriff.

The sun was barely at its zenith when the Tinkers called their midday stop, but Cassidy didn't think she could have lasted another fifteen minutes pedaling the bike. As she parked Carlotta's cart alongside the others, her leg muscles burned in protest. It was all she could do to climb down off the vehicle's high saddle without tripping or staggering once she got her feet back on the ground again.

"Pretty hard work, huh?" Rowena said sympathetically as she came around from behind the cart.

Checking first to be sure that no one was close enough to overhear, Cassidy allowed herself to wince and whispered, "This is worse than learning to ride!"

With a jingle of jewelry and a glint of sunlight off her rings, Carlotta came around the side of the cart. She beamed at Cassidy and Rowena. "You girls did real good; you're almost as strong as Teddy." As she began to unfasten the tarp that covered the cart she added, "You're welcome to eat with me and Sheila and Old Paul."

"We'd be glad to eat with you," Cassidy said.

"Can I help you with anything?" Rowena offered, turning back toward the cart.

"I'm just going to take my mare and water her," Cassidy said to them both. The horse, who was more than capable of finding water on her own, had been tagging along near the bike cart the second half of the morning, fascinated by the strange mechanical mount that Cassidy had chosen to ride in her place. Cassidy was glad Dragonfly was near enough that she didn't have to Call her. The Tinkers were surely familiar with Horsemen ways, but Cassidy didn't like to do anything that would call undue attention to herself or accentuate the things that separated her from them.

Hobbling a bit stiffly, she walked over to the grazing horse. It took a deliberate and concerted effort to hop aboard the mare without permanently injuring herself; the muscles in her calves and thighs screamed in protest at the maneuver. But astride the horse she felt more comfortable again. As Cassidy rode away from the cart, Carlotta was busily piling packets of food and utensils into Rowena's arms.

The small creek was at the bottom of a brushy ravine, and the gray mare had to wind her way around several old rotting logs and numerous snaggles of wild raspberry cane before they reached the water. Cassidy had not expected any of the other Tinkers to have made the rough descent down to the rocky little stream, since they carried plentiful water for the day in the casks on their carts. So she was surprised to find that someone else had beaten her and the horse down to the creekbed. A broad-shouldered young man with fair skin and short feathery blond hair was bent over the edge of the water, filling two metal buckets.

"Hi, Teddy," Cassidy said as the mare waded into the water. "What are you doing down here?"

The young man looked up from his task and smiled at her. Teddy wore a loosely cut blue shirt and pants, which only made his blocky body appear larger. He had big square even teeth and hair sun-bleached so light that it was nearly white. Although he was not quite as massive a man as Tad, he still had the muscular strength of a young bull. Cassidy could see how he'd been a big help to Carlotta before he had forsaken her cart to learn blacksmithing.

"Hi, Cassidy," he replied, his tone shy but friendly. He hefted the two buckets of water as if they were nothing more than a couple of berry pails, waving them in explanation. "Tad likes to soak his feet when we stop for lunch, but he hates to waste water from the drinking casks. So he sent me down here to fill a couple of buckets for him." He glanced from Cassidy's face to the big mare beneath her. The horse was completely ignoring both of them and was happily splashing around in the shallow water. "I guess you came to water your horse," he added needlessly.

When she had first been introduced to him that morning, Cassidy had noted several things about Teddy. One thing that was immediately apparent was that despite his size, Teddy was really quite gentle and shy. He tended to blush easily, and because of his fair skin it was readily observable. He was blushing slightly then, just at the novelty of talking with her. Teddy had also impressed Cassidy as being particularly kind-hearted, another quality she found especially pleasant in such a large man. And Teddy seemed to have a special interest in horses;

when he had first met Cassidy he hadn't been able to take his eyes off the gray mare.

Cassidy smiled at Teddy. "You can see that her idea of being watered includes giving herself a bath," she said, patting the mare's sleek neck with fond indulgence.

"She's really a beautiful horse," Teddy said. Then, as if embarrassed by his own sudden boldness, he ducked his big head to hide the way his broad and boyish face colored.

Allowing the mare to continue amusing herself in the creek, Cassidy favored Teddy with a look of friendly curiosity. "You really like horses, don't you, Teddy? Is that why you're apprenticing with Tad?"

Looking up then, seemingly only because he felt he had to in order to be able to politely answer her question, Teddy replied, "Tad really doesn't know much about horses."

Cassidy's brows rose in a puzzled arch. "No? I thought he was your blacksmith?"

Growing increasingly embarrassed but compelled by courtesy to overcome his shyness long enough to answer her, the big blond said, "You're thinking of a farrier. Tad isn't a farrier, he's a blacksmith." His ears were absolutely crimson by then; he had to duck his head again to be able to finish. "Some blacksmiths are farriers, too; and some farriers are blacksmiths. But not all blacksmiths are farriers and not many farriers are blacksmiths."

Cassidy had to stifle her amusement at Teddy's boyish discomfort in order to be able to follow his convoluted explanation. "Oh, I see," she said. "So you're going to become a blacksmith?"

His reddened face still averted, Teddy seemed absorbed in studying the gray mare's forelegs as the horse playfully pawed at the water. "I hope so," he murmured.

"Well, I think you ought to become a blacksmith *and* a farrier," Cassidy said, "since you like horses so much."

Grateful for her endorsement, Teddy managed to lift his eyes again. "We don't even have a farrier," he said. He hesitated a moment, then loudly cleared his throat. "I know Horsemen's horses are special, but do you think I could—could I pet her?"

Cassidy found the burly youth's shyness oddly endearing. She also felt a sort of kinship with Teddy, understanding as she did what it meant to long for something that seemed to stay forever beyond your grasp. "Sure," she said, "go ahead."

Cassidy urged the horse closer to the bank so that Teddy

could reach out and gently stroke the gray's long, water-speckled neck. The look of pure, unadulterated pleasure on his face as he gazed upon the object of his desire was a welcomed change from the kind of reaction that Cassidy had, as a Horse-man, inspired among the Villagers.

"Teddy," Cassidy asked as he continued to pet the mare, "why don't the Tinkers have horses? I would think it would be a lot easier than having the lug all of this stuff around from village to village with handcarts and backpacks."

But Teddy just shook his head, almost absently and without even looking up from his admiring study of the horse. "They'd be too much trouble."

Cassidy cocked her head. "Trouble? Teddy, horses can cover this kind of terrain a lot easier than people can; and you'd be able to haul a lot more stuff with horses."

The blond youth finally glanced up at Cassidy, his ears and cheeks still freshly pinkened. "Oh, I don't mean that kind of trouble," he told her. "I mean trouble with Horsemen." Then realizing to whom he was talking, the flush on Teddy's broad and fleshy face deepened even further. He had to hurry to fin-ish his explanation while he still was able. "And besides, horses can't travel on the river."

Sensitive to Teddy's embarrassment over what he must have perceived to have been a major gaffe, Cassidy was neverthe-less far too curious to just let the topic pass. "Trouble with Horsemen? You mean Horsemen might try to steal the horses?"

Almost squirming, Teddy dropped his hand from the gray mare's neck and looked up at Cassidy with a stricken look on his face. "I didn't mean you, Cassidy," he said hastily.

"I know you didn't, Teddy," she assured him in a soothing tone. Trying to calm him by shifting the topic away from the Horsemen, she asked, "But what did you mean about not being able to travel on the river? Horses can cross rivers without any problem; they're good swimmers."

But Teddy only seemed to grow increasingly flustered. In the direct light of the noon sun his flushed face looked as rosy red as Jimmy's shirt. "We don't cross the Long River," he said, "we go down it." Then, before Cassidy could even consider pressing him for further information, Teddy hastily stooped and scooped up the handles of the water buckets. "I'd better get these back to Tad," he said. He began to turn away, then paused awkwardly and looked back to where Cassidy sat astride the horse in the shallow waters of the creek. He smiled happily at her. "Thanks for letting me pet your horse."

In a few moments he had scrambled back up the briar-strewn slope bearing the two metal pails of water as easily as if they'd been empty.

All through her lunch with Rowena and Carlotta and the other Tinkers, Cassidy puzzled over the things Teddy had told her by the creek. She had immediately realized that the clumsiness of the brawny youth's conversation with her had nothing to do with evasiveness or any reluctance to reveal things to her. Teddy was merely shy. He had found it difficult to talk to her because he was simply tongue-tied around someone he didn't know very well. And that insight led Cassidy to another very important realization: She and Rowena could learn a lot from the Tinkers about the world they shared.

All of Cassidy's original cautious hope, the feeling of promise she had felt on that drizzly ridge when she and Rowena had first looked down upon the Tinkers' entourage and she had recognized the bicycles, returned to her then. She had to force herself to concentrate on the casual lunchtime conversation and remind herself to keep on eating the more-than-adequate meal. It was difficult for her to focus on matters as mundane as food when her mind was furiously racing again, considering all the possibilities.

As she chewed on a thick slice of cold meat, Cassidy reluctantly admitted to herself that at least part of the reason why it hadn't occurred to her sooner that the Tinkers could be willing and able to answer many of her questions was that she had been too suspicious of them even to consider it. Particularly of Click; her distrust of the tall dark-haired man was an especially obstructive reaction. Almost guiltily, she glanced around the noontime encampment. She caught sight of Click across the grassy clearing where he sat casually on the turf, sharing his lunch with Moira, Bonnie, and Willie. The large blond woman was tossing treats to her two scruffy little dogs, and Click was laughing at the creatures' greedy antics. He had rolled up his shirtsleeves, baring tanned forearms, and the clear yellow sunlight glinted off the metallic ornamentation on his leather vest.

In his tent the night before, Click had told them it would take about a week to get to the Long River. And down by the creek Teddy had just said that the Tinkers didn't cross the river, they went down it. Cassidy figured that gave her and Rowena another week to find out everything they could from those people. It would have to be done carefully because there was still too much the two women needed to conceal about themselves for their own safety. But Cassidy was confident they could manage it. After all, she thought dryly, her experiences with people like Yolanda and Misty had taught her everything there was to learn about deliberate obfuscation.

By the time the long, warm, summer afternoon had slid into evening, Cassidy was looking forward to stopping for the night. Although she had hoped for a chance to talk alone with Rowena, as well as the possibility of speaking individually to some of the other Tinkers, neither opportunity had presented itself after the lunch stop. Cassidy had alternated between riding the gray mare and taking her turn pedaling the bike cart for Carlotta. She found she wasn't able to ride the bike for as long of a stretch as she had in the morning; her aching legs just wouldn't permit it. But she and Rowena each took several shorter turns on the vehicle instead, and Carlotta seemed perfectly happy with their assistance.

The drier weather made travel considerably more pleasant even if the day had been fairly hot, and as the sun dropped lower in the sky the whole western horizon began to glow with a bright and fiery palette of red and golden hues. As Rowena pedaled Carlotta's cart over to where the other Tinker vehicles were being parked for the night, Cassidy slid down off her horse. She couldn't stifle a little groan.

· "Quite a day, eh?" Carlotta said, giving her an amused look.

"Yeah," Cassidy admitted, cautiously stretching her arms up over her head until she felt her spine pop. Normally she wouldn't have revealed any weakness in front of a stranger; but she liked Carlotta and realized that the woman was merely being sympathetic, not critical.

"I'm pooped," Rowena heartily concurred as she stiffly scrambled down from the bike's saddle. "If we keep this up, pretty soon I'll have thighs like match sticks!"

Both Cassidy and Carlotta laughed at the brunette's cheery hyperbole. Then the older woman said, "Well, you girls have done a very good job for me today, and I really appreciate it."

Glancing over at the packed bike cart, Rowena asked, "Is there anything we can do to help you set up for the night?"

But the ginger-haired woman just shook her head and made a shooing motion at them with her hands. "No, I can handle everything now. Why don't you two go down to the pond and clean up if you'd like to? Julie's making supper for us tonight—that is, if you're willing to eat with a bunch of old ladies."

Cassidy threw Rowena a quick look before replying, "Of course, we'd be glad to eat with you."

"Yeah, I feel like one of the 'old ladies' myself." Rowena groaned theatrically.

"Well, go on then," Carlotta repeated, waving her hands again. "We'll get to our cooking, and after we eat you can pick out a spot and set up your tent."

The rest of the Tinkers were already beginning the routine tasks of unpacking and setting up their campsite; firewood was being gathered, firepits dug and pots and other supplies hauled out from the backpacks and parked carts. Cassidy felt as if she and Rowena were the only two people in the whole group who didn't have a job to do as they cut across the little stretch of emerald turf selected for the night's stop. But the band had covered a lot of ground that day, and people seemed to be content if somewhat weary. Several of the Tinkers, including Tad and Teddy, called out greetings to the two women as, trailed by the gray mare, they made their way across the campsite.

There wasn't a creek or stream of any size in the immediate area where they had stopped for the day, but there was a large, long, sloughlike area beyond the camp, and along one edge of the marsh was a fair-size open pond. Some of the Tinkers, including Bonnie, had already gone down to the pond to draw water to replenish their casks. As she and Rowena walked down the gentle slope toward the water, Cassidy was a little disappointed to find that she and the brunette would not be alone. She had hoped to have the chance to talk privately with Rowena before they had supper.

"I almost wish I was naked again," Rowena said in a low whisper as they neared the pond. "It would sure feel great right about now to just be able to jump right into the water and soak!"

Cassidy flashed her a sympathetic grin. She knew how Rowena felt; she was sore and sweaty, too. Cassidy looked at the edge of the water, where several Tinkers were already gathered in the sedge grass. Suddenly she found she had no interest in joining them; she just wanted a little solitude.

"Listen, Rowena," she said quietly, "do you mind if I go out for a little ride before we eat? I want to see what the lay of the land ahead of us is like."

"Now?" Rowena said in surprise. "We're going to be eating pretty soon."

With effort Cassidy kept from smiling at the predictability of Rowena's priorities. "I'll just be gone a little while," she assured her. "I'll be back in plenty of time to eat."

"I don't care if you want to miss supper," Rowena retorted jovially, obviously excusing Cassidy. "Just remember you'd better get back here before dark to help me set up that darned tent!"

As they stood talking, Dragonfly had caught up to them. The horse had had an unusually undemanding day and had found plenty of time to graze. She regarded Cassidy with some interest as the woman mounted up. Cassidy hoped that no one else was watching her with quite the same avidity since it was not exactly the most graceful mount she had ever made. Although she got up onto the big horse's back on her first try, the muscles in her legs ached as if someone had soundly thrashed them with a strap.

"Don't get lost," Rowena called after her jokingly as the mare jogged off diagonally across the shallow slope.

Cassidy had no intention of getting lost or even of going very far. She did genuinely crave a little solitude, but as she rode away from the campsite she also realized that her explanation about surveying the surrounding terrain made a certain amount of sense. When the gray started up the wooded hill beyond the grassy slope, Cassidy let her pick her own course.

The path of the summer sun was at a high enough angle off the horizon that twilight was a prolonged period. The sun had been close to setting when the Tinkers had halted to set up camp, but darkness didn't come very rapidly that time of year. The shadows had deepened, spread low across the forested hills, and the busy chatter of the day's birds had given way to the pervasive sound of night insects; but the air was still awash in a honey-colored haze, a glow that hung over the ground like a spill of lamplight. Visibility was more than adequate for riding. As the mare paused on the crest of an oak-topped hill, Cassidy took a swat at the evening's first mosquito.

She would talk to Rowena later that night, Cassidy decided, gazing out over the gilded hills. They would have some privacy in their tent and it would be time enough. She wanted to tell her friend what Teddy had told her about going down the Long River, and to discuss possible ways to get more information from the Tinkers without arousing their suspicion. She also wanted Rowena's thoughts on just how much the two of them could safely reveal about their own situation. If it turned out that the Tinkers viewed the Warden of Horses with the same antipathy as did the Villagers, they would have to be circumspect about their real goal. It would be ironic, Cassidy thought, to finally find themselves in a position to actually get some help in finding their way to the Warden—and then not even be able to mention his name for fear of reprisal.

In spite of her sore legs Cassidy could have ridden much farther and lingered much longer in the forest. But she didn't want to worry Rowena, and she wanted to be able to get back to the camp in time to wash up at the pond before supper was ready. Carlotta and the others had been so nice to her and Rowena; she didn't want to offend anyone by being late. With a twinge of reluctance she turned the big mare and started her winding around the trees, back down the hill.

When Cassidy and the horse emerged from the trees at the bottom of the hill, the stretch of brush-tufted turf that stretched from the Tinkers' camp to the marshy edge of the pond was deserted. In the deepening twilight the campsite was aglow with cook fires and the warm still air carried the faint sounds of conversation, clanking metalware, and the tantalizing aromas of cooking food. Turning the mare toward the water, Cassidy smiled to herself as she heard the stacatto yips of Bonnie's two little ragmop dogs tormenting the tolerant larger dog.

The sedge grass at the margin of the pond was dark with shadow then, and Cassidy dropped down off the mare's back a few yards from the water so she could be sure of not soaking her new boots in the bog. Even landing on the soft sod she felt the jolt of hitting the ground again travel directly from the soles of her feet to her aching gluteals. Limping slightly, she carefully approached the marshy edge of the water. Someone who obviously shared her distaste for getting their feet wet had flattened down a path through the tough sedge grass and had laid down a few lengths of broken branches as a sort of crude platform at the very edge of the water. Side by side, Cassidy and the mare advanced. But while the horse just waded right in until the water was up to her cannon bones, Cassidy was forced to crouch gracelessly on the rough surface of the platform, cupping up water and sipping it from her hands while the big gray greedily sucked it directly from the pond's gilded surface.

"Careful—I think she's gaining on you."

The voice from almost directly behind her startled Cassidy so much that when she jerked up her head she nearly tumbled forward into the shallow pond. Still crouched on the wooden platform, she pivoted around, crablike, and glared up to find Click's long lean form silhouetted in sharp relief against the backlighting of the fading sunset.

"I'm sorry," he said immediately, stepping closer. "I didn't mean to frighten you."

Still staring at him, Cassidy clumsily got to her feet, struggling to keep her balance on the uneven platform of sticks. She saw that Click was shirtless and holding out his hands in an apologetic gesture.

"You didn't frighten me," she said. *Surprise, yes; but not frighten,* she thought to herself.

"I was helping Willie repack the axles on his cart," Click continued, his arms still held out from his body, "and I came down to wash off this axle grease."

By then he was near enough that Cassidy could see his hands and bare arms were smeared with dark oily stains. She could also see that the only thing he wore above the waist was the little leather thong that was knotted around his neck, and that his bare torso was cleanly muscled and his chest covered with whorls of dark shiny hair.

Dismayed to realize that she was still staring at him, Cassidy had to force the timbre of nonchalance into her voice as she said, "Then I'll just get out of your way so you can clean up."

"Actually," Click said, even as she stepped sideways off the platform of branches and began to back away from him, "I'm glad to find you here because I wanted to talk with you and Rowena about something."

Click paused, frowning slightly when he saw that Cassidy had frozen halfway across the strip of trampled sedge grass. The strange look of blank absorption on her face obviously made the Tinker leader reconsider the impact of what he had just said.

"Cassidy?" he inquired, his dark brows tenting quizzically. "Are you all right?"

It took Cassidy a few moments to tear her eyes away from the object of her sudden mesmerism; for once she had gotten near enough to Click she had finally been able to see exactly what it was that he wore hanging from the worn leather thong around his neck. Resting in a nest of glossy black chest hair, centered midway between his dusky-colored nipples, hung a bright brass key.

"Cassidy?" Click repeated, still puzzled as her eyes finally flicked up to meet his.

"Where did you get that?" she asked him, pointing at his chest.

His mouth shifted, the concerned frown replaced by a bemused little smile. "This?" he asked, using one finger to lift the key by its thong. "From a Finder."

Cassidy could feel her heart thudding in her chest, slowly and evenly but with a fierce emphasis that she recognized from her previous encounters with the *missing* things. It was like the cigarette lighter, the gun, the bicycles—but it was more. With every *missing* thing Cassidy felt that she was growing closer to the ultimate truth about that place. Like all the other found things, the key carried its own attendant chain of memories; but somehow that object seemed to represent something more, a vague but nagging hint of the larger mysteries that held the solution to her imprisonment there.

Cassidy couldn't stop herself. "Do you—do you know what it is?" she blurted out.

Still bemused, Click gave a little shrug, dropping the thong. "It's a key—just an ornament."

There were a dozen things she wanted to ask him then—including where the key had been found—since she had yet to see a single lock in that damned place—but she fiercely stifled the questions, too wary of what her interest might suggest to Click. If she continued to show such interest in the key he would certainly wonder why it was so significant to her; and that would bring up a whole host of questions she didn't want to have to answer. So she fought down her raging curiosity and excitement and managed to school her expression into as much innocent admiration as she could muster.

"I've never seen anything like it," she lied. "It's nice; I was just thinking that it's . . . nice."

There was something in the way Click's dark eyes narrowed, barely perceptible though it was, that made Cassidy hasten to divert him further from her interest in the key. "What did you say you wanted to talk to us about?" she said, edging past him and farther up from the pond.

Click paused a moment, his plain appraisal making it clear that he was still curious about her odd behavior. But then he lightly shrugged his bare shoulders again and said, "I had meant to talk with both of you, but I'm sure you can discuss it with Rowena later. I just wanted to let you know before tomorrow so that you'll have some time to decide what you want to do."

Then Cassidy, too, was effectively diverted from the matter of the brass key. She cocked her head at Click. "Why, what happens tomorrow?"

Click was still holding his greasy hands and forearms out from his body; the posture gave him an oddly supplicatory air. In the gathering darkness by the quiet pond the details of his features were becoming more difficult to see, but Cassidy could still discern the broader definition of his face—his tangled curly hair, his umber eyes, and the bold dark bar of his mustache. And for the moment she had temporarily forgotten her pervasive mistrust of him and was honestly curious about what he had to say.

"By midday we'll reach Briar Ridge, one of the villages where we trade. We usually stay there for a day or two, so that we can repair things for them as well as barter goods. I thought you and Rowena might wish to consider whether or not you want to accompany us into the village, or if you'd prefer to avoid it."

Click had delivered his explanation with the same calm equanimity he might have used to discuss the weather; but by the time he had finished speaking Cassidy felt as if her heart had suddenly stumbled to a jerky halt. She stared up into his dimly lit face, helplessly frozen with dismay as she struggled to conceal the chilling fear that had momentarily paralyzed her tongue.

How could he know? was the first coherent thought to rush through her mind. Cassidy was certain that she and Rowena must still be at least a full day's ride ahead of any possible pursuit from Double Creek. And the news of their flight could hardly have proceeded at any faster a rate; who could have gotten that far any quicker to have spread it? Therefore she couldn't think of any way that Click could have known that they were fugitives from village justice. But why else would he intimate that they might want to stay away from other Villagers? And what was even more surprising to her, why would he apparently be willing to help them evade detection?

When her heart resumed beating, the furious thudding made Cassidy feel literally weak in the knees. It took all of her concentration to remain standing steadily, and only by sheer dint of will was she able to speak calmly, even though the words felt dry and unwieldy on her lips.

"What makes you think we wouldn't want to go into the village with the rest of you?" she asked Click.

The silvered tips of his mustache lifted slightly, but the veiled amusement in his eyes was gentle, not sardonic. He made a small gesture with one oily hand. "You certainly may if you like," he said. "If you don't ride in on that mare perhaps they won't know that you're a Horseman."

The implied promise of relief pushed at Cassidy; she badly wanted to accept its comfort. She was a Horseman: That was the only reason Click had been warning her. He didn't know anything about what had happened in Double Creek; he just thought that she would want to avoid a farming village because most Villagers seemed to hate all Horsemen. That was all there was to it—wasn't there?

But as much as Cassidy wanted to believe that temptingly simple explanation, something wouldn't let her. Part of it may have been her ongoing paranoia, but another part of it was what she had seen in the ironic cast of the Tinker leader's dark and engaging face. Click knew—just how, Cassidy couldn't imagine, but that didn't change the fact that he *knew*. At the same time Cassidy realized that the man standing before her would not press the issue if she continued to feign ignorance. It was the realization of that fact more than anything else that made it possible—almost necessary—for Cassidy to overcome her distrust of him long enough to pursue it further. Unblinking, she looked up into those deep brown eyes.

"How did you know?" she asked him.

Cassidy did not need to specify precisely to what she was referring. Click did not insult her intelligence or try her patience by joking or pretending confusion over her simple question. He merely made another small gesture with his begrimed hands and said, "Bonnie recognized Rowena from Green Lake, from when she traded buttons and cloth there last year."

Skepticism creased Cassidy's brow. How could any of the Tinkers have remembered Rowena when the brunette had said she'd never even gotten to see any of the peddlers? But before Cassidy could voice that doubt, Click forestalled her interruption by holding up both greasy hands, palms out, before her.

"I doubt that Rowena would have seen Bonnie or any of the others," he explained quickly. "She was being . . . confined, supposedly as a punishment." The tips of his mustache twitched with momentary humor. "As I understand it, she did some serious damage to the village's clothing production."

Cassidy gave a silent little shake of her head. Rowena hadn't been kidding when she'd said she was infamous for her disastrous stint at the Green Lake clothing factory! But that had been over a year ago; certainly the Tinkers wouldn't assume Rowena was still being punished for that. Cassidy looked intently at Click, still not satisfied with his explanation.

"I don't understand," she said evenly. "What does that have to do with Rowena and me now?"

Click flipped his hands over, still holding their greasiness away from his bare chest. "Rowena may no longer be in trouble at Green Lake," he said calmly, "but I doubt that she stayed there much longer. Their mayor really has very little sense of humor."

Neither does Misty, Cassidy thought dryly. But what she said was, "That doesn't mean Rowena's still in trouble."

"No," Click agreed, "but you do." Cassidy actually opened her mouth to protest his assertion, but before she could get any words out he had simply gone on, his voice logical and matter of fact. "You're a Horseman, Cassidy, and yet you ride alone, without the company of others of your kind. That is not usual. You're traveling with a Villager, yet she doesn't have a horse. And the two of you were riding alone through some very rough territory, which is hardly the kind of journey anyone, even a Horseman, would undertake for recreation."

He paused briefly as if to assess the effect his observations would have on Cassidy. When she remained silent he gave her one of those small, gentle near-smiles of his and concluded, "I am assuming that you two ladies may have some reason for avoiding the local villages. You may correct me if my assumption is wrong."

Anger vied with trepidation as Cassidy grappled for a response to Click's canny summation of their situation. She realized that trying to deny what he had deduced would be pointless, and yet there was far too much frustration and anxiety churning up inside her for her merely to acquiesce. To her chagrin, she suddenly became aware that she had knotted her hands into tight fists as he had been speaking. Slowly and deliberately she unclenched her fingers.

"Are you going to tell the Villagers at Briar Ridge about us?" she asked him bluntly.

The half-smile played over Click's mouth again; once more

the splayed position of his dirtied hands gave the tall man an almost humorously harmless look. "We don't owe allegiance to the people of any village," he reminded her smoothly, adding "Besides, what do we know about the two of you—really?"

What indeed? Cassidy thought grimly.

"And so," Click continued calmly, as if the matter were one of only minor importance after all, "you can discuss this with Rowena and then decide what you wish to do. If the two of you would rather not go into Briar Ridge, some of our group always sets up a temporary working camp outside a village where we are trading, where they can practice their craft in peace while the necessary haggling is going on." He cocked an expectant brow at her. "You'd both be quite welcome to stay with that group instead."

Cassidy gazed steadily into that pleasant agreeable face, trying to penetrate the fathomless depths of Click's motives. She knew that it was probably just her own stubborn mistrust, but she couldn't figure out why he would bother to help her and Rowena, especially knowing as little as he did about them.

Unless he knows more than I realize. Somehow that possibility was even more troubling to her.

Cassidy was aware that she had been staring intently but rather stupidly at Click's face for an uncomfortably long time. She glanced down, her gaze skimming over his dark chest and the dim shape of the hanging key, and hastily murmured, "Thank you; we'll discuss it and decide by tomorrow."

As she hurried back up the grassy slope toward the bright firelight of the Tinkers' camp, Cassidy felt as if Click's eyes were on her back, pursuing her with their gentle mocking. She knew that was ridiculous; the moment she walked away he had probably immediately busied himself washing up in the pond, and she refused to give in to her paranoia by turning back to look.

But she still couldn't shake the persistent feeling.

And most confusing of all, she didn't find the thought of his interest entirely unappealing.

Chapter 5 ◀▥

The incident down by the pond and the implications of her conversation with Click considerably dampened Cassidy's enthusiasm for formulating plans to get more information from the Tinkers. In fact, as she sat eating her supper with Rowena and Carlotta and the others, she even temporarily considered not telling her friend about the key. The first little tidbits of information she'd gotten earlier in the day from Teddy, their discussion about horses and the Long River, suddenly seemed trivial and useless in the face of the threatening kind of knowledge Click appeared to possess. Cassidy's mind was in turmoil and once again she found herself eating only automatically, shoveling in food without regard for its taste or texture.

But later, by the time she and Rowena had set up their little tent and unfurled their bedrolls, Cassidy had finally regained a little perspective on the problem. And when she had, she realized that not only did Rowena deserve to share in everything Cassidy had found out, but that the pragmatic brunette was also her single greatest resource in helping to sort through the new information she gained and to make decisions about what they should do.

Although Cassidy was tempted to begin with the most dramatic news, her encounter with Click down by the pond, she resisted the impulse. She was afraid that her suspicions about what the Tinker leader knew about the two of them might impair Rowena's ability to clearly consider the other information, much as it had temporarily paralyzed Cassidy's own sense of purpose. So instead she told Rowena about what she had learned from Teddy down by the creek during their midday stop.

"I think I've heard of the Long River before," Rowena

mused. There was not enough light in the tent for Cassidy to be able to see the brunette's expression, but from the thoughtful tone of her voice Cassidy expected that there was a little frown of concentration on her friend's face. "You know, when Click mentioned the river last night the name seemed familiar to me; now I think I remember where I first heard of it."

Like Cassidy, Rowena lay reclining on her bedroll. The tent was too small and low to allow them much other choice of position when they both were in it. When the brunette paused she shifted a bit in the darkness. "Cassidy, have you ever heard anyone talk about the sea?"

"Sea? You mean like an ocean?"

"Yeah," Rowena said. "They call it the Gray Sea, or sometimes just the Big Sea. I know it's somewhere east of here, and I think it's at the end of the Long River."

Cassidy thought about that for a moment, then asked, "Do you think that's where the Tinkers are going then, to this Gray Sea?"

Rowena must have nodded; then, realizing that Cassidy couldn't have seen that, she said, "Yeah, that would be my guess. You said that Teddy told you they don't just cross the river, that they go down it. I think they might follow it all the way to the sea."

They both were silent for a few moments, each exploring her own thoughts. When Rowena spoke again her tone was slightly baffled. "Last night when Click said that we could travel along with them, he acted like he thought we were going to stay with them even after they reached the river."

"Yeah, that's the impression I got, too," Cassidy admitted.

"Then I wonder what's at the end of the Long River, besides the Gray Sea," Rowena said thoughtfully. "Do you think that's where the Tinkers live? There's got to be some reason why Click would think we'd want to go there."

"That's one of the things we've got to find out," Cassidy said. "I think there're a lot of other people besides Teddy who could answer our questions, but we've got to be careful not to make them suspicious about why we're asking."

Cassidy didn't need to see Rowena's grin; she could easily imagine it when she heard her friend's tone of voice. "Then we'd better not ask Click!"

By mentioning his name Rowena had provided Cassidy with the perfect opening. She still felt some misgivings but she quickly segued in.

"Yeah, well, I already had a little chat with him down by the pond earlier this evening," she said.

Cassidy could see the dim outline of Rowena's body shift as the brunette moved on her bedroll. "Oh?" she said with patent interest. "Is that why you were so late for supper—and why you were so gorked out while we were eating?"

"I was not 'gorked out,'" Cassidy protested automatically, She quickly moved on before Rowena had the chance to analyze her reaction. "Listen, did you know what he wears on that thong around his neck? It's a key."

That revelation at least had the desired effect on Rowena. "A key?" she echoed, surprised. "What the heck does he need a key for? Nothing here has a lock on it!"

"My thought exactly," Cassidy said. "He just considers it an ornament."

"Hey, wait a minute," Rowena said, her voice rising slightly with excitement. "Keys—they're another one of those *missing* things, aren't they?"

A sudden outburst of high-pitched yapping from across the camp by one of Bonnie's little dogs caused Cassidy to pause and keep silent. She and Rowena lay quietly in the darkness for a few moments, until peace fell over the Tinker camp and the only background noise was once again the soft soughing of the wind in the trees and the chorus of night insect sounds.

"He told me he got it from a Finder," Cassidy said then in a low voice. "Like Kevin, the one who found Yolanda's sunglasses and cigarette lighter."

If it had been possible to hear a frown then that expression was implicit in Rowena's next question. "How come you and I are the only ones who recognize what some of these things are for, Cassidy? I mean, they obviously know what bicycles are for—they must have built the darn things themselves. And all the stuff that you saw for the first time when you came to Double Creek, it was all stuff people there were using even if you hadn't seen it anywhere earlier. Why don't they know what these found things are?"

"Yolanda used the sunglasses and the cigarette lighter," Cassidy reminded her.

But that only seemed to add to Rowena's perplexity. "Yeah, but not to light cigarettes. Where the heck does all this found stuff come from if no one here made it?"

Although the question was a legitimate one and something that Cassidy herself had often fruitlessly mulled over, it was far too complex and frustrating to tackle at the moment. She had enough other difficult topics to go over with Rowena without the added headache of the ongoing puzzle of found things. Cassidy was about to tell Rowena just that and go on to something else when a sudden revelation struck her.

"Rowena," she said slowly and carefully, "do you remember the piece of T-shirt I found in the horse barn—the one with 'Adidas' on it?"

"Sure I remember it," Rowena replied promptly. "How could I forget the night you reminded me I know how to read and write!"

"Well, what if reading and writing are found things, too?"

"Wait a minute," the brunette interrupted, again shifting impatiently on her bedroll. "I think you're losing me. How can reading and writing be found things if we're the only ones here who've 'found' them? No one else here knows what it means to read or write."

"Just like they don't know what a key is for, even if they have one," Cassidy pointed out quietly. "Rowena, it's the same thing: The key, the cigarette lighter, reading and writing—they're all things that've come from the Slow World—*our* world. That's why no one here knows what they are."

But Rowena was only partially convinced. "I thought you said that everyone here came from 'our' world. And why are there so many other things here that you'd forgotten about until you actually saw them again—like saddles and guns and toilets—that everyone else here already knew about?"

Cassidy paused, as stymied by Rowena's convoluted phrasing as she was by the complexity of the question itself. "I don't know" was the only truthful answer. She had no idea how she had even come to forget almost everything she had ever known, much less why she had been able to recognize on sight everything in that crazy place.

Almost everything, she amended grimly, thinking involuntarily of the bizarre creatures she had seen on several occasions.

Fiercely pushing that disturbing memory aside, Cassidy forged ahead with the rest of what she had wanted to discuss with Rowena. "Click told me something when we were down by the pond," she said, "and he wanted me to discuss it with you and then let him know what we decide."

She knew immediately that she had Rowena's full attention;

the brunette leaned forward in the dimness of the little tent. "Decide about what?" she asked.

Cassidy quickly explained what Click had said about the Tinkers' stop in Briar Ridge. "Damn it, Rowena, he *knows* something about us. I'm not sure what, but I'm sure it'd be enough to cause trouble for us."

But to Cassidy's surprise Rowena seemed singularly undismayed; she seemed to have drawn an entirely different conclusion about the Tinker leader's offer. "Cassidy, if Click had wanted to cause trouble for us, he'd just haul us into that village tomorrow and turn us over to their mayor," she asserted. "He sure as heck wouldn't have bothered to warn us or give us the option of staying away from Briar Ridge."

"Don't tell me you trust him?" Cassidy asked in surprise.

Rowena made a shrugging motion, broadly enough that Cassidy could see it even in the dimness. "So far I do," she said noncommittally.

For a moment Cassidy could think of no response to that. Finally she said, "Well, what do you want to do about tomorrow then?"

The grin was back in Rowena's voice. "Stay out of Briar Ridge," she said immediately. "*Them* I don't trust!"

Later while Rowena slept, Cassidy still lay awake in the darkness. She tried to think about the nagging puzzle of the *missing* and the found things, about the kind of world from which she was certain she and Rowena had come, even about how they were ever going to find the Warden. But those thoughts were too insubstantial to stick; they seemed to have no weight or solidity to them and so they just kept floating off annoyingly out of her reach.

The only thoughts that wanted to stay, that kept coming around again and again despite her efforts to eradicate them, were of Click and the way he had looked when he had met her at the pond: the curly corona of his shaggy hair, the slow subtlety of his almost smile, the secret amusement in his dark eyes, and the way the little brass key had rested on the center of his bare chest.

When at last she fell asleep, those umber eyes seemed to follow her, gently mocking her for trying to resist the recollection.

Shortly before midday the next morning the group of Tinkers came to a halt. They had reached the point outside of

Briar Ridge where the trading party would break off and go
into the village, while the rest of the band would set up a temporary working camp. Cassidy was surprised to find that less
than half of the Tinkers would be going into Briar Ridge to
trade, and she asked Carlotta about it.

"This is one of our last stops on this trip," the ginger-haired
metalsmith explained as she busily separated and packed her
wares for the sojourn into the village. "Some of the others
have pretty well depleted their stocks of barter goods already.
Some of them, like Mitz, would rather use the time to work on
their craft." Carlotta shook out the links of a few segments of
shiny gold chain and added with a wry smile, "And some of
them, like Old Paul, just don't like Briar Ridge's mayor!"

Not coincidentally, the old cooper just happened to be passing by them at the moment, his cluttered handcart being
pushed for him by Toby, his wiry young apprentice. Old Paul
threw Carlotta a withering look and retorted, "The man is a
thief!"

"And he thinks you are a cheat, Paul," came the mild voice
from directly behind them.

Cassidy had been pedaling Carlotta's bike cart before the
halt had been called; she still sat on the vehicle's padded
leather saddle as they talked, her feet dangling. She turned so
she could face Click as the tall man came up alongside
Carlotta's cart. He gave them all a pleasant nod, even Old
Paul, who snorted and spat scornfully on the ground at Click's
teasing comment. But when Click spoke again his question
was addressed to Cassidy and Rowena.

"What have you ladies decided about the village?"

"We thought we'd stay here," Cassidy said casually, adding,
"At least if that's all right," as if it were not a matter of any
great importance to her either way.

Nodding agreeably, Click said, "I'm sure Paul and the others
will be glad for your company. Carlotta, Moira, and Jimmy
could use some help getting ready, if you have the chance."
Then Click was off, moving up the line of carts.

It took about half an hour for the Tinkers who were going
into the village to sort out their barter goods and repack them
for carrying or carting. Bonnie's little dogs ran around yapping
as usual at everyone and everything that moved; Cassidy
hoped the big blond woman would take them with her. She expected that everyone would eat lunch together before they split
up, but apparently it was traditional for a village to provide a

welcoming meal for the traders. Once the group had departed, she and Rowena ended up eating lunch with Toby, Old Paul, and the others who had remained behind.

Most of the Tinkers who had elected not to go into Briar Ridge were those whom Cassidy and Rowena did not know very well yet. They had shared supper the night before with Julie, a plump middle-aged weaver who fashioned everything from cloth to rugs from various fibers. Of course they knew Old Paul; everyone knew the prickly old cooper, but Cassidy wasn't sure she wanted to have to count on his hospitality for two days. Paul's apprentice, Toby, was a serious-minded man of about Cassidy's own age, and she figured Old Paul would keep Toby busy. Cassidy knew only slightly the rest of the Tinkers who had stayed behind.

Of course, there was no edict that said she and Rowena had to stay in the camp the whole time. Cassidy figured they both could mount up on the gray mare and go do a little scouting around if they wanted to. But she also realized they wouldn't learn as much that way as if they stuck around and were able to talk to some of the Tinkers. At least that was the basic reasoning that made the two of them stay behind the rest of that long and warm summer afternoon, while the other Tinkers were in Briar Ridge.

But the way the afternoon turned out, there really wasn't any opportunity for either Cassidy or Rowena to talk with any of the Tinkers who had remained behind. The craftsmen had stayed to work, and while there was no shortage of things for her and Rowena to help with, it didn't leave much chance for informational chats.

One of the things that hampered Cassidy's efforts to learn more was that she felt certain unavoidable constraints in just how to proceed. She was cautious about asking overly obvious questions—such as the location of the Warden's garrison—since she was certain the Tinkers would assume that as a Horseman she would know such things, even if she actually didn't. There were even many fundamental things about the Tinkers themselves of which she was ignorant. She was still unclear on exactly what they took in exchange from the Villagers for all of the varied wares they bartered. She supposed the farmers offered foodstuffs, for there certainly was never any shortage of good things to eat in the Tinkers' camp. And the Villagers probably also supplied much of the raw materials for the Tinkers' crafts, such as leather, wool, and cotton. But beyond that, she hadn't noticed that the itinerant tradesmen were carrying with them much of anything that they hadn't made themselves.

Cassidy and Rowena spent most of the afternoon helping gather firewood to fuel one of the portable forges. Tad and Teddy had gone into Briar Ridge, but another of the forge carts belonged to Henry, the Tinkers' soft-spoken coppersmith. He had let some of the other traders take his pots and pans into the village while he remained behind to work on more cookware. Cassidy figured Henry's product was probably one of the most sought-after barter items in the rural villages.

Cassidy found the coppersmith of interest for several reasons. Physically he was an unimpressive specimen, slightly built with thinning light brown hair and soulful brown eyes. For a Tinker he dressed very conservatively, his shirt and trousers a neutral tan color and simply cut. But Cassidy sensed a secret good humor beneath the man's saturnine exterior, and he was the first to pitch in willingly to scour the surrounding forested hills for dry firewood.

Given Henry's tractable nature, Cassidy might have considered him a good potential source of further information. But while he proved quite willing to talk as they worked, the only thing he seemed interested in talking about was his craft. Fascinating as copperwork might be, it was basically irrelevent to Cassidy's goals. And once they had gathered sufficient firewood and he had stoked up his forge and laid out the tools of his trade, his work turned out to be much too noisy to allow much conversation. Although it was interesting to watch the skill and deftness with which the unassuming little man hammered the bright sheets of metal into such utensils as mugs and cooking pots, shaping the copper as easily and smoothly as if he were working with something as malleable as Moira's clay, he proved to be a total disappointment in the matter of providing any useful information.

Cassidy ended up the day mildly frustrated at the way all of the Tinkers in the working camp had become so engrossed in their crafts. Even the evening meal left little opportunity for idle talk. Only one large communal cook fire was laid and food preparation was minimal. Most of the mealtime talk was taken up with the business of trade potential in Briar Ridge and the results of the afternoon's work, with no real chance for small talk or private conversations. No one even lingered around the fire's banked ashes for extra mugs of coffee.

"Jeez, I think I even miss those yappy little dogs of Bonnie's," Rowena groused sleepily as she and Cassidy crawled into their bedrolls that night.

"I wouldn't go that far," Cassidy responded.

But as she lay on the edge of sleep Cassidy was willing to admit to herself that she did miss the presence of some of the Tinkers who were spending the night in the village. She told herself that it was not because of any sense of friendship or other affection; it was merely because they were the people who had posed the best potential as sources of information.

And I sure as hell don't miss Click, she thought with finality.

The base of Cassidy's throat burned with a piercing sting. As she adroitly squashed the offending mosquito with the back of one hand, she thought for what must have been the tenth time in as many minutes that perhaps she had made a mistake by agreeing to go along with Mitz that morning. Just ahead of her on the brushy slope the diminutive gray-haired woman who strode briskly along, stirring up the humming cloud of mosquitoes that had then been feeding on Cassidy, seemed oblivious to any such doubts.

At breakfast that morning Cassidy had been seriously considering just taking the gray mare out for the day. Rowena's services had been appropriated by Chrissy, the group's cutler, when Rowena had expressed admiration for one of the black woman's finely honed knives. Cassidy hadn't volunteered to help when the small woman offered to show them how to make hafts and handles out of antler. Hiking up to the crest of the wooded hill behind Mitz and her lop-eared dog under a sky the color and weight of slate, Cassidy had plenty of time to wonder if she'd made the wrong choice by not staying in camp with Rowena and Chrissy.

Mitz had come by Carlotta's bike cart as Cassidy was restowing her and Rowena's bedrolls and tent. She was a seamstress by trade, but she was also proficient in other crafts. With her bright and shrewd eyes and her colorful outfit of brilliant yellow shirt, black vest, and dark brown pants, Mitz reminded Cassidy of a meadowlark. And she was the nominal owner of the third camp dog, the long-suffering object of Bonnie's dogs' tormenting.

"If you're willing, I could use some help," she'd said forthrightly to Cassidy. "Toby says that there're some willow breaks down near the slough that lies just over that hill. I'm going to go cut some switches for weaving wicker baskets, and I'll need some help carrying them back into camp."

The way Mitz had put it, it seemed more of a statement than a request; Cassidy could think of no graceful way to demur, especially in favor of doing something as frivolous as riding her horse. So armed with a pair of heavy shears and a ball of coarse twine, Cassidy found herself following the limber little woman up the long incline, batting aside branches and swatting hungry mosquitoes.

Despite the overcast sky, the air was warm and humid. Cassidy's new shirt was plastered to her back by the time they had crested the hill. They pushed through a copse of thick bushes and second-growth trees on the crest and then started down the other side, the oat-colored dog trotting on ahead of them. The hill was a little clearer on the other side, leading down to the boggy ground of a rush-choked marsh that filled the hollow at the bottom of the slope. No open water was visible in the slough, but the sound of peeper frogs rose up like a soprano chorus from the depths of the sedge grass and cattails, and dragonflies and lacywings skimmed over the tips of the vegetation, their wings iridescent even in the sunless air.

Just as Toby had told Mitz, the low land around the slough was lush with the waving green spears of young willow trees. "This will be perfect," Mitz said as she led the way down to the bottom of the hill.

"Perfect" wouldn't have been the term Cassidy would have chosen; she was sweaty and full of mosquito bites. But as her eyes swept over the boggy ground, which was broken by the vigorously growing clumps of willow and a few young poplars, she decided the marsh was probably more interesting than learning how to make handles for cutlery. And there was always the possibility that the energetic little seamstress would turn out to be garrulous and add something to Cassidy's knowledge.

The ground around the clumps of willow was spongy but firm enough to walk on without getting their boots wet. Mitz cropped off a few long spears and inspected them for strength and flexibility. Then she showed Cassidy how to select the best of the whips from the willows' profusion of branches.

"They don't have to be real long," she explained, cutting off a few more shoots, "but they should be straight and the diameter should be uniform. Otherwise they won't make a nice even weave."

After dislodging a few inquisitive gnats by wiping her cheek on her shirtsleeve, Cassidy experimentally wielded her own shears. "What about the leaves?" she asked Mitz as she began to gather the severed whips on one hand.

The gray-haired woman had already begun to work in earnest, snipping off the gleaming green shoots with a practiced rhythm and methodically gathering them into a tight bundle in her other hand. "We can strip the leaves off later," she told Cassidy. "And I leave the bark on until I'm ready to trim and use them."

Cassidy wasn't able to work at Mitz's pace and her movements weren't nearly as smooth and economical as she sheared off the long supple branches; but she worked steadily and tried to follow the seamstress's specifications when choosing the shoots. And although her fingers quickly grew sticky from the willow sap, and the mosquitoes and gnats found her increasingly attractive, Cassidy didn't find the job difficult. It was even fairly pleasant at the edge of the marsh, in spite of the insects. Once her shirt began to dry and didn't stick so annoyingly to her back and arms, the morning weather even seemed rather comfortable.

Once Mitz had accumulated a fairly good-size pile of cut branches, she moved a little farther down the breaks to another clump of willow. Her long-eared dog, wet and muddy from the belly down, flopped down on the soft sod, his tongue lolling. When Cassidy had pruned off all of the suitable shoots from the clump where she had been working, she moved along with Mitz.

"That's good," Mitz said, favoring her with an approving nod. "Carlotta was right when she said you two were good workers."

Feeling a little ambivalent about the idea of the Tinkers evaluating her and Rowena's performances, Cassidy changed the subject slightly. "Do you make wicker baskets to trade?" she asked. "I don't think I've seen anything like that in the camp."

Mitz replied without even glancing over from cutting whips. "Wicker needs time to cure. I've already bartered off everything I'd brought with me."

"Wicker must be popular then," Cassidy said, stooping to set down another handful of cut whips.

"Baskets and bushels are," Mitz said. "But there're a lot of other things you can make out of wicker—even furniture. Villagers aren't interested in that sort of thing, though, so I don't bring anything like that to trade."

Cassidy was so busy cutting shoots, cropping and grasping the long sprigs with increasing dexterity and enough concentration, that at first she didn't even notice that Mitz had paused in her own work. It was only when Cassidy had to duck her head sideways to dislodge another mosquito that she saw Mitz had stopped lopping off the branches and stood regarding her with a mildly speculative expression on her face.

"If you're curious about wicker weaving I'd be glad to teach you once we reach the river."

Still cutting whips, Cassidy made a polite demur: "I wouldn't want to bother you . . ."

The older woman gave a little shrug. "It's no bother; it's a long trip and there'll be plenty of time."

Cassidy hesitated then, the shears held suddenly motionless in her hand. Again the assumption was being made that Cassidy and Rowena would continue with the Tinkers on their journey down the Long River. Uncertain how to respond, Cassidy fumbled for something noncommittal.

"Sure, okay—if we decide to go along with you."

But Mitz didn't immediately resume her pruning. The corners of her mouth crimped slightly, as if Cassidy had said something amusing. "I wouldn't think that would take much deciding," she said wryly. "It's a pretty long walk to the Iron City, even on horseback."

Suddenly Cassidy felt unnervingly light-headed. She had to concentrate very distinctly to be able to slowly and precisely snip off another willow shoot, and it took all of her force of will to keep from just looking right at Mitz and gaping stupidly. Instead she fiercely reminded herself to *breathe* as she carefully and deliberately cut another whip and added it to the small bunch in her other hand.

If there was one thing Cassidy had learned in all of her crippling ignorance in that world, it was that when someone presented you with a massive non sequitur you neither agreed nor disagreed with them; you just waffled and hoped like hell that their next statement would help clarify matters. So Cassidy tried to neither confirm nor dispute Mitz's assumption about their destination because she didn't want the seamstress to know that she had never even heard of the Iron City. Keeping her face averted as, with a false nonchalance, she studied her next likely willow whip, Cassidy said, "What makes you think that's where Rowena and I are going?"

Mitz was no longer paying any attention to the clump of willows. She was looking at Cassidy with open bemusement on her face. "Where else would you be taking her?" she asked. Then, before Cassidy could even try to fabricate another suitably indifferent response, the little woman lifted one hand in a restraining gesture. "Oh, you don't have to deny it, Cassidy. I can promise you that no one here has anything against people of her kind." Mitz dropped her hand and lifted her shears again. "And I know that as a Horseman you have your duty to your Warden, as well."

Cassidy's mind was roiling like a bank of stormclouds. Her sense of confusion was almost a physical thing, like vertigo; she was relieved when Mitz turned back to her pruning, giving Cassidy a few unguarded moments in which to try to compose herself again. As she stood there in the willow breaks, the shears clutched forgotten in her hand and her thoughts tumbling wildly, she could only seize upon one thing: *Rowena— they think Rowena is the crazy one here!*

And hard upon the heels of that realization came a second one: The Tinkers must think that Rowena had the Memories. Why else would it be Cassidy's "duty" to take her anywhere? Cassidy flashed back to Yolanda and the obsession the woman who had first found her had had with anything Cassidy might have remembered from her past. Once Yolanda came to believe that Cassidy had possessed what Yolanda had called the Memories, she had been determined to take Cassidy to the Warden. "Everything we have has come from the Memories," Yolanda had told Raphael, her impatient apprentice. And Valerie, the Trooper Cassidy had encountered outside Double Creek the night of the fateful fire, had been equally adamant about her going to the Warden once the woman realized that Cassidy dreamed and had seen the monsters.

But if the Tinkers thought that Rowena had the Memories and that Cassidy was taking her to the Warden . . .

Then the Iron City must be where the Warden is.

And the Iron City lay at the end of the Long River and the Tinkers' journey.

Bending to drop another bundle of freshly cut willow shoots, Mitz glanced over at Cassidy and then paused, giving her a longer look. Misinterpreting the frank distress she must have seen in Cassidy's expression, the seamstress's face softened slightly and she even gave Cassidy a little smile. "Mercy, girl, you look like someone's just waved a noose at you! You're not dealing with a bunch of pig-headed farmers anymore. I told you, we don't meddle in Horsemen's affairs." Mitz's voice dropped, becoming more kindly. "We knew what you were when we offered to let you travel with us. This isn't safe country for two people to cross alone. Besides," she concluded with another wry smile, "I wasn't just joshing you: It *is* a long walk to the Iron City. Better that you two just come down the river with us."

Cassidy's heart was pounding so hard that she was certain it must be audible to Mitz. "We'll certainly consider that," she managed to murmur. "Thanks for your help."

To Mitz, the little misunderstanding seemed to be completely over then and she didn't appear to notice that Cassidy was still in any distress. She wielded her shears again, lopping spears with fresh enthusiasm as she said, "Well, you're helping us, as well. We can cut enough willow here for me to make baskets all the way down the river, till we get home."

Hands trembling, Cassidy lifted her own shears and snipped clumsily at a branch, hoping that Mitz wouldn't notice the way she was still shaking. Hope, fresh and unexpected, sang with the adrenaline through her veins. The Tinkers were going home. And if the Iron City was where they would find the Warden of Horses, then perhaps she and Rowena would be going home, as well.

It was late that evening before Cassidy was able to tell Rowena about the amazing things she had learned from Mitz.

In the waning hours of the afternoon, the trading party returned from Briar Ridge. Apparently their mission had been a successful one; at least they didn't return with much of the goods they had gone into the village with, and Cassidy noticed several sacks of staples such as flour and potatoes in their place. Also, much as she had assumed, the Tinkers returned with cured sheepskins, fleeces, and rolled bales of unbleached cotton.

Amid all of the bragging, complaining, and other chatter, there was a brief communal discussion about the merits of breaking camp and moving on farther that afternoon. The Tinkers who had come back from trading seemed to favor the idea; those who had remained behind were disinclined to give up the rest of their day's work just to travel a few hours more.

In the end the camp stayed put, although very little work was accomplished once the traders had come back.

Cassidy honestly hadn't missed Bonnie's annoying little dogs, but it was nice to have the big blond woman around again. Carlotta, who seemed to have done very well in her bartering, was full of jokes and good humor as Cassidy and Rowena helped her repack the bike cart. The metalsmith hauled out more of her most exotic jewelry and ornaments to show them, and even offered to pierce Rowena's ears for her. Cassidy half thought the brunette might go through with it, taken as she was with the Tinkers' flashy style of dress. But in the end Rowena just told Carlotta she would have to think about it.

Cassidy did not consciously try to avoid Click—or at least that was what she told herself. She just didn't want to have to deal with any more little surprises from the tall dark-haired man, at least until she'd had the chance to discuss her latest discoveries with Rowena. And so she was glad to be able to stay on the fringes of the big communal meal the Tinkers prepared that night, nearly on the opposite side of the camp from Click.

But Cassidy could not keep from shooting surreptitious glances at Click as he held forth with Tad and Willie and the rest of his friends. Click's subtle sense of humor seemed especially mellow that night, and he good-naturedly accepted the jovial barbs of the other members of the trading party as they shared supper. The flickering firelight played over the dark ringlets of his hair and winked from the metal conchas and rings on his leather vest. And once—just once—when she did not drop her eyes quickly enough, Click looked directly across the breadth of the cook fire and met her gaze with an ironic little lift of his arched brows.

Rowena probably would have happily sat there all evening, sharing the camaraderie of their Tinker hosts. Cassidy had to be rather blunt and clumsy in convincing Rowena that she was really tired, and wouldn't Rowena come and help her set up their tent and bedrolls? It wasn't until they were pulling their gear out of Carlotta's bike cart that there was enough privacy for Cassidy to be able to hiss that she had to talk to her about something important.

When they were finally ensconced in the tent, far enough from the center of camp to have at least nominal seclusion,

Cassidy was finally free to tell Rowena everything that Mitz had revealed to her that morning out in the willow breaks.

For a few moments after Cassidy had finished speaking, Rowena was silent, and the dominant sounds in their tiny tent were the ebb and flow of unintelligible conversation from over at the Tinkers' fire. Then Cassidy finally realized that Rowena hadn't responded because she was choking with laughter and trying valiantly to keep from laughing aloud.

"Jeez, I don't believe it!" Rowena managed to sputter out. "They think that *I'm* the one with the Memories?"

Disappointed with what she took to be Rowena's failure to grasp the importance of her revelations, Cassidy said, "Well, don't let it go to your head."

Still struggling to stifle her laughter, Rowena leaned closer, reaching out to touch Cassidy's arm in the darkness. "I'm sorry, Cassidy," she said, having to muffle another snort of humor but sounding contrite nevertheless. "I just think it's hilarious that after all of the time we spent worrying about how we were going to find the Warden and how were we going to get these people to help us without them getting suspicious about who we were, now you tell me they're ready and willing to take us right to him!"

Rowena deteriorated into helpless choking sounds again, so Cassidy pushed on. "You won't think it's so hilarious if they decide you're worth more to them than to the Warden," she told Rowena sternly.

Hiccupping into temporary sobriety, Rowena peered at Cassidy in the dimness of the little tent. "What do you mean? Do you think the Tinkers care anything about people with the Memories?"

"It's possible," Cassidy maintained stiffly.

But Rowena seemed unconcerned about that likelihood. "No one believes in the Memories anyway, except for a few kooks—and Horsemen. Cassidy, they have no idea what you know, what *we* know." Her grip on Cassidy's forearm had automatically tightened as she spoke. "What, you think they'd try to barter me off like a copper pot or a bolt of cloth? None of those yahoos would be interested—unless I could remember how to make a better chicken coop or hay rake." Rowena was shaking her head; Cassidy could see the movement against the lighter backdrop of the tent's canvas. "To the Tinkers this is all Horsemen's business, the Warden's business. All we have to do is keep being helpful and keep our mouths shut and they'll gladly take us right to him."

Cassidy wished that she could share Rowena's robust confidence or even her active sense of irony about their circumstances; but something kept damping down her ability to accept all this as just an amazing windfall, a good piece of luck. It just couldn't be that simple.

Dropping Cassidy's arm, Rowena flopped back down onto her bedroll with another chuckle. "I guess we should have thanked that Woodsman after all," she told Cassidy. "If we hadn't fallen into his trap and gotten taken for everything we had, we'd probably still be out in the woods somewhere, eating rabbits and heading in the wrong direction!"

Cassidy had to smile at that, although she was glad that in the darkness Rowena wouldn't be able to see her. "Yeah?" she shot back, punching a little cushioning into her bedroll. "Well, I wouldn't pledge him my undying gratitude just yet. We still have a long way to go before I can 'present' you to the Warden."

But Rowena's only response was a wide yawn.

Despite the heavy meal she'd consumed and the cathartic if somewhat mixed feelings produced by her discussion with Rowena, Cassidy found sleep elusive that night. It wasn't a problem of noise, for the camp's sounds quickly died down after she and Rowena had gone to bed. And those sounds, even the snippy yapping of Bonnie's dogs as they challenged some shadow, were more comforting than disruptive to Cassidy. The problem was the same stumbling block that kept her from being able to share Rowena's congenital optimism about their fate. Cassidy just didn't believe in good luck.

Finally, when hours of restless wakefulness had brought her nothing more than a stiff neck and the need to urinate, she gave up on her bedroll and quietly crawled out of the tent. The moon had long since set and the Tinker camp was shrouded in thick shadow. The only light seemed to come from the faint glow of the big cook fire's dying coals, and that did little more than paint a pale rime on the nearest tents and anonymous bundles of supplies.

Shivering a little as her bare feet sliced elliptical trails of dark silver over the dew-drenched sod, Cassidy slowly crept around the edge of the camp, looking for the nearest thicket of brush. As she reached the bushes she felt her heel connect with a dead twig, snapping it like a dry bone. She froze, expecting to have set off a chorus of canine yapping. But nothing in the camp stirred.

Hastily squatting to relieve herself, Cassidy felt a vague sense of uneasiness replace her nagging insomnia. Silently she berated herself for the paranoia. *First I don't trust the Tinkers—now I don't even trust the night.* Then automatically, like the tip of a tongue blindly and helplessly reaching to touch a sore tooth, Cassidy's thoughts went again to the Tinkers' leader.

Click was the stone in her boot, Cassidy realized with a certain glum clarity of introspection; the reason she could not believe in their good fortune. She didn't trust Click.

Or is it that you don't trust yourself?

Shaking off that thought like an annoying mosquito, Cassidy slipped back out of the bushes and began to glide soundlessly over the wet grass. She was only a few yards from their tent, draped in the thickest of the shadows, when she suddenly halted, her bare toes digging into the cool turf. Across the camp from her, strolling slowly and almost casually with his back to her, Click was moving like a lean and limber shadow.

Although the simplest explanation would have been that Click was just out there for the same reason that Cassidy had been, she immediately and instinctively knew that was not the case. He just didn't act like a man out looking for some bush to piss behind. Rather, as he glided quietly over the dew-spangled sod, Click looked like a man who was searching for something.

Perhaps searching was not exactly the right word, either, Cassidy decided as she stood, still frozen in place, wrapped in her cloak of shadow. It was more like Click was watching, a nocturnal guardian prowling in the warm shroud of darkness that hung over the Tinker camp.

Cassidy watched him for a few moments longer, as he moved steadily and surefootedly around the perimeter of the camp. His thumbs were hooked in the waistband of his trousers, giving his gait a casual air; but from the tautness in the long lines of that lean body Cassidy could see that Click was completely alert, his gaze sweeping out in concentric arcs over the shadowy brush. Afraid then that he might suddenly look over across the camp and spot her standing there, Cassidy crept the last few yards to her tent and ducked beneath its flap.

Sleep finally came to her, but it took its own sweet time.

Even after she had closed her eyes, what she had just seen kept playing relentlessly behind her lids. And the image of Click guarding the camp in silent solitude during the long hours before dawn disturbed her in a way she could not understand.

Chapter 6 ◀▥

Rain rolled in the next morning and the bad weather clung for several days. The air was still warm but the wet conditions made travel unpleasant, and the Tinkers' usual good cheer was often tested. Cassidy and Rowena continued to take turns helping Carlotta pedal the bike cart, but none of them could keep up the job for very long. The rain made the grass and dead leaves slick and the ground, especially on the slopes, became slippery with little runnels of water. Rest stops, although more frequent and very welcome, were abbreviated by the steady showers. Even night camps were relatively cheerless affairs with the band huddled together to take advantage of any natural covering and the air heavy with the smells of wet canvas and damp woodsmoke.

Most of the Tinkers remained philosophical about the dreary weather, although some grumbling was an ongoing occurrence. Relief that they were reaching the end of their trading tour was the general consensus. Carlotta had had a good season, and her spirits were more easily maintained than some. She even offered again to pierce Rowena's ears, and this time Rowena agreed.

"I suppose next thing you'll be wanting a tattoo," Cassidy had groused; but by evening she had relented and inspected the tiny gold studs in Rowena's earlobes with a certain grudging admiration.

To distract herself from the foul weather, Cassidy spent some of her own free time with Sheila, the cobbler. The woman worked extensively with leather, and Cassidy was curious what sort of clothing she made. As well crafted as it was, nothing Cassidy saw compared to the beautifully dyed, incised, and ornamented leather tunics and trousers she had seen worn by the Warden's Troopers on the night of the fire back in Double Creek. But Sheila must have known something of Horsemen and Troopers—probably far more than did Cassidy—and she didn't question Cassidy's interest in her handiwork. She even showed Cassidy some of the handsome leather bridles and halters she made for village trade.

Desire to reach the Long River seemed to hang over the Tinker camp like the promise of sunshine. While Cassidy still viewed their destination with some wariness and uncertainty, everyone else was openly looking forward to it.

"I'm glad this is the end of it," Old Paul muttered the night they set up camp near Pointed Rock, the village that would be their final stop. "If I never have to haggle with these tightwad farmers over another keg or barrel, I could die a happy man."

A fine drizzle was falling as Cassidy and Rowena helped Carlotta secure the bike cart's load for the night. Since they were so close to the village, Cassidy expected the trading party to go into Pointed Rock that evening for the traditional hospitality meal. She was puzzled when it became obvious that wouldn't be the case.

"Maybe they don't want to have to haul their stuff into the village in the rain," Rowena suggested as the two of them helped Jimmy and Teddy scour the wet, gloomy hills for firewood.

Glancing over to be sure they were far enough from the two young men to not be overheard, Cassidy said, "What the hell—it's probably going to be raining again tomorrow anyway."

During their supper with Carlotta, Julie, and Mitz, hunched close to the cook fire in their damp and rumpled clothing, no one offered any explanation for the decision not to go into the village that night. And because of the weather there was very little after-dinner conversation. Tents had been erected early and most of the Tinkers got under cover as soon as they could. Restless and disinterested in crawling into their own tent so early, Cassidy talked Rowena into taking a little walk with her after they had helped Carlotta with the supper pans and dishes.

The remnants of cook fires still sputtered and smoked as they cut across the dimly lit campsite. Several of the Tinkers were poking around in their carts and at the canvas-covered piles of backpacks that were stacked beneath them, making sure their goods were secured for the night. They exchanged greetings with both Sheila and Moira as they neared the edge of the encampment. Beneath Tad's forge cart, Bonnie's pair of raggedy little dogs held down Mitz's long-eared mutt in mock battle, growling ferociously at the amazingly tolerant larger dog.

Her clothing had been damp all day; Cassidy was beginning to think that traveling naked had had its advantages. Their clothes barely had time to dry out overnight in the tent before they had to go out again in the morning for another soaking. But somehow that night's fine drizzle felt less irritating. Perhaps it was just that Cassidy was preoccupied, thinking about what they should do when they reached the Long River and had to make a choice about staying with the Tinkers. That kind of nagging concern left little room for complaints about the weather.

Shooting a surreptitious look toward Rowena's half-shadowed face as they passed the hissing coals of the last cook fire, Cassidy realized that her friend seemed to harbor few such doubts. It was far simpler for Rowena; she trusted the Tinkers. The brunette was already certain that they should accompany the band down the Long River to the Iron City instead of trying to travel there on their own.

Intent on her thoughts, Cassidy hardly noticed her surroundings as they walked past the last cart in the line of parked vehicles. It was Old Paul's and the wizened little cooper was standing beside it, muttering to himself as he fussed with a strap on the tarp that covered his wares.

"Do you need some help?" Rowena called out.

"What I need is a month of sunshine," the old man grumbled, giving the strap a final sharp tug. Then he turned toward them, eyeing them critically. "And where would you two be going in the rain?"

Although Cassidy had long since learned that Old Paul's crochety manner was mostly just harmless bluster, it suddenly seemed a little too frivolous to admit to him that they were just out taking a walk. So before Rowena could offer the old man the truth, Cassidy said, "Just out to check on my mare."

The cooper gave a deprecating grunt. "Not much use, that horse," he said. Wiping his gnarled and stained hands on the damp front of his trouser legs, he added with a certain nasty relish, "And you can't take a horse down the river."

Cassidy honestly had no intention of picking an argument with the brusque old man. But his comment about the mare cut too close to the core of the upcoming dilemma she had just been mulling over. Without thinking, she responded, "Well, maybe Rowena and I aren't going down the river."

Beside her, Cassidy saw Rowena's head turn in surprise; but to her credit, the brunette did not blurt out any contradicting opinion. It was left to Old Paul to point out to Cassidy the inherent foolishness of her assertion.

"Hah!" He snorted. "You think the two of you are going to ride that horse all the way to the Iron City? Even if you did make it alone, it would be weeks before you reached the sea."

Cassidy was tempted to continue the conversation just to try to cadge more useful information out of the cooper; but she reluctantly realized that it wouldn't be worth it to antagonize Old Paul in the hopes of learning something more about their destination. Just as she was about to make some placating, totally insincere response to the old man's harsh prediction, another voice joined the conversation, a voice increasingly familiar to Cassidy with its calm and reasoning tone.

"Horsemen ride to the Iron City all the time, Paul," Click said, stepping out from the near darkness on the other side of the old man's cart. He was looking directly at Cassidy as he concluded, "I think you underestimate the speed at which a horse can travel, my friend."

Old Paul merely snorted again and spat on the wet ground. The somewhat theatrical display of disgust was only pretense when the old cooper used it around Click; Cassidy had noticed that the old man held the Tinker leader in genuine affection. "And I think these ladies underestimate what lies between here and the sea," he retorted. He fixed Cassidy and Rowena with a stern and beady-eyed stare for a moment before he concluded, "There's worse things in these woods than Woodsmen!"

That said, Old Paul made a show of hitching his trousers up on his bony hips and then stalked off toward the center of the camp, his wet boots squishing on the soft sod.

"I hope we didn't make him mad," Rowena said as the old cooper stepped stiffly off.

The silvered ends of Click's mustache lifted in amusement. "Don't worry, Rowena," he said, "the rain has already done that."

Shifting uncomfortably, Cassidy tried for a quick and graceful exit. The one thing she didn't need that night was a little chat with Click, no matter how nonchalant Rowena seemed about the interruption.

"Well, I guess we'd better go check the mare," she said, not meeting Click's eyes, as if to acknowledge his gaze would be to be trapped there.

Those dark eyes, lit from within by some secret subsurface mirth, regarded the two of them with equal solemnity. "Old Paul may not have much appreciation for horses," he told them, "but he is right about one thing, you know. It's still a long way to the Iron City, and the woods can be dangerous."

Irritation, that sense of automatic annoyance she had not allowed herself to feel earlier at Old Paul's comments, then caused Cassidy to look up directly into Click's face. "We know how to travel in the woods," she said.

"What did Old Paul mean?" Rowena quickly asked, interrupting the incipient confrontation between Cassidy and Click. "What's in the woods that's more dangerous than Woodsmen? Bears?"

But Click took an oblique tack, not precisely answering Rowena's question. He shook back his wet hair, the dark ringlets dripping. "Paul's an old man," he said, "and he's seen a lot of things. After all, even the Woodsmen aren't really dangerous; they just prefer their solitude."

Yeah, solitude and women's panties! Cassidy thought sourly, remembering the indignity inflicted upon her and Rowena. Giving Click another sharp look, Cassidy nudged Rowena with her elbow and said, "Come on, let's go check on my horse before we get any wetter." But before she could turn away and reasonably ignore his presence, Click spoke again.

"Most of the group will be going into Pointed Rock tomorrow morning," he said. "Once again you both are welcome to come with us if you wish. Or if you prefer to stay with the camp—" He made a small inclusive wave at the darkened huddle of carts and tents. "—I'm sure your help would be most welcome."

Was Click making fun of them? Cassidy glared up at him, a single drop of moisture coursing from her hairline across her forehead to dangle inelegantly from the tip of her nose. "Maybe you'd like us to just march into that village," she said, her tone nearly an accusation. "Then you could explain to those Villagers just why you're—"

This time it was Rowena who elbowed Cassidy, so abruptly and so roughly that she almost had to take a step sideways to keep her balance.

"We'll just stay with the camp again," Rowena said with de-

liberate politeness. "There's a lot of things we can do and I'm
sure we'll be of much more help here."

Wincing, Cassidy gave Rowena a baleful glare; but she still
obediently nodded in agreement.

"As you prefer," Click said smoothly. And that time Cassidy
was certain he was laughing at her.

But Cassidy didn't have a chance to make any further ri-
poste. Rowena had seized her firmly by the upper arm and was
practically dragging her away from Click, past the shadowy
bulk of Old Paul's cart and out beyond the edge of the camp.
The brunette walked rapidly and ruthlessly. When they were finally out of earshot, Rowena spun Cassidy around on the slick
sod and with surprising force gave her arm a frustrated little
shake.

"For crying out loud, would you cut that out, Cassidy?" she
demanded. "Quit trying to always pick a fight with him!"

"With who?" Cassidy replied, ineffectually fumbling for an
air of genuine and affronted innocence.

Rowena dropped her arm but still stood glaring at Cassidy
with exasperated reproach. "What is it with you and this guy
anyway?"

Relenting, Cassidy dropped her gaze; but she pointedly
rubbed her upper arm. "I don't trust him," she insisted.

Rowena fixed her with a long and direct look of patent disbelief, but she didn't openly challenge Cassidy's explanation.
"Okay, so *don't* trust him," she said. "But let's not get ourselves killed just to prove your point!"

A few minutes later, as Cassidy stood leaning against the
grazing mare's warm and steaming shoulder, finger-combing
out the tangles from the long silver mane, Rowena offered her
an appeasing thought.

"I'm sure no one expects you to leave your horse behind,"
she said, patting the gray's solid rump as the horse casually
cropped the wet grass. "They know you're a Horseman. I think
Old Paul is just trying to be a pain in the ass."

"Yeah? Well, he's succeeding," Cassidy muttered. But she
took comfort in the logic of Rowena's observation and by the
time the two of them headed back for the camp and their tent,
the brief bit of tension between them had gone.

The trading party left for the village early the next morning.
The rain had finally stopped, although the sky still sagged low
with pendulous gray clouds and the hills were shrouded in fog.

Nearly all of the Tinkers went into Pointed Rock, leaving a mere half-dozen craftsmen behind at their camp. To Cassidy's surprise, even Old Paul and Henry the coppersmith joined the group going in to trade.

Because so few of the Tinkers had remained behind, there wasn't really much of a working camp atmosphere among them. With no one to work a forge, there was no need for a big supply of firewood. No one even asked for their help, so Rowena and Cassidy felt at loose ends for much of the morning. Then after lunch Ben, the Tinkers' cartwright, announced that he was going to replace the troublesome wheel on Willie's cart and that he'd need some help unpacking all the canvas and other goods that were loaded in it.

Rowena quickly volunteered to help, earning herself an appreciative nod from the stout, gray-haired man. Cassidy could also have volunteered but some impulse held her back. She still felt strangely restless, and since the rain had stopped the afternoon seemed like the perfect opportunity to do something that she had been longing to do for nearly a week: just get up on her mare and ride.

The truth, however, sounded a little too self-indulgent to confess, so Cassidy quickly came up with a plausible excuse. "Yesterday afternoon when we went through that big meadow, Mitz said she wished she'd had the time to stop and cut herself some yarrow to dry for tea," she told Rowena—and anyone else who may have been interested. "Well, she won't be able to get back there now, but it'd be less than an hour's ride on horseback. As long as it's stopped raining, I think I'll ride back and cut some of it for her."

Once she was alone on the gray mare's back, Cassidy felt the resurgence of all of the old sense of empowerment and confidence that seemed to have eluded her of late. That was one of the big problems with having joined up with the Tinkers, she reflected as she let the mare scurry up a wooded slope, Dragonfly climbing with the strength and agility of a stag running a deerpath. Too much time spent walking and pedaling a bike and not enough time joined with her horse. And joining was not too dramatic a term for what Cassidy felt when she was mounted on the big gray. The bunch and flow of the horse's muscles beneath the silver silk of that glossy coat seemed to be conducted directly through the snug fabric of her new pants, connecting with the muscles and blood and nerves of her own body in a way that was at the same time both exhilarating and soothing. She was a Horseman; together she and the mare were like one living thing.

When Cassidy reached the long narrow meadow valley she had crossed with the Tinkers the previous afternoon, she found it lying draped in a veil of thin but persistent fog. She could still see the trail of bent and flattened grass where they had passed on foot and with the carts, and the occasional score mark in the wet sandy earth from the wheels. The glen looked curiously empty then, with only her and the gray mare for occupants.

Cassidy slid off the horse's back and studied the growth of the various weeds and wildflowers that dotted the meadow. Because of the overcast weather there wasn't much color visible, but she recognized the yarrow's tall feathery foliage and its flat clusters of tiny grayish-white flowers, as well as its pungent smell. The stems proved to be tougher than she had expected, and she wished that she'd thought to bring Mitz's shears with her as she tugged and twisted at the spicy green stalks. The mare ignored her, wandering off to rip up mouthsful of the coarse grass with her customary gusto.

The hills surrounding the narrow valley were quite steep and thick with evergreens and old-growth trees. Being in the serpentine-shaped meadow was like being at the bottom of a huge green trench, with the thick gray coils of the sagging clouds seemingly suspended directly from the tops of the big trees on the nearby hills. The fog hung in trembling streamers from the lower tier of those same trees, floating down the hills over the wet meadow grass.

As she twisted and yanked off the tough stems of yarrow, Cassidy thought about how the terrain had been gradually changing in the time she and Rowena had been traveling with the Tinkers. The hills had become larger and more steeply pitched. There were fewer clearings and meadows, both upland and lowland, and less open brushy land. The nature of the forest had been changing, as well, with more evergreens and hardwood trees, most of them old growth in size. And there was one thing that Cassidy had never really noticed until she had ridden back to the meadow that afternoon, probably because it was the first chance she'd had in quite a while to cover that much ground in so short a time. The overall axis of the land was changing, and the general slope and fall of the land was toward the east—toward the Long River and ultimately toward the Gray Sea.

Cassidy had originally thought that after she'd picked Mitz's yarrow, she might ride on beyond the meadow. But by the time she had accumulated a fair-size bundle of the pungent weed and had tied it on both ends with a length of twine, so that she could sling it over her shoulder like a leafy bedroll, she no longer felt much interest in going on past the valley.

After approaching the gray mare, who cocked a quizzical ear at the weird object slung over her back, Cassidy hopped up onto the horse's back. A vague feeling of uneasiness had descended upon her, almost unnoticed, as she had finished picking the yarrow. Once she had mounted up she looked up and down the length of the misty meadow, feeling more than a little foolish for her anxiety.

I've been living in a camp for too long, she told herself firmly, *if a little solitude is all it takes to make me this spooky.*

And the big mare seemed completely unperturbed, except perhaps at being disturbed from her grazing, as Cassidy swung her back in the direction of the Tinker camp. The damp air was calm and the woods were quiet as they made their way back up the hillside. The only thing to ruffle the gray fringe of fog that clung around the trees was the movement of the passage of the horse and her rider.

Just when Cassidy had convinced herself that she was woefully out of practice at being out on her own, and that certainly if anything was lurking around, the mare would have been more excited, she heard the distinct sound of a branch breaking somewhere in the forest behind them. An innocent sound in itself, it still made Cassidy jump as if it had been a gunshot. She spun around on the mare's back, but she saw nothing but a dark fog-blurred wall of green down the slope they had just climbed. Dragonfly swiveled one ear back, more in response to Cassidy's abrupt movement than anything else.

Okay, it's probably nothing but a squirrel or a fox, right? Cassidy lectured herself; but she still kept turning to look back in the direction from which the sound had come. After all, the mare wasn't worried, so how bad could . . .

Another cracking sound, more muted but just as close, interrupted her deliberate self-reassurances. And although she could still see nothing in the thick and misty forest behind them, Cassidy recognized what she was hearing: It was the sound of something moving through the trees—something big, and either rather clumsy or just incautious. Something that didn't need to be afraid of one woman on a horse.

Cut that out! Cassidy admonished herself, even as she tightened her legs around the gray's barrel. After all, the horse wasn't afraid; why should she be? If there was anything back there that . . .

Another series of crunching, trampling noises truncated that line of thought and brought with them a sudden realization that made Cassidy stiffen on the horse's back. Adrenaline, unexpected and unwelcome, sent its tingling terror sluicing into her veins and she felt her pulse begin to accelerate, her heart thumping against her sternum.

Four times already she had seen something—some *things*—that had horrified her and been beyond all rational explanation. Cassidy realized then that on three of those four occasions the gray mare had not been with her. And on the fourth occasion, the night of the fire in Double Creek when she had ridden with Mike along the river-bottom pasture and had seen those roiling putrid creatures of the darkness—well, she had been on the mare that night, but the horse had not been afraid.

Great! Cassidy thought grimly, tightening her heels against the gray mare's sides. *Of all the horses in this miserable place, I have to get one who's not afraid of monsters!*

With a loud grunt at Cassidy's sudden imperative urging, the big horse bounded forward, plunging ahead heedless of the hazards of the narrow slippery path that wound its way upward between the massive trees. The ground there was still slick from the rain and treacherous from rotted leaves. But Cassidy didn't care; she had more faith in the mare's natural speed and agility than she had compunction about driving her with such reckless haste. She just crouched over the gray's pitching withers and buried her face in the whipping strands of the horse's long mane.

Once they were galloping full out, with wet branches tearing at her sleeves and slapping her across the knees, Cassidy could no longer hear anything that might have been following them. The only sounds she could hear then were the swish and snap of errant boughs, the muffled thump of the mare's hoofbeats, and the insistent thudding of her own pulse in her ears. But she didn't mind the minor annoyance of being thrashed by a little foliage—not with the images of those hideous stinking *things* so fresh in her mind. She didn't even notice the way the twine-bound bundle of yarrow swung and bounced against her back; she probably wouldn't even have noticed if the whole bunch had fallen off.

It was difficult to say just how long Cassidy would have continued to push the gray mare if the rutted and twisting trail along which they were racing hadn't finally bottomed out into another long narrow glen. Once they had burst out into a relatively open area, Cassidy's burgeoning panic forced her to glance back over her shoulder to see if whatever was chasing them had gained on them. And when she did, what she saw suddenly made her precipitous flight seem not only useless but also completely foolish.

A hundred or so feet behind them the object of her terror crashed out from among the trees and leapt into the narrow valley. Rather, the *objects* of her terror, for the creatures that had inspired such fear in her were a whitetail doe and her two nearly grown fawns.

Sensing Cassidy's chagrin, the gray mare pulled down to an abrupt walk, snorting loudly through her distended nostrils. At that sound the trio of deer also slid to a halt at the edge of the clearing, their big winglike ears pointed forward and their huge dark eyes popping, much as if they were as amazed as was Cassidy to have found themselves following a horse and rider. Then, with an agility that even the mare couldn't have hoped to match, the three deer turned and bounded back off into the trees. Within seconds they had disappeared completely.

It took several more minutes for the urgency of the adrenaline rush to finally dissipate from Cassidy's veins. Feeling relieved and embarrassed, she let the horse amble idly for a while, not even minding that the gray took advantage of the opportunity to crop at a few twigs as she made her way up the incline of the next hill at a considerably more sedate pace.

Finally becoming conscious of the way the twine from the yarrow bundle was cutting into her neck, Cassidy shifted the burden on her back. Her shirtsleeves and the legs of her pants were wet from the fog-drenched foliage and her damp hair felt like a tangled mop. As she urged the mare on again at a more collected gait, Cassidy remembered Old Paul's gruff assessment of the dangers of the forest. For the first time the idea of traveling down the Long River with the Tinkers didn't seem like such an unattractive proposition.

A half hour later when she rode over the crest of the last hill and started down the slope to the Tinkers' temporary camp, Cassidy actually felt quite glad to be returning. She was even thinking, with a surprising and unfamiliar sense of satisfaction, how nice it would be to please Mitz with the unexpected gift of the yarrow. So absorbed was Cassidy in those thoughts that it took a few moments for it to register with her that something was wrong with the scene below her.

What had been a nearly deserted camp, populated only with the half-dozen Tinkers who had stayed behind, was full of people again. The traders had come back from Pointed Rock.

Cassidy hesitated for a long minute on the edge of the encampment, trying first to figure out what the hell was going on before she put herself back into the thick of it. Everyone in the camp seemed to be bustling around doing something: folding tarps and tents, packing carts, stacking goods for the backpacks. She saw Rowena over at Willie's cart helping Ben and the tentmaker replace the newly repaired vehicle's contents. And unlike the jovial atmosphere after the successful trading session in Briar Ridge, the mood of the entire group seemed decidedly downbeat.

Slipping down off the mare's back, her pants still tacky with half-dried sweat, Cassidy unslung her bundle of yarrow and started across the campsite. She greeted Bonnie and Wanda and a few of the others, but their responses were brief and perfunctory and they seemed absorbed with their packing. Probably no one had even noticed her absence, Cassidy realized. She cut directly over to Willie's cart.

"What the hell is going on?" she asked, coming up behind Rowena and causing the brunette to jump in surprise.

Glancing around to be sure no one was close enough to overhear, Rowena just shrugged helplessly and said, "They came back about an hour ago. We're going to move out yet this afternoon."

"I assume the trading didn't go well then," Cassidy said.

Carlotta had come up behind Cassidy, probably looking for her and Rowena to help with her cart, and she heard Cassidy's pithy remark. "Not exactly one of our more successful bartering sessions," the jeweled woman said quietly, nodding sympathetically at her briskly packing companions. "But we're only about a day's travel from the river. Click wants to move out yet this afternoon."

Following Carlotta and Rowena back to the bike cart, Cassidy slowly swung the bundle of yarrow by its twine cinch and ventured a question of the older woman. "What happened in the village? Why did you come back so early?"

At first Cassidy thought that Carlotta wasn't going to answer her. The metalsmith loosened the fastenings of the tarp that covered her cart and began to retrieve the trade goods she had piled on the sod beside the vehicle. Cassidy and Rowena started to help her, and they all worked in silence for a few moments. Then Cassidy realized that Carlotta was merely waiting for an opportune moment, until the other Tinkers who were working nearest them had turned their attention elsewhere and would not be likely to overhear.

"There was trouble in the village," she said quietly, "and strangers." She gave her head a rueful little shake, sending her hooped earrings jangling. "They weren't especially interested in bartering, and we aren't interested in their affairs."

Villager's affairs: The phrase leapt out at Cassidy and reminded her of Mitz's profession of support the morning they had been out in the willow breaks. Cassidy felt the familiar nagging twinge of warning go through her once more, and she exchanged an anxious if surreptitious glance with Rowena over Carlotta's bent back.

"Anyway," Carlotta went on matter-of-factly, straightening again with another load of metal tools to stow in the cart, "we may as well move on today. Click figures it could be raining again by morning."

Cassidy's eyes fell on the twine-bound bundle of yarrow, lying where she had set it down against the bike cart's wheel. "Listen," she said to Carlotta, "I picked this stuff for Mitz today. I'm just going to run over and give it to her before we get started."

Not waiting for a response from either woman, Cassidy turned and began rapidly striding away across the breaking encampment. She didn't care if Rowena and Carlotta thought she was acting weird. She couldn't help but think that perhaps Mitz could tell her more of what she needed to know about events in the village.

It wasn't so much that Cassidy wasn't watching where she was going; she didn't run into Click out of carelessness. Rather, the Tinker leader deliberately intercepted her course, and because she was so preoccupied she didn't realize that he was alongside her until he reached out and began to try to take the bunch of yarrow from her hands.

"Is this for Mitz?" he asked, even though he obviously knew the answer. "I'll give it to her for you. We're just about to get moving now."

Cassidy was momentarily startled by Click's sudden appearance at her side, but she refused to relinquish her hold on the yarrow. She looked up directly into his face; he was close enough that she could clearly smell the leather and soap scent of him, even over the tang of the yarrow. She hadn't particularly wanted to talk to Click, but since he had presented himself to her she figured that he rather than Mitz could answer her questions.

"What went wrong in the village?" she asked him. "Carlotta said there was trouble."

Click kept his hold on the bundle of yarrow; he also kept on walking, and so since Cassidy refused to yield up the bunch she was forced to walk along with him. He moved quickly but almost casually, much as if the two of them just happened to have been strolling along in the same direction for a pleasant little chat. He shot Cassidy only a brief glance before speaking, but the look in those deep brown eyes was both solemn and compelling.

"It's been a bad summer for trouble," he said, but Cassidy detected no hint of facetiousness in his tone. "It's a good thing we're almost to the river."

Unsatisfied with that and becoming increasingly concerned, Cassidy persisted. "Carlotta said there were strangers in the village; were they looking for us?"

Her bluntness caused Click to finally slow his pace. He didn't let go of the yarrow, but at least he looked sideways so he was facing her. One dark brow climbed in a sharp arch. "Do you expect someone to be looking for you?" he asked her.

Cassidy could have kicked herself for blundering into that admission. She had been so suspicious of Click that she had entirely forgotten that he probably knew a lot less about her and Rowena than she imagined.

"Villagers are always suspicious of Horsemen," she said, her fingers tightening on the bundle of yarrow. "They seem to think we're all thieves and cheats. But it's not only me they'd be interested in."

Click said nothing but he had at last come to a halt. They were standing beside the blackened remains of one of the camp's old firepits, uncomfortably close to where the line of carts and Tinkers hefting backpacks was assembling. He looked directly at her. Click had a way of canting his eyebrows that asked the necessary questions for him.

"I know you've figured out what Rowena is," Cassidy continued, her voice pitched so low that it was nearly a harsh whisper. "I don't think you want to see some superstitious

bunch of farmers interfere with what she and I have to do."
She paused briefly, then concluded, "If you did want that, you
could have given us up long before this."

The combination of confession and an appeal to Click's
sense of honor seemed to be working; at least he didn't respond with some wry comment. To seal the offering of her
confidence, Cassidy suddenly released her hold on the yarrow,
completely freeing the bundle into Click's hands.

The tall man took a half step backward from her, holding
the bunch of pungent herb like a wand. For a long steady moment he looked directly into her eyes, and for the first time she
really saw how all of the lines of his sleepless nights had been
etched so deeply into his face. "Go help Carlotta, Cassidy," he
said then. "I'll see that Mitz gets this. We have to be getting
under way now."

Turning without a backward glance, Cassidy quickly re-
traced her steps across the empty campsite to where Carlotta's
bike cart waited as part of the growing caravan of Tinkers. She
didn't know if her ploy with Click had worked or not, but she
and the Tinker leader shared one common pressing concern:
They both wanted to leave the village of Pointed Rock behind
them as quickly as possible.

The afternoon remained gray, the low clouds hanging sul-
lenly in a sky the color of tarnished pewter. Droplets of water
still dripped from the grass and weeds and leaves, and the
faintest smudge of fog still blurred the damp air in the glens
and wooded valleys. The longer steeper hills made travel more
difficult, especially with the heavily laden carts. But Cassidy
had never seen the Tinkers push on with such sober determination. Even though they would never be able to reach the Long
River before dark, they certainly seemed eager to put as much
distance as possible between themselves and Pointed Rock before night fell.

As the gloomy afternoon wore on into an equally gloomy
evening, Cassidy's feelings of frustration and unease were
joined by a deep weariness. She was not exactly surprised
when the band did not follow their usual custom and stop well
before dusk. Traveling with the Horsemen and Villagers had
taught her how to squeeze every hour of light out of a day on
the trail. But she was still concerned about what had happened
back in that village and increasingly discouraged to find out

how physically fatigued she was growing as the group pushed
on into the somber twilight.

Cassidy wished that there was someone she could talk to
about her concerns—even Rowena would have been a big
help, although the brunette knew as little as did Cassidy about
what had happened to send the Tinkers prematurely out of
Pointed Rock. As it was she could only trudge gamely on, taking her turn with Carlotta and Rowena at pedaling the bicycle
and looking forward to the chance to finally stop for the night.

It was nearly full dark by the time they halted to set up
camp. Too tired and hungry to even complain, Cassidy helped
Rowena and Jimmy and Teddy gather firewood. She was
sprawled out at Carlotta's cook fire with Rowena, Julie, and
Chrissy, thinking about how grateful she was that it hadn't begun to rain again and nursing along a second cup of coffee,
when Mitz joined them.

The diminutive gray-haired woman got right to the point.
"Click gave me the yarrow you cut for me," she told Cassidy.
"It was very thoughtful of you and I appreciate it." At the very
edge of the fire's light, Mitz was not clearly visible, but
Cassidy could see that the woman was holding out something
to her. "Here," she continued, "for you and Rowena. If this
weather keeps up, they'll come in quite handy."

Surprised, Cassidy automatically reached out and took hold
of what the seamstress was proffering. Her fingers closed over
folds of soft, tightly woven material. "Thank you," she said,
"but you didn't have to—"

But Mitz merely waved down Cassidy's polite protest.
"They aren't exactly gifts," she pointed out. "The two of you
have done more than your share of work since you've been
with us." Turning to leave, Mitz threw off over her shoulder,
"And when we go down the river, I'll show you how to weave
wicker."

The garments Mitz had given them were short, hooded
cloaks fashioned from finely woven gray wool. Cassidy had
seen many of the other Tinkers wearing similar cloaks in the
rainy weather during the past week; she knew they would
prove more than handy if the wet conditions persisted. She and
Rowena both tried on the cloaks as they sat by Carlotta's cook
fire. And later, when they had crawled into their little tent,
Cassidy folded hers to use as a pillow, where the garment
proved to be firm but springy.

That night, exhausted and uneasy, Cassidy dreamed. It was

the first dream she could remember having since they had joined up with the Tinker band. She dreamed that she was galloping on the gray mare, speeding along as urgently as she had that afternoon in the forest. But in the dream she was not being chased, she was chasing after something. Other people—Rowena, Click, Carlotta, Bonnie, Mitz, Old Paul—were walking along in the same direction that she was riding, but she just galloped on by all of them without a word. And in the way of dreams, the thing that she pursued remained ever beyond her, something both elusive and unknown.

Out of the soundest sort of sleep, deep within the dream, Cassidy was dragged into wakefulness by someone firmly and insistently shaking her shoulder.

"Cassidy? Quickly—you have to go."

The voice that hissed in her ear was so familiar to her that at first the urgency of its message never connected with her dream-drugged brain, and all she wanted to do was burrow her face more deeply into the soft folds of her new woolen cloak and resubmerge herself in sleep. But the annoying shaking persisted.

"Rowena, you, too! Come on, the both of you."

Suddenly making the connection, her shoulders jerked with a violent little twitch as Cassidy realized the person trying to rouse her was Click. She lifted her face from the folded cloak, blinking up stupidly at him in the darkness. For a split second all she could think was *What the hell is Click doing in our tent in the middle of the night?*

Beside her, Rowena was groggily stirring, murmuring something incoherent as she, too, was reluctantly dragged into wakefulness. Cassidy's eyes felt gritty from sleep, and once her initial sense of surprise had passed, irritation took over.

"What the hell is going on?" she muttered at the dim shape that was crouched over them, framed in the narrow triangle of the tent's opening.

"Shh!" Click reprimanded her. "Get your boots on; you both have to go—quickly now!"

Automatically beginning to obey even though she was still half asleep, Rowena was fumbling around the edges of her bedroll, groping for her footgear. Slightly more awake and considerably less compliant, Cassidy abruptly sat up and nearly bumped heads with Click.

"What the hell is going on?" she repeated in a loud hiss.

Thrusting her boots at her, the dark-haired man reiterated in a low and urgent whisper, "You both have to get out of this camp at once." He had Cassidy by one arm then and was forcibly drawing her from the tent. "I want you to get on your horse and *ride!* Now!"

Baffled and clumsy with sleep, Rowena tumbled out of the tent after them. "Where are we going?" she asked with a yawn.

"*Why* are we going?" was Cassidy's question, even as she jerked her arm free of Click so that she could stumble into her boots.

Outside the tent the night air was cool and damp, vaguely phosphorescent with hanging fog. It was impossible to see anything, but Cassidy hastily looked around anyway. Across the camp from them, Bonnie's two obnoxious little dogs began to yap, and other Tinkers had begun to stir.

"Call your horse," Click insisted, less concerned then with muting his voice than with getting them to obey him swiftly.

All of Click that Cassidy could see was the outline of his tall lean form, a black sylph against the choking deep gray of the fog, and the faint glitter of the metal rings and conchas that decorated his vest. But she stared sharply at him anyway. "Not until you tell me why the hell we're about to go pounding out of here in the middle of the damned night!" she retorted.

Suddenly Click had her by both arms, pulling her so close that she finally could see his face, even if it still was inked with shadow. Those umber eyes were not amused then, they were narrowed to a piercing intensity. His fingers felt like metal bands digging into the flesh of her upper arms.

"There's been trouble in Pointed Rock—trouble in the villages up and down these hills," he said, his voice low and hoarse. "Things that people don't understand. Trouble brings Troopers, and these farmers like the Troopers even less than they like the trouble."

Click paused a moment, the fierce grip of his fingers abruptly and deliberately loosening on her arms. When he went on his voice had moderated slightly. "There were sheriffs in Pointed Rock. They were looking for someone to blame for their troubles. And now it would seem they are looking for you."

Startled in spite of herself, Cassidy just stared dumbly at him for a few seconds. She had been so worried about imagined danger from the Tinkers themselves that she had practically forgotten that she and Rowena were still essentially fugitives from village justice. By then the word could very well be out about them, even so far from Double Creek. And any Villager who knew could pose a threat to them.

Cassidy didn't have to Call Dragonfly; the horse suddenly appeared at the edge of the camp, luminous as a ghost in the heavy mist. The mare nickered nervously at Cassidy. Rowena was still struggling into her new cloak as she stumbled across the drenching grass toward the horse. Click released Cassidy but for a moment, torn by ambivalence, she could not turn away from him. Then he was reaching inside the dark leather edge of his ornamented vest and offering something to her, pressing it insistently into her hand.

"Take it," he hissed softly; and for an instant she thought she saw the old spark flicker in his eyes. "Just don't use it unless you have to."

Cassidy's fingers closed awkwardly over the cool metal shape of what she instantly recognized was a gun; a small gun, a pistol, and not a rifle like Allen's.

"Go!" Click commanded, more loudly again. "Follow the river and we'll find you again."

Cassidy pulled on her new cloak as she ran. She reached the mare in a few strides and without even breaking momentum she leapt up onto the horse's back. It took a few brief fumbling seconds more to help Rowena vault astride behind her. Cassidy did not look back as she urged the mare forward, away from the Tinker camp and into the foggy darkness.

Two things were familiar and reassuring to Cassidy as they galloped off over the wet ground: the solid heat and powerful bulk of the gray's body beneath her, and the clinging companionship of Rowena behind her, once again sharing Cassidy's fate. Those two things helped partially to ameliorate the frightening danger of the less familiar things, the threat from the Villagers and the odd hard pressure of the pistol she had thrust into the waistband of her pants beneath her cloak.

Grateful for the horse's superior night vision, Cassidy let the mare choose her own route as they climbed the first hill out of the camp. The horse ran easterly, just as Click had advised them. With Pointed Rock behind them, Cassidy hoped they would at least have the slight advantage of a lead. If they were lucky and the Villagers stopped first to search the Tinker camp, then maybe . . .

No sooner had that hopeful thought kindled in Cassidy's

mind then she heard a sudden commotion in the wooded gloom immediately to their left. Like the phantom pursuit that had so thoroughly terrified her only the previous afternoon, the disturbance sounded like something large moving rapidly and heedlessly through the brush and trees. Only this time Cassidy was certain it wouldn't turn out to be just a few startled white-tail deer.

"Cassidy?" Rowena said anxiously, almost into her ear. The brunette's hold around Cassidy's waist was like a deathgrip.

"I hear it," Cassidy said, urging the mare to veer right, angling away from the thrashing sounds in the darkness. She and Rowena both had to tighten their legs around the gray's broad barrel as the horse dodged a rotting deadfall and began bounding up another slope, the incline treacherous with the detritus of scattered branches and wet loose shale.

Cassidy recognized that the terrain had grown rougher in recent days as they had neared the Long River. She just hadn't expected to have to go galloping full tilt across that same terrain in the middle of the night, with the ground soaked from the rain and the fog shrouding every obstacle like a trap. The gray mare's agility was incredible; even with two riders she wound through the darkened forest without slackening her stride. Perhaps the only thing Cassidy could have faulted the horse for was her recklessness. Crouching lower over the steep withers, Cassidy winced as a dripping bough of white pine delivered a soaking, stinging slap to the side of her head.

It took a minute or two more of evasive flight, the horse dodging and feinting at breakneck speed, before Cassidy was confident that the sounds of their pursuers were growing fainter. *Where the hell did they come from?* she wondered, as a little flock of some kind of small bird, haplessly rousted from their sleep in the brush, exploded shrilly into the fog around them. *It's almost as if they knew which way we were going to—*

"Cassidy!" That time Rowena shouted, her arms clutching Cassidy's body even more tightly.

But Cassidy had not needed the warning for she, too, had heard the ominous crashing sounds pummeling through the forest toward them, again from their left. *Damn!* Where were all those Villagers coming from, and how the hell did they know just where to intersect them to force the gray mare back around?

Grunting as if in exasperation, the horse veered sharply right

again. Cassidy had now lost all concept of which direction
they were headed, and the commotion behind them was so
close that she felt if she were to turn back and look, she would
have been able to see their pursuers even despite the intervening fog, darkness, and trees. But Cassidy was not afraid; not
yet. She knew what village horses were like and she was confident the gray mare could outdistance any of them, especially
under these adverse conditions. Even if they were being driven
back toward the camp, their capture was still far from a certain
thing. But the whole string of unpleasant surprises was making
Cassidy feel increasingly apprehensive about what else they
might encounter before the night's ordeal was over.

They had pulled ahead again, the big mare plunging down
a steep slope slippery with pine needles and studded with the
stumps of long-dead trees, before Cassidy even dared to catch
her breath. Her new cloak was soaked through from the wet
branches, but she did not feel the chill. She kept her fingers
burrowed deeply into the long silver strands of the horse's flying mane, just beginning to allow herself to believe that no
matter what direction they were headed they had again outdis-
tanced the Villagers, when the first faint hint of the odor hit her
nostrils.

That stench—there was no other word for a smell like
that—was so terrifyingly familiar that for one awful heart-
stopping second Cassidy thought that the mare had somehow
run right over—right *into*—one of those hideous black hanging
things that she had seen before in the trees. All of the fear that
she had managed thus far that night to keep at bay came surging up in Cassidy, overwhelming her. Adrenaline, sharp and
cold like a sliver of ice, sluiced into her veins, and she had to
grope frantically to keep her grip on the horse's mane.

Villagers—even sheriffs, even if they had guns—were one
thing, she thought. Monsters were something else entirely.

Cassidy was certain that Rowena could also smell the foul
stink. There was no opportunity to discuss it, but Cassidy
heard the woman behind her make a disgusted sound at the
stench that had by then enveloped them.

Where are the damned things? Cassidy thought desperately.
And how fast were they—could they outrun a horse? She no
longer even felt the branches that ripped at her arms and legs.

As if in reply to her unspoken question, a new sound pierced
the foggy blackness. It was the shrill whinny of a frightened
horse and it came from somewhere back behind them, back

where they had last heard the sounds of the pursuing Villagers. The terrified cry set Cassidy's nerves stinging and caused her own adrenaline-fueled pulse to hammer even harder. Clutching the gray's mane so tightly that the strong strands of iron-colored hair nearly cut through the skin of her fingers, Cassidy tried to drive the horse even faster. But she had forgotten one thing, the thing she had learned the day she and Allen had faced the bear: She had forgotten that she rode a warhorse.

Instead of running away even faster, the mare did the exact opposite of what Cassidy would have expected or wished for. Snorting loudly, as if to forcibly expel from her nostrils the fetid stench that filled the damp air around them, the horse dropped her haunches. She slid to a bumpy halt, her hooves slicing furrows in the soft bed of slippery dead leaves that covered the ground. Cassidy felt Rowena's arms jolt loose from their hold on her waist; then Rowena's hands were frantically grappling for a grip on Cassidy's cloak. As the brunette fumbled to grasp the wet fabric, the mare abruptly pivoted and reared up onto her hind legs, bellowing out that eerie sound of challenge she had made when she had charged the wounded bear. Even as she desperately clung to keep her seat, Cassidy could feel the hair on the back of her arms and neck climb to stiff attention at the sound.

Behind Cassidy, Rowena slipped helplessly from the mare's back. Since she slid down she landed feet first, and since the ground was soft, Cassidy was certain that she wasn't injured. Besides, Cassidy had bigger things to worry about then. She was still on the mare and the damned horse was plunging back into the woods, right toward the source of the terrified whinny they had heard.

Toward the Villagers, Cassidy thought incredulously, bending low over the long arched neck. *Toward the damned monsters!*

Another frightened whinny reverberated through the murky soup of fog. Then there were other sounds, panicky and high-pitched, some of them too terrifyingly agonized to have been horses. Human sounds: shouting, then screaming, then something beyond screaming. Somewhere still ahead of Cassidy in the blackness of the wooded hills, sharp cracks like tree limbs being sundered shattered the night air. There was a storm of sounds then: frantic whinnies, cries of pain that could have been either animal or human, the staccato snap of ripping, cracking wood.

And then, too suddenly, a near silence.

Almost paralyzed with fear, Cassidy clung to her galloping horse, an unwilling passenger on a journey into hell. The cloying stench, a miasma like rotted flesh, hung so thickly then that it made her gag. She didn't understand how the horse could bear to run back into it. Wet branches from the brush and hanging boughs of trees slapped and snatched at Cassidy, but she was numb to their punishment.

What the hell happened? The sudden cessation of all of the furious sounds had frightened Cassidy almost more than had the initial commotion. What kind of struggle had been played out there in the deep blackness of the foggy forest—and what had ended it?

Beneath her Cassidy felt the big mare abruptly slow. The change in gait nearly unseated her, and she had to use her hold on the horse's mane to pull herself upright again. The mare shook her head, anxiously and angrily, sending the tangled mass of her mane jerking in Cassidy's hands. Then the horse exhaled loudly, her sides bellowing out and her nostrils flaring.

When the gray began moving forward again, she stepped carefully around something that was lying on the ground. It was something big, but because the gloom was so utter and deep there among the trees, they had to pass almost directly over it before Cassidy could see that the something was the body of a horse. Horrified, she saw that another dead horse lay only a few yards ahead of them. But the second horse wasn't lying amid the wet scuffled leaves; its body was about four feet off the ground, impaled on the shattered stump of a pine tree whose trunk had been a good foot in diameter.

I guess this is why Click gave me the gun, Cassidy thought numbly, groping at her waistband for the pistol.

Before she realized what she was doing, Cassidy found herself slipping down from the mare's back. Ahead of them for as far as she could see in every direction the dim mist-covered forest looked as if a tornado had torn through it, whipping up the leaves and dirt, snapping off the trees, pulverizing the brush and branches. And across the whole scene of devastation were splattered dark gobbets of blood and the glistening droplets of something slimy and foul.

Gripping the pistol in front of her like a sword, Cassidy moved forward, numb with disbelief yet inexorably drawn as she stumbled across the carnage. There were four more dead horses; two of them were gutted with their entrails strewn about the mangled brush like gory garlands. Blood and the stink of death had finally superseded the foul stench of the hanging black things.

Cassidy had to walk at least another fifty feet across the ruined landscape, back to where the terrified horses had perhaps first thrown their riders, before she found the first human victim of the slaughter. Once more she found herself wondering how the hell the gray mare could have run *toward* that massacre. Averting her pistol and reluctantly bending lower to see through the clinging fog, Cassidy briefly studied two unfamiliar and brutally slain men. The next body was that of a woman with blond hair; for one heart-stopping moment Cassidy thought of Meggie, her friend from Double Creek. But the woman, too, was a stranger.

Then Cassidy could see no more bodies in the immediate area. Hesitating, she just stood there for a moment, the pistol dangling uselessly in her hand. There had been six horses; there should have been six riders. Should she keep searching for the rest of the Villagers? They weren't her responsibility. She tried to tell herself that. Her responsibility was to Rowena, who was somewhere back there in the woods, probably frightened and confused. Her responsibility was to get both of them the hell out of there before those creatures—those hideous *things* that could shatter trees as if they were mere matchsticks and gut a horse as if it were a rabbit—could come back again and finish the job.

Gulping a deep breath, Cassidy abruptly turned and began winding her way back through the path of devastation toward where she had left the gray mare. Her woolen cloak hung on her like a wet shroud, spattered with dirt and bits of slime. As she edged a wide berth around the mangled bodies of the two dead men, who lay tangled together as if they had somehow embraced their violent deaths trying to defend each other, she stumbled over a twisted root hidden in the darkness and nearly fell.

Except that the root groaned.

Swiftly and automatically, Cassidy brought the pistol up and pointed it at the sound. She froze for the space of a few thudding heartbeats. Then, chagrined, she dropped down on her knees beside the bloodied body that lay half buried in a drift of dirt, leaves, and shattered wood. The man was twisted in an unnatural position, his head and upper body nearly covered by debris. Cassidy had to dig like a dog through the litter before she could even get her hands under his shoulders to pull him over onto his back. And when she had, she sat back abruptly on her heels, her mouth dropping open in fresh shock.

For the man was Allen, the sheriff of Double Creek.

Chapter 7 ◀▥

Later Cassidy was surprised to find out just how close the mare had brought her back to the Tinkers' camp. There had only been one wooded hill and a shallow ravine between their encampment and the scene of the carnage. In fact, after Rowena had been so unceremoniously unhorsed by the gray mare, the brunette had only had to walk for a few minutes through the foggy underbrush before she had seen the light of the lanterns carried by the group of Tinkers who were out searching for them.

When the Tinkers found Cassidy in the shattered clearing she was still kneeling over Allen's unconscious body, unmindful of the dirt and slime that had spattered her clothing, trying to staunch his bleeding with her woolen cloak. She felt dazed and curiously drained, and although she was relieved to see the wavering procession of approaching lanterns, she had not responded when they had called out her name. She hadn't even looked up from her ministrations to Allen until a hand landed on her shoulder and gently shook her. Then she had lifted her face into the foggy pool of yellow light and seen Carlotta's concerned face bending over her.

Much of the rest of that night became a blur to Cassidy. She had refused to leave Allen; Tad finally had to pick her up as if she were a stubborn child and carry her slung in his huge arms back to camp. As the big bald man lifted her, she had seen Bonnie and Mitz crouching over Allen's prostrate form, hastily conferring in grave murmurs. They had to fashion a litter from a couple of stripped saplings and two cloaks to be able to transport the unconscious man.

Although Cassidy had been more than willing to leave that devastated stretch of forest, she refused to give poor Tad any

cooperation until the blacksmith could show her that both
Rowena and the gray mare were unharmed. Once they had returned to the Tinker camp, Cassidy pushed off all attempts by
Carlotta and even Rowena to offer her comfort or clean clothing. She went directly to the makeshift pallet where Allen lay
and elbowed in past Mitz and Bonnie.

"Is he going to live?" she demanded.

In the almost phosphorescent yellow light of the semicircle
of lanterns that had been set up around the sheriff's body, Bonnie's broad and expressive face was etched with concern. "I
don't know, Cassidy," she said with equal candor. "He's lost a
lot of blood."

From the other side of the recumbent body, Carlotta looked
across at Cassidy, her eyes soft with sympathy. "You know
him, don't you?" she said.

Cassidy fumbled at the edge of the pallet, groping for Allen's cold blood-smeared fingers. "Yeah," she said, her voice
nearly without inflection. "His name is Allen; he's the—"

"Sheriff from Double Creek," Carlotta finished for her.
"Yes, I know him, too." Looking down at Allen, she shook her
head with a sad fondness. "No taste in clothes, but he had a
good eye for metalwork, and he was an honest man."

Bonnie was conferring with Mitz and Moira, firing off instructions at them so rapidly that Cassidy's numbed mind
could not follow all of it. But when the blond woman attempted to pull Cassidy back out of the way so that she could
begin to cut off the ragged bloodstained remains of Allen's
clothing, Cassidy would not be moved. So Bonnie just worked
around her, deftly snipping with her big steel scissors and
gently tugging away the coarsely woven cloth as Cassidy sat
beside Allen on the ground with one of his limp and callused
hands still clenched in both of hers.

The lanterns' artificial light danced off the gold highlights in
Allen's russet hair and beard, giving his slack face a misleading sort of sunniness. But Cassidy knew even before Bonnie
had shorn away his clothing that the big man's wounds were
grievous. She had seen him the way he had been out there in
the shattered woods, left for dead with half his drab farmer's
garb torn from him and his body lacerated and bleeding. There
she had done the only thing she could think of to save his life,
pressing her own cloak into those wounds and setting her fists
against the hemorrhaging, even though she had been shaky and
light-headed with fear and anxiety. There she had rediscovered

a man she had never expected to see again, a man who mattered very much to her, the sole survivor of a slaughter that defied all explanation.

Mitz returned bearing a steaming pot of something that smelled like pungent tea. Moira and Carlotta followed with rags, towels, blankets, and a collection of small glass unguent jars. As the women gathered around the prone body to clean and dress Allen's wounds, Cassidy felt someone touch her gently on the shoulder.

"How is he?" Rowena asked softly.

Cassidy made a nonspecific shrugging motion, trying to prevent the gesture from turning into an involuntary shudder of cold and weariness.

"Jeez, what could have done that to him?" Rowena wondered aloud.

From what Cassidy could see of his ghastly injuries, by all rights Allen should have been dead. The entire right side of his body, from armpit to midthigh, looked as if someone—some *thing*, Cassidy thought grimly—had slashed his flesh with sharp curved blades. The wounds varied in shape from short arcs to semicircles to near-full circles, all comprised of deep stablike incisions. Amazingly, it didn't appear as if any vital organ had been penetrated; that was probably the only thing that had kept him alive until Cassidy had found him. But what, if anything, would keep him alive from that point on was still an open question.

Hypovolemic shock, Cassidy thought dully; the phrase had sprung from somewhere in that same deep pit of memory that had yielded up the other apt recognitions: bicycles, cigarette lighters, firearms. But it was one *missing* thing Cassidy could very well have continued to do without.

Leaning back slightly to allow Mitz better access to the wounded man, Cassidy felt her shoulders bump against Rowena. The brunette had settled on the ground right behind her; now Rowena leaned companionably against her, sharing the warmth of the blanket in which she had been draped.

When Bonnie and the other women had finished dressing Allen's wounds with their various salves and clean towels, they wrapped him in blankets. Other than a few irregular inhalations, the injured man had not stirred; he hadn't even groaned. Cassidy looked down at his pale and expressionless face, trying to find some spark of the vitality that had always driven the Allen she had known. But there was nothing.

A vague shape bent over her, holding something in outstretched hands. It was Sheila, pushing a steaming mug of coffee at her. As she looked up and reached automatically to take it, Cassidy was surprised to find that the eastern sky was already tinged with the faint glow of dawn.

"Willie and the others are coming back," Sheila said quietly to Bonnie. "I guess I'll start cooking some breakfast."

Methodically scanning the hillside that lay east of the encampment, Cassidy picked out the single file of a half-dozen Tinkers, led by the big overalled man. They trod slowly, dark shapes against the gauzy gray light on the slope, each with a shovel slung over his shoulder. Cassidy did not have to ask where they had been or to what task they had been bent. Perhaps "village affairs" were none of their concern, but the deaths of Villagers were a grim reality that had to be dealt with. When she thought of what she had seen in that plundered forest, Cassidy could easily understand the sober gait of the returning men.

Cradling the hot coffee mug in both hands, Cassidy scanned further. Dragonfly was at the edge of camp, standing calmly but not grazing. Not a dozen yards from where the mare kept her dawn's watch stood five more horses, their lowered heads equally quiet. In the thin and murky light Cassidy could see that they, like the gray mare, were big, long-legged, and powerful horses, and like her they wore no tack. Not village horses then.

A short distance up the slope, keeping some council on the wet and fog-draped grass, Click stood deep in conversation with five strangers. There were three men and two women, and even from that distance Cassidy could see the distinctive ornamentation of their dyed and incised leather clothing that marked them as the Warden's Troopers.

"Trouble brings Troopers," the Tinker leader had told Cassidy. But as her fingers tightened around the almost painfully hot ceramic of the coffee mug in her hands, she wondered if Click hadn't gotten that backward. It was beginning to seem to Cassidy that Troopers brought trouble—first at Double Creek the night of the fire and again here, with the unspeakable slaughter in the woods.

All around Allen's pallet the Tinker camp had already begun to break into its prosaic rituals of morning. Tents were struck, cook fires stoked, and the damp air was redolent with the smells of smoke and frying fat. Life went on even in the echo of death. But Cassidy was scarcely aware of the change, scarcely even aware of Rowena who was still huddled beside her, cautiously sipping at her own mug of coffee while the sunrise gained momentum in the misty eastern sky. Sitting beside the pallet, her mug of coffee still cradled undrunk in her hands, Cassidy's attention was focused on the shadowy figures who stood on that quiet hillside.

It did not surprise Cassidy when, some long minutes later, Click began to walk back down the incline toward the camp. His low boots left long, darker scythe-shaped sweeps in the silver of the dew-drenched sod. He went first to the line of carts, parked shrouded in their damp canvas covers. There he paused to speak briefly with Willie, who was still cleaning and oiling the blades of the shovels the burial party had used. Then Click cut across the camp to Bonnie's cook fire where, delicately wreathed in smoke, he held a short but intense discussion with the blond woman, Mitz, and Carlotta. Carlotta in particular seemed concerned about something; Cassidy saw the metalsmith make several empathic gestures toward the pallet where Cassidy kept her watch. Cassidy was also not surprised when, after all of that was done with, Click crossed the remainder of the camp and came over to where Allen lay.

Click's face was somber, the silvered bars of his mustache bracketed by a deep set of lines, his eyes thoughtful and grave. He dropped down into a squat beside Cassidy, with a short nod for Rowena and a brief appraising glance for the body beneath the blankets.

"They tell me that you probably saved his life," he said to Cassidy.

"I don't know," she said honestly. To her, Allen looked so barely alive that the assertion seemed premature.

Click glanced down at Allen again. "Is he the man who was looking for you?" he asked her.

Dropping her gaze, Cassidy gave a brief nod. For some reason that only made what had happened seem all the worse to her, as if by running away from Double Creek she and Rowena had brought all that had happened down on Allen. But Click had a natural way of putting things in perspective.

"Well, I would guess that was his job," he said.

Cassidy was still looking down at the unconscious body that lay swaddled on the pallet when Click spoke again. "The Troopers want to talk with you about what happened out there," he said quietly. "You don't have to speak with them if you don't want to." As Cassidy's head jerked up, her eyes narrowing, the dark-haired man went on. "You may be a Horseman, but you're traveling with us now; that puts you under my jurisdiction, not theirs." He made a small gesture with one hand held palm up. "I told them that I would ask you, but that it would be your decision."

Cassidy lifted her eyes to the eastern hillside where the three men and two women stood, as calmly as if all the day were theirs as the rising sun began to fragment the shining mist which floated around them. To her there didn't seem to be much choice, and she had a good many questions of her own.

"I'll talk to them," she said, handing over her cooling mug of coffee to Rowena and pushing herself up. She managed to gain her feet more by sheer determination than by strength. Once standing, she had to step sideways to keep from swaying, but she ignored Click's offer of a steadying hand, just as she waved down Rowena's obvious intention to follow her.

"You weren't even there," she reminded the brunette, adding more softly, "Just stay here with Allen, will you?"

Cassidy started walking out of the camp, her legs growing more steady as she went. She was halfway across the wet turf to where the Troopers stood before she realized that she still had Click's gun sticking out prominently from the waistband of her pants. But she dismissed any possible concerns about the propriety of wearing the weapon to their meeting with one simple overruling thought: *Considering what these people have been dealing with, I don't think one Horseman with a pistol is going to spook them . . .*

She didn't Call the gray mare, but as soon as she'd cleared the edge of the Tinker encampment the horse came to her, nickering softly and pushing her big head against Cassidy's chest, expecting to have her ears rubbed. Cassidy indulged the horse for a moment. Troopers would certainly understand the bond that bound her to the leggy gray. When she finally gently shoved the mare away and continued walking, the horse tagged her up the slope like a large and docile dog.

As Cassidy approached the group of Troopers, she confirmed her first impression of them, which was that they had ridden far and hard, and had not liked what they had found at the end of their journey. One of the two women was black, but other than gender and color they could all have been poured from the same mold, no matter what their age or physique. There was some quiet strength to them, a self-assurance and sense of balance that sustained them despite their drawn faces and the men's stubbled cheeks. Glancing them over as she drew up to them, she tried to determine who might be their leader.

"My name is Cassidy," she said by way of introduction. "Click said you wanted to talk to me."

The largest of the three men was not the tallest, but he was built like a stone fence. The decorated leather of his fringed tunic was stretched across a chest as broad as a barrel. His graying hair was closely cropped, the same color as the stubble of whiskers on his face, and when he nodded at Cassidy she could see that his eyes were nearly the same gunmetal shade. He looked her up and down with the blunt sort of appraisal at which Cassidy had long since learned not to take offense. But if he was wondering why a Horseman was traveling with a band of Tinkers, he didn't vent his curiosity.

"My name is Cobb," he said. "The Tinker told us that you were out there last night." The gray eyes narrowed, iron-colored slits beneath his bushy brows. "What did you see?"

Cassidy looked up directly into his stolid face. "Dead horses," she said. "Dead people. Trees smashed apart like piles of tinder."

One of the other Troopers, a tall thin woman with twin braids of chestnut-colored hair, intervened then. Her voice was insistent but not sharp. "What happened out there, Cassidy?" she persisted.

Looking over to the tall woman and then beyond her, to the other three Troopers in turn, Cassidy fixed them all with a taut grim stare. "You tell me," she said. "You tell me what can gut a horse like it was a rabbit and hang it up off the ground on a tree stump, or what can carve a man up like a ripsaw. Tell me what the hell stinks so bad that you almost gag just breathing its rotten smell—just tell me what the hell it is that you're looking for."

For the space of several hard thumping heartbeats no one moved or spoke, and Cassidy realized that her last words had nearly been shouted, with her leaning angrily forward, her hands clenched into fists. But none of the Troopers had flinched in the slightest. Looking at the five of them, Cassidy had trouble imagining them flinching at much of anything, much less one dirty, irate woman.

It was neither Cobb nor the woman with braids who finally responded to Cassidy's outburst, but the second woman, the black one. She had gleaming nappy hair that was shorn as short as any man's, but her eyes, wide and dark and fringed with heavy lashes, were entirely feminine. She regarded Cassidy with an expression that was calm but not unsympathetic.

"The ones that stink so bad aren't really the dangerous ones," she said matter-of-factly. "They're just scavengers, like carrion birds. They only eat what the other ones kill."

Cassidy's mind had unwillingly summoned up the vivid image of the filthy hanging things, their black and loathsome bodies streaming with slime, pulsing as they . . .

"Other ones?" she said. "What about the other ones?"

But the woman didn't directly respond to that. "What did you see out there?" she asked instead, repeating Cobb's initial question. "Did you see the actual attack?"

Cassidy stared at her in silence for a moment, then shook her head. "No, I didn't even see those stinking things this time—I just could smell them afterward."

The black woman nodded. "You probably scared the scavengers off, or at least your horse did." Closely studying Cassidy's face, she added perceptively, "But you've seen them before, haven't you?"

Cassidy hesitated, automatically prepared to conceal the truth—which to her still seemed entirely incredible. There on that quiet hillside in the rising light of day and thinning fog, such things as monsters seemed to belong to an entirely different realm of existence, completely removed from the simple intrinsic rhythm of dawn. But as she looked at the Troopers' faces, sober faces scorched by fatigue and worn down by a dreadful knowledge whose burden few could share, she suddenly realized that those people and the others of their kind were perhaps her only hope of solving the bizarre mysteries she had found in that world. She realized, as well, that they were also her best link to the Warden, who was still her best hope of ever finding her way home again. And so she gnawed at her lower lip for a moment, but then she told them everything.

"I've seen the rotten ones twice before," she said. "Once when I was back in Double Creek, in a ravine; and then again less than two weeks ago, but just out in the middle of nowhere. Both times they were just hanging in a tree." She paused, deliberating a moment, but then confessed, "I thought I was going crazy—except I couldn't figure out how anyone could have hallucinated anything that smelled that bad."

Cobb gave a little grunt and the black Trooper actually cracked a small smile. But when Cassidy didn't just go on, the woman's expression sobered again and she urged almost gently, "What else, Cassidy? What have you seen of the others?"

As her mind flashed back to the night in Double Creek when she and Mike had ridden along the river-bottom pasture, that memory jogged something in Cassidy's mind. She thought of the Troopers she had seen that night, Valerie and Walt and the others, and then she considered the Troopers before her. *Hunters,* she had thought that night weeks ago—and she knew she had been right. And what all of them had been hunting were . . .

"Monsters," Cassidy breathed softly. "That's what they are, aren't they?" Once the word had been spoken, Cassidy would not back away from it. "I saw one in a river the first night I was here, like a big snake gliding through the water. And the night the barns burned in Double Creek, I saw these—these *things* racing through the air, like great big coils of greasy black smoke." She looked from one Trooper to the next, directly into their haggard faces. "They're monsters—but what in the hell *are* they?"

For a few seconds no one moved, no one responded. Then Cobb shook his head and scrubbed a callused palm across the peppery stubble that dotted his chin. "We don't know that yet," he admitted.

Cassidy felt an involuntary little shudder of revulsion run through her. "They're like something out of a nightmare," she murmured softly.

Several of the Troopers stirred restlessly then. On the hillside pale shafts of sunlight were angling obliquely through the mist. Before Cassidy, the black woman caught her attention with a direct compelling stare. Despite her soft-spoken demeanor, it was becoming obvious to Cassidy that the woman was the most doggedly pragmatic of the Troopers, and rather than speculate on what they didn't know she quickly went on instead to another line of questioning.

"The man who survived," the Trooper asked, "could he have seen something? As far as we know, this is the first time they've attacked humans."

Cassidy immediately thought back to all of the strange disappearances of animals in Double Creek and in Silverstone; and of all of the "troubles" in villages all along the chain of hills. How long had it been going on, and did any of the Villagers realize just what they might be dealing with? Cassidy became so immersed in thought that for a moment she didn't even remember that the woman had asked her a question.

"The man who was injured?" the Trooper prompted helpfully.

"He's the sheriff from Double Creek," Cassidy said. She hesitated, then continued reluctantly. "But he hasn't been able to speak. He's been unconscious since I found him; I don't know if he'll even live."

Cobb reached out and lightly touched Cassidy on the arm. "Listen carefully, Cassidy," he said gravely, "because this is very important. If this man lives, he could know more than anyone else does about these creatures and what they can do. We have to find out what he saw if we're ever going to learn what they are and how they can be stopped." His thick blunt fingers tightened on her arm; Cobb's gray eyes were hard and bright like silver as he charged her. "I want you to swear to me—swear on your blood—that if he lives you will take this man to the Warden in the Iron City."

Momentarily speechless, Cassidy just gaped up into Cobb's intense and sober face. "Me?" she blurted out. "But what about you? Rowena and I are trying to get to the Iron City ourselves—can't you take us all with you?"

As she stood beseeching Cobb, Cassidy noticed for the first time that the Troopers' horses had stirred and come across the hillside to within a few yards of where they all stood. Called or not, the horses waited with an ill-concealed impatience, their curved ears swinging to catch every little sound from the forested hill behind them.

The woman with the chestnut braids stood absently stroking one of the horses, a bay mare with a starred face. When Cassidy made her plea to Cobb, the woman replied, "There's no way the man could travel with us. You've said yourself he's seriously injured. And we're not going directly to the Iron City."

Cobb's fingers still gripped Cassidy's arm. The look on his face was no less intense but his tone had moderated slightly. "Go down the Long River with the Tinkers, Cassidy," he said quietly. "Keep this man alive. Bring him safely to the Iron City and you'll have earned the Warden's gratitude."

Even as Cobb was speaking, the other Troopers had begun to mount up. Given their appearance of long-driven fatigue, Cassidy was amazed at how lightly and swiftly the leather-clad men and women were able to spring back astride their horses. She looked from the mounted Troopers to the big man who still stood beside her.

"We were already on our way to the Warden before any of this happened," she told Cobb plaintively. "Isn't there any way you can take us with you?"

Cobb was sympathetic but he still shook his head. As he dropped his hand from her arm, he said, "We have no choice, Cassidy; and you're far safer with the Tinkers. If you go down the river with them, I promise you you'll get to the Iron City long before we will."

As the gray-haired man turned away from her, Cassidy made a frustrated grab for the sleeve of his fringed leather tunic. But in one quick and easy motion he had vaulted astride his own horse, leaving her reaching for nothing but mist and sunlight.

"Rowena and I could ride with you," she called after him. "Rowena has the Memories—she has to get to the Warden!"

The other Troopers had already begun to move away, their big horses striding up the slope, long legs slicing trails through the dew-drenched grass. Cobb held his cinnamon-colored gelding back for a moment as he looked down at Cassidy with an expression of honest regret.

"Stay with the Tinkers, Cassidy," he repeated. "Keep the sheriff alive. You'll get to the Warden safely, and long before we will."

He had already let the big gelding swing around again before he looked back at Cassidy and added, "Besides, your friend isn't the one with the Memories, Cassidy, you are."

Apparently her look of open-mouthed dismay was too much for even a harried Trooper to resist. Cobb swung his gelding around yet again and made one last pass by where she stood.

Cassidy glared up at him as he rode by her. "How did you know?" she demanded.

Cobb shrugged, while his big gelding shook his head impatiently, eager to follow his fellows. A brief smile flirted with that broad and craggy face. "When you said those creatures were like something from a nightmare," he explained then, "I knew that you know what it is to dream."

When Cobb let the cinnamon-brown horse leap forward, he

quickly scaled the hillside. Within seconds he was alongside the other four horses; moments later all five had disappeared into the trees at the crest of the hill.

For a long moment Cassidy merely stood there, watching the gap in the dark trees through which the mounted Troopers had disappeared. If she allowed her mind free rein, only one vivid image dominated: the utter devastation in that bloody stretch of woods where she had found Allen's savaged body. What *were* those ghastly creatures? And why had she already had so many encounters with them and yet always emerged unscathed? Unwillingly she remembered that night along the river-bottom pasture when one of the greasy black air monsters had passed right over her—*right through you,* she reminded herself fiercely—without harming her. And yet five Villagers had just been slaughtered and Allen lay near death by the same creatures. Why had she been spared again?

The thought of Allen brought with it a pang of guilty concern. Cassidy turned, looking back down the long grassy sweep of the dawn-lit slope, still wreathed in the barest veil of mist, toward the Tinker camp. From that distance the pallet where Allen lay was just a tiny rectangle, his big body nothing more than an indistinct mound under the blankets. Had she and Rowena been at least partially responsible for what had happened to Allen? Or had the sheriff, as Click had suggested, merely been doing his duty?

The gray mare watched Cassidy pivot. Then the horse approached her, jaws slowly grinding as a few stray wisps of grass dribbled from her mouth. She gently butted Cassidy's chest with her forehead, her long forelock sprouting like an errant fountain of hair across the front of Cassidy's filthy shirt.

Cassidy absently rubbed the bases of the mare's curved ears. The Troopers had told her to stay with the Tinkers. The Warden was in the Iron City, and they had said that going with the Tinkers down the Long River would be the fastest and safest way for her to get there. But what were she and Rowena going to do once they got there, once the convenient fabric of misleading half-truths and outright fabrication with which they'd been covering themselves began to fall apart and they had to explain the truth to a total stranger?

How are we going to convince the Warden to help us search for a world that no one else here even remembers? Cassidy thought glumly, cradling the mare's big head in her hands. She could not keep herself from adding *Especially if Allen dies . . .*

Exhaling noisily, the mare pushed at Cassidy's chest. With a final hug, Cassidy shoved the long head aside and started walking back down the hillside.

In the encampment breakfast was over and packing up was well under way. From her vantage point on the slope Cassidy had a clear view of all of the activity. But the Tinkers' actions were not distraction enough to keep her mind from returning to her previous conundrum as she walked.

Now that she and Rowena finally had a definite chance to reach the Warden of Horses, Cassidy wondered if he would actually be the solution to their problem, after all. Would he understand or believe that what everyone there called the Memories were really the remnants of another life in another place? Or would he prove to be as maddeningly obtuse as had been the village's farmers?

Automatically stepping over a rough hillock in the wet grass, Cassidy swung her arm, smacking her palm against the dewy crown of a Queen Anne's lace flower and sending droplets flying. Maybe some of the people there were more receptive to crazy ideas than others, she reflected. At least Cobb had known what dreams were—and he knew that the knowledge of dreams was a Memory. And Yolanda, Valerie, and those Troopers had all acknowledged the value of Memories to the Warden.

We've got to get out of here, Cassidy told herself desperately. *I want to go back to the real world!*

She was so engrossed in her thoughts that she hadn't even noticed Click coming toward her from the edge of the camp until she had almost walked smack into him. When she did glance up, seconds from impact, she was startled to see him there right in front of her. And because she didn't realize how grim a frown was frozen upon her own face, she immediately misinterpreted the grave look of concern that dominated Click's lean dark face. Cassidy jerked to a halt, staring up at him with anxious dread.

"Is—is he . . . ?" she stammered.

Click's brow arched more sharply; then he understood her assumption. "Your sheriff? No, he's the same," he said quickly, his hand automatically going out to touch her shoulder in a gesture of reassurance. "I was just worried about you. Are you all right?"

Cassidy finally realized that she probably looked like hell. Between the night's hasty flight, the filth and blood of the forest massacre, her vigil over Allen and finally the confrontation with the Troopers, she felt utterly depleted. If she looked half as bad as she felt, no wonder Click was concerned.

"I'm okay," she assured him, for the first time genuinely touched by his obvious interest in her welfare. She hesitated a moment and then decided that she would have to tell him at least something of what had happened with the Troopers. And, much as she hated to admit it, she and Rowena and Allen were all relying on Click's cooperation then, more heavily than ever before.

"I'm afraid I wasn't able to tell the Troopers anything really useful," she said, keeping just close enough to the truth to make it possible for her to look Click directly in the eye. "But they think Allen may have seen something out there— something to do with all of the troubles around here." She couldn't bring herself to use the word "monsters." She concentrated on a point just slightly below direct eye contact, a point somewhere around Click's silver-winged mustache. "If he lives, they want us to take him down the river to the Warden."

Click considered that for only a few seconds; then he nodded and said, "We would have done that anyway. If we'd left him back at Pointed Rock he'd undoubtedly die."

Click started slowly walking again, but since he'd kept his hand on Cassidy's shoulder she was more or less obliged to walk along with him. Click shot her an oblique glance and then said matter-of-factly, "Rowena told me that you've saved this man's life once before."

Rowena has a big mouth! Cassidy thought; but what she said was, "Sort of, I guess. A bear was after both of us, and I shot it."

That suddenly reminded Cassidy that she still had the pistol that Click had given her, tucked forgotten in the waistband of her trousers. She started to reach for it, saying "Wait, I still have your gun."

But Click's hand slipped smoothly from her shoulder to the hand that was reaching for the pistol, staying it. "Keep it," Click said simply. "I have another."

Cassidy wanted to protest, but she saw that they were almost to the pallet where Allen still lay. Several people were standing around his motionless body, so Cassidy was reluctant to start an argument over the firearm. As she and Click approached, Bonnie looked up from where she was squatting at Allen's side. Bonnie was so huge that Cassidy often wondered

how the woman ever made it to her feet again once she had
crouched down that low. But the big blond woman had always
surprised her, proving to be amazingly agile for her size.

"He's about the same," Bonnie said, before either of them
could ask.

"Can he travel?" Click asked.

Bonnie shrugged, her redundant chins bobbing. "Well, if he
lives or if he dies it won't be from the change of scenery."

One corner of Click's mustache twitched. "I take it that was
a 'yes,' " he said dryly.

Cassidy looked up to see Rowena and Willie approaching
with the big man's cart. The cart had been emptied of all of its
canvas goods and other supplies, and its bed was deeply layered with bedrolls and blankets. It occurred then to Cassidy
what Click must have been discussing with Willie after he had
come back from talking with the Troopers. It also made her realize that Click had not been misleading her when he had said
that the Tinkers would have taken Allen along with them regardless. And for the second time in as many minutes, Cassidy
found that she was strangely grateful to Click for his support.

While the rest of the camp finished loading up their gear, including the redistribution of the things that had been in Willie's
cart, Tad, Teddy, Click, and Willie lifted Allen's unconscious
body into the cart. As they carried him from the pallet Allen
made a soft deep sound, like a weak groan of protest. But that
was all. Once he was ensconced in the cart, carefully packed
to Bonnie's exacting specifications, he remained silent except
for the quiet and regular hiss of his breathing.

Rowena went to help Carlotta pedal the bike cart, but
Cassidy insisted on staying to help Willie with his cart. The
big canvas-worker just made a clucking sound of disapproval
when she tried to grab hold of one side of the push bar.

"You don't look like you could push this cart ten feet without falling flat on your face," Willie said, although not un-
kindly.

"You should be riding, not pushing," Bonnie added, looking
up from making the final adjustments to her own cart.

Click had been walking up and down the line of Tinkers,
checking carts and backpacks. At Willie's cart he easily hefted
his own heavily laden pack frame up onto his shoulders and
said to Cassidy, "Climb up and ride in there with your sheriff
for a few miles; someone should watch to see that the bumps
don't jostle his dressings and start his wounds bleeding again."

His lip never lifted, but Click's dark eyes betrayed a hint of humor to Cassidy. "Then if you still feel like pushing the cart, Willie will trade places with you."

Too tired to be offended, too weary even to argue further with him, Cassidy climbed up into the cart. Squeezing in carefully alongside Allen's legs, she sat on the blankets with her back braced against the side of the cart. She remembered the cart starting forward, but she didn't remember much more. Long before the Tinkers had climbed the first hill, Cassidy had fallen into an exhausted sleep.

It was nearly noon when the band reached the bank of the Long River. It may very well have been the fact that the cart had stopped moving that finally awoke Cassidy. Then she sat up abruptly, stretching stiffly and blinking into the bright sunlight, to find that they had reached the river.

Cassidy wasn't sure exactly what she had expected. As a sort of defense mechanism in that oddly skewed world, she had developed the habit of not expecting anything. But she realized she had not anticipated anything as settled or organized as the wharf on the Long River.

The river itself was easily the largest Cassidy had yet seen there, a good hundred feet from bank to bank at that point. There were steep bluffs on either side, heavily forested headlands that broke off abruptly into crumbling dropoffs of clay and rock. A winding loop of road led down to the bank where a small collection of rather crude-looking wooden buildings marked the wharftenders' little settlement. A long wooden wharf covered the whole near bank of the stream. From the wharf, extending out like a huge and roughly hewn parquet floor, rode a flotilla of big log rafts, all tethered aft and stern and side to side to each other and ultimately to the wharf, and all gently nodding and bumping in the river's current.

Cassidy had apparently slept through the initial exchange of greetings, for when she lifted her heavy head over the edge of Willie's cart she could see that the wharftenders were already well into an animated conversation with Click, complete with expansive gestures toward the fleet of rafts. She saw about a dozen workers, all tough and wiry-looking men and women, as businesslike as any Villager as they took to their tasks. Yet the Tinker influence was also clearly evident there, as well: All of the wharftenders wore unique and brightly colored clothing.

Bending back over Allen, Cassidy nearly bumped heads

with Bonnie, who had leaned in from over the other side of the cart. The enormous purple-clad woman had her hand against the side of Allen's neck, feeling his pulse. Embarrassed by her obvious failure to have monitored Allen's condition during the trip, all Cassidy could do was meekly ask, "How is he?"

But the look Bonnie gave her was tolerant, even affectionate, as she replied, "The same; maybe even a little better." Lifting the edge of the blanket that covered Allen's chest, Bonnie felt for something beneath it. "His dressings are dry and his pulse is stronger." She patted the blanket back down and shot Cassidy another look. "He looks like he'll live. So do you," she added.

Further embarrassed by Bonnie's concern, Cassidy clambered stiffly out of the back of the cart. To change the subject, she nodded toward the wharf and asked, "Who do all those rafts belong to?"

"While they're moored here they belong to the wharf-tenders," Bonnie said, stepping back from the cart. "But once we're on the river they belong to us."

Cassidy took that to mean that the Tinkers rented the rafts rather than owned them outright; but before she could ask Bonnie to clarify it for her, she found herself talking to thin air. The big blond woman had already started back to her own cart. In fact, nearly all of the Tinkers were already busy, pushing the first of their carts down across the wooden planking of the wharf toward the waiting fleet of rafts.

Since each raft was about ten or fifteen feet wide and about fifteen or twenty feet long, Cassidy didn't think it would take too many of them to accommodate all of the Tinkers and their goods. Certainly the group couldn't have filled up all of the rafts that were docked at the wharf; there must have been at least thirty. Cassidy assumed the wharftenders rented the vessels to anyone who had cargo to haul down the Long River. And from the appearance of the workers' clothing, they obviously enjoyed a healthy bargaining history with the Tinkers, at least for some of their goods.

From where she stood by Willie's cart, Cassidy could easily and automatically sense the presence of the gray mare; but it took her several moments of scanning the area surrounding the wharf to pick out exactly where the horse was. Around the cluster of houses and sheds the earth was hardpacked and essentially bare, but a short distance off, near the base of the clay bluff, the weeds and grass grew lushly. The mare was grazing placidly along the edge of a rough post-and-rail fence. It took Cassidy a few seconds more to register that on the other side of that fence, regarding the horse with an almost comic sort of intensity, were a half-dozen big coffee-colored mules.

Mitz walked across Cassidy's field of vision, carrying a small bundle under one arm. Seeing what Cassidy was staring at, the little gray-haired woman smiled. "Barge mules," she said, "for hauling loads up the river."

It had simply never occurred to Cassidy that people might have cause to bring goods up the river, as well, or that heavily loaded rafts didn't just float upstream against the current. She had been concentrating for so long on going down the Long River that she had never even considered the alternate possibility.

A little abashed by her own ignorance, Cassidy glanced down to see that Mitz was checking on Allen's condition, much as Bonnie just had. The packet that the seamstress had been carrying and that she had set down in the cart contained more bandaging materials. Looking up from her examination, Mitz gave Cassidy the same sort of kind and tolerant look that Cassidy seemed to be earning more and more lately.

"Why don't you go help Rowena load Carlotta's cart?" she suggested. "Moira is going to help me change his dressings, and we'll be loading this cart last."

Hesitant, but also a little relieved for the obvious dismissal, Cassidy threw one last look at Allen's peaceful form and then started off across the packed-dirt lot toward the wharf itself. She still felt mildly guilty about not having helped at all with the morning's travel, even though nothing in the Tinkers' attitudes toward her had encouraged any such remorse. Quite the contrary, both Rowena and Carlotta greeted her with genuine pleasure as she reached the bike cart just in time to help them push it across the wharf's rough planking.

"Jeez, you still look like hell—but you look a lot better than you did last night," Rowena said after a frank appraisal of Cassidy's appearance.

"Thanks," Cassidy shot back, suddenly conscious of her dirty clothing and tangled hair. But her sarcasm was completely unconvincing as she put her shoulder to the back of the overloaded cart and helped shove.

"How is your friend?" Carlotta asked as she and Rowena continued to pull on the bike cart's shafts.

Wondering just how Allen had gone from being the sheriff

of Double Creek to being her "friend," Cassidy shot Rowena a suspicious glance. But she realized that both the metalsmith and Rowena were genuinely interested in the answer, so she quickly replied, "He's still unconscious but Bonnie says he's better."

The three of them had to pause a moment while several wharftenders rushed to the aid of the cart directly ahead of them, which belonged to Old Paul and was so heavily loaded that the wizened little cooper and his apprentice could barely control it and also negotiate the narrow wooden ramp to the raft. Much of the supplies and equipment that had been carried in the backpacks was already stowed on the same raft. Even as they waited for Old Paul's cart to be put aboard, Cassidy realized that it would not take those efficient workers long to load the entire Tinker group. She glanced back over her shoulder at the line of carts behind them and then beyond to the patch of grass beside the rail fence where the gray mare still grazed.

With an astuteness eerily reminiscent of Mitz's earlier perception, Carlotta glanced back and followed Cassidy's line of sight. "Still worried about your horse?" she asked gently.

Cassidy shrugged as if to dismiss the question, but as she looked back toward the river she couldn't keep from adding, "I guess Old Paul was right about one thing—she sure can't ride on one of these rafts. I don't think I'd be able to get her to even set foot on the ramp!"

"No, but she can follow us down river along the bank," Carlotta assured Cassidy. "See the pull path from the barge mules? Well, it runs along this bank of the river all the way from here to the Iron City."

Once Carlotta had pointed it out to her, Cassidy could see that there was indeed a rutted but broad dirt trail near the water's edge, leading away from the wharf and eventually disappearing from view around the first bend in the wide river.

"No wonder Click wasn't concerned by Old Paul's grousing," Rowena said with an impudent grin. "That darn path looks more comfortable than these crazy rafts—I may just decide to walk to the Iron City myself!"

As soon as Old Paul's cart had been loaded onto the raft, the wharftenders came back to help with Carlotta's bike cart. Cassidy was willing to step back and let them do most of the work. Although none of the men or women was big or burly, and their gaudy attire even lent them a certain foppish air, they all proved to be as tough as nail kegs and quite adept at muscling around recalcitrant carts. As they took over, Cassidy left the wharf and walked quickly back past the cluster of buildings, toward the mule paddock where Dragonfly was calmly grazing.

Even from that short distance, Cassidy felt curiously removed from the bustle at the wharf. As she approached her horse, she could look back and still clearly see all of the activity both on the wharf and on the rafts. She could even hear the voices of the Tinkers and the wharftenders, especially when they were raised to shout some instruction or question. But as she stepped alongside the big gray and ran her hand along the horse's warm sleek side, she felt as if what was happening down at the river had nothing to do with her.

The mare lifted her head from the grass, blowing loudly through her nostrils and causing the most persistently curious of the barge mules on the other side of the fence to spook back in brief alarm. With their big lop ears and the lighter rings around their eyes and muzzles, the mules already had a look of perpetual startlement about them. But as Cassidy affectionately scratched the mare's withers, the mules crowded closer to the fence again, as if torn between caution and jealousy.

"I think you have them enchanted."

The familiar voice from almost directly behind her caused Cassidy to jump involuntarily. Her head jerked around to see that once again Click had managed to catch her woolgathering.

"Then again, perhaps it's just your horse," the Tinker continued as he came up alongside the mare. She sniffed his arm with polite disinterest; she had not been surprised by him. "I doubt that they get to see many horses out here."

Cassidy was at something of a loss with Click then. Her old sense of all-abiding suspicion no longer served her quite so well, and she hadn't yet found the reaction with which she wanted to replace it. She firmly told herself that she still didn't trust the Tinker leader, even if Rowena seemed content to. But it no longer seemed exactly fair to mistrust him, either, not after what had happened in the last twenty-four hours. And so Cassidy was left without an appropriate mind-set concerning the tall dark-haired man who now stood beside her.

Which isn't such a good thing, she thought ruefully as she looked up into his weathered but handsome face, *when you remember sex—even if he doesn't!*

Hastily casting about for a neutral topic, Cassidy said, "It looks like almost all of the stuff is loaded; how many rafts will you have?"

Click didn't even have to glance back toward the wharf to be able to answer her. "Six altogether," he said. "Five that will carry most of the cargo and then one where most of us will ride."

Relaxing slightly, and frankly tempted by the rare opportunity to gain more information so easily, Cassidy decided to push her luck with another question. She waved toward the rafts. "How many people does it take to handle one of those things on the river?"

"Usually just one," Click replied. Even as he spoke, he automatically reached out and brushed an irritating horsefly off Dragonfly's hip. "They're constructed with a keel and rudder assembly, so it's mostly just a matter of keeping them pointed in the right direction. There are only a few places on the river where the currents can be troublesome."

Trying to feign simple curiosity, Cassidy asked, "And how long does this trip usually take?"

The edges of Click's mustache lifted slightly. "That depends on how much of a hurry you're in." But before Cassidy had time to grow irritated by what seemed to have been a deliberately flip answer, he went on. "If you ride straight through, it can be done in less than a week." He spread his hands. "But we're accustomed to stopping overnight; most of us still prefer to sleep on solid ground."

For a moment all Cassidy could think of was the huge serpentlike water monster she'd seen on her first night with Yolanda and the Horsemen. And that had been in a far smaller stream than the Long River. She didn't care what the Tinkers were accustomed to—she was damned if she was going to be out on that river at night. Trying to school her expression to near neutrality, she merely said, "You moor the rafts and come ashore at night then?"

Click nodded, giving the mare's broad hip a friendly pat. "I think that will work out best for your sheriff, as well."

Looking down at the ground near the toes of her boots, where the mare had casually resumed cropping grass, Cassidy said, "I wanted to thank you for helping him. I know that it isn't—"

The touch of his hand upon her shoulder interrupted her.

"We would never fail to offer help to anyone in need," he assured her; and although his voice was perfectly grave, in those deep umber eyes there lurked that incipient spark of humor that made Cassidy suspect Click was referring not only to Allen. "And besides," he continued, his hand dropping easily from her shoulder, "from what the Troopers told you, it would appear that he's of some value to the Warden." The spark in his eyes grew stronger; it was a damned *twinkle* by then. "So perhaps kindness has nothing to do with it and we are just serving our own best interests by taking him with us to the city."

Suddenly even less comfortable than she had been, Cassidy started to step sideways, around Click. "It looks like the rafts are almost loaded," she said, looking toward the wharf, "so I guess maybe I'd better get back and—"

Click took one long-legged sidestep that neatly interposed his body between hers and the direction in which she had tried to make good her escape, and she abruptly found herself staring directly into the metal conchas and rings that decorated his vest.

"Cassidy, wait," he said—rather needlessly, she thought, since she'd already effectively been brought to a halt by his deft maneuver. His hand slid inside his vest, and when it reappeared a moment later he held something concealed in his closed fingers. "I have something for you."

For a few seconds, irrationally but nevertheless automatically, Cassidy believed Click was about to present her with another gun. It took her that long to realize that whatever he held wrapped in his long fingers was something much too small to be a weapon. When she still didn't reach out voluntarily to take his offering, Click took one of her hands in his other one, turned it palm up, and then opened his fingers to deposit his gift.

"I would have given this to you sooner," he said as he did so, "but with everything that's happened, there never seemed to be a good time."

But to Cassidy, Click's words seemed barely relevant, and his explanation so far removed from the small object she held in her hand that they might just as well have been spoken in some language she couldn't understand. For Cassidy then everything—even the blood in her veins, the air in her lungs, the swift spark in her nerves—simply ceased to move from the moment she stared down at that little bit of metal.

It was a key, similar to the one that Click wore on the leather thong around his neck, but with one important difference. Stamped onto the head of that key, in raised stylized letters, was a single word: FORD.

Cassidy felt light-headed, almost frighteningly so, and yet the sudden defection of blood from her brain also left her with a bizarre feeling of euphoria. She was only marginally aware of Click speaking; his words seemed to come at her from some great distance, hollow and meaningless.

"When I saw it in Pointed Rock, I thought you might like it," he said. As he stood gazing down into her face, his expression changed from quizzical to concerned within a heartbeat. "You seemed so taken with the one I wear . . ." He trailed off with a frown.

Cassidy could only have guessed at what Click must have been seeing on her face. She was no longer really aware of his presence beside her. She was also no longer really aware of the presence of the mare, the mules, the sod beneath her feet, or anything else beyond the simple reality of the small metal key in her hand. And even that key seemed to be receding even as she stared at it, as if it were slowly being pulled away down some long narrow tunnel of vision.

Click's hands went to her shoulders. "Cassidy? Are you all right?"

Cassidy stood at the precipice of that fathomless abyss of memory, that unplumbable depth across which she thought she might never again pass. And in that moment when she felt unconsciousness rushing up to meet her, she stepped willingly over the edge, into the darkness.

Click was still holding her by the shoulders, calling her name, when she fainted.

Chapter 8 ◄▬▬

Of the rest of that day, her first afternoon spent on the Long River, Cassidy remembered nothing. By the time she woke up again she was lying on the ground wrapped in her own bedroll, blinking up past the drooping flap of her and Rowena's familiar little tent at a patch of night sky that was framed by the dark boughs of trees. Her head ached with a ferocious intensity she had not experienced in a long time.

Wincing, Cassidy closed her eyes again and tried to stifle some of the stabbing pain that seemed to radiate from behind her eye sockets. She could smell the mingled aromas of woodsmoke, cooked food, and old canvas. Nearby were the background sounds she had learned over the last week to associate with the Tinker camp: the clicking of utensils, the murmur of voices, a random yap from one of Bonnie's scruffy little dogs. Reassured by their familiarity, she again tried to open her eyes.

That time the pain remained bearable and Cassidy slowly sat up, poking her head out through the flap of the tent. She was sitting near the edge of the camp the Tinkers had set up on the bank of the river, right on the other side of the dirt path used by the barge mules. To one side of her little shelter spread the dark shapes of the other tents, the blaze of cook fires, and the fire-lit figures of the various craftspeople she had come to know. And on the other side, just beyond the mule path, spread the deep liquid ribbon of the river where the big loaded wooden rafts were moored like a chain of floating shadows.

Just sitting quietly for a moment, Cassidy tried to cast back through the throbbing ache in her head far enough to be able to recover the memory of the last thing that had happened to her. She felt as if she'd been kicked in the head, but she didn't think that she . . .

And then the faint firelight caught the glint of something that lay suspended on the front of her shirt, hanging from a fresh leather thong around her neck. Incredulously Cassidy reached up and touched the irregularly shaped little metal talisman that had proven literally to have been the key to the past. For then Cassidy *remembered*.

The key that Click had given her was a *car* key—*a goddamn Ford of all things*—and when she had seen that name embossed upon it she had remembered cars. Not just cars really; trucks, buses, vans, motorcycles—anything with an internal combustion engine—you name it and she had remembered it, like a crazy crash-course auto show inside her head. But that hadn't been all.

Absently rubbing her temple but not even particularly aware of the still-considerable pounding there, Cassidy reran the incredible flood of memories *(Memories?)* that the key had unleashed. It was not just cars and trucks, it was almost everything else that had been *missing*, everything that her aching mind had been searching for, everything that still belonged only to the world from which she and Rowena had come—the world to which she was then more determined than ever to return.

The incredible kaleidoscope of images was painfully rich, like the strobing of a light that persisted behind her lids long after she had closed her eyes, once she had gazed directly into the brilliance of it. Cassidy deliberately tried to squelch the cascade of memories before she became nauseated or actually fainted again.

She tried to concentrate on just the car key. It had literally unlocked a vast area of her memory. Was that part of the reason why the sight of the other key she had seen earlier hanging from Click's neck had made such a profound impression on her, far more than had the other found things? Gingerly touching the raised lettering of the Ford logo with the tip of her index fingers, Cassidy thought, *Well, if nothing else I sure as hell was right about found things—they're things that have come from our world.* But how the hell had they gotten there? And, more important, how the hell had *she?*

Her eyes jerked from the key to the fire-lit Tinker camp. Not thirty feet from her she saw Moira, Willie, and Bonnie sipping coffee around a cook fire, and on the ground only an arm's length from them, still bundled in his blankets on his pallet, lay the insensate form of Allen, the sheriff of a village called Double Creek.

Where the hell am I? Who are all these people? And who the hell am I?

There was no way then that Cassidy could still view anything in the same way. Nothing was the same. Even the dramatic discoveries she had made back in the village, the things she had shared with Rowena, such as reading and writing—even sex—hadn't rocked her as elementally as had that simple little bit of stamped metal that hung from the thong around her neck.

Cassidy's gaze jumped again, from the shadowy figures in the Tinker camp to the encampment's periphery where she automatically tracked down the subtly felt presence of the gray mare. Her scan quickly centered on the long sweep of coarse grass that grew between the dirt of the mule path and the river's edge. Even though she knew that the horse was there, it took a few seconds for her eyes to be able to pick out the big mare's leisurely grazing form, a deep silver shape against the even darker pewter of the water's surface. Almost as if she had felt Cassidy's eyes rest upon her, the mare stopped chewing for a moment. But she never lifted her head, and when the moment had passed the horse resumed her grazing as if nothing had happened.

Not everything had changed, Cassidy realized then. The horse was the same, her horse in both that world and whatever one the two of them had come from. And Cassidy knew that she was still a Horseman—whatever that might be.

Letting her eyes drift back toward camp, Cassidy sat quietly just inside the flap of her tent and thought about what had been happening to her. From the time she and Rowena had joined up with the band of Tinkers, Cassidy had felt that their sense of purpose, their commitment to discover the full truth, had somehow been compromised. It wasn't that the Tinkers hadn't treated them fairly; in fact, they had been treated very generously. And maybe that was part of it. Cassidy had feared that Rowena was gradually coming to accept the way of life there. The buxom brunette seemed to fit in so comfortably with those craftsmen in a way she never had with the farmers in the village. Cassidy wondered if it was really still so important to her friend to find her way back to that increasingly vague other world from which they'd come.

If Cassidy was totally honest with herself—something she

found remarkably easier to do now that she had the goading throb of her old headache back again—she would had to have admitted that she had felt herself growing more comfortable there with the Tinkers, as well. If things had just kept on going along as they had during their days on the trail perhaps she, too, would have begun to think less and less often about their original mission. Perhaps she, too, could have envisioned a lifetime of the itinerant bartering, working wicker baskets with Mitz and sharing coffee over a cook fire with Click. If things had just stayed the same.

But the events of the last twenty-four hours had broken that complacency and ruptured Cassidy's temporary sense of safety. That world was not her world. The world where she belonged was filled with the images she had seen in that maelstrom of memories: cars and electric lights and television and jet planes. The world where she found herself trapped was filled with people who couldn't read or write, or at least remember that they once had; people who peddled pots and pans like a band of gypsies; people who didn't even know what sex was.

And that world was filled with monsters.

Once again, urgently and fervently, Cassidy renewed her vow to herself to find her way out of it.

Pulling herself up onto her knees, Cassidy took one last glance at the key that hung from her neck; then she lifted its leather thong and slipped the little miracle back inside of her shirt. She got cautiously to her feet, her head spinning. She stood at the edge of the tent for a few moments, experimenting with her sense of balance. Only when she was certain that she wouldn't fall flat on her face once she tried to walk did she start slowly forward toward the nearest cook fire.

Bonnie looked up with a maternal smile as Cassidy approached, and Willie and Moira immediately greeted her with offers of food and drink. Demurring, Cassidy waved off their attempts to feed her. Instead she stepped carefully around their fire and looked down at the dimly lit pallet where Allen lay. Dropping down beside him, Cassidy reached out and touched him almost tenderly on one hairy cheek. She felt that for the first time she was able to see him for what he really was, a remarkable man who would have been considered a hero in her world.

"How is he?" she asked Bonnie.

"A better question would be, how are you?" Moira interrupted, still trying to get Cassidy to accept a mug of coffee.

"For a while there we seemed to have had two casualties on our hands."

"I told you she was just tuckered out," Willie said gruffly, slapping at a mosquito that seemed to have taken some particular liking to the thick flesh on his beefy forearm. "Told Click that, too." He shot Cassidy a look. "He thought you'd fainted," he confided somewhat disparagingly.

Cassidy found that she liked the version Willie was espousing much better than she liked the truth and so, regardless of what appearances might have been, she quickly agreed with him. "Yeah, I should have just stayed in your cart, Willie."

The big man grunted in satisfaction, but Cassidy could see that Moira and Bonnie both were too shrewd to be anything but skeptical. Bonnie calmly ladled soup into a bowl, remarking mildly "Well, whatever the problem was, I'm sure a little food will improve it."

Relenting, Cassidy moved over to the cook fire and took the proffered bowl. "How is Allen?" she persisted, fumbling with the spoon. "And where's Rowena?"

"Rowena's over eating with Carlotta," Bonnie said. "She'll be back to check on you, I'm sure. And your sheriff friend is a little stronger." The massive blond leaned forward over the fire, snagging the last two biscuits from the pan right in front of Willie. Cassidy was certain the woman was in danger of setting her bosom on fire by bending so low. "He was even conscious for a little while after we took him out of the cart," she went on, dropping the biscuits into Cassidy's lap.

Which is more than could be said for me, Cassidy thought ruefully. She paused with a spoonful of soup halfway to her lips. "Did he say anything?" she asked.

"Oh, he said plenty," Willie said gruffly, shooting Bonnie a baleful glare for stealing his biscuits. "He wanted to know where the hell he was and what the hell had happened to him."

"He doesn't seem to remember much about the attack," Bonnie explained, "but I think that's still mostly from the shock. Maybe when he's had a chance to get back a little more strength, he'll remember more."

Leaning in closer to the warmth of the fire, Cassidy began to eat. As she spooned up the soup and chewed on the biscuits, she slowly came to admit two things. One thing was just how tremendously relieved she felt that Allen seemed to be recovering. She still felt painfully responsible for what had happened to him. And the other thing was that it no longer really mattered so much whether the sheriff would be able to recall anything useful to tell the Warden, at least not as far as Rowena and herself were concerned. For thanks to Click, Cassidy herself now held knowledge—Memories, or whatever you chose to call them—far more valuable than anything Allen might have seen in that embattled stretch of woods. No matter what happened with Allen, she and Rowena could still go to the Warden alone.

If Rowena still wanted to go, that was.

Setting aside her soup bowl only half emptied, Cassidy abruptly got to her feet, nearly bumping into Moira in her clumsy haste. "I think I'll go look for Rowena," she said.

Frowning, Bonnie glanced down at the uneaten soup. "Aren't you going to finish eating first?" she asked, the sternness of her tone a poor disguise for her unmistakable concern.

Cassidy spread her hands guiltily. "I'll have some more later," she promised. "I'm really not hungry yet—all I've done is sleep."

She turned and stepped over a bundle of Bonnie's cooking supplies and started off across the camp. Negotiating the dimly lit and cluttered encampment was a real test of skill for a person with a nagging headache who also still felt vaguely dizzy. But as the various Tinkers recognized and greeted her from around their cook fires or the open flaps of their tents, Cassidy just acknowledged their hails with a wave or a nod of her head and kept on walking.

She quickly discovered that without the familiar shapes of the Tinkers' different carts to guide her, it was far more diffi- cult to tell one group's firepit from another. With all of the carts and craft goods still lashed to the rafts, the only equip- ment that had been brought ashore was the tents, bedding, and food for the overnight stay. She almost walked right past Rowena because the brunette and Carlotta were the only two people left sitting around the remains of their cook fire. It was only the faint twinkle of the metalsmith's elaborate earrings that made Cassidy turn and look again more closely.

"Well, it's good to see you up and about again," Carlotta said heartily. "Have you had something to eat yet? We have some leftover beans with saltpork and plenty of potatoes and bread."

"You still look kind of shaky," Rowena told her as Cassidy dropped down beside her. "Did you just get up? Here, let me fix you a plate."

"No, that's okay," Cassidy hastened to tell them, "I've already eaten over with Bonnie."

"Did she tell you about Allen?" Rowena asked, pouring a mug of coffee for Cassidy even over her protests, and thrusting it at her.

"He's a strong man," Carlotta said, cradling her own mug in her hands. "I think there's every chance he'll survive now. And if he never remembers what happened to him out there—" She shrugged. "—well, perhaps that's for the best."

Cassidy just nodded politely as Carlotta spoke, scarcely even glancing in the woman's direction. She was trying to get Rowena's attention without having to be obvious about it. Unfortunately, Rowena seemed more interested in polishing off the last of the honeybread she'd been having for dessert than in noticing Cassidy's stare. Finally Cassidy had to dig the toe of her boot sharply into Rowena's thigh to get the brunette's attention.

"I need to talk to you," she hissed under her breath, dropping her head as if she were looking for a place to set down her coffee mug. "Now!"

Carlotta was looking rather quizzically at both of them from across the fire, so Cassidy hastily said aloud, "You know, I think I'd better try to get plenty of rest tonight. I'm still pretty tired. But first I'd like to check on my horse."

"Uh, yeah," Rowena quickly responded, throwing Cassidy a puzzled look. "I think maybe I'll go with you. I'd like to check on Allen again anyway."

Instead of cutting back across the encampment, where many of the Tinkers were already preparing to settle down in their own bedrolls, Cassidy briskly led Rowena to the edge of the camp. There they skirted some clumps of brush and several large trees and then headed in the direction of the river. Even that close to the camp there was hardly any reflected light, and Cassidy had to concentrate on covering the uneven ground without stumbling, but she didn't slacken her pace until they had nearly reached the mule path.

"Jeez, wait up, will you?" Rowena complained, tripping over a tree root as she hustled to keep up. "What's the big hurry anyway?"

Cassidy looked back toward the camp and then rapidly scanned all around them in a wide arc. Even then she didn't immediately reply; she just grabbed Rowena by the arm and practically dragged her across the rutted earth of the pull path.

Near the water's edge where the first two rafts had been moored to the bank, a lantern had been hung from the low branch of a poplar tree. Its wick had been trimmed low, but it still cast a small circle of pale yellow light, enough for Cassidy's purposes without making the two of them too conspicuous as they stood there beneath it.

As Cassidy released the brunette's arm, Rowena automatically rubbed the released limb, giving her friend an uncharacteristic look of irritation. "What the heck's the matter with you?" she asked plaintively. Then her hazel eyes narrowed slightly and her tone softened. "Are you feeling all right, Cassidy?" she asked, obviously misinterpreting her friend's behavior. "I know you've been through a lot since last night . . ."

"You don't know the half of it," Cassidy muttered under her breath. More audibly she said, "I'm sorry, Rowena, but I had to talk to you—alone. I've discovered something really important, something that's going to help us get out of here."

"Is this something to do with Allen?" Rowena asked, both curious and hopeful.

"Not exactly." Hooking her forefinger around the thin leather thong around her neck, Cassidy pulled the key back up and out through the collar of her shirt. Displaying it between thumb and forefinger, she held the key out for Rowena's inspection. "See this?" she said, unable to keep the eagerness from creeping into her voice.

Rowena bent forward and peered at the key in the overhead lantern's weak light. For several long moments the brunette said nothing, and the dominant sounds along the river's edge were only the rhythmic song of the peeper frogs and the night insects. Then Rowena looked up into Cassidy's face. "It's a key," she said, obviously puzzled by her friend's apparent urgency. "Like the one Click wears."

Impatiently Cassidy thrust the key closer to Rowena's face. "Click gave it to me earlier today, at the wharf. But it's *not* like his—look at the writing on it."

Lines of perplexment furrowed Rowena's normally smooth brow. " 'Ford,' " she read. Then she shrugged, looking up again. "So? What does that mean?"

Ice spilled into Cassidy's veins. It was not the same chilly rush that came with adrenaline; it was the cold sluice of an unthinkable disappointment. Looking intently into Rowena's face, Cassidy had only one awful thought: *She doesn't recognize it— she doesn't remember.*

Cassidy had, of course, just automatically assumed that the car key would trigger in Rowena the same sort of recognition and the same outpouring of images and memories that it had ignited in her own mind. It had quite simply never occurred to her that there was anything that she could remember which Rowena might not. Could it be that Rowena's growing sense of contentment there among the Tinkers had already dulled her ability to recall things from her previous life? And then a horrifying thought hit Cassidy.

Is she becoming just like everyone else here?

Trying to suppress that sickening fear and to keep her hand from trembling, Cassidy tilted the key slightly into the light. "Look at it again," she said in a slow and measured voice. "Doesn't the word 'Ford' mean anything to you? Don't you remember what this key is used for?"

Rowena cooperated by bending closer and really scrutinizing the key; but her brow remained furrowed and there was no glimmer of recognition in her eyes. "No," she finally had to admit. "Should I know what it's for?"

Cassidy tried to contain the magnitude of her despair; she didn't want Rowena to see how important it was to her, or how upset she had been by the brunette's failure to recognize the significance of the key. "Ford is the name of a kind of car, Rowena," she said softly. "This is the ignition key from a—"

Cassidy broke off then, not because she couldn't think of how to explain to Rowena what a car was, but because Rowena's wide-set eyes had suddenly grown as big as saucers. "Holy *shit!*" she breathed in astonishment. "Cassidy—I *know* what a car is!"

Cassidy's sense of relief and amazement was so profound that she actually felt her knees buckle beneath her. Both with joy and in an effort to maintain her balance, she threw her arms around Rowena's shoulders and gave her friend a hearty hug while Rowena pounded Cassidy on the back in excitement.

When the two of them were finally able to speak again, Cassidy quickly explained to Rowena what had happened to her since Click had first laid the key in her hand. She didn't think she could have described to Rowena every image that had washed through her mind in that tremendous tidal wave of memory; she didn't even try to. But, her voice often breaking with emotion, she told Rowena about as much of it as she could. And to her immense gratitude and relief, Rowena understood it all. Perhaps the brunette's memories had not been triggered as easily as Cassidy's had been, but they definitely were still there, and she was capable of making the appropriate associations once Cassidy reminded her of something. And there was another happy consequence to sharing everything with Rowena; as Cassidy spoke she realized that her persistent headache had nearly vanished.

When Cassidy had finally reached a lull in her somewhat breathless recitation, Rowena bounced forward again and gave her another spontaneous hug. "Jeez, Cassidy," she said with a happy grin, "you were right about the found things—they really *are* stuff that came from wherever we did." She gave a tug on the Ford key that hung from the thong on Cassidy's neck. "This proves it!"

"Yeah, and it's too bad we don't have a nice little Ranger pickup truck right now," Cassidy quipped in reply. "We could drive down to the Iron City in style."

Glancing around them in the faint circle of lantern light, Rowena frowned, her brows tracing another quizzical arch. "But how do you suppose found stuff gets here?"

Cassidy had often wondered about that very thing. "I don't know," she admitted. "Maybe people have it with them when they're brought here."

"You mean like in their pockets?"

Cassidy shook her head in mild exasperation. "Maybe—but listen, what really matters is that this explains why everything here seems so—so off-kilter."

"Yeah," Rowena agreed, her tone still one of wonderment, "like the paved streets in the village; it's all starting to make sense now."

Cassidy nodded. "Yeah, they had paved streets but no cars or trucks; and toilets but no electricity."

"Hey," Rowena interrupted her excitedly, "do you remember how you said you kept catching yourself reaching for something on the wall whenever you walked into a dark room? Electricity—you were reaching for a light switch!"

Suddenly and unexpectedly, they both dissolved into helpless laughter at that thought. Some of their hilarity was due to the genuine irony of Cassidy's unthinking reflex, which had persisted into a world that had no use for it; but a good part of it was just due to the simple need to relieve some of the tension that had been wrought by the enormity of what Cassidy had revealed.

"The houses," Cassidy forced out, nearly gasping, when she could catch enough breath to speak again, "those *boring* houses! Don't you see? They were all the same because all they probably had to go on was one person's version of the one house he could remember." Sobering slightly as she regained some control again, Cassidy went on, "And remember Allen's rifle, how it didn't look quite right? Well, I think that's because it was made by someone who had an imperfect memory of how a rifle was made."

"That must be why it didn't work very well, either," Rowena said.

But Cassidy's mind was already racing ahead, even as her hand automatically brushed the waistband of her pants, where for a time she had carried the pistol that Click had given her before she had stowed it safely with her gear. That gun looked right, Cassidy thought; which meant that if it wasn't a found thing, it must have been made by someone who'd had a better memory—or someone who'd had the Memories.

Rowena's mind had been racing, as well. "I wonder how come the Villagers have some things like indoor plumbing but not things like cars," she mused. "Why would someone remember something like toilets but forget something like trucks?"

Again Cassidy was reminded of what Yolanda had said to Raphael: "Everything we have has come from the Memories."

"Maybe it's not just a matter of what someone remembered," she said quietly. "Maybe it's a problem of technology, too."

Rowena cocked her head. "What do you mean?"

"Well, it's a lot simpler to make a toilet than it is to make a truck, even if you remember the principles behind how each one of them works. And think of all the refined products that go into something like a car; even the fuel oil they burn in these lanterns is pretty crude stuff. How could you make a car, even if you could remember how to, without things like plastics and rubber and gasoline?"

"But they can make things like glass," Rowena reminded Cassidy, "and paints and dyes."

"Yeah—and wicker and leather and copper pots, too," Cassidy said. "But don't you see, Rowena? All of that stuff was made for hundreds of years before anyone even invented cars; it's all really pretty basic stuff."

Cassidy could tell from the expression on Rowena's face

that her point had been understood and taken; but she could also tell that the brunette had suddenly thought of something else. "What?" Cassidy asked, a little warily, for Rowena's eyes contained a strange gleam that had very little to do with the lantern's light.

"Cassidy," Rowena said, "I don't suppose that with everything else you've remembered, you've figured out where the heck we come from—or even where the heck we are right now?"

Cassidy had been afraid she'd recognized the hope behind that oddly intent glimmer in her friend's eyes. Her temporary ebullience faltering, Cassidy could only shake her head. "I don't have the faintest idea," she admitted. "That . . . that isn't the kind of stuff I remember."

For with all of the tremendous variety and rich imagery of what she did remember, Cassidy still had gaping holes in what she could recall. Nearly everything that had come back to her when she had seen the car key had been *things*, not places and certainly not people. Despite the clarity and aptness of his image, even the origin of her namesake, the elusive Butch Cassidy, remained completely beyond her reach.

Rowena hesitated, reading Cassidy's expression with her head cocked in a tentative pose. In the lantern's weak and shimmering light Cassidy could see the brief sparkle of the brunette's tiny earrings. "Then I don't suppose you know—" Rowena began.

"No . . . I don't know who I am."

That omission in particular was one that Cassidy had deliberately avoided examining, for she had known—even in that first incredible light-headed moment when she had gazed down upon the key lying in her hand—that it would not be the kind of memory she would be given.

At least not like that. At least not yet.

Rowena shrugged almost casually, but from that moment on their mood of hopeful excitement was somehow broken, and both women realized that there simply would be no way to retrieve it again that night. Cassidy slipped the metal key back inside the collar of her shirt and said briskly, "Come on, let's go check on Allen."

Rowena didn't disagree, and the two of them started back across the mule path toward the camp. The cook fires were all burned down to winking beds of coals by then, and most of the Tinkers had settled in for the night. Other than a few murmured bits of conversation and the faint sighing of the wind in the trees, the only sounds seemed to belong to the frogs and the insects. With a surer sense of direction than earlier, Cassidy led the way around the tents and the small bundles and stacks of camp supplies to where Bonnie had set her fire. Coming upon the site in the near darkness, Cassidy could see that there still were two people crouched down by the bundle of blankets where Allen lay sleeping. It wasn't until she and Rowena were almost up to them, however, that she could see for certain who they were.

Mitz barely glanced up at them before she resumed what she had been doing, and Cassidy was embarrassed once she realized just what that was. Because the injured man had very little physical control yet, the Tinker women kept Allen's midsection wrapped in towels; Mitz was calmly tugging off a wet, urine-soaked one off his groin and replacing it with a dry covering. Click knelt on the other side of the supine man, lifting him as Mitz required.

As the gray-haired little seamstress pulled the blanket back up over Allen, Click sat back on his heels and looked up at Cassidy and Rowena. Cassidy had no idea where the dark-haired man had been earlier in the evening, but she noticed that both his low boots and the bottoms of his trouser legs were wet. Unexpectedly unnerved by the quiet scrutiny in those deep umber eyes, Cassidy dropped down to her knees at Allen's feet and tried to keep her gaze on the recumbent man.

"Bonnie said that he was awake for a little while," she said, to neither Mitz nor Click in particular.

Mitz favored her with a sympathetic smile. "He's better, that's for certain," she said, wadding up the soiled towel in one hand. "But I still wouldn't expect too much of him just yet."

With a little nod to Rowena, Mitz then stood and started to walk away. Cassidy glanced after her, but then her attention returned to Allen as Rowena also dropped down beside him. Click's steady appraisal was making Cassidy uncomfortable and as she reached out one hand to lightly touch Allen's blanketed leg, she felt the need to speak again just to break the silence.

"Willie said that he didn't remember anything about what happened, though." By default, Cassidy supposed that the comment had to have been directed at Click that time. But his response wasn't exactly what she was anticipating.

"Are you concerned that he won't be of any help to your

Warden when we reach the city?" the Tinker leader asked quietly.

Cassidy had to look at Click then; it was either look at him or look at Rowena, and if she had looked at the brunette she was afraid that the two of them might have betrayed themselves to Click. "Oh, no," Cassidy said in perfect honesty, "I don't care about that; I just want him to be all right."

Click's eyes softened then; and having been buffeted by that tidal wave of memories, Cassidy suddenly found that she could no longer react to the man in the same way she had been. For having remembered the other world—the Slow World—had made her appreciate just how extraordinary a man Click was in his own.

"He'll be all right," Click said simply; and for a moment his steady stare would have made it impossible to have believed anything else. He tilted his shaggy head to give Rowena a sudden little wink. "I can tell you that with great certainty," he went on, the silvered wings of his mustache quirking, "because I know for a fact that none of these women take kindly to having someone die on them."

Early the next morning Cassidy was again kneeling beside Allen, helping Bonnie as the big woman changed the dressings on the man's extensive wounds. Cassidy had been surprised by how much better the ugly lacerations looked already and by how much they had healed in barely more than a day's time. When she commented on that to Bonnie, the blonde just said, "The wounds are deep but the cuts were very sharp. All we have to do is keep them clean."

And keep them from getting infected, Cassidy thought; but she didn't voice that concern to Bonnie because she wasn't sure yet just how concepts like infection played in that world, even though memories of things like ampicillin and Keflex and other antibiotics flickered through her mind. *Shit, they don't even have aspirin,* she reminded herself glumly. *Remind me not to break a leg!*

Seeing and touching Allen's undraped body was affecting Cassidy in a more familiar manner again, and she had to carefully school her expression to keep Bonnie from noticing anything odd about her reaction. She tried to let the older woman do most of the actual physical contact, but she could not keep herself from looking—and remembering. Since she finally understood her own normal sexual feelings, she realized the attraction she felt toward Allen. She tried to tell herself the feeling was not romantic. But she admitted to feeling a great affection and friendship for him, and in his present condition she also felt a powerful desire to comfort him—and in that desire there was a definite physical component. She wanted to be able to touch Allen in a way that would make him understand. It presented a confusing sort of emotional dilemma that seemed especially bizarre when played out against the mundane backdrop of morning in the Tinker camp, with people all around them cooking breakfast, shaking out bedrolls, and striking tents.

As Bonnie removed the last of the old dressing material that had covered Allen's upper rib cage, it adhered slightly to his skin, held by a crust of dried serum. Only then did the injured man stir. He gave a soft groan and then abruptly opened his eyes, blinking up at both Bonnie and Cassidy as if he had just awakened from some unscheduled nap. His sun-colored eyes were still somewhat sunken into the net of lines that stress and time had spun around them, but there was perfect cognizance in his gaze as he looked up into their faces.

"Cassidy," he said, his tongue thick from disuse.

Surprised by the degree of relief she felt just to again see recognition on that familiar face, Cassidy reached down and gently squeezed his hand. His fingers, blunt and callused, tightened on hers.

Allen tried to speak again, but all he got out before Bonnie shushed him was the single word "Why . . . ?"

"Shh, don't you wear yourself out now trying to talk," the big blond commanded him. "And don't be trying to sit up." She enforced the last admonition with graphic eloquence, placing one fleshy hand directly in the center of his bare chest and holding Allen down. His hand slipped from Cassidy's, but she didn't think he looked as if he were about to attempt going anywhere yet.

When Bonnie seemed equally satisfied that Allen had taken her point and would remain lying quietly, she released him and, with the grace that rode so amazingly upon her bulk, rose to her feet. Looking down at the two of them, she said to Cassidy, "Why don't you start putting the ointment and clean dressings on him? I'll go fix up something he should be able to eat." With a rustle of her long purple dress she headed off to her cook fire.

For the first few moments after Bonnie had left them, nei-

ther Cassidy nor Allen seemed to know precisely how to react
or what to do. Cassidy looked down at the ground at a point
somewhere slightly askew from Allen's blankets, while the big
man looked up quizzically at her. Then, even though she felt
anything but competent at nursing care, Cassidy covered the
awkwardness of the moment by picking up Bonnie's jar of
ointment and digging her fingers into it. Still strikingly aware
of Allen's nakedness, she tentatively bent forward and lightly
touched her greasy hand to the arc-shaped wound just above
his right knee.

At first Allen said nothing, and Cassidy even began to gain
a little confidence as she slowly and gently began to work her
way up his thigh, scooping out more unguent as she needed
and spreading it over the partially healed lacerations. She
found that if she concentrated on the simple motions of her
ministrations, it did not trouble her quite so much that Allen
was lying there naked, or that the low oblique rays of the rising sun—the same sun that poked through the tree branches
and danced across the river's surface—gilded like polished
copper the golden hairs on his body. Or at least it did not trouble her until Allen's hand came up, intercepting hers where she
worked across his hip, and his fingers closed over hers.

"Why did you run?" he said, his voice a soft hoarse croak.

It was not what Cassidy would have expected him to say,
and in her surprise she looked down directly into his gold-
ringed eyes. "Why were you chasing us?" she shot back automatically.

Allen winced; the apology that Cassidy had never and would
never hear from his lips was suddenly displayed in the language of his big body. "Had to," he said then, his voice still
hoarse. "Misty's orders."

Cassidy didn't exactly pull her hand away from his; she just
steadily and firmly resumed spreading the ointment, and Allen
either had to release her or be pulled along with her fingers.
She had also dropped her eyes from his, but her voice was
calm and level as she said, "Then you can understand why we
had to run."

It was obviously an effort for Allen to speak, not only because of the disability of his physical condition but also because he was amazingly clumsy at having to deal with her
from a position of weakness. It made Cassidy wonder afresh
just what the hell had happened back in Double Creek when

Allen had returned after the fire to find that she and Rowena were gone.

"You didn't do anything wrong," he rasped. "If you'd've stayed—"

Cassidy moved his right arm, carefully but purposefully, and began to spread Bonnie's ointment across his ribs. "You weren't there to stick up for us this time," she said. "If we'd've stayed there, we would have been hanged long before you ever got back."

And Cassidy could see that although Allen wanted to disagree with her, to protest her analysis of the situation, he was unable to do so. He was too honest a man to try to deny that she was right.

After finishing with the ointment, Cassidy reached for the clean cotton dressings Bonnie had left at the edge of the blanket. Somehow then it was easier to have to touch Allen, because something in the balance between them had changed. She no longer felt quite so guilty about the feelings she had toward him, or even for the advantage she had of remembering sex when he so obviously didn't, because in a way Allen had owned up to what he apparently perceived as a weakness of his own. He had failed to be there to protect her and Rowena when they had needed him.

As she began to place the dressings around Allen's thigh, Cassidy glanced out across the camp. She was quickly able to pick out Bonnie's queen-size purple form bent over her cook fire; the woman was busy stirring something in an iron pot. Cassidy realized she wouldn't have much more time to speak to Allen in private. Pausing for a moment, she looked back down into his familiar bearded face, studying those deep-set eyes with blunt intensity.

"What happened out there in the woods?" she asked quietly.

Just as she had never before seen the admission of regret on Allen's rugged face, so, too, had Cassidy never before seen such painful fear. She instantly regretted her question as she felt the big body shudder beneath her hand. Allen's eyes squeezed shut as if from an involuntary reflex, and he turned his head away from her.

She wanted only to reassure him then, to comfort him, to at least apologize for having asked such an untimely question. But before Cassidy could do anything, Bonnie's generous shape suddenly was bending over them, bearing a steaming bowl of what smelled deliciously like hot soup. The blond woman quickly assessed the progress of Cassidy's redressing of Allen's wounds as she dropped down beside them again.

"Almost done, are you?" she said heartily. "Well, I can finish up here now. Why don't you go, Cassidy? I think your friend Rowena is looking for you."

Feeling both relief and reluctance at the dismissal, Cassidy gave Allen's uninjured thigh a gentle squeeze. His eyes were still closed as she said, "I'll see you again later."

Crossing the camp in search of her own breakfast at Carlotta's fire, Cassidy felt a sense of remorse that was even more disabling than her ongoing guilt at her part in Allen being wounded in the first place. She knew that whatever had happened in that woods had been something horrible. The aftermath that she had witnessed had been awful enough, and she at least had the added advantage of having seen the monsters before. What if Allen had not even known before that night that the creatures existed?

Chapter 9 ◀▥

Cassidy's first full day on the Long River and her first conscious experience traveling by raft went smoothly and rapidly. It didn't take her long to understand why the Tinkers chose to return home by way of the river rather than going overland through the wooded hills. The big rafts easily rode the river current, even heavily laden with the packed carts and other goods. As Click had explained to her, one person could guide a raft quite handily, and the vessels' pace was steady and brisk. On the river's bank, whenever the gray mare paused too long to graze along the mule path, she would have to trot for a few minutes to catch up again, a situation that had never arisen when the Tinkers had been traveling on land.

The Long River was broad but fairly shallow; they often had to navigate around sandbars and even the occasional small island, although none of those was much larger than the deck of one of the rafts. The land on either side remained wooded, but it seemed to Cassidy that the terrain was less hilly, or at least that the hills were becoming lower again. Other than the rutted mule path, they didn't pass any sign of human intervention that day, and even the path remained empty and bare, long since washed clear of any footprints. If the Troopers had ridden that way, Cassidy thought as she watched the smooth greenish water slide past the side of the raft, they had not followed the barges' pull path.

After the days of travel on foot in the hills, industriously hauling carts and carrying backpacks, the leisurely respite of river travel seemed an almost decadent luxury to Cassidy. She was content that day just to sit for long periods on the raft's log side rail and enjoy the pleasure of the warm sun and the beauty of the passing scenery. Because she hadn't felt comfortable with the thought of spending the whole day so close to either Allen or Click, she had offered to help Willie pilot one of the cargo rafts rather than sharing space on the passenger raft with most of the other Tinkers. But since really very little help was needed in guiding the raft, other than acting as an informal lookout for obstacles in the river, Cassidy got to spend most of her time relaxing and thinking.

The things that Cassidy had to think about were not always particularly relaxing subjects, but it still was easier for her to sort out her thoughts without the close proximity of the two men who had been causing her the most anxiety lately. If she put all other considerations aside, she was finally willing to admit to herself that she was attracted to both Allen and Click. *Not romantically, of course*, she told herself primly; that would have been a worse than useless emotion there. But she was attracted to their more universal qualities, their courage and intelligence, their fairness in the way they had both treated her and Rowena, and, at least in Click's case, by his ironic understated wit.

There's nothing wrong with liking them, she reminded herself. She would just have to be careful not to jeopardize her own or Rowena's future by her affection for either of the men.

The day slipped by with pleasant speed. Because of the logistics problems involved in docking the little fleet of rafts, the group didn't pull in to the bank to make cook fires for lunch. Instead they had a cold meal that had been prepared earlier that morning, eating while they continued to drift down the river. Cassidy shared her lunch with just Willie for company, even though none of the other rafts was ever more than a few dozen yards away at any given time. It was a nice sort of separation because it gave the illusion of privacy without the inconvenience of any real distance.

As the sun began to sink on the western horizon and the river's surface took on a gleam like molten metal, the Tinkers began to scout for a good mooring site for the night. The rafts' stubby keels made some clearance necessary, at least to get the first of the vessels up to the bank. But because traveling on the water was so much easier than packing along overland and because almost everything could remain permanently stowed on the rafts, they had the luxury of waiting until it was nearly dark to make camp if they needed to.

Once the six rafts were securely moored, both to the bank and to each other, Click supervised the moving of Allen off the passenger raft. Cassidy had not seen the sheriff up close all day, and so when she started to help set up their encampment she was pleasantly surprised to find that the injured man appeared fairly alert. He even wanted to sit up, although Bonnie effectively discouraged that notion.

"Tomorrow—if you're stronger" was all the concession the blond woman would offer him.

And when Allen looked to Click for reprieve, the dark-haired man could only spread his hands in a theatrical gesture of helplessness. When it came to Allen at least, it seemed the weighty blonde was in charge.

Between the passenger arrangements on the rafts and the relatively close confines of the night camp, Cassidy also hadn't had much chance to talk with Rowena since the night before. So she was especially pleased when her friend volunteered both Cassidy's and her own services in going out to gather firewood before it became totally dark. At Rowena's call, Cassidy willingly left the gray mare's side, where she had been inspecting the horse's legs and feet in what was a normal evening ritual for her.

Rather than cut directly into the woods, particularly that close to dusk, the two women chose to walk upriver a ways along the mule path to look for firewood. There were enough large trees with snags and deadfalls for the supply of dry branches to be plentiful even close to the path. Like most of the other places where they had traveled in that world, there didn't seem to have been enough demand for firewood to have kept up with the plentiful and perpetually self-renewing supply. They hadn't gone very far from where the camp was being set up, not even far enough to have been out of earshot of some of the louder Tinker voices, when Cassidy noticed that Rowena seemed to have something on her mind.

All too often, Cassidy realized then, she had become so obsessed with her own concerns, with her own memories and discoveries, her own fears and hopes, that she had failed to pay attention to her best friend's feelings. Rowena's generally sunny disposition and stout-hearted loyalty tended to feed into that failure; the woman had proven so reliable that Cassidy was often guilty of taking her for granted. But as they bent to break and gather branches in the deepening shadows beneath the big trees, Cassidy glanced over at Rowena and saw that the brunette seemed troubled about something.

Cassidy had never been effective at small talk; it was, she

thought, probably a deficiency that she had carried over with her fully formed from her former life. She couldn't think of any oblique way to slide into her inquiry, so she just paused in her task and put the question bluntly to Rowena.

"Is something wrong?"

Rowena was about as useless at evasion as Cassidy was at chitchat, so she appeared to welcome the query. She let the bundle of sticks she held slip to the ground at her feet. "Cassidy," she said quietly, "do you remember the time you asked me about monsters?"

I should have known, Cassidy thought as reluctance warred with self-recrimination in her mind. It was the one thing she and Rowena had never discussed again, even after Cassidy had several more very up-close-and-personal experiences with the damned things, even after the attack in the woods when Allen had nearly gotten killed. *I should have told her—especially after I found out for sure that they were real.*

Holding her own bundle of dead branches to her chest, as if they could serve as some sort of a shield against blame, Cassidy nodded. "Yeah, I remember. You told me they were just figments of these people's imaginations."

That got the desired quick grin from the brunette. "I said the same thing about the Woodsmen, if you remember," she reminded Cassidy.

But Cassidy sobered. Her friend deserved to know everything she did. "What about monsters?" she asked.

Rowena glanced back down the path toward camp, where the gathering darkness rendered the Tinkers' busy figures into moving silhouettes and the still air carried the faint thudding of tent pegs being driven. The reaction was not, Cassidy realized immediately, a precaution against being overheard; rather, Rowena was thinking about someone specific who lay in that camp.

Looking back into Cassidy's face, Rowena asked, "What happened to Allen out there, Cassidy? I think he remembers, but he doesn't believe it; and I think you know, even if you didn't see it."

Cassidy just gazed steadily into her friend's face for a moment, remembering the brunette's faith and courage. "Well, I can tell you one thing," she said softly then. "It sure as hell wasn't Woodsmen."

As she had with Cobb and the other Troopers, to explain fully to Rowena, Cassidy had to go back to what she had seen on her first night in that new world. She then went on to tell Rowena every extraordinary thing she had seen since she had first crouched on that riverbank and stared out over the black water in mute amazement at something that had been too unlikely to have been believable. She told Rowena about the carrion eaters, the loathsome hanging creatures that she had seen both in the ravine and along the rabbit run. And she told her about the huge apparitions that had streamed overhead along the river-bottom pasture the night of the fire in Double Creek. It was difficult to find the words to describe much of what she had seen, but she did her best to convey the astonishing appearances. And even though she had not seen any of the creatures two nights before, the night of the slaughter outside Pointed Rock, she shared with Rowena what she had been able to learn from the Troopers, including her own belief that the existence of the monsters explained most of the bizarre occurrences that had been plaguing the villages. And much to Cassidy's surprise, for the first time the whole story seemed less crazy for the telling rather than less credible.

Throughout the entire remarkable recitation, Rowena had remained silent, her guileless hazel eyes fixed on Cassidy's face. Interpreting the brunette's stunned silence, Cassidy felt a deep pang of guilt and remorse.

"I should have told you sooner," Cassidy admitted, still embarrassed that she hadn't been totally candid. But she had misinterpreted the reason for Rowena's dismay.

Rowena touched Cassidy's shoulder, her expression of amazement considerably softened with sympathy. "Jeez, Cassidy, I wish you had," she said earnestly. "That way you wouldn't have had to go through all of this alone. I don't know what I could have done to help, but at least you would've had someone you could've talked to."

Still feeling guilty, if then for a slightly different reason, Cassidy just ducked her head. "On top of everything else, at first I thought I must be going crazy," she said.

Cassidy could see Rowena's mind working, rapidly mulling over what she had just learned. "What I don't understand," she said, "is if these things have been so close, why haven't *I* ever seen them?" A specific realization hit Rowena, making her eyes widen even further. "Jeez, I'd been in that same ravine with the goats a hundred times—I never saw *anything!*"

Cassidy shrugged helplessly. "I don't know," she said. "Why do *I* keep running into the damned things? It's almost as if . . ." She trailed off, reluctant still to reveal the possibility that she was considering.

But Rowena wasn't easily dissuaded. "What?" she insisted.

Cassidy met her eyes again. "What if it has something to do with the Memories, Rowena? What if the monsters have something to do with finding out the truth about how we got here, and why?"

Rowena's mind automatically filled in the blanks: *What if the closer we get to the truth, the closer the monsters will get to us?*

"Shit," the brunette murmured.

For a moment they both fell silent, a gap into which the sounds of the nearby Tinker camp seemed to flow with an unnatural clarity. Unconsciously Cassidy lowered her voice when she went on.

"I really believe that even the Troopers don't know any more about these creatures than what they told me," she said. "And I think they really are hoping that Allen can tell them something more."

Rowena studied Cassidy's face for a moment, plumbing the familiar features for the answer to the question she still felt compelled to ask. "Allen did see something, didn't he?" she said softly.

Cassidy nodded. "I asked him about it this morning," she confessed, a bit reluctant to admit to the questioning because of the resulting distress that it had provoked in the injured man. "He just froze up; he wouldn't say anything—but I could see it in his eyes."

Rowena gnawed briefly on her full lower lip. "Jeez, Cassidy, I never saw Allen afraid of anything," she said.

But Cassidy had thought a lot about that very thing during the day as she had ridden the raft down the river. She immediately shook her head. "I don't think he was afraid of what he saw, Rowena; I think what he was really afraid of is that they could actually exist."

"Heck, me, too!" Rowena said.

For a few moments both women stood silently again. Cassidy could see that Rowena's eyes had gone to the river, gazing out over the dark and glistening surface of the water as it soundlessly slid by. Cassidy was certain that they both were thinking the same thing. Then, in a voice marked by her typical unsinkable humor, Rowena confirmed it by saying "Hey, thanks again for telling me all this, Cassidy. It sure will be fun sailing down this river now that I know about those water monsters!"

"Yeah? Well, you might want to stay out of the woods, too."

They both were still standing there staring out over the water when a sudden voice behind them completely startled them.

"Are you having trouble finding wood?"

Rowena and Cassidy spun around to find Toby standing not a dozen feet from them, his arms filled with dry branches, a quizzical look on his innocent face.

Traveling on the Long River made it even more difficult than before for Cassidy to separate herself from the band of Tinkers. By day on the water the group's rafts were never far apart, and at night the quick and simple camps were closely set for convenience. But the very conditions that made it almost impossible to be alone, or even alone with Rowena, also made it easy to avoid being put in the position of being alone with either Allen or Click.

It wasn't that Cassidy didn't want to see them; she just wanted to avoid the awkwardness of close contact with either of them. As long as there were others about, she was perfectly happy to spend time with Allen. She gladly helped Bonnie with the sheriff's meals and the management of his wounds. By their third day on the river, when the stout blonde had finally determined that it would be safe for Allen to sit up for a few hours each day, Cassidy even rode on the passenger raft most of the afternoon so that she and Rowena could help keep him company. She realized that although he was still frighteningly weak, he was also in danger of becoming fatally bored; and she and Rowena seemed to be the most adept at keeping him entertained because they knew the most about his normal life and interests.

In many ways Click was less of a problem for Cassidy. First of all, she didn't have to feel guilty about anything that might have happened between them, even if her and Rowena's presence might have endangered the Tinker camp outside of Pointed Rock. And second, even though there wasn't much work connected with the piloting of the rafts, all of the Tinkers, Click included, seemed to be keeping themselves quite busy with their crafts as they rode down the river. Not that Click precisely had a craft—at least Cassidy had never seen any particular handiwork in which the dark-haired man seemed to engage—but just being in charge of everything was a job that hadn't ended for him when they'd taken to the river. Click spent most of his days roaming from raft to raft, seeing that there were no problems and that everything ran smoothly. And so while she saw him frequently, Cassidy never saw him for long and she never saw him alone.

By the fifth day on the river Cassidy could see that the terrain was changing even further. While the land along the river was still mostly wooded, it had definitely become less hilly, and twice they had passed vast marshy estuaries where smaller streams flowed into the Long River. Both had been on the far bank, so the mule path that Dragonfly followed had remained uninterrupted; but Cassidy couldn't help but wonder if that would eventually become a problem.

Despite Old Paul's dire warnings, Cassidy hadn't had to worry much about the horse yet on their trip down the river. The gray mare was almost always within easy sight, and she seemed to enjoy the simple freedom of being able to wander at liberty. There was always ample grazing, so much so that the horse spent very little time eating at night, a pattern that she had been forced into when Cassidy and Rowena had been pushing her hard when they had fled Double Creek. And for all of Old Paul's grumbling and Cassidy's own misgivings about what might have lurked in those unfamiliar woods, she had to admit that the mare had not only been perfectly safe, she also seemed entirely content with the travel arrangements.

And so it was not exactly concern for the horse's welfare that prompted Cassidy to stay ashore that fifth morning when the Tinkers cast off their rafts from the night's mooring. "I'd like to do a little riding today," she explained to Rowena. "I don't want to get out of shape."

Rowena grinned at her from the deck of the passenger raft. "You just think she's getting too fat and lazy," she teased.

"Yeah, her and me both," Cassidy agreed.

Vaulting astride the gray mare, Cassidy felt an instant sense of calm, a reassuring feeling of centeredness that had been difficult for her to maintain during the days she had lived afoot and on the rafts. Squeezing the mare's broad barrel between her knees, she also had to agree with Rowena that the horse was putting on weight. *We probably all are,* she thought ruefully. *Tinker cooking!*

After all of the rainy weather that the Tinker band had been forced to endure on their trek through the wooded hills, the warm clear days they'd enjoyed since they reached the Long

River were like a special gift. In fact, as Cassidy let the mare lope lazily along the dirt pull path, she thought that it had been a long time since she had allowed herself to feel anything so closely bordering on contentment. Everything, from the friendly heat of the sun on her shoulders, to the excited chittering of the birds, to the rhythmic solidity of the mare's body between her legs, seemed to compound Cassidy's unfamiliar mood of well-being. From her vantage point on the bank she could easily see all six of the Tinkers' rafts gliding steadily on the greenish sun-gilt water. She decided as she rode that she would spend the day ashore with the mare.

I'm a Horseman, Cassidy thought firmly. With the Iron City and their encounter with the Warden drawing nearer every day, she felt it would be well to keep that fact uppermost in her mind.

The thought of what might lie ahead for her and Rowena did not seem quite as intimidating as it once had, before Click's gift of the car key had unleashed Cassidy's latest and most extensive flood of memories. She was certain that she and the brunette were somehow closer than ever to finding out the truth about their inexplicable presence in that world. And since she then had such a far more detailed memory of what their own world was like, Cassidy felt more confident than ever before that they would have something with which to bargain for their freedom, when or if it came to that. *Because someone brought us here,* she told herself determinedly. *So there must be someone who can take us back again.*

At the midday meal Cassidy let the mare swim out to alongside the passenger raft so that she could board the vessel. The horse enjoyed swimming and the river's tame current didn't present any real challenge to her. Even after Cassidy had disembarked onto the deck, the gray amused herself by following the raft for a while, swimming alongside, slurping up mouthsful of water and splashing with her upper lip.

Old Paul, looking up from his plate of cold food, merely snorted at the horse's antics. But Click couldn't keep from teasing the old cooper.

"I'd say you were wrong, Paul," the dark-haired man said wryly. "It looks as if horses can go down the Long River after all."

Cassidy ate her lunch with Rowena, Mitz, and Allen. When the seamstress reminded Cassidy of her standing offer to teach her how to weave wicker, an activity that had already been keeping Mitz occupied for several days, Cassidy felt a moment of indecision about her choice to spend the day on her horse. She was grateful when Rowena quickly spoke up and said that she'd like to learn the craft if Mitz would be willing to teach her instead. Even Allen surprised Cassidy with an observation of his own.

"Cassidy is a Horseman, Mitz," he told the gray-haired woman with a hint of solemn irony. "I'm afraid you're too late to try to make a Tinker out of her."

From her seat on the big logs that formed the side rail of the raft, Cassidy looked across to the makeshift chair that had been fashioned out of wooden crates, where the burly sheriff sat on his mound of blankets. Even dressed in Tinker garb and with some color returning to his bearded cheeks, Allen was still far from being his old self. His recovery was progressing remarkably, but he was far from his usual strength. He was lucky that Bonnie would permit him to walk from the raft to the campsite on his own. It would be awhile before he would be fit enough to mount up on a horse again. That thought brought to Cassidy a twinge of sympathy for Allen, because she understood just how badly the big man missed his self-sufficiency. He was used to taking care of people, not being taken care of.

When she stood and scanned the riverbank for the gray mare, intending to return to the horse's back, Cassidy noticed that she had acquired a companion at the rail. Teddy stood alongside her, watching the mare sampling some coarse grass at the water's edge. Perhaps it was the unshuttered wistfulness in the big blond boy's eyes; perhaps it was the memory of how endearingly grateful he had been the day she had first let him pet her mare. Or perhaps it had something to do with the way that Allen, a man who belonged on a horse's back almost as much as did Cassidy herself, was confined to the raft. Whatever the reason for the impulse, Cassidy found herself turning to Teddy and offering "Would you like to take a ride on her with me?"

Teddy was so surprised by Cassidy's proposal that for a few moments all he could do was gape speechlessly at her, his pale blue eyes widening. Then bright splashes of pink color bloomed on his cheeks as he blushed with embarrassment and excitement.

"C-could I?" he stammered eagerly. Cassidy wasn't certain if Teddy was asking her, since he was glancing hastily around the raft as he spoke, as if he were seeking some kind of group consensus.

"Go on, if she'll have you," Tad told him, waving Teddy off as if he was shooing away some large but harmless insect. "I can do without you for a while; there's not much blacksmithing to be done on this raft!"

"Go ahead, Teddy," Click agreed, managing effectively to conceal his amusement at the boy's enthusiasm. He added with a straight face, "Just see that you keep on heading in the same direction we are."

"But h-how will we get on her?" Teddy asked Cassidy anxiously, glancing from the horse on the bank to the smooth greenish water that was slipping by the side of the raft.

"You aren't afraid of getting your legs wet, are you?" Cassidy teased him, even as she silently Called the mare.

The big blond boy watched in happy fascination as the gray splashed into the river and propelled herself forward until the water was deep enough to swim. She had no difficulty catching up to the raft or keeping alongside it as Cassidy slipped over the rail and onto her slick wet back. Then Cassidy held out her hand to Teddy in a self-explanatory invitation to join her astride the horse.

As shy as he was by nature, Teddy was so enamored of the big mare that he barely hesitated. Swiftly and with surprising agility, he stepped down from the side of the raft onto the horse's back, right behind Cassidy.

"Hang onto me, Teddy," Cassidy instructed, turning the mare toward the riverbank. When he seemed hesitant to respond, she added, "Otherwise you're going to slide right off, especially when she climbs out of the water."

Accustomed to riding double with Rowena, Cassidy didn't really notice any difference with Teddy as her passenger as long as they were still in the river. But as soon as the mare's feet hit the river bottom and she began to rise up out of the water, Cassidy could feel the difference in the height and weight and breadth of the young man's body. The horse seemed completely unimpeded by the added load; in fact, she seemed to take particular delight in bounding up onto the bank like a huge wet dog. But Cassidy was immediately aware of the unfamiliar feeling of Teddy's arms around her waist, Teddy's wet thighs against hers, and Teddy's broad chest bumping lightly against her back.

As they began to ride along the rutted mule path, the mare's sleek and dripping body still as slick as Moira's potter's clay, Cassidy could sense the joy and excitement that coursed through Teddy at actually being astride the object of his admiration. What a simple way to make someone happy, she thought in wonder; she wished she'd thought of it days earlier. And although Teddy's inexperience made it necessary for him to grip Cassidy with his arms nearly as much as he gripped the horse with his legs, she found that she didn't mind in the least. No man in that world had ever held her in such an embrace; yet there was simply nothing provocative about it. To Cassidy, Teddy was like a child, and his plain and unfettered elation was like the pure and guileless pleasure a child would feel.

For nearly an hour they rode along the mule path, sometimes pacing the rafts, sometimes jogging on ahead to see what lay around the next turn. Cassidy knew Teddy would have happily ridden with her all afternoon, but she reminded herself that without any previous riding experience behind him, the poor boy was going to have some very sore muscles the next day if she let him ride much longer. However reluctant she was to spoil his fun, she finally had to end his adventure.

"Maybe we can do it again before we get to the city," she offered as she maneuvered the swimming mare so that Teddy could climb back onto the raft. "That is, if your saddlesores will let you!"

Blushing an appropriate shade of crimson, Teddy blurted out his gratitude to Cassidy as the gray calmly paddled alongside the raft.

"I think you've committed yourself to that ride for certain," Click said to her before Cassidy could turn the horse back toward the bank. Squatting casually by the raft's log side rail, he gave the mare's wet neck a gentle pat. "And I could use your help tomorrow morning with something, as well, if you would."

More curious than concerned about Click's request, Cassidy looked calmly across into those deep brown eyes. "Sure, what is it?" she asked.

"By tomorrow we'll be reaching the first set of rapids," he told her. "If you're willing, I'd like to ride ahead and check on conditions in the river before the rafts reach that point."

The request seemed so simple when compared to all of the possibilities suggested by Cassidy's paranoid imagination. She was not so far removed from her mistrust of Click that such an innocuous-sounding favor would have been high on her list of his most likely demands. Thus her instant acquiescence had more to do with a sense of relief than merely any desire to do him a good turn.

"Sure," she said quickly, "any time you want to go."

It was only later as she let the mare amble lazily along the sun-dappled mule path in the waning hours of the afternoon, while the last of the moisture evaporated from her damp pants and boots, that Cassidy admitted to herself that there was also another component to her agreement. She *was* willing to do Click a good turn; she felt as if the Tinker leader had earned it from her.

The next morning dawned cloudy but the air was still dry and pleasantly warm, even by the time the Tinkers broke camp. As Cassidy helped Carlotta and Rowena clean and pack their breakfast dishware, she scanned the sky. From north to south in long rows, thick gray clouds lay like earth plowed over in wide furrows. Not rain clouds, Cassidy decided with relief; but a change in the weather was coming.

"Plowman's clouds," Allen remarked when she and Rowena stopped by Bonnie's cook fire to see him. "They mean the weather's on the move."

"I'll be glad when we get back to the city," the bulky blonde said as she scraped a pan. Her two little dogs scampered around her feet, quarreling over the scraps. "I'm ready for a regular roof over my head again."

As curious as she might have been about the Tinkers' homes and the Iron City, Cassidy didn't feel that then was the best time or place, or even that Bonnie was necessarily the best person, to ask about it. So she sat silently with Allen and Rowena while the sheriff finished the mug of tea he was still obliged to drink in lieu of coffee. But as soon as Bonnie had moved out of earshot, Allen had a comment of his own that surprised Cassidy.

"I'd settle for my own roof, in my own village," he said over the rim of his mug, "although Bonnie's chances look better than mine."

Cassidy and Rowena exchanged a guilty glance. If it was true, as Click had said, that Allen had placed himself in harm's way by coming after them, then it still did not necessarily follow that they'd had the right to carry him off, farther from his own village. It was true that the Tinkers and maybe even

Cassidy herself had saved his life; but since that night the burly man had had no choice in what had been happening to him. And they were bearing him farther and farther from his home, to a place where he very likely didn't even wish to go.

The only thing that rescued Cassidy from further self-recriminating ruminations was Click's timely arrival at Bonnie's cook fire. The tall dark-haired man, his boots and trouser legs damp from the morning dew, strode up and greeted them all with his typical bonhomie. He mooched the last of her coffee off Bonnie without a moment's shame, and discussed the day's planned route with Allen as if the big sheriff was his second lieutenant and old friend rather than being his unwilling ward. Watching him in action, Cassidy was suddenly struck by how well she had come to know Click in such a relatively short time. And surreptitiously studying his hard lean frame, from the cut of his trousers, to the metal ornamentation on his vest, to the silvered bars of his mustache, only one comparison came to mind.

He really is the king of the gypsies, Cassidy thought with her own secret sense of amusement. Then she caught herself in surprise, because the descriptive phrase and its connotation was something she was certain she would not have been able to come up with even a few days earlier. For a moment that realization so occupied her that she nearly missed the fact that Click was addressing a question to her.

"Well, Cassidy, are you ready to get started?" he asked.

"Sure," Cassidy replied, getting to her feet. She led their way through the breaking camp to the grassy edge of the pull path without even looking back to see if Click was following, because she was certain that he was. As she came up alongside Dragonfly and gave the horse's mane an affectionate tug, she saw that he was right behind her.

Willie walked by on his way down to the rafts, a huge roll of tent canvas balanced on each shoulder. "Measure how deep the draw is if you can," he called out to Click as he went past.

"You can count on it, Willie," Click called back.

Touching the mare's withers, Cassidy vaulted up onto her back. Then, when she had settled herself into position, she reached back down to offer Click a hand. But much to her surprise, even though he took her hand, it was obvious that the dark-haired man hadn't needed it. He sprang smoothly up onto the horse's back behind her with the casual agility of someone who'd been doing just that all of his life.

As Click shifted himself so that he was centered behind her, Cassidy tried to conceal her chagrin. The man's obvious skill should have come as no surprise to her; just because she had never seen him ride a horse didn't mean he didn't know how. The discovery did, however, force Cassidy to reevaluate her previous sense of just how well she thought she knew him.

"All set?" she asked dryly.

"As ready as you are," Click replied. And had Cassidy been able to see his face, she knew she would have seen that little spark of humor in his eyes.

Cassidy let the mare move out on the mule path at her own pace, which was measured and contained at first, even though the horse seemed filled with energy. Click sat easily behind her, his hands resting on his own thighs, only the barest brush of his knees forming any contact with her body. Even at a walk it was a far cry from riding double with Teddy or even with Rowena. Click seemed to find his own balance with the mare and his presence did not intrude upon Cassidy's. It was almost like riding alone except for her constant awareness of his larger form behind hers, and the subtle smells of leather and soap and smoke that clung to him.

Because of the thick masses of low-lying clouds, the morning was slow to brighten. But the air was calm and warm enough, and the beauty of the river and the surrounding woods did not depend on the sunlight for its appeal. Riding ahead of the rafts, Cassidy and Click found the river and its banks undisturbed. Birds flitted along the path before them and the surface of the opaque water occasionally exploded with the leap of a fish or frog. From the safe distance of the opposite bank a solitary white heron watched with obvious curiosity as the horse and her riders passed.

After ten or fifteen minutes at an easy walk, Cassidy allowed the mare to break into a jog trot. The rhythm of that diagonal gait caused Click's body to settle against Cassidy's, although he still kept himself well balanced on the horse's back. And although Cassidy doubted that he needed to hold onto her to keep his seat, it seemed only natural and comfortable that Click's hands should move from resting idly on his own legs to lightly bracket Cassidy's hips.

Click appeared to feel no pressing need to make small talk, a fact for which Cassidy was strangely grateful. It was somehow more companionable just to ride along in silence, listening to the natural sounds of the river and the land all around them.

The front of Click's thighs fit neatly against the backs of hers, and his chest and belly lightly touched her back at predictable intervals in the mare's swinging stride. His hands on her hips were an almost reassuring presence, harmless and friendly. When she inhaled she could tease out the familiar scent of him, even over the smell of the horse, the forest, and the river. And the oddest, most satisfying aspect of all of it was that up until even a couple of days earlier, Cassidy could never have conceived of ever being that comfortable with him.

Even at a jog the big mare was impatient, and despite its rather rutted surface the pull path was clear and the ground was sandy and yielding. "You want to lope?" Cassidy asked. Click's response brought an unseen grin to her face.

"Are you asking me, or the horse?" he said.

"I don't have to ask the horse," she responded, glad that he could not see the amusement on her face.

"It would be my pleasure," Click said.

It was the gray mare's pleasure, as well, and in her exuberance at being allowed to extend her gait she even threw in a few mild high-spirited bucks for good measure. At the sudden shifts in momentum and direction, Click's arms slipped up around Cassidy's waist for support. He may have been agile and not inexperienced in riding, but he didn't seem to have the desire to take any unnecessary chances of being unceremoniously unhorsed.

Within moments the mare had settled down and leveled out into a smooth ground-covering canter, her big body rocking easily along the dirt path. Cassidy stroked the sleek neck, empathizing with the horse's eager energy. And even though the horse's rangy lope was at least as steady as her trot, Click's arms remained lightly encircling Cassidy's waist.

Once again, just as she had when she had ridden the mare the day before, Cassidy marveled at the simplicity of that elusive emotion, happiness. It had been so elementary just to get up on the horse and ride; and it had hardly been any more revolutionary an idea to offer to share that pleasure with Teddy. And yet both actions had brought Cassidy something she thought she had forgotten how to find. They had made her happy.

And although some part of her still fought against the realization, riding out that morning with Click was making Cassidy happy, as well. Why was she so reluctant to admit that to herself? Was it because the touch, the warmth, the scent, the very nearness of his body was pleasant to her? And if so, what was wrong with that?

Sex is what's wrong with that! her nagging little internal voice told Cassidy with its customary acerbity. In a way she almost felt as if she were *using* Click somehow; because even though he seemed to be enjoying their ride as much as she was, it couldn't have been for all of the same reasons.

Cassidy hated trying to argue with that annoying little voice in her head; for some reason it always won. Instead she tried to shift the focus of her whole dilemma away from Click specifically and generalize the question. Why was there no sexual context to anything those people did? That was perhaps the single most frustrating mystery of the place. Forgetting electricity or the internal combustion engine was one thing; even forgetting how to read and write. But how could they just have *forgotten* sex?

Cassidy was so thoroughly immersed in thought and lulled by the rhythm of the mare's rolling canter that she was a bit startled when Click spoke nearly right into her ear, even though his words were soft.

"There's the beginning of the first set of rapids," he said, raising one arm to point past her shoulder, "right beyond that deadfall on the other bank."

Cassidy brought the mare back down to a walk again even as she turned her gaze in the direction in which Click had pointed. The river there seemed broader than before, but she could clearly see across the expanse of gliding greenish water to the opposite bank, where the blackened skeleton of a huge downed pine tree jutted out into the stream like a broken wharf. From the way the water swirled and foamed around the deadfall's partially submerged limbs, Cassidy realized that the current was much stronger there than it had been upstream.

The gray mare shook her head and blew loudly through her nostrils, a theatrical and totally unnecessary gesture aimed purely at expressing her displeasure at having had her little run terminated. But as the big horse carried them farther along the dirt path, Cassidy could see how rapidly the nature of the river was changing. Broader and shallower, the stream also ran more swiftly and as the surrounding terrain began to drop the water seemed to race to keep up with it.

"The Tinkers call these the Folly Falls," Click said to the back of Cassidy's head. When she turned her head slightly, she could see that the silver-tipped swag of his mustache was lifted in his typical ironic humor. "They aren't the worst rapids on this river, but since they're the first they'll quickly demonstrate to you whether or not you've adequately secured all of your cargo."

Glancing around again to where the widened river churned noisily over a series of broad steplike drop-offs, Cassidy asked, "Ever lose anything off the rafts here?"

Cassidy knew without having to turn again that the tips of Click's mustache had quirked even higher. "A few things," he said, adding "the first time."

Cassidy stopped the mare when they reached the head of the rapids. The mule path itself was slightly sloped there and more deeply rutted and eroded, apparently from the increased effort on the part of the draft animals hauling barges up the drop in the river. As she watched the pale green water slip by, foaming around the occasional protruding rock, Cassidy could appreciate the added skill it would take to pilot the rafts down that stretch of the river. Up until that point they had hardly needed the keel and tiller mechanisms on the vessels; but the rapids were going to provide a bit more challenging ride.

Behind her, Click swung one leg back over the gray's rump and twisted off, landing lithely on his feet at the horse's side. He didn't appear in the least bit cramped from the hour's ride. If not for the light tracing of horse sweat and dirt on the inner thighs and seat of his pants, it would have been hard to tell that he'd even been on a horse at all.

"I'm going to wade out into the river and check out the draw in a few places," he said, gesturing toward the rapids.

Dubiously eyeing the expanse of rushing water, Cassidy wondered if that would be particularly safe; but what she said was "Do you need any help?"

Click had taken a few steps away from the horse and was already standing balanced on one foot, tugging at his other boot. "Not really," he told her. "This is actually quite simple and it won't take long." He switched to the other foot, pulling off his second boot. "Why don't you just let your mare graze, and enjoy the scenery."

It was especially beautiful along that part of the river, Cassidy had to acknowledge. Over the past few days she had noticed that there had become more evergreens in the forest, which made a nice contrast to the deciduous trees and bushes. And the same spine of rock that had created the rapids also added an interesting series of shale ledges and outcroppings to the forest floor. Even as she slipped down from the horse's back, Cassidy scanned the tall treetops for the source of one particularly resonant bird call.

When her gaze casually swept back along the riverbank to where Click was standing, Cassidy was both surprised and embarrassed to find that the dark-haired man was matter-of-factly shucking off his clothing. That was, of course, an entirely logical thing to do, since he was going out into the river. There was no need for him to ride back to the rafts in wet clothes. In fact, when Cassidy thought about it, it would have been pretty silly for Click to have waded out into the water fully dressed. And after all, nudity meant nothing to those people. Or at least that was what Cassidy kept telling herself as she watched Click calmly step out of his trousers.

There was nothing sexual in the man's actions; she was confident of that. But as Click deftly folded the trousers and dropped them on top of his boots and shirt, Cassidy could not honestly say that she operated under the same neutrality. His rangy body was as supple as she had imagined, but more muscular than it had appeared beneath his casual clothing. Varying graduations of suntan lent his skin a layered look, well browned on his hands, arms, throat, and face, lighter golden on his chest and back, and pale on his buttocks and legs. He never even gave Cassidy a backward glance as he stepped through the sedge grass at the edge of the bank, wearing nothing but the little brass key on its leather thong around his neck.

"Enjoy the scenery," indeed!

Trying for an air of nonchalant indifference, Cassidy glanced idly about at the forest, the cloud-furrowed sky, and her own placidly munching mare. She didn't want to look toward the river for too long; she especially didn't want to give the appearance of seeming to stare. But as Click began wading out into the rapids, regardless of the fact that he was naked she was still concerned about his safety.

The current caused churning little eddies to form around Click's legs as the tall man moved slowly and steadily into the river. He seemed to feel for secure footing before taking each step. By the time he was a few dozen feet from the bank, the emerald-tinted water was lapping around his pale buttocks. Momentarily mesmerized by the subtle play of muscle along his hips and spine, Cassidy had to force herself to look away.

Damn! I wish I could just "forget" about sex again, she thought ruefully. *At least for this morning!*

Turning to the gray mare, Cassidy began methodically checking the horse's legs and feet for scrapes or bruises. Anything to keep from watching the sleek motion of Click's naked body gliding through the water. *After all, I've got to ride all the way back to the rafts again with him sitting right behind me . . .* As she crouched by the horse her mind automatically segued back to the puzzling question that had occupied her earlier, and she happily welcomed the diversion. Only then when she thought about it again, something different happened. Instead of continuing to look at the same pieces of a baffling puzzle that just did not seem to fit, she abruptly reversed the equation in her head.

What if I'm looking at this whole question backward? she thought suddenly. *What if the question isn't why have these people forgotten about sex—what if the real question is why should they remember it?*

The implications of that fresh perspective so riveted Cassidy that for a few moments she was completely unaware of anything in her immediate surroundings—the solid earth beneath her feet, the feel of the mare's leg against her hands, the beating of her heart—much less Click's nudity. Why should those people remember sex? What good would it do them there? If all of them had, like her and Rowena, come from somewhere else—the Slow World, Allen had called it; the real world, as Cassidy preferred to think of it—and yet had all somehow been made to forget everything about that world, then sex would only have been a complication.

The gray mare blew through her nostrils, jerking Cassidy out of her thoughts. The horse wanted to move forward to graze, Cassidy realized belatedly. She released the mare's leg and glanced out over the river, where Click had moved downstream and was still wading slowing and carefully in what was then nearly chest-deep water.

Okay, so it isn't like people here don't have any feelings at all, Cassidy resumed musing, leaning back against the mare's shoulder. She had at various times seen them express every sort of emotion: fear and courage, anger and affection, generosity and greed. But then perhaps that was merely a matter of survival. People everywhere, even in such an oddly circumscribed world, couldn't have effectively coped with all the vagaries of daily life without the buttress of such emotions.

But they don't need sex, she realized. Purely from a survival standpoint it was necessary only to perpetuate the species. And that wasn't exactly a problem there, since everyone had merely been brought from somewhere else—presumably somewhere where procreation still existed. Why muck things up by introducing sex into the picture?

Simultaneously excited and depressed by the irrefutable logic of her conclusion, Cassidy turned again toward the river in despair. *Great—there's no reason for them to ever remember sex,* she thought glumly as she watched the water swirl around Click's half-immersed figure as he continued to explore the rapids. *In fact, sex is probably the most important thing for them to forget.*

Cassidy had long been troubled by the gaping chasm in her memory and by the punishing headaches that seemed to accompany her every attempt to regain anything from her past. But with that fresh insight she was also struck anew by the sinister implication of what could be nothing less than the depressing confirmation of what she had long suspected.

We aren't supposed to remember ...

Dragonfly took another step forward, still grazing, again jolting Cassidy out of her glum speculations. She glanced over to see that Click was returning, approaching the bank again, the swirling greenish water of the river coming only to his mid-thigh. The dark-haired man still moved deliberately but with an almost casual sort of grace, much the way he moved on dry land. Once in the shallows he looked back out over the rapids, studying them for a few moments as if committing some feature of them to memory. Then he came sloshing through the sedge grass and back up onto the bank again.

There was really no point in trying to not look at him anymore, Cassidy realized with a certain wistful resignation. Once he was standing practically right in front of her, he would naturally expect some sort of ordinary eye contact with her; she could hardly stare off into the trees or over the river if he was speaking to her. He would be puzzled if she seemed uncomfortable or embarrassed, no matter that his naked body still gleamed from his foray into the river, or that droplets of water hung like diamonds in the dark hair that grew across his belly and on the long muscles of his thighs ...

"Well, Willie will be glad to hear that we shouldn't have any problems going down the Follies this time," Click said. He glanced back toward the river and made a gesture, holding his hands out as if he were taking the measure of something. "The water's at a good depth, even at the bottom end."

Caught taking some measure of her own, Cassidy quickly blurted out, "Guess all that rainy weather we've had has been good for something."

Click's genial little almost-smile curled at his upper lip as he bent to pluck up his shirt. Using it like a towel to briskly blot up the remaining water from his arms and chest, he remarked, "It might make for an interesting ride farther downstream, however. These first rapids are usually just a nuisance because the river's the widest and shallowest here. The next sets are likely to be a little more—" He paused, selecting his word with a certain relish. "—rambunctious."

Trying to look Click in the face and not to follow the movements of his shirt as he scrubbed it across his belly and upper thighs, Cassidy asked, "How many more sets of rapids are there?"

"Three after this," he said, bending to dry his lower legs. "We'll probably hit the first of those later this afternoon."

Cassidy fixed her eyes on the place where Click's head would be and then waited for him to straighten up again before she said, "Then we must be getting close to the city, huh?"

Click nodded. "If all goes well, we could be docking there as early as tomorrow evening."

As she stood there studying his face, Cassidy suddenly wished that she hadn't started the topic in that direction; or at least that she hadn't done it until Click had gotten completely dressed again. For she could tell from his particular thoughtful expression as he calmly looked back at her, his damp shirt drooping idly from his hand, that they were about to have a serious conversation about something. And a serious conversation with Click could prove to be trouble enough without the added distraction of being confronted by that lean and engaging body.

"Even before we reach the city we'll begin to encounter some smaller settlements along the river," Click said.

"Like the villages?" Cassidy asked, keeping her eyes on his face.

"Not precisely." Almost absently, he had gathered the dangling tails of his shirt with his other hand, thus temporarily if not purposely shielding his midsection from Cassidy's view. To her bemusement she discovered that even naked Click still smelled of woodsmoke and leather, unless that scent was concentrated in the damp fabric of his shirt. It was then that she realized the solemn expression on Click's cleanly planed face was not just thoughtful; he was also clearly concerned about something.

"I know you are eager to reach the city, Cassidy; eager to see your Warden." His umber eyes were calm but somehow they seemed to hold an undercurrent of warning. "But I also know that you've never been to the Iron City, and I would be failing you as a friend if I didn't urge you to be cautious."

For a moment Cassidy just stood there staring mutely at him, rendered speechless more by his declaration that he considered himself her friend than by the knowledge implicit in his warning. "I'm always cautious," she said, regaining her composure.

To her surprise, Click took a step forward, resting one hand on each of her shoulders. His shirt hung between them like a flag as he looked down directly into her eyes from the advantage of his superior height. "I know you are eager for answers, Cassidy, but it is dangerous to assume too much—especially in the Iron City." The argent tips of his mustache twitched. "For someone with the gift you possess, it's too easy to want to trust the wrong people."

Cassidy felt light-headed with surprise and dismay; the touch of Click's hands, as gently as they rested upon her shoulders, weighted upon her like the press of hot irons. *He knows,* she thought, looking up helplessly into those solemn brown eyes. *He knows that it's me . . .*

As if he had plucked the words directly from her roiling mind, Click said, "Yes, Cassidy, I know it's not Rowena." Before a single word of protest or denial could leave her mouth, he raised one hand from her shoulder and gently laid his forefinger across her lips. "I know you're the one who has the Memories."

Her heart pounding, Cassidy shook her head, dislodging his finger. "How did . . . ?" she began; but Click's interception was too smooth and compelling to be so easily overridden.

"The key," he said simply. His strong sinewy forefinger hooked around the leather thong that circled her neck, slowly and delicately drawing up the bit of stamped metal from its resting place beneath her shirt. Cradling the key in the palm of his hand, his eyes still steady upon hers, he went on. "The morning we reached the river, while you were still asleep with Allen in Willie's cart, I showed Rowena what I had gotten for you. I asked her if she thought you'd like it." His one brow canted evocatively. "After what you'd been through, I didn't want to upset you with something inappropriate."

Cassidy's pulse had settled into a thudding rhythm, her heart banging steadily against her ribs like the drum of hoofbeats. It seemed so loud in her own ears that she half believed Click must have been able to hear it, as well; it filled the small space between them like thunder. Her focus had become so narrow, so intense, that when she looked up at Click all she really saw of him was the rich warmth of his unblinking eyes.

"She told me she thought you'd like it," he continued. "But she didn't react to it—not like you did." Click paused, his voice dropping lower, like the deep strength of the river's hidden currents. "It's made you remember something more, hasn't it?"

Several very powerful and conflicting emotions warred in Cassidy then, wrenching her from the near trancelike state induced by Click's overwhelming nearness. She felt shock and alarm at what he had discovered, and concern and suspicion regarding his motives in discussing it with her. She tried to take a step backward away from him, but found herself bumping right into the gray mare's substantial body.

"Rowena never said anything to me about you showing her the key first," Cassidy blurted out, almost accusingly.

Dropping his hands from her, Click spread them, his shirt waving like a flag of truce. "I asked her not to," he explained mildly. The old humor, dry and ironic, glinted in his eyes. "I wanted it to be a surprise."

"It was," Cassidy assured him.

For a few moments neither of them spoke or barely even moved, other than the slight rocking of Cassidy's body as she tried to will her breathing to return to its normal rate. Behind her the mare snorted greedily into the grass, shaking some insect off her neck with a desultory toss of her mane. Then Click took a casual step sideways from Cassidy and shook out his shirt, preparatory to tugging it on over his head again.

As the dark-haired man dressed, Cassidy just stood watching him, no longer even concerned about trying to avert her eyes or divert her thoughts. For when she looked at Click then she no longer even noticed his nudity. All she saw was a man who could either be an incredible danger to her and Rowena or an invaluable ally. And she wanted—she needed—to know for certain which he would be.

After pulling on his second boot, Click straightened and

gave his whole body a little shake, the metal rings and conchas on his leather vest jingling, as if to properly settle all of his clothing again. When he looked across into Cassidy's face, he seemed mildly surprised and genuinely concerned at the distressed expression that he found there.

"No one else knows," he assured her. Cocking his head, he regarded her with a bemusement that was gentle and not at all mocking. "Did you think I would have brought you all this way just to keep you from your Warden now?"

Not certain just what she believed, but unapologetic about neither the strength nor the persistence of her wariness, Cassidy just replied, "I don't know—have you?"

Click shook his head, his eyes lit with a certain rueful deprecation. "Ah, Cassidy," he said gently, "I've already told you: We would never fail to help anyone in need."

But Cassidy could not keep from recalling that at the same time Click had told her that, he had also told her that taking her to the Warden might just be serving his own best interests. And she could not keep from wondering if by "we" Click was still referring to the Tinkers.

Chapter 10 ◀▥

Just as Click had predicted, the rapids he called Folly Falls posed no serious problems for the Tinkers' rafts. Three people were stationed on each vessel to help with the navigation as they negotiated the more turbulent stretch of the river, but it was more of a precaution than a necessity. Once Bonnie, Moira, and Click had taken the lead raft down the channel, it was relatively easy for the five other craft to follow their route. And with the increased speed of the current on the rapids, they all quickly passed beyond the potentially troublesome section of water. By the time they took their midday meal, the rafts were again riding smoothly on the steady glide of the big river.

Cassidy again rode on the raft that Willie piloted, where Rowena had joined them before they had entered the rapids. As she shared a meal of cold sandwiches and fruit with the big burly man and the brunette, Cassidy became particularly aware of the fact that Rowena had been regarding her with a certain surreptitious curiosity ever since she and Click had ridden back to the rafts that morning. Cassidy doubted that Willie or any of the other Tinkers could have detected anything amiss, but Rowena had become too astute a judge of Cassidy's moods to have missed the subtle signs of her preoccupation and uneasiness. And although Cassidy had been perfectly able to follow all of Willie's instructions and to keep her attention focused on her job as their raft had navigated the rapids, her mind was still on the implications of what Click had revealed to her by those same rapids earlier that morning.

Glancing up from the bound stack of cured hides upon which she sat, Cassidy threw Rowena a quick look. Somehow she didn't think she'd have any problem getting the brunette to come out of camp with her that night for some private conversation.

By midafternoon the sky began to clear. The dragging windrows of thick gray clouds had been gradually lifting and thinning all day until finally bright blue sky appeared in bands between their tattered remains. Then sunlight began to shoot down in broad shafts, sparkling like swaths of glitter across the calm greenish water of the river's surface.

By the time the rafts reached the second set of rapids, the sky was nearly cloudless and the sun had begun to descend behind the treetops. As Click had described, the river at that point was not as shallow or as wide, but the rapids were indeed more "rambunctious." In fact, Cassidy's first impression as she watched the lead raft enter the head of the swiftly running descent was that the blocky vessel had suddenly been sucked into some kind of chute. There were no protruding rocks, no visible foaming or churning, and no sounds of gurgling water. The raft just took off, borne down the rapids by a nearly invisible current that seemed to have snatched the craft from its fellows and then instantly ferried it, dipping and bobbing, to a point much farther downstream.

Cassidy was especially grateful to have the solid and stolid bulk of Willie at the tiller as their own raft was caught by the same current. Since there really weren't any hazards to navigate around, she and Rowena were left free to just hang on and enjoy the ride. And despite her initial misgivings when she had first seen the lead raft sucked down the rapids, Cassidy actually did enjoy it. Their ungainly rectangular craft suddenly shot through the water, the rough wooden deck planks pitching unpredictably beneath her feet. She and Rowena both ended up practically on their hands and knees, as the whirling water hit the keel and fought with Willie for the control of the rudder. But both women quickly realized that they were in no real danger, and in spite of the raft's somewhat rowdy bucking, its speed was more exhilarating than frightening. And, of course, being able to see that the raft that had gone ahead of them was already placidly gliding on the quiet water below the rapids considerably ameliorated any concern.

As Willie guided their raft through the remainder of the fast water and they smoothly coasted along with the last of the rapids' added momentum, Cassidy and Rowena got to their feet again. Willie shot them both a look of amused tolerance.

"Not quite like riding a horse, is it?" he said as he adjusted the tiller.

"Probably a lot safer, at least for me," Rowena said with a plucky grin.

Cassidy looked back upstream to where the next raft was already racing down the stretch of rapidly moving water. "Click said that there were three sets of rapids on this part of the river," she said.

"Yeah, two more to go," Willie agreed, his huge and weathered hands playing over the polished wood of the helm, automatically making some minor course change to bring them in line with the lead raft. "But I suspect we'll save those for tomorrow."

"Why?" Rowena asked the big man, her brows rising quizzically. "This wasn't so bad; are the others worse than this?"

"They can be," Willie said laconically. He glanced back, checking the position of the other rafts, before he added, "The last two sets of rapids are pretty close together, and it'd be almost dark by the time we'd reach them. So I expect we'll wait till morning."

Rowena gave Cassidy a cheerful little shrug and moved around the stacks of cargo to the stern of the raft where she could wave at Carlotta and the others on the craft coming up behind them. But Cassidy just stayed where she was for a few moments, staring out without really seeing across the calm and glistening greenish-gold surface of the sun-painted river.

Tomorrow . . . Click had told her that by the end of the day tomorrow they would reach the Iron City. But he had told her other things, as well, things that had tempered her former eagerness with apprehension and confusion and had made her determination to seek the Warden seem as much of a risk as a means to salvation.

Willie's expectation proved correct, and the Tinkers put in to the bank and made their camp early that evening. With the clearing of the sky some heat had returned to the last part of the day, and the land along the riverbank was fairly low and marshy. They had passed several more estuaries and stretches of swamp during the late afternoon and had to settle for the best piece of higher ground they could find to lay out their camp. But because they still were surrounded by boggy land, the contingent of mosquitoes and other biting insects was especially impressive that night. The gray mare's tail was almost constantly in motion as she grazed along the edge of the mule path, and the cook fires were intentionally laid with some green wood in the hope that the added smoke would bring some relief from the bugs.

Cassidy and Rowena ate with Carlotta, Mitz, Old Paul, and Toby. Before the meal the spry little seamstress offered them all some additional protection from the bugs. As Cassidy batted away yet another whining insect, Mitz dug into her bundle of supplies and produced a brown glass bottle.

"Rub on some of this," she instructed, anointing her own palm and then passing the bottle on to Cassidy.

Rowena wrinkled her nose suspiciously. "Whew—that smells awful!" she complained.

But Cassidy, already slathering the pungent liquid onto her arms and neck, didn't much care what it smelled like as long as it worked.

"The smell will tame down pretty quickly," Carlotta assured them, taking the bottle from Rowena.

"Besides, what does it matter what it smells like," Old Paul said gruffly, "if we all smell like it?"

With the whole camp wreathed in the hanging smoke of greenwood fires, even the strong herbal scent of the oily potion wasn't detectable for long. And by the time they had finished eating, even Rowena had to admit that Mitz's lotion had proven an effective repellent for the mosquitoes.

"Although I still think the stuff stinks," the brunette said as she passed Carlotta her empty dishes.

Cassidy had been well aware throughout the meal, just as she had been all afternoon on the raft, that Rowena was eager to talk with her alone. She also knew that they probably would not get a better opportunity. So when Rowena stood, Cassidy immediately got to her feet, as well. What they hadn't anticipated was Carlotta's intervention.

"Going over to see Allen?" the metalsmith asked. Without even waiting for a reply, she held up a plate piled with thick slices of the same delicious fruit bread she had just served them for dessert. "Take him some of this," she said. "The man needs to build his strength."

While Cassidy reached hesitantly for the plate, Old Paul grunted into his coffee mug. "You think Bonnie isn't feeding him over there?" he muttered at Carlotta.

But Carlotta ignored the old cooper and just made a shooing

motion at Cassidy and Rowena. "Go ahead, then; Toby and I will clean up here."

As they turned away from Carlotta's fire, Cassidy exchanged a glance with Rowena. Cassidy felt a little ambivalent because she really did want to see Allen, as well. In fact, she definitely wanted to talk to the sheriff again—she just hadn't planned on doing it in Rowena's presence, any more than she had planned on talking to Rowena in Allen's presence. Carefully balancing the fully laden plate as they skirted Tad's cook fire, they both nodded greetings at the blacksmith, Teddy, Henry, and Willie.

At Bonnie's cook fire only the massive blond woman and Allen remained. Cassidy found herself both relieved and oddly disappointed not to find Click there. The sheriff looked up from his seat on a mound of bedrolls, his bearded face framed by stray wisps of smoke.

"Carlotta sent this over for you," Cassidy said, offering Allen the plate.

Bonnie looked over sharply from her position across the fire from them, where she sat rinsing cups with water from a jug, her two little dogs collapsed at her feet like twin dust mops. She said nothing, but her opinion of Carlotta sending food over to her cook fire was obvious. Allen noted the big woman's pointed glance but seemed unperturbed by it.

"That was nice of her," he said, taking the plate from Cassidy. "Bonnie's filled me up pretty good right now, but I'll save this for later."

Cassidy found his tactful solution impressive. *No wonder he was a sheriff,* she thought. *Is a sheriff,* she corrected herself. *Is, not was.* For Allen was still a sheriff, even if they had been carrying him farther and farther from his territory and his jurisdiction. Uncomfortable with that reminder, Cassidy didn't even notice that Allen had set the plate aside, and so he surprised her by suddenly pushing himself up, getting unsteadily but determinedly to his feet.

When he was standing directly in front of her, Cassidy was once again reminded of Allen's size. Even though he still was pale and weakened by his ordeal, he carried himself with a certain natural dignity. He also looked down at her, right into her eyes, and there was no mistaking the familiar resolve on that bearded face.

Bonnie looked up at Allen, her eyes narrowing suspiciously. "And just where do you think you're going? she asked him.

Allen had never impressed Cassidy as a man given to bursts of humor, secret or otherwise, and so she was surprised to detect a certain note of good-natured sarcasm in his voice as he replied, "Where do you think, Bonnie?" He gestured toward the ground. "Or would you prefer me to do it right here?"

Bonnie made a scoffing sound. "Just try it! I've already had enough of cleaning up after you to last me a lifetime," she retorted. But remembering the big woman's endless patience and gentleness with Allen when he had lain helpless, Cassidy was certain that Bonnie's seeming scorn was only a matter of form. "Look at you," she continued. "You can hardly stand up without falling flat on your hairy face." She waved at Cassidy and Rowena. "If you're going to try staggering out into the bushes, at least take one of them with you, to come back here for help if you collapse somewhere with your fly open."

Rowena was grinning openly at Bonnie's withering assessment of Allen's capacity, but Cassidy saw in it the perfect opportunity to get him somewhere they could talk alone without it looking odd. And if she still needed to talk to Rowena alone, too, well, that might be possible later.

"Don't worry, we'll keep an eye on him for you," Cassidy quickly assured Bonnie, stepping away from the cook fire and ahead of Allen. She saw Rowena hesitate for a moment, looking slightly puzzled before she seemed to comprehend Cassidy's intention and moved to follow them.

"Don't you try to walk too far," the big blonde called after them, once again her bluster a transparent veneer for her true concern about Allen's well-being.

None of them spoke as they made their way the short but cluttered distance from Bonnie's fire to the edge of the camp. Allen moved with the stiff, foreshortened gait of an ancient man; in fact, his slow and painfully precise steps as they threaded their way around tents and little caches of supplies made Old Paul's usual shuffle seem spry by comparison. Glancing sideways at him in the smoke-smudged dimness, Cassidy could still see the deep lines that Allen's ordeal had etched into the pallor of his bearded face. *Job or no job, it was still because of us,* she couldn't help thinking.

Cassidy had fully expected Allen to head for the nearest clump of brush once they had cleared the edge of the Tinker camp. The fact that he didn't, and instead veered clumsily but purposefully toward the pull path at the river's edge, made her suddenly remember the painful associations that the darkened forest must have held for him. It was not until Allen had stopped, his eyes quickly sweeping the immediate surrounding area before settling on her face, that Cassidy could see something of his expression. And then even though the gloom prevented her from reading his face with complete clarity, she saw enough in it to realize that relieving his bladder was the farthest thing from Allen's mind. He had come out there deliberately, and he had wanted her and Rowena to come with him.

"Click tells me that by the end of the day tomorrow we should reach the Iron City," Allen said without preamble.

Beside her, Rowena blinked quizzically; but Cassidy simply said, "Yeah, that's what he told me, too."

Cassidy wished that she could have seen Allen's expression more clearly then, because as his voice dropped his tone became one of focused intent. "Did he also tell you that you might very well be in danger there?" Before Cassidy could respond the big man held up one hand, warding off any interruption, and continued with a quiet earnestness. "Cassidy, I know you want to go to the Warden—I know it's what you've wanted all along. And you have every right to go. But you shouldn't make the assumption that because you're a Horseman the two of you will be welcome there—or even safe."

Momentarily taken aback by how closely Allen's warning echoed the one she had received from Click only that morning, Cassidy was not able to respond before Rowena did. "You don't have to go there with us, Allen," the brunette said. She shot Cassidy a quick look before she continued firmly, "I don't care what those Troopers said; we don't have any right to make you come with us."

The arch of Allen's brow was sharp enough that his puzzlement was clearly evident even in the dimness, even before he spoke. "Troopers?" he said. "What do Troopers have to do with this?"

Several possible responses occurred to Cassidy then, most of them involving some protective editing of the truth. But as she looked from Rowena's concerned face to Allen's baffled one, somehow trying to maintain a viable cover story seemed an increasingly feeble concern in light of the magnitude of the problem they were facing. She could not help but to think that all of her previous deceptions had only helped to cause many of the hardships all three of them had endured. Now that they were nearly to the Iron City, she quite simply could see no other way to try to minimize the dangers and maximize their chance for success than by just resorting to the plain truth.

.Cassidy looked up directly into Allen's face. "She's talking about the Troopers I met outside Pointed Rock the other night, the Troopers who were chasing the things that nearly killed you."

Only her expectation of his reaction enabled Cassidy to keep from visibly flinching as Allen shied away from the impact of her words. His head jerked up and his whole body froze. His face, defined in that faint light only by the contrast between the pallor of his skin and the darker hue of his hair and beard, seemed if anything even more ghostly as he stared down at them.

Her voice softening, Cassidy asked him, "Did you know that the Troopers have been hunting those things?"

An involuntary shudder ran through Allen's broad frame. As if by extension of that tremor, he shook his head, briskly and emphatically. "No," he said hoarsely, "not until that night."

Gently but matter-of-factly, Cassidy persisted. "You'd never seen any of those creatures before?"

"No," Allen repeated, still shaking his shaggy head. He glanced sideways, a brief darting look that took in Rowena's concerned face. "There's been trouble," he said stolidly, as if still reluctant to admit even that, "but we thought—Misty thought—that it was Horsemen."

Then, as if considering for the first time just how ludicrous that theory appeared in light of everything that had happened, Allen made a self-deprecating noise. "That's why she was so suspicious of you," he added needlessly.

Cloaked in the pall of smoke and darkness, Cassidy had almost forgotten how close to the camp they still stood until the sudden sound of metal clanging against metal startled her. Someone cleaning pots, she thought, willing her pulse to slow again. She could not be sure how long this opportunity to speak in private might last. Looking up into the dimly defined oval of Allen's bearded face, she said softly, "What happened out there that night, Allen—what did you see?"

That time the broad-shouldered figure did not recoil from her question, although he did not answer her immediately, either. Allen seemed to be searching for words with the same methodical urgency that a man dangling over a precipice might use to search for the handholds with which to pull himself back up from the edge. And when he did speak his deep voice was husky and harsh.

"Misty charged me with finding you again, so I rode out searching for you. But none of the villages along the way had seen any sign of you. When I got to Pointed Rock and their sheriff told me about the troubles they'd been having, I asked him about strangers. We knew the Tinkers couldn't have gotten far. I would have waited until morning, but some of the Villagers were afraid that we might lose our advantage, or that the Tinkers might reach the river before we could catch up with them." Allen paused to clear his throat, but when he continued his voice still contained the same rasp. "We split up in the woods so that if you ran we could ride in relays. I knew they'd never be able to outrun that mare of yours," he added, in a tone which almost suggested that he was counting on that very fact.

When Allen did not immediately resume speaking, Cassidy was torn between pressing him out of a sense of urgency and holding her peace out of a sense of compassion for the obvious pain he felt having to relive what he'd been through that night. While she wavered, the big man scrubbed the back of one hand almost absently over his bearded cheek and reluctantly went on.

"We had just about caught up to the second group of Villagers when it started. Screaming—the horses were screaming. Our horses began panicking; we could hardly control them, much less get them to go forward. Then it didn't really matter because those things were coming toward us."

That time when Allen paused, Cassidy was quite certain he would not go on again unless he was prodded to. He swayed slightly, like a man trying to keep his balance in a high wind. She could not relent; but because she did not want to prolong his distress, she tried to assist him.

"I know what those things did," she told him quietly. "I saw it all before I found you. Just tell me what they were—what did they look like?"

In the warm smoky balm of the summer evening air, the pain evident in Allen's very posture was obscenely out of place, like the repellent sight of one of those foul black things hanging from the limb of a tree. But he looked directly at Cassidy, unflinching and unblinking. "They looked deformed," he said, "like things that couldn't be alive because nothing could be that grotesquely put together and still live. They were like nothing real." He held out both hands, spacing them about two feet apart; they were amazingly steady and did not shake. "Some of them were little things, like animals that weren't finished right. I think those were the ones with all of the teeth. But most of them were big, like great big snakes or clouds of smoke. Those were the ones that tore everything apart." He suddenly looked away from Cassidy's face, his eyes abruptly squeezing shut as if closing off the images. "That's all I remember. The little ones came after me and that's all I saw."

Driven to somehow comfort him, Cassidy was disconcerted to find herself frozen by the very strength of the compassion that so compelled her. How could she physically display her understanding of what he had gone through without further upsetting him? Fortunately for Allen, Rowena did not suffer from such ambivalence; as soon as he had given the last of his painfully horrifying description, the brunette closed the short distance between the two of them and put her arms around his big body in a supportive hug.

"I'm sorry," Cassidy said then, with utter sincerity. "But I promised those Troopers that I'd ask you what you'd seen. They've been hunting those things, but they've never gotten close enough to get a real look at them, and they said they've never seen them attack humans before. They thought that if we could take you to the Warden—"

She broke off then, because from over Rowena's shoulder Allen's shaggy head lifted, his expression a cipher in the darkness. "If I survived, you mean," he said.

"Yeah," Cassidy agreed. "If you survived."

Dropping his arms, Allen stepped back from Rowena. He seemed deliberately composed as, his face still obscured in shadow, he studied Cassidy for a moment. "You've seen those things, too," he said. It was neither a question nor an accusation, although she interpreted it as something of both.

Cassidy hesitated but only briefly. "Some of them," she admitted, "but never that close—never like that. And they never attacked me."

And then, looking up into the dusky shape of that familiar broad face, Cassidy made a decision. She had known from the moment she had first laid eyes on Allen that the sheriff would be either a major impediment or a major ally to her in her quest; she just hadn't realized that he could come to be both. She was no longer certain just where his loyalties lay, or if he would try to help or hinder them. All she could be sure of was that almost everything he had done since the night he and his fellow Villagers had rescued her from the flood, including introducing her to Rowena, had been instrumental in bringing her to that point. For that if for no other reason, she felt he deserved to know the truth.

But before Cassidy could say anything further, Allen spoke again, his voice low but matter-of-fact. "If you get to see the Warden once we reach the city, what are you going to tell him?" he asked her.

Momentarily stymied by the implication in his question, Cassidy blurted out, "Actually I was thinking more of *asking* him some things rather than telling him anything."

Allen just gave a little grunt. "You still believe in the Slow World."

"Wait a minute," Rowena interjected. "What do you mean *if* we get to see him? Why wouldn't we get to see the Warden?"

Allen shook his shaggy head, in that case a gesture more of exasperation than of negation. He looked to both of them in turn, asking, "What do you know about the Iron City?"

Deciding that candor would be the most effective course, Cassidy said, "Practically nothing; up until a couple of days ago we didn't even know that's where the Warden was."

But to Cassidy's surprise, Allen's response to her confession was thoughtful, not deprecating. "I guess I just keep thinking that as a Horseman you must know these things," he said, almost to himself. He briefly stroked the end of his beard with the tips of his fingers. "But since you were already a Horseman when you came here, you really don't know."

"Then tell us," Rowena said. "Have you ever been to the city or seen the Warden?"

Allen shook his head again. "No," he said, "but I know that it's not a safe place for strangers. People are different there. And," he added significantly, "you don't just ride in and expect to get to speak with the Warden, Horseman or not."

For the first time in well over a week, Cassidy spared a brief rueful thought for her lost fetish, the talisman Valerie had given her. Perhaps the tiny bit of horsehair, beads, and feathers had been worth more than even all of the knowledge she and Rowena possessed. But she temporarily bypassed Allen's negative assessment of the city itself and said instead, "But you must know something about the Warden—you're a sheriff. If he's the leader of all the Horsemen, then you must have had some dealings with his representatives."

Allen made a coarse sound of scorn. "He may call himself the ruler of all the eastern territories," he told them, "but that's never been of any use to us. The Troopers may serve him until death, but most of the Horsemen we have to deal with aren't Troopers, and they seem to serve only themselves. They cause more trouble than Troopers can cure."

Cassidy sensed that the direction of the conversation was beginning to veer uselessly into old enmities; she attempted to redirect Allen's attention to their own situation. "Well, those things out there—monsters, or whatever you want to call them—are going to cause more trouble than all the Horsemen put together ever could," she reminded him. "And while it's true that Rowena and I have our own reasons for wanting to see the Warden, after what happened to you out in those woods, I would think you might want to have a word with him yourself."

Cassidy could see that her words had hit home by the way the man's broad shoulders stiffened. And while Allen's antipathy toward the Horsemen and their Warden might not have lessened, it was clear that he still felt a deeply ingrained sense of duty to his village. As he looked from her to Rowena and then back again, Cassidy could read the resolve in the jut of his bearded chin.

"You know I don't understand the things you believe," he said to them both, "all this talk of Memories and the Slow World. But I don't doubt that you believe it." He paused, his lips compressing for a moment beneath the rusty-colored swag of his mustache. "I don't understand what happened in that woods, either," he continued, his voice lowered to a gruff rasp, "but not understanding it doesn't make it any less real." He stirred slightly, shifting his aching muscles as he drew himself up to his full height. "Troopers are fond of swearing on their blood; well, I'll not swear any Horseman's oath, but I will promise you this: I'll go with you both to the Iron City—to the Warden, too, if he'll see us. I'll tell him everything that I've seen." His shaggy head canted then, taking in both of them again. "And I promise that I'll help you in any way that I can."

As Cassidy stood there in that smoke-tinged darkness, looking up at the broad outline of Allen's resolutely erect body, she thought that they could hardly have asked the man for anything more.

* * *

Later that night after they had crawled into their bedrolls beneath the A-shaped shelter of their little tent, Cassidy silently debated the wisdom of recounting to Rowena her conversation with Click. Allen had already imparted to them essentially the same warning about the Iron City as the Tinker had given her; and Cassidy questioned the wisdom of letting Rowena know that Click had seen through her cover story. She wasn't comfortable about keeping information from the brunette, especially after their recent discussion about monsters. But she rationalized her decision to say nothing by telling herself that it would be far easier for Rowena to continue to act normally among the Tinkers if she didn't realize how much of the truth Click really knew.

Cassidy dreamed again that night. Surprisingly, it was not a nightmare. She dreamed that she was riding Dragonfly, loping easily along a broad path through the forest. In the way of dreams, they didn't seem to actually be going anywhere, but that was of no concern to her. Someone was riding double with her on the horse, but Cassidy didn't know who it was, and she either couldn't turn to see or simply didn't even try to. The fact that she didn't know who it was didn't upset her, however, and she was content to just keep riding on.

In the dream Cassidy merely thought to herself, *When we get to the city I will know who it is.*

The next day was hot and humid, grown uncomfortably muggy long before the sun had climbed even halfway up into the cloudless sky. All of the Tinkers seemed especially eager to break camp, as if they were in a hurry to dispense with what very well might prove to be their last day of travel on the river. Out on the water, the breezeless air seemed particularly cloying and clouds of insects hung over the smooth greenish surface like a shifting veil of living fog. On the bank along the pull path the gray mare frequently dove into the nearby clumps of brush to help dislodge the more persistent of the biting flies.

"Coastal weather," Willie grumbled as he poked around the periphery of the raft, checking the security of the ropes that anchored their cargo.

At the tiller Cassidy briefly scanned the flat brilliance of the midmorning sky. Rowena had stayed on the passenger raft with Allen and most of the other Tinkers, so Cassidy and Willie rode alone. Cassidy enjoyed the big canvasworker's company, and she was pleasantly surprised that he had offered her the control of the raft while he prepared for the run down the rapids. The helm's wooden haft was smooth and worn beneath her hand, and the blocky craft slid placidly along after the lead raft.

In response to Willie's comment about the weather, Cassidy offered, "Mitz said there's a front coming through."

Bent over to tuck in the edge of a canvas tarp, Willie replied without glancing up from his task. "In a day or two maybe, but I intend to be under my own roof again by then."

Watching the big man methodically test another knot, Cassidy asked with deliberate ingenuousness, "Just where is your house, Willie? In the Iron City?"

In the muggy heat the perspiration had already glossed Willie's broad forehead with a pebbly cap of glistening droplets, and the bulging muscles of his bare forearms were sleek with sweat. He made a deprecating sound at Cassidy's query. "No one with any sense lives in the city," he said.

Reminding herself to look forward to align the raft's prow, Cassidy made a minute adjustment on the tiller before she went on. "But the Warden lives there," she pointed out.

Willie was tugging at one of the ropes where it had been secured to a metal cleat on the raft's deck; he did not look up as he said, "Well, I don't happen to credit the Warden with much sense. Besides, his compound is well out of the city."

Cassidy had grown increasingly puzzled by those people's attitude toward "the ruler of all the eastern territories." After Allen's scornful remarks the night before, Willie's blunt assessment seemed particularly disparaging. Were the Horsemen the only ones who had any respect for the Warden? Click had been civil toward the Troopers outside Pointed Rock, but Cassidy had to admit that the Tinker leader was the one who had seemed the most skeptical of all of what went on in the Iron City.

"So you don't live in the city then?" she persisted, swatting at a whining mosquito.

Willie had made his way to the front of the raft and was using the toe of one boot to poke at the thick wooden chock blocks that braced the big wheels of his cart. He looked over at Cassidy then, mild amusement evident on the smooth surface of his sunburned and perspiring face.

"I take it you've never been to the city before," he said.

"No," Cassidy admitted, too curious to dissemble.

"It's a foul place, Cassidy," Willie said, wiping the back of one huge hand across his streaming forehead. "No one lives there by preference." He began to count off on his thick stubby fingers. "There's the workers from the factories and foundries and mills; the gangs and thieves who are too ignorant or lazy to earn an honest living; the Troopers that are assigned there; and, of course, the Warden's followers."

With her recently enhanced memory of a far more sophisticated technology, Cassidy had at least a vague impression of the kind of place Willie was describing, even if she still didn't remember any specific cities from her own world. She had already deduced that the Iron City must have been the local center for smelting and the refinement of other crude materials. All of the metal and glass and other manufactured goods she had seen in that world must have come from somewhere far more advanced than the simple farming villages in the hills. But she still was puzzled by Willie's patent scorn.

"Most of us live outside the city limits," Willie continued, leaning back against the wheel of the tethered cart, "with the other craftsmen and tradespeople in the southern enclave beyond the marsh bridge." Suddenly he spat, the stream of saliva arcing over the edge of the raft to land soundlessly in the river's smooth green water. "That's still a sight closer than I'd prefer," he concluded, "but a man's got to be near his sources if he hopes to practice a craft, I guess."

Cassidy was still considering his statement, her gaze idly drifting out over the gnat-covered water, when her eyes caught sight of something on the river's bank that nearly made her lose hold of the tiller. She jumped up from the box she'd been sitting on to pilot the raft and pointed out across the river.

"Willie, look! What the hell is that?" she exclaimed.

Willie looked in the direction that Cassidy had indicated, but he gave the riverbank only a cursory glance. "That?" he said. "That's just some Woodsman's idea of a little joke."

Staring harder as their raft slowly glided past, Cassidy could then see that Willie had been right. What had first appeared to her to be three people—three *bodies*, Cassidy amended grimly—suspended from the high limb of a cottonwood tree, hanging by their necks on ropes out over the water, proved upon closer inspection to be merely three dummies: old clothing stuffed with leaves and dead grass to mimic the human form, like three ghoulish scarecrows.

"Some joke," Cassidy muttered darkly. *I wonder if that's what they want the clothes for?*

"The Woodsmen have an odd sense of humor," Willie said, coming back to reclaim the tiller, which Cassidy gladly relinquished to him. As he dropped down onto the wooden crate, he added, "There are far worse things than a few Woodsman's amusements along this river."

Wonderful, Cassidy thought glumly as she automatically scanned the adjacent mule path for sight of her mare. But the horse, seemingly oblivious to the trio of macabre fabrications that dangled overhead, was still ambling placidly along the path, her long tail swishing busily.

It was less than an hour later when they reached the next set of rapids. Willie had explained the day before that the last two drops in the river occurred close together, so that the Tinkers basically considered both sets of rapids as one extended run. And although no one, least of all Willie, seemed overtly anxious about navigating those last two sets, Cassidy had noted that during the course of the morning the big man hadn't been the only Tinker double-checking the security of their raft's load.

As several of the other vessels tacked sideways, delaying a bit to allow the raft carrying Click, Bonnie, and Moira to assume the lead again, Cassidy brushed the gnats out of her eyes and contemplated what she could see of the river ahead of them. Although the water surrounding their raft still looked calm and almost stagnant she could see where the river narrowed, and the first drop was at least deep enough to make the greenish plane of the surface of the water seem simply to vanish at the mouth of the rapids. But if the river proved a little "rambunctious" and she got splashed, Cassidy figured that wouldn't necessarily be the most unwelcome thing on such a hot sticky day.

Upstream, the lead raft nosed into the current and was suddenly swept past and into the rapids. The raft and its passengers and cargo rose high enough above the surface of the water not to completely disappear from her line of sight, the way the surface of the river seemed to; but Cassidy was still surprised at just how swiftly the current created by the drop in the river could carry the blocky craft. Tacking sideways, Willie managed to hold their raft back as, one by one, the other vessels headed into the rapidly flowing water and were propelled through the rapids. When he finally eased off on the tiller and allowed the prow of the raft to slip into the center of the river, they were the last vessel in line.

Even as the current caught them and the raft shot forward, Cassidy could see the first raft a few hundred feet ahead of them, gliding calmly where the river's surface had leveled off again in the lull between the two sets of rapids. Their own trip down the first drop was so short and swift that she didn't have enough time to consider anything else. The high water level in the river had made the run both faster and smoother than it might have been in a drier year. Within moments their own raft had joined the others that were sailing smoothly on the slower water. Cassidy realized that she hadn't even gotten a single drop of spray on her.

Directly downstream the river appeared to take a bend to the left. At first Cassidy thought that it must be some kind of an optical illusion, however, for she could clearly see by the tall growth of the trees on either bank that yet farther down the river its course definitely veered to the right again. It took her a few moments and some study to realize that the second set of rapids was a long elliptical curve.

"This last one's the trickiest," Willie said unnecessarily, calmly tending his tiller.

No shit! Cassidy thought as she watched the lead raft abruptly shoot forward again, caught in the current of the second drop. Both the sudden acceleration and the speed at which the vessel moved surprised Cassidy, since from what she could see of the river's surface, the raft hadn't appeared to have been close enough yet to the drop for the current to have been that swift or strong. But appearances aside, there was no mistaking the powerful surge of the ungainly wooden craft as it raced into the rapids.

The next raft in line, piloted by Tad, was already being pulled into the current as the first raft swung around the descending curve in the river. From the speed at which the first vessel was being borne downstream it could have been as light and insubstantial as a leaf floating on the water, but the manner in which the raft rode the river was anything but delicate. Cassidy watched anxiously as the stout wooden craft was literally tossed, bucking and rolling, down the long chute of water.

At the lead raft's tiller Click stood braced, rocking with every pitch and yaw of the raft's plank deck. Bonnie and Moira clung to the ropes that secured their cargo as sprays of water sloshed over the side rails of the raft and soaked their clothing. The raft bobbed wildly, its blunt square prow plowing down into the roiling greenish water and then shooting back upward again as the stern of the craft dipped down. Watching the dark-haired man wrestle for control of the helm, Cassidy was glad to have a man of Willie's heft at the tiller of their raft.

By then Tad's raft had been caught up in the rapids, as well, enduring the same rocking and buffeting as the first craft. But Tad's task seemed even more difficult because of the nature of his raft's cargo. The added weight and bulk of such items as his forge cart and much of Ben's and Henry's supplies made the second raft ride lower in the water. In the turmoil of the rapids the extra draw seemed to give fresh encouragement to the river's surging current, and the vessel wallowed dramatically. The anchoring ropes strained and for a few seconds Cassidy was certain that the top-heavy forge cart was going to break free on the tilting deck. But Teddy and Ben managed to keep the load secured as a wave of spray washed over them and the raft shot ahead into the lower rapids.

The third raft carried Wanda at the tiller. She had tacked back and forth across the river, fighting the increasing current for as long as she was able, to give Tad more room to get out of her way. But when her vessel had been drawn close enough to the mouth of the rapids, she no longer had any choice and she had to turn her prow into the current to avoid losing control. The rapids took the third raft with as much alacrity as it had the first two. Cassidy was glad that the cargo on that raft was composed mainly of the smaller, less bulky items, centered well and tightly lashed to the deck. Not that she doubted Wanda's piloting skills; the plump woman had already proven to be one of the Tinkers' most adept rafters. But her crew consisted of Jimmy and Sheila, and neither of them would have been strong enough to have held down a load of freight the size that Tad's raft was carrying.

Cassidy was relieved to see that for all of its uncontrolled rowdiness, the lead raft's ride down the rapids was finally coming to a more peaceful end. She was still looking downstream when a sound from Willie made her gaze jerk back toward the other rafts. It hadn't been an exclamation or even a word, but Cassidy instantly understood the burly man's reaction. Halfway down the roiling descent of water, Wanda's raft was surging up out of the river like a fish leaping from the water.

Stupefied, Cassidy watched as the entire vessel seemed to rise up out of the rapids, water streaming from its wooden deck and sides, almost as if its keel had ridden up onto some kind of submerged ramp that had then launched the raft up and out of the river. An added burst of acceleration propelled the craft forward, shooting it ahead into the sweeping current. At the helm Wanda hung onto the tiller, fighting not only for control of the rudder but also to keep from being thrown over the side.

As the raft plunged back into the river, sending water surging in all directions in a tremendous wave from beneath its boxy hull, the rapids snatched it once more. The whirling current rocked the raft from side to side, and Wanda had to throw all of her strength into steadying the tiller. For a few moments the lurching vessel seemed to straighten itself. Then the wooden craft shuddered so hard that Cassidy could see the stacks of cargo actually shift, and then the prow of the raft was swinging around. Out of control, the raft began to spin down the rapids.

Cassidy watched helplessly as the fourth raft, the one carrying Allen and Rowena and most of the other Tinkers, was sucked into the rushing current at the top of the rapids. At its helm Carlotta had delayed the raft as long as she had been able, hoping to give Wanda more room to maneuver. But it had been Wanda's raft and not Carlotta's whose course had been interrupted, and so when the passenger raft entered the rapids and quickly lurched forward it began to gain on the preceding craft—which was still whirling helplessly in the churning current.

With the distance between Wanda's disabled craft and the passenger raft closing dangerously, Willie was finally forced to straighten his rudder and turn their raft into the rapids, as well. Cassidy dropped to the deck and grabbed hold of the cargo lines as the surging water made the deck drop from beneath her. A curtain of spray broke over the rail and hit her full in the face as she struggled to see ahead to the other rafts. Somehow the water didn't feel as refreshing as she'd thought it might.

Blinking and coughing, Cassidy looked down the long whirling chute of water. Tad had finally piloted the second raft clear of the rapids; it was steadily drifting toward Click's lead raft in the calmer water below. But Wanda's raft still spun dizzily, completely out of control, as Jimmy and Sheila clung desperately to the lines and water poured over the deck.

Carlotta's raft had nearly overtaken Wanda's; in fact, for a moment it even looked as if the fourth craft were about to pass the disabled third one. But then as Cassidy watched in dismay, the spinning cargo raft spun around and collided with the passenger raft as that vessel came abreast of it. The impact was somewhat blunted both by the rotation of the one raft and the relatively equal speed of the two vessels, but it still was enough to jolt the passenger raft abruptly sideways. And as the wooden deck shifted rudely beneath them, several people on board went slewing over the side rail and into the roiling rapids.

"Rowena!" Cassidy cried, feeling the deck of their own raft buck beneath her as Willie grappled for control of the rudder.

The brunette had been one of the people swept from the passenger raft. Bounding and bucking, their own raft was drawing perilously near to the two that had collided. Straining to see past the nauseating lurch of the deck planks, Cassidy saw at least three other people tumbling down the river in the drop of greenish water: Mitz, Old Paul, and Allen.

"Cassidy!" Willie bellowed at her. "Just stay there—hang on!"

Until the big man shouted at her, Cassidy hadn't even realized that she had already begun to crawl forward toward the side rail. Hesitating, she looked back over the pitching deck to where Willie stood braced, his soaking clothing plastered to his broad body as he clutched the wooden tiller in both hamlike hands.

"No—don't!" he commanded her. "We can get past!"

Willie had accurately anticipated what Cassidy had been about to do, but he had misinterpreted the reason. Even Cassidy herself had not realized until that moment why she was about to go over the rail. Their raft still raced forward toward the two craft that were jostling roughly together right ahead of them. Just when another collision seemed inevitable, Willie hauled hard about on the tiller handle, wrenching the rudder to the side. Caught in the powerful sweep of the current, the raft did not respond promptly or dramatically, but it did respond. And as the bounding craft dodged clumsily around the two rafts ahead of it, Cassidy released her hold on the cargo line and dropped over the rail into the river.

Her first thought as she sank beneath the surface of the rushing green water was that the trip down the rapids might well prove to be a smoother ride without benefit of a raft. But when she tried to right herself in the turbulent current, she discovered that the river had its own ideas about just where she could go. Gasping for air, Cassidy lifted her head out of the water and quickly oriented herself. To her relief she found that she was safely clear of Willie's raft and that the other two rafts still bumping against each other ahead of her had left Rowena and the others in their wake.

"Rowena!" Cassidy shouted, settling for just being able to keep her head above water as the current whisked her along.

She was relieved to see that the four people whom she had joined in the water all seemed unharmed. Considering their ages, Mitz and Old Paul were doing a commendable job of treading water, even if that also required just letting the rapids carry them along. And Rowena had proven to be a strong swimmer. She had gone immediately to Allen's side and had, over his obvious protests, grasped his shirt collar in one hand while she used a modified backstroke to tow the injured man along after her.

Once another collision had been averted, Willie had redirected his raft, angling the craft away from the rock-studded banks of the rapids and back into the center of the stream. As he pulled on the tiller he shouted something to Cassidy. Relaxing slightly once she was relatively certain that they all would be able to ride out the rest of the rapids, Cassidy twisted around in the water to face Willie as his raft pulled away.

"You didn't have to jump off!" Willie shouted at her. "Be careful!"

Yeah—fine time to think of that! Cassidy thought as her attention returned to the other swimmers.

Far heavier and yet at the same time more buoyant than the five swimmers, the three rafts began to pull away more rapidly down the river, with the passenger raft and Wanda's renegade vessel still running side by side. Once the rafts had pulled away, the swimmers had the river to themselves. Or at least so Cassidy had thought.

She was steadying herself, riding on the swift current while she kept an anxious eye on the other people ahead of her, when she first felt something brush against the soles of her waterlogged boots. Initially she assumed that she had touched bottom and that the object had been a big rock. But instead of being something she just passed over, the pressure beneath her feet persisted. Something bigger, then, she thought, not particularly alarmed. She even tried to use the object as a launching point from which to propel herself farther ahead through the water. When her feet touched it again she decided it must definitely be something big—maybe a ridge of rock in the river-bed or even a submerged log.

. . . That was no log . . .

The instant the memory hit her, the thing beneath Cassidy simultaneously rose, forcing her whole body upward. As she automatically bent her legs against its pressure, she found herself actually kneeling on the vast firm surface that then shuddered beneath her, racing along just beneath the surface of the rapids.

Cassidy wanted to shout, to cry out some warning to the four people who still floated ahead of her, helplessly borne along by the river's powerful current. But even as her shoulders broke the surface of the water and she leaned forward, her hands plunging down in a purely reflex motion to try to keep her balance, she could not seem to force a single word from her mouth. Then as the greenish water tore at her outstretched arms, Cassidy's hands clutched at the thing that carried her, her fingers grappling frantically at the rough sandpapery surface of something that was both huge and sinuous and that slid through the turbulent river as smoothly as a shadow.

"Oh, my God—look out!" Cassidy cried out.

Several yards ahead of her in the water, where the four other swimmers rode the swirling crest of the current, heads snapped around at her warning. Then their eyes widened in surprise.

"Holy shit!" Rowena exclaimed. "Cassidy, look out!"

"Get down!" Old Paul shouted.

But the huge surging thing that had risen beneath Cassidy's body and upon which she had ridden like a Horseman upon a mount had suddenly dropped away from under her, abruptly plunging her back into the river and so startling her that for a few seconds she could not comprehend why everyone else was still looking back toward her in such alarm. Old Paul's emphatic instruction further baffled her; she was already submerged in the river again—how much farther *down* could she get? She didn't want to get down, she wanted to get *out*.

She would have told the old fart that, too; in fact, the words were nearly launching off her tongue when she heard someone else shouting—someone *behind* her. Then Cassidy's own head snapped around and she looked back upstream, practically right into the prow of the rapidly approaching sixth raft.

"Dive! Get down out of the way!" Ben shouted from the deck of the last of the Tinkers' craft.

It was too late to try to evade the raft, although Cassidy

hoped that Rowena and the others ahead of her would have time to. Cassidy took the only option that was open to her. After filling her lungs with one last desperate gasp of air, she doubled over and plunged deeper into the churning green water. As she kicked toward the bottom she wasn't concerned about drowning; she wasn't even concerned about just what might lie beneath the surface of the rapids. She was concerned about only one thing, and that was being run over by Ben's raft.

The deep current snatched at Cassidy, twisting her body as she struggled to reach the bottom. Then the greenish haze of water all around her suddenly darkened to a hueless murk and she felt something hard smack her painfully in the ankle. The blow spun her farther around and she temporarily lost her orientation. But before she could try again to drop deeper, the water overhead abruptly brightened. The raft had passed over her.

Lungs burning, Cassidy let herself shoot back to the surface. She came up only a few yards behind the stern of Ben's raft, but that was far enough. Gasping and sputtering, she shook her wet hair back out of her eyes and hastily scanned the whirling surface of the rapids for the others who had been in the water with her. To her considerable relief she saw that all four appeared unharmed, riding the current off to the side of the last raft as it sped past them down the river.

"You idiot!" Rowena shouted at her, still hanging onto Allen's collar—an assist that the injured man no longer appeared to be resisting. "Are you all right?"

Right on both counts, Cassidy thought, but she gave Rowena and the others a quick wave and shouted back, "Yeah, it went right over me." She didn't bother to mention that some part of the raft, either its keel or the hull itself, had whacked her in the ankle in the process.

As the five of them were pulled along the rest of the way down the rapids behind the last of the rafts, Cassidy swam to catch up with the others. Her ankle throbbed, but she was certain the injury would prove to be more painful than debilitating. She was floating alongside Mitz and Old Paul when the river finally leveled out again and the current spat them out into the broader calmer waters below the rapids.

Cassidy watched as Rowena towed Allen with all of the sustained strength and skill of a lifeguard. She was relieved and grateful that the sheriff had had such a competent companion when he'd gone over the edge of the raft, and she felt somewhat embarrassed that she'd thought it necessary for her to go to his aid, as well. She had jumped into the water without really thinking, and all she had accomplished was nearly getting herself killed.

Oh, and don't forget that nice little ride on the water monster, Cassidy, her nagging little inner voice reminded her.

Shaking that thought away along with the annoying wet strands of hair that were plastered over her forehead, Cassidy followed Mitz and Old Paul as the two elder Tinkers paddled doggedly toward the nearest raft. Once she was no longer being bounced along down the rapids, her saturated clothing and boots felt like an anchor, making swimming an increasing effort. Getting out of the water again was becoming a very appealing idea.

On the quiet water downstream of the rapids, the six rafts were converging again, herded together like unruly sheep that had made a rebellious but unsuccessful bolt for their freedom. While Teddy, Toby, Bonnie, and the others grappled with the tangled tether lines and wrested skewed cargo back into place on the dripping decks, Click leapt from raft to raft, assessing the damage. Carlotta leaned over the stern of the passenger raft, encouraging Mitz forward until she could grasp the old seamstress's arm.

Cassidy swam over to Willie's raft, willingly accepting the assistance of the muscular arm that reached over the rail for her. As the big man pulled her from the river like a drowned rat, Cassidy glanced over to be certain that the others who had also taken a dunking were being safely hauled from the water.

"You didn't have to jump," Willie repeated, his growling tone a poor cover for his obvious concern. He took in her bedraggled appearance with a grunt. "We weren't likely to hit them," he went on, "and even if we had, you still would've been a sight safer on the raft than in the water."

Cassidy just shrugged meekly and said nothing. It seemed easier to just let them all think that she had acted out of fearful alarm rather than to admit the truth: that she had jumped into the river because she wasn't sure if the others knew how to swim, and she had been afraid that they would drown. In retrospect that bravado looked not only needless but a bit presumptuous, as well, so she would rather have had Willie and the other Tinkers just think that she had acted impulsively out of fear.

On the passenger raft Click was bending over Allen, speaking quietly to the larger man where he sat on a wooden crate with Carlotta and Chrissy hovering anxiously around him. Rowena was already grinning with the good humor that is particular to the survivor of a disaster as she and Mitz compared the sodden condition of their clothing and teased Old Paul about his equally disreputable appearance. Before Cassidy looked away again Click's head suddenly lifted and he turned, his eyes meeting hers. It was the briefest of glances, but somehow its directness made Cassidy feel very uncomfortable, as if she had in some way been responsible for the near disaster that had just occurred on the lower rapids. She dropped her gaze and was looking down at her own dripping clothing when Shelia called from one of the other rafts.

"Click? Better have a look at this," the cobbler called.

As the Tinkers' leader turned to make his way back across the checkerboard of rafts, hopping nimbly from deck to deck, Cassidy got a better look at exactly what it was that Sheila waved aloft. At first glance it had looked like a broken scrap of timber, but then Cassidy noticed the metal fittings still bolted to the somehow familiar wooden shape.

"No wonder I lost control of the raft," Wanda said, gesturing at the object that Sheila held out for Click's inspection. "The rudder's been snapped clean off the tiller."

Beside Cassidy, Willie made another grunting sound. "Must've been an old snag she hit," he said, "or a rock shelf. No wonder we had so much excitement back there."

Cassidy heard Willie's words but they really didn't register with her. Her eyes were no longer on Wanda's once-renegade raft. The moment she had identified the sheared-off stub of the craft's rudder, her gaze had shot back over to the deck of the smoothly gliding passenger raft. There two complicit pairs of eyes moved to meet hers: Rowena's wide with sudden comprehension, and Allen's narrowed stoically.

Willie could blame rocks or submerged stumps all he liked; in fact, Cassidy would have preferred it if the other Tinkers had unanimously agreed with his assessment of why Wanda's rudder had snapped. But Cassidy still remembered the way the blocky wooden raft had suddenly surged forward before it had been jolted and lost control; and she also still remembered the powerful lift of that rough and gritty surface that had risen beneath her knees.

She had seen the raw grain of the clean break in the wooden shaft of the rudder, and she knew that nothing had simply snapped it. The rudder's shaft had been bitten off.

Chapter 11 ←▦

Once Tad and Teddy had made the necessary temporary repairs to the damaged rudder on Wanda's raft, they continued down the river. Despite a generous drenching, none of the cargo had been permanently damaged. After Bonnie had outfitted with dry clothing Cassidy and the others who had taken an unwitting swim, it would have been difficult to tell that anything untoward had happened on the rapids. To Cassidy's relief there was no further discussion of her own rash actions, and even Rowena's only comment was wryly self-deprecating.

As they changed out of their wet clothes, the brunette had confided to Cassidy, "Remember how I said these rafts were probably a lot safer than riding your horse? Well, forget it—the horse is looking better and better all the time!"

In fact, the gray mare was probably the one most unperturbed by the unexpected turmoil on the rapids. The horse had been able to trot along the rutted mule path, easily keeping up with the runaway rafts. Watching the mare amble along the riverbank, pausing only to crop at twigs and branch tips, Cassidy found herself wishing she had decided to ride the horse rather than the rafts that final day.

Below the rapids the river gradually broadened, although the current still remained slightly faster than it had been upstream. The string of rafts glided smoothly over the shimmering surface of the translucent water, while clouds of gnats and other insects boiled up into the muggy air. The flat yellow disc of the summer sun began its slow descent across the cloudless afternoon sky as Cassidy sprawled out on a bale of hides on the deck of Willie's raft. She was lost in that muzzy haze between fatigue and dozing when they encountered their first sight of other river traffic.

"Timbermen," Willie said, gesturing toward the three long craft that had appeared ahead of them sailing slowly along near the far bank of the river.

Batting insects away from her face—if not for the consistent annoyance of the bugs she probably would have fallen asleep on the hides—Cassidy studied the trio of long crude vessels. They were so heavily laden with logs that it was difficult to tell just what they looked like beneath their cargo, but the bargelike craft appeared to be larger, more elongated versions of the Tinkers' type of raft. The three vessels were linked together like pack mules by short lengths of stout chain, and there didn't even appear to be anyone riding on the middle one. On the leading raft two men and a woman, all of them bare-chested and perspiring in the heat, manned long poles with which they appeared to be directing the craft. They seemed oblivious to the swarming insects that had been irritating Cassidy. The third raft was piled so high with neatly stacked logs that it must have nearly been wallowing on the river bottom. At its stern two more shirtless men were stationed at crude but effective rudders.

"Are they going down to the city, too?" Cassidy asked Willie.

"Likely," Willie said.

Cassidy was curious and would have asked him more about the Timbermen; but within a few minutes the lighter, faster Tinker rafts had passed by the heavy timber carriers. And after that they began to encounter other types of river traffic. Other rafts appeared, some smaller and more sophisticated than their own and carrying passengers or small loads of cargo. But many of the rafts were even cruder and most were much larger, piled with a variety of raw materials from the rural outlands. In addition to logs Cassidy noted stacks of baled hay and straw, huge piles of bagged grain and cob corn, and even pens of live chickens and pigs. To Cassidy, the people who piloted those cargo rafts looked more like the somber and single-minded Villagers she remembered from Double Creek than traders like the eclectic Tinkers. There was also the occasional small boat, most nothing more elaborate than a rowboat, carrying one or more passengers and perhaps a small cache of cargo.

A few of the people on the other craft returned waves of greeting as their vessels met or passed, but for the most part the men and women they encountered on the river seemed more interested in tending their vessels than in exchanging pleasantries.

As the river grew ever wider and the other craft more numerous, the Tinkers broke from their single-file pattern and formed their rafts into a loose bunch. Rowena even forsook the passenger raft and took advantage of Willie's invitation to hop over when the two vessels briefly paced each other. There she sat with Cassidy on the bale of hides, taking in the changing sights with increasing interest. She was as fascinated as was Cassidy with the variety of river craft and the people who piloted them.

"What's that up there?" Rowena asked Willie at one point, indicating over the prow of the raft.

Cassidy followed the direction of Rowena's raised arm and picked out some sort of large structures downstream on the riverbank. From that distance she couldn't make out any details, but a big column of thick grayish smoke rose up into the calm and heavy air above one of the buildings.

"Lumber mill," Willie said, giving his tiller a little nudge.

Used to the beefy man's terse answers, Cassidy merely studied the site more closely as the current carried them nearer. The marshy forest that had covered the surrounding land was bluntly interrupted by the mill's sprawl. She could also see several of the huge timber carriers moored along the river at a wharf constructed of rough planking.

Cassidy's gaze automatically swept back and scanned the bank parallel to their raft for the familiar form of the gray mare. From that distance the horse was a miniature figure, stepping along the mule path like a silver toy against the darker backdrop of the wooded bogs. For the first time in days Cassidy began to feel some anxiety about being separated from the horse. She was beginning seriously to consider swimming back to shore and joining the mare when a reassuring voice from across the opposite side of Willie's raft jolted her out of her distracted musings.

"You needn't worry about your horse coming to any harm," Click said from the helm of his raft as it paced Willie's. It was as if he had read the troubled thought directly from her mind. As Cassidy and Rowena both turned to face him, Click went on. "The pull path runs directly to the harbor."

Reluctant to concede her anxiety, Cassidy still felt compelled to ask him, "What about all the people between here and there?"

But Click gently shook his head. "No one would ever interfere with a horse; not here under the Warden's jurisdiction." He paused for a moment, lightly stroking the polished haft of the tiller that lay beneath one callused hand. In the humid air his dark hair had become a riot of curls and his tanned skin gleamed with perspiration. And when he looked over across the bulk of Willie's cargo at her, it seemed as if he had indeed read Cassidy's mind. "You, on the other hand, might attract some unwelcomed attention if you were to go ashore here," he advised her. "It's best to let the mare go on alone." He winked. "That way we won't have to worry about either one of you."

Not completely mollified by Click's assurances, Cassidy looked back toward the bank where the mare had paused to rip up some grass. *If there's any "interference" with her,* she thought resolutely, *I'll be over the side of this raft too quickly for anyone to have to worry about me.*

As both the afternoon and the little fleet of rafts proceeded, Rowena and Cassidy saw plenty of new sights as they neared the city. After the lumber mill other industrial structures became more common along both banks of the river. Willie laconically pointed out grist mills, tanneries, foundries, and other types of processing facilities. Cassidy thought the big man made a peculiar but effective tour guide for their first trip down the Long River.

As they glided closer to the city, the entire nature of the river changed. With the increase in other craft and the industries that lined the banks, Cassidy began to notice a distinct decrease in the greenish translucence of the water, and there was a persistent sort of sour odor to the air. She had never really thought about it when they had been out in the isolation of the countryside; she had always just taken the purity of the air and water for granted. By contrast, the people and commerce of the Iron City seemed to be taking their toll on the surrounding environment. Somehow Cassidy had just assumed that pollution was a concept unique to her own world. But the naïveté of that notion was brought home to her with a graphic bluntness when Rowena made a face and pointed over the raft's rail side, and Cassidy looked down to see the pale and partially decomposed carcass of a dead chicken floating by with other debris on the opaque water.

As the sun slid lower into the western sky, long shadows reached out across the river's murky surface. The air was still uncomfortably hot and humid and the cloudless sky had turned the color of one of Henry's copper pots. Mosquitoes multiplied, undeterred by the distinctly unpleasant smell that hung over the water.

The city itself was visible from some distance off, partially by virtue of its size and location and partially by virtue of the dingy smoke that rose up over the sprawling harbor district. Although she hadn't ceased worrying about her horse, Cassidy had to admit that Click's assessment of the situation on the bank seemed to have proven true. The pull path did indeed run essentially uninterrupted along the entire northern bank of the river, even past the worst of the mills and smelters and other effluvious enterprises of industry. And the mare had passed quite undisturbed along that path, although several times she had attracted curious glances from workers along the river. The few teams of mules she had encountered seemed far more interested in her than she had been in them. After seeing what the river water had begun to look like, Cassidy would have been less than enthused about having to take another swim in it.

"There're the docks," Willie told them, pointing toward a point downstream along the river's northern bank. The extensively developed and visibly congested area could hardly have been overlooked, or mistaken for anything else. And farther yet downstream, almost lost in the murky haze of sunset where the river's mouth opened widely upon a vast pewter-colored stretch of water, lay the Gray Sea.

Standing beside Rowena on the raft's plank deck as the setting sun painted them both an unflattering shade of ocher, Cassidy got her first real look at their portal into the Iron City. Even though it was evening, the large and disorderly sprawl of wooden wharfs and jetties was crowded with activity. There must have been at least a hundred other vessels arriving, departing, or moored for unloading at the complex of docks. To her astonishment, Cassidy noted several huge stern paddle-wheelers, boats that from their towering black smokestacks and the clouds of gritty smoke that belched from them could only have been steam powered. Artificial light spilled from the wide doors and square windows of most of the big warehouselike buildings that were stacked like giant crates on the slopes leading down to the river. Everything from horse-drawn wagons, to handcarts, to burly men and women simply hoisting their loads over their shoulders was being utilized to move cargo about from the teeming network of piers to the vast buildings and the city beyond.

Cassidy exchanged a look with Rowena, seeing that her friend was also simply overwhelmed by the sheer numbers of people and the size of the settlement. It all was somehow familiar and yet so totally and incomprehensibly alien to Cassidy. For the most part, what she had been able to remember was *things*, not *places*. She knew what should be in a city and yet would not be there: cars, buses, electric lights, the drone of jet planes overhead. And yet she could not have anticipated what she saw. Her partial and imperfect memory of a world as advanced from that one as a flintstone was from a cigarette lighter had not really prepared her for the sheer visceral shock of that much humanity. After the pastoral peace of the wooded hills, the villages, and even the river, the confusion and noise and smell of the city's docks were like a large dose of some foul and unexpected medicine.

Taking over the lead again, Click slowly but precisely maneuvered his raft amid the river's other traffic, threading a path for the other Tinkers around the various incoming and outbound vessels and gradually working his way toward the periphery of the broad spread of wharfs. From that section of the docks they had a clearer view of the wide delta of the river's terminus and of the limitless expanse of sea that stretched beyond it, lacquered by the setting sun.

There were a hundred questions Cassidy would have liked to have asked Willie then, especially before she and Rowena would have to leave the sanctuary of the raft and step off into the strange new world that awaited them beyond the docks. But the relatively cumbersome nature of the raft made navigation difficult there, and the busy cross traffic on the harbor's oily waters seemed to absorb Willie totally in the task of piloting his raft along behind the others. And so Cassidy kept her silence.

As they gradually drew in closer to the docks, Cassidy could see that despite the surface appearance of disorganization with all of the activity on the wooden wharfs, there did seem to be a definite protocol to docking there. Craft like their rafts that were propelled only by the whims of the current and the skill of their helmsmen were given the right of way over boats that were artificially driven, no matter what their relative sizes. Thus even one of the massive steam-powered paddlewheelers veered aside and allowed the Tinkers' little procession to pro-

ceed ahead of it when they had entered the watery maze of
piers.

Once they had passed the outer pilings and had lost the advantage of the river's current, wharftenders came alongside the
rafts and tossed down tow ropes. With the lines securely fastened to each raft's prow, several of the half-stripped, perspiring workers acted like human barge mules to propel and guide
the Tinkers' vessels from the mouth of the harbor deeper into
the network of wharfs. Cassidy watched in fascination as the
brightly garbed men and women who commanded the traffic at
the docks coaxed the blocky rafts into the appropriate mooring
space.

Taking her lead from Willie and the other Tinkers, Cassidy
attempted not to appear inordinately interested in all of the
goings-on around them. Never mind that she had never seen
anything even remotely like it in all of that strange world; she
forced herself to assume the same detached nonchalance that
she saw all around her. Only the yapping of Bonnie's little
dogs broke the calm. But Cassidy and Rowena both still kept
scanning the docks, surreptitiously taking in the surprising variety of people and things that they saw there. If Cassidy had
thought the backward little village of Double Creek had been
a technological marvel when she had first arrived there, she
never imagined anything like the Iron City existed in that
world.

Just as she had deduced, the city was obviously the center,
at least for the region, of material refinement and available
manufacture. Almost everything there at the docks and the adjacent warehouse district, from the sheer number and variety of
people, to the amazing flotilla of water vessels, to the size and
sophistication of the buildings, reinforced Cassidy's assumption that the city was where the real material base of the whole
region lay. It was also, she had to keep reminding herself, the
place where they would find the Warden of Horses, the man
whose belief in the Memories had made him Cassidy's goal
since the day she had first heard Yolanda speak his name.

The wharftenders began mooring the rafts, tethering them in
a row along the dock with thick stained ropes, which they
deftly snubbed to the worn and heavy timber uprights. The
opaque and vaguely greasy surface of the river, as dark as yesterday's coffee in the recesses of the wharf as the evening
shadows deepened, wavered slightly beneath the hulls, causing
the rafts to bob gently against their restraints. Several of the

Tinkers were already climbing up from the vessels' decks and onto the stout planking of the pier. But Cassidy hesitated for a moment, fascinated by the sight of two lamplighters, both adolescent girls in tight-fitting shirts and trousers, as they came down the length of the wharf bearing long torch poles with which they ignited the oil lamps that were set on every dock post.

"Jeez, it really stinks around here!" Rowena said from beside her, jolting Cassidy out of her contemplation of the lamp lighting. "This is worse than that time back in the village when Paula's sausage went bad!"

Although Cassidy had been fortunate enough to have missed that culinary milestone, she nodded absently in agreement. She glanced back toward the raft's stern where Willie was fast becoming nothing more than a large blocky silhouette in the falling dusk. She assumed that some of the Tinkers would remain with the rafts until all of their cargo had been unloaded, although she saw that Moira, Chrissy, and some of the others were already starting to walk up the broad wooden pier toward the warehouses. She and Rowena didn't really have any possessions to pack up except for what few things they had earned on their journey, but Cassidy still hesitated, torn between the desire to get off the raft and find her horse and her sense of responsibility to Willie. She was scanning along the row of tethered rafts, looking for Allen's familiar form, when she was startled by a voice from directly above her on the wharf.

"Cassidy? Your mare is up by the glaziers' warehouse," Click's smooth tones assured her.

Cassidy looked up at the tall man who stood beside the raft, backdropped by the confusing clutter of the busy docks and weakly lit by the pale light of the setting sun. Click bent slightly, extending a prompting hand to her.

"Come on then," he urged quietly. "There's no need for you to stay down here on the docks."

When Cassidy didn't immediately respond to his gesture of help, Click turned slightly and helped a far more cooperative Rowena hop up from the raft's deck and onto the pier. With the brunette beside him, the dark-haired man once again leaned toward Cassidy with the same proffered hand. "Bonnie will bring your things," he added, as if that might have been the reason for her reluctance to leave.

Cassidy finally accepted Click's assist, but even as he

locked hands with her and easily tugged her upward, she asked him, "Where's Allen?"

"With Mitz and Tad," Click replied with a calm nod in the direction of the huge buildings beyond the wharfs, "right over there."

Squinting into the fading daylight, Cassidy tried to differentiate the bearded sheriff from the milling mass of other people who still crowded the docks. It was that precise stage of twilight when neither the fleeing natural light nor the freshly guttering glow from the long row of oil lanterns meant to replace it was particularly useful. And so even as Click started to walk away from the raft, trying to draw Cassidy along by the arm after him, she resisted and hung back, her eyes sweeping over the crowd of unfamiliar people.

"I want to go to the Warden," she said doggedly.

"In the morning," Click said. "Come with us to the enclave for tonight."

But Cassidy shook her head, stepping sideways to neatly lever her arm free of his hand. Click didn't try to hold her but he did take a step after her, his palms spread in a mild appeal.

"I want to see him now—tonight," Cassidy insisted, growing annoyed that she still hadn't been able to pick out Allen or even any of the other Tinkers from all of the workers teeming on the docks.

"That won't be possible," Click said, his tone remaining surprisingly even in the face of her obduracy. If he viewed Cassidy's pigheaded behavior with any irritation, no hint of that had leaked into his voice. "In the morning I'll take you to the garrison myself, and see if they'll let you speak to the captain of the Troopers. She's the only one who can grant you access to the Warden."

Once again Cassidy could not help thinking that her mission there would have been a lot easier if she still had Valerie's little token. Unsatisfied by Click's answer, she took a few more abrupt steps away from him. If she had chosen to remain logical, she would have had to admit that she had been warned. Even Allen, who had pledged to her and Rowena his total assistance, had told her that it would be difficult to get to see the Warden. She could hardly have expected Click to tell her anything different. Still, the whole situation was becoming increasing nettlesome to Cassidy. Striding on ahead of the Tinker leader and Rowena, she started briskly up the pier, dodging impatiently around brightly clad wharftenders coiling ropes, stacks of crates and sacks, and an old woman with a pushcart who seemed to be peddling something fried and spicy.

Heedless of the many people she passed, Cassidy reached into her mind for her innate link with the gray mare. The horse was indeed nearby, just as Click had assured her, and was not in any distress. As Cassidy's bootheels clattered over the wharf's wooden planking, she was forced to admit that of the two of them, the mare definitely had always had the better temperament.

Just before she reached the foot of the pier, where the stout posts and wooden planking of the wharfs gave way to a wide and lamp-lit paved lot in front of the first row of warehouses, Cassidy recognized the brilliant yellow of Mitz's shirt just ahead of her. When she slowed down to look more closely she could also see Allen, Old Paul, and several others whom she knew among the people moving there. A little abashed by her rude behavior, she glanced back over her shoulder to see that Click and Rowena were close behind her. But as she started to turn again toward the end of the wharf, a commotion on the paved lot caught her eye.

A big metal two-wheeled cart came clattering along over the pavement, propelled at a furious pace by a tall, husky, red-haired woman. Cassidy was instantly prepared to step back out of the cart's way because she could tell even at a glance that it was filled almost beyond capacity with garbage; and the woman who was pushing it gave every indication, both by her aggressive demeanor and her speed, that she was used to being given a clear path. The redhead was dressed, as were many of the wharf's occupants on that muggy evening, in what Cassidy took to be a common outfit for the city: loose-fitting cotton trousers and a tank-top sort of sleeveless upper garment of a thin and brightly patterned fabric. As the cart rumbled past her, Cassidy noticed that it was closely followed by two similarly dressed men, each of them carrying a big barrel-shaped container that looked like a wooden trash can, balanced on their beefy shoulders.

The stench that rose from the metal cart as it was wheeled past her convinced Cassidy that it contained more than just ordinary refuse; it reeked like offal. And unless she missed her guess, she was about to witness the source of one of the main causes of the water pollution in the terminal Long River. The woman pushing the cart and the two trashmen behind her were headed directly toward the nearest open mooring slot on the pier. As the burly men swept by her, sweat gleaming on the tanned skin of their bare arms, Cassidy took a wide step aside to avoid them. But even as she was moving, she pivoted around, watching them pass with eyes widened in shock.

One of the wooden barrels tilted slightly in its carrier's grip, bits of debris carelessly dribbling from its filthy lip. But Cassidy paid no notice to the little scraps that splattered onto the plank decking of the pier, no more than did the sweating trashman who pushed past her. There was only one thing Cassidy could see at that moment, something thin and deathly pale that dangled limply from the mouth of the same barrel. Something that looked like a tiny arm.

"Wait!" Cassidy had automatically spun around, and the command was out of her mouth even before she was aware that she had already taken off after the man bearing the trash barrel. But the man never slowed his pace, and so he was nearly up to the edge of the pier before Cassidy caught up with him.

The hefty redhead had already tilted her cart, dumping its load of refuse into the water of the harbor. She turned with a puzzled look on her face when she saw Cassidy grabbing for the back of her fellow trash hauler's shirt.

"Wait!" Cassidy barked again, hauling back so hard on the man's tank top that he nearly dropped the container he was carrying. He turned around to glare down at Cassidy from his superior height as she reached up to try to pull the barrel from his hands.

"What the hell?" the red-haired woman demanded irately, rounding on Cassidy as if to knock her away.

Only some outside intervention prevented the whole scene from turning into an impromptu brawl. Cassidy felt a strong arm close around her shoulders from behind, pulling her fingers free from the trashman's shirt and preventing her attempt to wrest the barrel from his grasp, even as a maddeningly calm voice said, "Here now—there's no need for that."

Freed from Cassidy's grip, the trashman took a step backward and glared at her anew, holding the filthy barrel to his chest as if it contained some valuable treasure that he had just thwarted Cassidy's attempt to steal. "What is she—crazy?" he huffed at Click. "She almost made me spill this!"

Cassidy was peripherally aware that Rowena had also come up behind them, but she didn't even spare the brunette a glance. Furious, she struggled against the implacable steel of Click's hold. "Make him dump it out!" she insisted.

The second trashman, standing off to the side, shifted his own reeking barrel on his broad shoulder and looked at the scene being played out before him as if Cassidy were speaking in some foreign language. While he and the big redhead exchanged a quizzical look, Click tried to reason with Cassidy.

"It's just garbage, Cassidy," Click said quietly, still holding her immobilized. "Let's just let—"

"It's not just garbage—there's a *baby* in there!" Cassidy exclaimed, writhing ineffectually against the arm lock Click maintained around her shoulders.

For a moment the three trash haulers just looked at each other in silent communion, their puzzled irritation plain. Then the red-haired woman shrugged and said to Cassidy, "So?"

Sudden enlightenment appeared to have visited the trashman who held the offending barrel, and he looked as if he believed he had solved the mystery of Cassidy's bizarre behavior. "What, is it still alive?" he asked her with a baffled frown. Then, before Cassidy could respond or even imagine what she was about to do, the burly man tipped the container so that part of its contents tumbled onto the worn planking of the wharf at their feet.

Cassidy's body stiffened against Click's and behind them she heard Rowena gasp as, along with an ooze of foul fluid and what looked to be the fatty trimmings from some rancid meat, the limp and grayish body of a naked infant thumped out onto the pier. Was the baby dead? Cassidy had to think so— she saw no movement in the tiny form—but she still was completely unprepared for what happened next. Bending to reach down, the trashman deftly snagged the pale body by its little feet. In the same motion he swung the baby in an arc up into the air and brought it down headfirst onto the stout planking, so hard that Cassidy heard the distinct and sickening crack of the infant's skull impacting with the wood.

"There," he said to Cassidy, flipping the maimed baby back into the barrel. "Now are you satisfied?"

For a few seconds Cassidy was simply so horrified that she was stunned into immobility. She was not jolted out of her state of shocked paralysis until Click began to pull her backward, away from the trashmen and the edge of the pier. When he attempted to move her, she began to struggle in earnest.

"Wait! That was a *baby*, you bastards!" she snarled. "A *baby*, not some piece of—"

To add to her outrage, Cassidy felt the palm of Click's hand clap firmly over her mouth, muzzling her. As she jerked and thrashed to get free of his hold, she felt Click bump into an astonished Rowena as he steadily towed Cassidy backward across the wharf.

"No—Cassidy, *no!*" he hissed fiercely in her ear, all the while dragging her away from the ugly confrontation. "Let it go!"

With a sense of desperation Cassidy noted that the whole incident had hardly attracted much notice on the wharf; perversely, she wished that it had. She *wanted* someone to have noticed the outrage—that it had been a *baby*, damn it, not just another chunk of offal! But despite her best efforts she could not break Click's powerful grip on her or even slow his determined pace as he swiftly drew her back toward the warehouse area where the other Tinkers waited. She tried to kick him in the knees, but all she succeeded in doing was tripping herself up badly enough that he ended up almost having to carry her along. And all the time he kept up a litany of softly urgent admonishments directly into her ear.

"Cassidy, behave yourself—just let it go! This isn't like one of your villages. The baby was dead; it doesn't matter now. Just calm down and—" Click broke off with a muted grunt as one of Cassidy's jabbing elbows finally connected with his chest. But he refused to release her and continued in a firm whisper, "Don't be a fool! Calm down before the wharftenders think you were trying to steal something. If you get in trouble I can't help you—I don't have any jurisdiction here."

The threat of outside interference was finally enough to compel Cassidy to cease her struggling. But even as her furious efforts ebbed and she managed to get her feet back under herself, Click still loosened his grip only with caution. By then he had dragged her well onto the paved lot in front of the first row of warehouses, where she could see Allen and the Tinkers waiting beneath one of the oil lamps, all with expressions of puzzled concern on their faces. Even Rowena, who had followed her and Click in mute submission, seemed perplexed by the ferocity of Cassidy's reaction.

As soon as she was permitted the freedom, Cassidy spun around within the corral of Click's arms. Glaring up into his face she snapped, "Take your damned hands off me, you son of a bitch!"

Behind him, Mitz started to step forward, but the slightest of nods from Click stayed the gray-haired woman. Looking down steadily into Cassidy's flushed face, Click dropped his arms and she immediately stepped back from him, as taut as an angry cat.

"I've had enough of this shit," she said, her voice amazingly level despite her fury. "Take me to the Warden—*now*."

It was Allen who intervened then, separating himself from the group of Tinkers and coming up alongside Click to face Cassidy's wrath. "Cassidy, it's not that simple." His shaggy head was bent so that even in the artificial light of the street-lamps she could see the look of gravity in his sun-colored eyes. "First you have to go to the garrison commander and request that—"

"The hell with that," she said, her tone as cold and brittle as frost. "What the hell kind of place is this anyway? Take me tonight—or I'll go by myself. I don't care how I get there."

"But the Warden won't see you if—" Allen started. But Cassidy ruthlessly cut him off.

"He'll damn well see me," she said, "if he wants the answers."

For a few moments neither Allen nor Click responded. Then the sheriff just shook his bearded head and began to turn away from Cassidy.

"You bastard—you promised that you'd help us!" Cassidy threw after him hotly. She was not surprised to find that she'd clenched her hands so tightly into fists that her fingernails were cutting into her own flesh.

Allen turned back toward her, those solemn eyes unblinking in his weary face. "Cassidy, I don't know how I can."

But to Cassidy's considerable surprise, it was Click who acquiesced. Giving Allen a brief but comradely pat on the shoulder, the dark-haired Tinker stepped forward again to look down squarely and steadily into Cassidy's angry eyes.

"Call your horse," Click said. "I'll take you to your Warden."

Of her first journey through the rank and dimly lit streets of the Iron City Cassidy would later remember very little. Astride the gray mare, with Allen mounted behind her, she grimly followed Click as he and Rowena preceded the horse on foot up one of the potholed thoroughfares that led away from the docks. The mare's hooves clopped hollowly on the uneven pavement, the sound rebounding off the dark canyon of the warehouses' walls. Her spine still rigid with anger, Cassidy just looked straight ahead at the outline of Click's shaggy head, her mind far too agitated to register most of what they passed. There was only one image that persisted in her thoughts, the scene playing and replaying itself over and over again as she rode into the unfamiliar warren of filthy streets. And that image—the obscenity of the sweating trashman dashing the infant's skull against the pier—goaded her beyond all reach of caution.

As they passed through the warehouse district with its huge looming buildings, they shared the streets with a smaller group of people who were nevertheless very similar to those who had populated the busy wharfs. Handcarts and even a few wagons rumbled by, briefly illuminated in the guttering light of the oil lamps. Everyone seemed bound somewhere on some specific errand, and no one paid much notice to one more horse and four people. When they had traveled a few blocks away from the docks, the fetid smell of the river was no longer as obvious, but the melange of odors that replaced it was hardly an improvement. The muggy air was hung with a miasma of rotted garbage, stale smoke, manure, and ammonia fumes.

Beyond the warehouses the dim shapes of the buildings grew more irregular, although their fronts still formed a solid wall along both sides of the street. Some light and various noises leaked from some of them: the grinding and clacking of factories, unintelligible voices and sporadic bursts of the deeper grumbling of some sort of unseen machinery. Cassidy sat erect on the gray mare, looking directly ahead between the twin curves of the horse's ears. The presence and occasional touch of Allen's body behind her meant nothing to her; it meant as little as giving a ride to Teddy, or less. Cassidy's anger had given her a focus that was so narrow that little other emotion could intrude.

Even as her mind gnawed over the memory of what had happened on the docks, Cassidy realized that the incident had shocked her for two reasons. One reason was that the presence of an infant in that world seemed to fly in the face of all of her previous assumptions. Where had the baby come from? Whose child had it been? Not knowing the answers to those questions was nearly as disturbing as the fact of the trashman's casual brutality. Was regard for human life so low in the Iron City? Taken together, the two factors fused to propel her beyond her usual sense of wariness. It was one thing that people like her and Rowena had been brought there against their wills and stripped of all memory; but who would bring a mere infant there? And why had it died?

The mare suddenly tensed between her thighs, drawing to a halt and jarring Cassidy from her thoughts. Just ahead of them on a cross street four riders emerged from the shadows of the buildings. Even in the gloom she could see that they were Troopers.

Before she could even consider a response, Click acted. The Tinker leader murmured some brief instruction to Rowena, who had been walking right beside him, and then he stepped forward alone into the intersection. Four oil lamps, one posted on each corner of the intersecting streets, granted both Click and the leather-clad riders quadruple sets of shadows, filling the litter-strewn surface of the pavement with an eerie texture of dark and light.

Too far away to be able to hear clearly what any of them said, Cassidy could only wait in tense silence as the dark-haired man conferred with the quartet of Troopers. Around them the continuous rumble and hum of the city formed a sort of artificial alternative to the chorus of night insects that would have been its counterpart back in the hills. Would the Troopers detain them? Cassidy wondered. She became increasingly anxious as the exchange continued. No voices were raised and Click's demeanor retained its customary calm even when he turned to gesture toward the gray mare and her riders. But the Troopers, two men and two women each mounted on big, powerfully built horses, would clearly have had the advantage had they chosen to act.

Temporarily shaken from the insular little world of her anger, Cassidy tried to concentrate on the meeting being played out in the intersection before her. Did Click know those Troopers? That seemed unlikely, and yet there was some subtle suggestion of recognition in the riders' manner. Cassidy was still puzzling over that, and trying to decide whether it would be to their advantage if the Troopers did know the Tinker, when Click gave the four Horsemen a short nod and abruptly stepped back from their mounts. To her surprise the four Troopers urged their horses forward again and rode off across the intersection without so much as a backward glance.

As Click approached them again Cassidy could not keep herself from staring inquiringly at him. But all that he said to them, with a vague wave of his hand, was "Keep your wits about you; the gangs have been troublesome here." Then he began walking again, the heels of his low boots tapping dully on the pavement.

As they moved still deeper into the murky maze of the city's streets, the shapes and junctures of the buildings became even less regular and the sounds of industry faded to a kind of eerie stillness. The stench, unfortunately, had only grown stronger and more indefinable, several times leading Cassidy to peer down apprehensively over the mare's shoulder at the rough pavement below in anticipation of just what the horse might be stepping through. Oil lamps still lit both sides of the street, but their faint glow seemed unequal to the task of taking on the thick shadows that cloaked every alley and doorway. Cassidy found herself wishing for the return of her protective shield of rage because with every step the horse took, she felt more and more the sense of being utterly vulnerable in that alien place.

Well, not completely vulnerable, Cassidy had to concede, watching the tall silhouette of Click's back as he continued to lead them through the city. He did not appear to be afraid, she thought, or perhaps he was just unwilling to reveal any fear in front of them. Cassidy was mulling over that possibility when she first heard the scrabble of many footsteps coming from one of the intersecting alleyways.

Click did not hesitate; he continued striding briskly up the center of the gloomy street even as the poorly defined forms of several people spilled out onto the littered pavement from the darkness of the alley. The people—an odd assortment of a half-dozen men and women all clad in grubby clothing that was tattered and unpatched—started moving up the street parallel to them, keeping well to the murky shadows that shrouded the fronts of the buildings. Involuntarily Cassidy tightened her knees around the gray's barrel. For the first time on their trip through the city's streets she felt fully aware of the warmth and bulk of Allen's body behind her on the horse, and she was curiously grateful for the sheriff's presence there regardless of his weakened condition.

Cassidy found herself thinking back to what Willie had told her only that morning about the inhabitants of the Iron City. Were these motley people some of what he had referred to as "the gangs and thieves that are too ignorant or lazy to earn an honest living"? She darted another sidelong glance in their direction and was relieved to see all six of them turn away and start down another narrow alley, where they quickly disappeared from sight and where even the scuffling of their footfalls soon faded.

Only then, when Cassidy's attention was returned to the street ahead of them, did she notice something that she had not been aware of earlier. Click was still walking steadily along, seemingly as indifferent to the group's disappearance as he had been to their sudden emergence from the alleyway. But his right arm, which had been bent at the elbow with his fingers just touching the edge of his leather vest, casually dropped to his side again. Exhaling shakily, Cassidy remembered the little pistol the Tinker had given her—and his calm assurance that he had another.

Twice more on their journey across the city they encountered roving groups of ragged-looking people with suspicious demeanors. And there were many more times when Cassidy had the sense of being observed from the darkened gaps between buildings or from their shadowy doorways, although she could never see anyone there. She sat alertly on the mare, her muscles aching with tension as her eyes swept the confines of the dimly lit street. She didn't know if it was what Click would have called "keeping her wits" about her, but she did take some small comfort in the continued self-assurance of the tall man's gait and from the touch of Allen's thighs against her own.

They didn't encounter any more Troopers, although once Cassidy heard the rapid clatter of shod hooves on the paved surface of an adjacent street. If the Troopers patrolled the city then the effort didn't impress her as being very organized. The worst part of that was that Cassidy didn't know if she should be concerned by that lapse, or grateful for it.

Finally the buildings lining the street upon which they traveled began to thin out, the structures interspersed with gaps of darkened and empty land, all featureless under the humid cloak of the summer night. Even the streetlamps had disappeared. Had they gone all the way across the city then and were they about to come out on the other side? Instantly and without volition, Cassidy felt her suspicions return. In her sense of urgency incited by her outrage on the docks, she had trusted Click completely. She suddenly began to wonder if she had made a mistake, for she realized that Click could have been taking them anywhere. Her body stiffening with that thought, Cassidy was on the verge of urging the gray mare forward to confront the Tinker leader when something made her hold her peace.

They were leaving the city behind them then. The street broadened into a road, still paved but hemmed by trees rather than buildings, and the faint odors that rose around them were things far more familiar and comforting: grass and wet earth and the musky peat of natural decomposition. Willie had told her that the Warden's compound was "well out of the city." After they had walked for a good ten or fifteen minutes, Cassidy began to relax again. By the time they had walked for half an hour, she had begun to wonder how Willie defined "well out."

At last Cassidy grew aware of something so simple and familiar that it was an instant reassurance to her. She heard the sound of horses nickering and smelled the warm scents of crushed grass and the sweet fragrance of horses' bodies. Ahead of them on the darkened ribbon of the broad roadway she heard the soft clang of iron-shod hooves. Faintly backlit, the dusky silhouettes of several riders approached them. From their bearing she took them for Troopers; as they drew closer the absence of tack and the clothing they wore confirmed it.

It was only when Click had led them a little closer that she was able to see that the Troopers had ridden out through a wide metal-barred gate, whose aperture spanned the road and served as the single opening in what otherwise appeared to be a formidable stone wall. Oil lamps flickered at the gate's posts, offering a dim light to the road and those who stood met upon it. In that light the mounted Troopers loomed over Click like huge shadowy centaurs.

For the first time since they had encountered the four Troopers inside the city, Click turned and offered an explanation to Cassidy and the others. The silvered tips of his mustache lifted slightly as he said with an economical gesture and his typical gift for understatement, "The Warden's garrison."

Once again, as in that city intersection, Cassidy had the distinct sense that Click and these Troopers knew one another. The central of the three riders, a lithe but capable-looking man with touches of gray just barely visible in the cropped hair at his temples, looked down gravely at Click and said, "What brings you to our gate at this time of the night, Tinker?"

Click made another small gesture, one Cassidy had become

familiar with, the equanimical spreading of his oddly graceful hands. "We've come to see your captain," he said.

All three Troopers devoted a long and bluntly appraising look first to Rowena and then to Cassidy and Allen on the gray mare. One of their horses, a broad-chested dun, snorted loudly and pawed at the pavement. Cassidy was struck by the irony of it; the horse had recognized one of his own kind, even if the Troopers were less easily swayed.

"Come back in the morning," the central Trooper told them gruffly, "and we'll see."

As many times as Cassidy had already found herself unwittingly seduced by Click's easy charm, she still was surprised at the simple skill with which he kept the three Troopers from just turning away and riding back through the garrison's gate. A few softly spoken words from the dark-haired man gave him their complete attention.

"Has your captain been so successful in her hunting then," Click asked them evenly, "that she no longer needs to seek information about her quarry?"

Before any of the men could speak in response, Cassidy watched in bemusement as Click did what he had done to her more than once: He simply deflected all protest by continuing on in that same quiet and rational tone. "Because if you tell me that your Warden has no further concerns about what's been happening in the hills," he said with the very slightest cant of one brow, "then we would be most relieved to just go on our way and leave you good men in peace."

The other two Troopers, younger men than their leader, exchanged quick, almost reflexive, glances with the gray-templed man. The older man shifted slightly on his horse, and when he spoke Cassidy could detect that only by the most studied effort was he concealing his irritation.

"Who are these people then, Tinker?" he asked Click, indicating Cassidy and the others with the barest nod of his head.

Before Click could speak, Cassidy felt Allen's body suddenly stir behind her, and the big man dropped somewhat clumsily to his feet on the ground beside the mare. Standing there, he steadied himself by leaning into the horse's flank and squarely faced the trio of mounted men. "I am Allen," he said, "the sheriff of the village of Double Creek in William's Territory."

Gesturing, Click continued the introductions with the same infuriating calm that Cassidy could not help but believe he was purposely wielding against the Troopers. "Cassidy, a Horseman of these territories," he said, "and Rowena, a craftswoman and her friend."

Cassidy felt a twinge of inappropriate amusement at the unwarranted status that Click had just bestowed upon them both; but then she supposed it was in their best interest to be presented in the best possible light before those men. From the Troopers' reaction, however, she suspected it would take more than mere titles to convince them. The three men on the big horses still looked decidedly skeptical. But Click was not finished with them yet.

"They've come a long way, down the Long River from Pointed Rock," the dark-haired man said. Continuing to speak even as he stepped toward the gray mare, he looked up directly at the Troopers. "They've come because they have information important to your Warden." Listening to his smooth voice, Cassidy had no indication what Click intended to do until he suddenly reached for Allen's shirt and tugged up the garment's hem. Pivoting aside to stand clear of Allen's body, Click held up the tail of the shirt with a near flourish as he concluded, "I think your captain will want to see this for herself."

The light from the gate lamps was guttering and weak and Click had bared only a portion of Allen's torso; but the character and the gravity of his partially healed wounds were a mute and powerful testimony to what he had endured. For a few seconds the Troopers simply gaped at the pattern of fresh scars on the bearded man's side. Cassidy had no idea what kind of news might have reached the city, or if knowledge of the monsters was universal among the Warden's Troopers, but Allen's injuries defied rationalization and gave the three men little choice.

Cassidy could see the gray-templed Trooper suppress his reservations with an almost insurmountable reluctance. But whatever his doubts, the man finally gave Click a curt nod and said, "Follow us then."

As the three big horses wheeled around in unison, reversing themselves on the road, Click lowered Allen's shirt again and with his characteristic consideration helped the sheriff tuck it back into place. Then Click threw Cassidy an odd look that she could not decipher, a look that seemed to encompass both encouragement and challenge, before they followed the Troopers.

Out of concern for Allen, who remained afoot but accepted

the support of the gray mare's sturdy body, Cassidy kept the horse to a measured pace. Rowena dropped back and walked beside Allen, close enough so that her shoulder was nearly touching his arm. They passed into the wavering pool of yellow lamplight and then through the open iron gate into the compound beyond.

In a totally unfamiliar place with nothing more than a few randomly spaced oil lamps for illumination, initially Cassidy had difficulty orienting herself inside the garrison. Her first impression was that they had entered some kind of large stableyard because in the near darkness they were surrounded by the sounds and smells of horses. But as they continued to follow the three mounted Troopers up the roadway she became aware of many other people moving about in the immediate area, some on horses but most on foot. It wasn't until they approached the corner of a long single-story building and the lantern light became stronger that she had any idea just how big the compound was or how many Troopers it contained.

Other riders cut around them, headed outbound on the same road, leather-clad men and women mounted on sleek long-legged horses riding past them with hardly a sideways glance at the odd new arrivals. And from the nearest low building and the dark sweep of land that stretched beyond it came the reassuring presence of more horses: horses munching feed, shifting their feet, blowing softly through their nostrils. The gray mare stepped sedately but alertly, her long ears constantly swiveling.

Cassidy wasn't even aware that the three Troopers who led them had stopped until the mare also came to a halt. They stood in what appeared to be some sort of broad courtyard, surrounded on two sides by the stables and on the other two sides by the two wings of a large, two-storied, L-shaped wooden building that she thought might be the barracks. The Trooper with the graying temples slid from his horse's back and beckoned to them with one terse gesture.

Glancing up at the building, Cassidy slipped from the mare's back. The barracks had a plain wooden face, fronted by a long narrow porch and checkered at regular intervals with small square windows, most of them dark. Light from some of the windows and from a few oil lamps on posts spilled across the courtyard, but it was not strong enough to get a good sense of detail about the place. Preoccupied, Cassidy stepped forward behind Click, Allen, and Rowena to the front step where their escort waited for them.

"The captain's been conferring with the Warden," the senior Trooper explained. Cassidy could see from the veiled tautness of the well-disciplined man's expression that it was information he was reluctant to divulge to them. "Wait here, and I'll see if they wish to speak with you."

Click settled his shoulders against one of the porch's wooden columns with a stoic air as the gray-templed Trooper opened the barracks' door and a fresh flood of light spilled out across the entryway. As the man entered the building, two more people emerged through the opened door. One of them was another Trooper, a leather-clad woman with a solemn long-jawed face and dark shoulder-length hair. But it was the man who walked behind her who caused Cassidy's head to snap around in amazement. For although the muscular young black man did not wear the typical garb of the Warden's Troopers, Cassidy knew for a fact that to do so had long been his ambition: The young man was Raphael.

Too stunned to speak, Cassidy could only gape at him as Raphael glanced over and suddenly noticed her. She could see the identical jolt of recognition in those wide dark eyes, but he masterfully tried to conceal it as he just kept right on walking behind the woman Trooper. And for a few moments there on that shadowy porch there evolved an almost comic duel of cross purposes, with each of them frantically debating whether to acknowledge the other, and each visibly grappling with the possible adverse outcomes of such an acknowledgment.

As Raphael followed the Trooper right past them and down the steps off the porch, Cassidy felt a brief if unreasonable panic that someone else might recognize him, as well. She had to remind herself that Rowena and Click had never met the cocky young Horseman. And it had been so dark that night out on the prairie that even though Allen had taken a shot at the thief who had "stolen" Gabriella's foal, the sheriff couldn't have gotten a good look at Raphael. And so as if by some unspoken but mutual agreement, Cassidy and the black youth studiously avoided looking at each other as Raphael passed right by them and then on into the broad and dimly lit courtyard.

Then Raphael had achieved his goal after all, Cassidy thought; he had come to the Warden as a full-fledged Horseman. Her reaction to that was tinged with ambivalence. Her problem with Raphael seemed to remain the same nettlesome one that had always vexed her: She couldn't be certain if he was friend or foe. Then something else occurred to Cassidy; if

Raphael was there, was Kevin there, as well? She conceded she would have been far happier to have seen the odd-eyed boy than she was to see his companion. She was still pondering that possibility when the door to the barracks swung open again and the gray-templed Trooper filled its frame.

Cassidy could have predicted what the man would say before he ever opened his mouth because he no longer took any pains to conceal his mistrust for them. Not that she had any quarrel with that; Cassidy found both the candor and the skepticism refreshing, especially after the bland sort of indifference she had initially encountered in so many people of that world.

"The Warden is with the captain, but they'll see you," the Trooper announced, reluctantly stepping back inside the doorway to allow them entry.

But when all four of them began to move forward, the Trooper held up his hand. "Not you, Tinker," he said gruffly to Click. "Just them."

For a split second Cassidy hesitated, unpleasantly surprised to find that now that push had come to shove she actually trusted Click more than she trusted the Troopers. But Click urged her onward with an almost imperceptible little gesture, his dark eyes bright with the latent irony of the situation.

"I'll just wait out here," Click said, as if that had been his preference all the while.

After that there was no time for further deliberation because the senior Trooper was headed back into the building, leaving Cassidy little choice but to follow him or lose all credibility.

The interior of the barracks was unremarkable, a softly lit montage of bare wooden floors, plastered walls, and the subliminal murmurs of distant voices behind a series of closed doors. Their reluctant guide led the way down a short broad hallway and paused outside the last door. Although he didn't knock or even say a word as far as Cassidy could detect, the door promptly swung open just seconds after he had reached it.

Cassidy had not realized how hard her heart had been thumping until the sudden splash of light from within the room spilled out into the hallway and she caught herself involuntarily taking an almost painfully deep breath. Someone, either Rowena or Allen, touched her gently on the shoulder from behind, and Cassidy stepped forward into the room with the reflex obedience of a timid horse being loaded into a trailer. Suddenly and with a useless desperation she wished that she and Rowena had taken more time to rehearse just exactly what they were going to do when that moment arrived and they actually stood before the Warden of Horses. But then the Trooper who had opened the door for them, a whip-thin woman with long black hair as glossy as a raven's feathers, threw her a curious look, and Cassidy hurried to catch up with the gray-templed Trooper.

Inside the room Cassidy tried to take her cue from their escort, who halted and then stood silently but alertly. The room they had entered was not a very large one, and most of the center was taken up by a long, heavy, wooden table surrounded by matching chairs. Several oil lamps on wall brackets accounted for the strong illumination, and the room smelled faintly of their smoke and of leather and horses. The size of the big table suggested it could easily have accommodated at least a dozen people, but there were only three people in the room when they had entered it, the thin woman at the door, another taller woman, and a man.

The man sat at the table with his back toward them; a woman stood behind him with her curly head bent as she looked down over his shoulder at something that was spread on the table. The elaborately incised and dyed leather of her fringed tunic marked her as another Trooper, and yet there was something in her very bearing as much as the simple fact of her presence there that marked her as the captain of the Troopers. Then the woman lifted her head and threw back a glance toward the doorway and, to Cassidy's astonishment, she found that the woman was also someone she knew: The captain was Valerie.

Recognition rested comfortably upon the spare planes of those elegant high cheekbones, though there was also puzzlement in the longer look the curly-haired woman gave Cassidy. "The Horseman from Double Creek," she said, extending her hand. "But why didn't you just give the guards my token?"

Cassidy was dimly aware of Rowena and Allen shifting behind her, no doubt puzzled by the captain's greeting. But before Cassidy could offer an explanation, the man who was seated at the table first seemed to notice the interruption. Visibly preoccupied, he turned in his chair and glanced almost absently over his shoulder at them.

For Cassidy then, everything else in the room just seemed to vanish.

Later she would not have been able to describe the clothing he wore, not even under the threat of death; nor would she have been able to relate exactly how his chin lifted just so, or the way the silky wealth of his light brown hair dangled incorrigibly over his high forehead. Because with that single distracted glance the man they called the Warden of Horses had instantly bridged the abysmal chasm that had sundered Cassidy's memory for so long. And with that bridging intense pain, like a crushing cloak of blackness, descended over her, snuffing out her consciousness like dark water closing over a frail flame.

I know him, Cassidy thought, as she felt the wooden floor bounce up to smack her in the head.

And because she knew him, she remembered everything.

PART TWO ◀▬▬

Chapter 12 ◄▦

Dragonfly was a good horse, a special horse. She had trained a lot of horses but the big gray mare was the best. Sometimes it almost seemed as if the horse could anticipate what she wanted even before she would ask for it. That was why when Joel asked her about using the mare in the rehab program, she had readily agreed to give the gray a try. That was how she had met Andy Greene.

Andy was special, too—at least that was the current politically correct term for people like him. It had not been the term she would have picked for the young man the first time she had seen him; "tragic" would have been more apt. But Joel's commitment to the riding therapy program had already yielded some impressive results, and despite her initial misgivings she was determined to give Andy that chance.

Joel firmly believed that horses and horseback riding could reach something hidden inside those profoundly unreachable people the Center's dedicated volunteers kept bringing out to the farm. "AFB," the woman from Reiners had told her, leading Andy forward in much the same way as you would push along a bicycle; "autistic from birth."

She had looked at the young man with a mixture of pity and dismay. "Andy," she tried helpfully, "my name is Cathy. Would you like to pet one of the horses?"

But Andy didn't speak; Andy didn't move. Andy didn't even blink, not even when, with a nod of encouragement from the volunteer from Reiners, she took him by the arm and gently tugged him forward. He would walk as long as he was led, but the moment she stopped leading him he simply ceased to move. He was like a zombie.

The worst part about it, she later admitted to herself—and not without a certain self-conscious twinge of shame—was that Andy was gorgeous. His wide uncomprehending eyes were the rich pure color of melted chocolate, fringed with a fashion model's lashes, and his soft sunny-brown hair framed a face of boyish but classically handsome lines. Even that compliant body, so will-less and undirected, was distressingly beautiful, with the limber bounty of a youth just cresting manhood. Whatever cruel fate of genetics or birth had rendered him trapped like a sleepwalker within his own mind had ironically also given him a face and form that so casually mimed perfection.

Who said that nature didn't have a sense of humor? she had thought ruefully.

And so Andy Greene was a challenge. Many of the program's other pupils had profound physical handicaps; several were severely retarded. But no one else was quite like Andy; no one else was so physically present and yet so mentally absent.

"Thanks a lot!" she had muttered to Joel after that first day.

But Joel had merely laughed at her. "Cath, I know you won't quit on him," he had said confidently.

And the trouble was, Joel was right; she had always been too damned stubborn to give up on anything or anyone. Even when days had passed without any visible signs of progress she had persisted, leading the automatonlike young man around after her as she worked in the barns or with the other pupils, lifting his unresisting hand to make him stroke a horse's neck or to wield a brush. Until finally one day something happened.

She had been working with Dragonfly, tacking up the gray mare for another pupil's therapy session. But when she began to lead the horse away, after having first patiently backed Andy up out of the way, he had suddenly taken a step forward again and reached for the mare's rein. It had seemed impossible, but it was almost as if he actually had acted to keep her from leading the horse away from him.

That was the beginning of a long and painfully incremental period of progress with Andy. He hadn't suddenly begun to react to things; even the incident with Dragonfly had not triggered that. But there definitely was something about the gray mare that had broken through to him, to whatever unfathomable little world in which his mind still lived. He wanted to be near the mare. She was the only thing he would spontaneously touch, the only thing to which he seemed capable of responding. It began with the simplest of things, like stroking her or even just leaning against her side. Then came the astounding day when Andy had taken the dandy brush from Cathy's hand and had begun, quite capably, to curry the mare.

If she had allowed herself to hope or believe that those little responses signaled some kind of change in Andy's overall condition, she would have been woefully disappointed. But she was too cautious a woman to have made that mistake. After she had taken him on as a pupil in the riding therapy program, Cathy had done her homework, dogging the staff from Reiners Center with questions about Andy's situation and reading everything she could lay her hands on about autism in general. So she knew that there was no cure for what he had, not really any treatment—not even any explanation. But sometimes there was palliative care, something that would at least temporarily ease the symptoms of what he suffered. And the key to that care had proven to be the gray mare.

There were other pupils in the program who made astounding progress, and their victories remained like emotional trophies in Cathy's mind. There had been Joey, so mentally impaired that he had been thought incapable of being toilet trained, who suddenly responded for the first time to such hygienic disciplines after he discovered that it was a hell of a lot more comfortable to ride horseback without the bulk of a diaper. And Monica, a paraplegic whose first slow solo trot around the riding ring on a plodding gelding brought tears of joy to her eyes. And Cindy, the deaf and blind girl who spoke her first words in over ten years when she was allowed the freedom of a horse's back. By contrast Andy's progress may have seemed minuscule; and yet to Cathy it had been the most remarkable of triumphs.

And so there had come the day when, against Joel's better judgment and therefore without his knowledge, Cathy had eased Dragonfly over to the wooden fence where she had left Andy standing complacently. The day when, suddenly and astonishingly and with only the slightest of physical cues from Cathy, Andy Greene had stepped onto the lower fence rail and from there had pulled himself up onto that broad gray back. The day when, without saddle or reins or any visible means of control, he had ridden Dragonfly around the schooling ring, the mare gathered beneath him like a dressage horse.

That had been the day when Cathy first had to admit to the existence of something that simply defied comprehension, the day when she had looked up into the utter blankness of that perfect face and glimpsed the transformation behind those

*chocolate-colored eyes. For a few amazing minutes the boy
and the horse had been one.*

*That had been the day when Cathy Delaney had first
thought the unthinkable.*

The first crimson glow that flared behind her tightly closed
lids brought with it a staggering bolt of pain, like a pair of hot
pokers piercing her fragile skull. *Great,* Cassidy thought groggily, fighting off consciousness, *why should this time be any
different?*

Only that time was different. Even as she lay defensively
curled up, groaning and trying to beat back the aching advent
of awakening, Cassidy could not forget that. In fact, she realized as her torpid brain insistently stirred back to life that forgetting was something that just wasn't going to work for her
anymore.

Someone bent over her, a presence sensed if not seen, and
a familiar hand gently touched her forehead.

"Cassidy? Are you okay?" Rowena asked in a deferentially
soft tone.

Because she was lying on something comfortable, probably
a bed, and because she knew for a fact that once she opened
her eyes her entire skull would simply split wide open, Cassidy
didn't immediately respond. She just concentrated on taking
slow shallow breaths and wondered why no one had ever bothered to explain to her that death was going to be such a headache.

"Cassidy?" Rowena repeated, a touch more anxiously.

Cassidy slitted her lids and squinted up into the vague
outline of her friend's face, wincing at the almost incendiary
brightness of the quiet room where she lay. "Where's my
horse?" she mumbled thickly.

"She's fine—you're the one who scared the shit out of me,"
Rowena said. "You feel like sitting up?"

To Cassidy's surprise the burning pressure inside her head
actually receded somewhat once she completely opened her
eyes. She turned her head, cautiously scanning her surroundings. She was lying, fully dressed for once, on a wide firm bed
in a large sunny room that was furnished with the basic accou-
trements of a bedroom. "Where am I?" she said.

Rowena appeared to realize then that Cassidy might not remember. "We're in the Warden's house," she said, adding in a
cheerfully deprecating tone "Jeez, Cassidy, after all it took to

get us here, if I'd known you were going to take one look at him and hit the floor—"

"I *know* him," Cassidy interrupted, her voice an urgent hiss.

The brunette looked down quizzically at her. "What do you mean, you—"

Cassidy cut her off by reaching out and grasping Rowena by the arm, using the hold to pull herself up into a sitting position on the bed. "Where's everyone else—where're Click and Allen?" she demanded.

Increasingly perplexed, Rowena just shrugged. "I don't know where Click is; I haven't seen him since we went into the barracks last night. But Allen was here with us most of the night. I think he's out in the garden."

Swinging her legs over the side of the bed, Cassidy fought down a transient wave of light-headedness. Still gripping Rowena's arm for support, she kept firing off questions. "What time is it? And where's the Warden?"

"Nearly midmorning," Rowena said, surveying Cassidy's face with a look of genuine concern. "And I don't know where the Warden is; I haven't seen him since they brought us here— Cassidy, are you sure you're all right? Maybe you hit your head harder than—"

But Cassidy shook her head briskly, a motion of both denial and impatience. "Maybe I finally hit my head hard enough," she said resolutely. "Listen, Rowena: I remember now who I am."

The brunette's hazel eyes widened and for a moment she was speechless with shock. "Holy shit!" she whispered.

Leaning forward over the edge of the big bed, Cassidy said, "My real name is Cathy Delaney, and I—"

"No, wait," Rowena interrupted her, lifting one hand as if to stop Cassidy's flow of words. "I think we better find Allen; he should hear this, too."

Cassidy recognized the expression on Rowena's face; it was the same sort of ambivalence Cassidy herself had felt the night before when she had wondered if finally reaching their goal, the Warden, would turn out to be a wonderful or an awful thing. "Okay," she agreed, awkwardly gaining her feet.

It took Cassidy the length of the generous and airy room to become really steady on her feet again. She followed Rowena to a broad bay window on the far side of the room where full-height glass casements opened out onto a narrow stone walk and a strip of green lawn. Beyond the lawn, still damp with the morning's dew, lush beds of flowering plants curved symmetrically across the grass, backdropped by a thick wall of trees and shrubs.

Allen had been standing beside the egg-yolk yellow flowers of a vigorous patch of rudbeckia, his hands locked behind his back, his leather boots stained with a dampness that revealed many a turn around the dewy grass made during his solitary contemplation in the Warden's garden. He turned as he caught sight in his peripheral vision of their approach, his shaggy head lifting.

"Are you all right?" he asked Cassidy immediately, unwittingly echoing Rowena's words.

"That remains to be seen," Cassidy replied. She looked up directly into the sheriff's bearded face, forcing herself to ignore the fresh tracery of stress lines that she could see etched around the corners of his eyes and mouth. "Allen, I know you don't believe in all the things that Rowena and I have been saying, but something else has happened. I've remembered more."

Automatically Allen's eyes shifted, scanning the breadth of the bright and sunny garden. The morning was pleasant, the quiet air cool and far less humid than it had been down on the river. There didn't appear to be anyone else out on the vast lawn, but with the same reflex to seek privacy Cassidy also turned, glancing back toward the big brick house from which they had come. It was the Warden's house, Rowena had told her. Somehow Cassidy had expected something more pretentious, a palace or at least a mansion; but it was just a house, even if it was a large and handsome one.

"Memories?" Allen asked reluctantly, his voice pitched purposely low.

Not "Memories" but memory, Cassidy thought, still staggered by the implications. But what she said to Allen, looking up into those wary but steady gold-ringed eyes, was "Yeah, the Memories that just might explain everything."

With another quick glance in the direction of the silent sun-washed house, Allen gave a little jerk with his bearded chin and then began to walk, steadily and intently, along the colorful bed of flowers. Cassidy and Rowena fell into step behind him, their boots sinking soundlessly into the soft green grass. Birds shot up out of the garden ahead of them, flitting toward the trees in a bright flash of feathers.

As they walked Cassidy was relieved to realize that even the prickling remnants of her headache had receded. She felt the familiar sense of the gray mare's nearness, the horse's serenity resting comfortably with her. She was far less comforted by thoughts of the task that lay ahead. How was she going to tell Allen what she had remembered when they shared no common beliefs about their backgrounds? How was she even going to explain it to Rowena, when what she remembered seemed impossible to Cassidy herself?

Allen paused when they reached the end of the flower bed, where a tall hedge of what Cassidy thought might be rhododendron formed a barrier between the garden and a row of trees. *Because Joel had a rhododendron hedge on the farm* . . . Beyond the trees a tall stone wall snaked along the gentle slope; and beyond the wall spread some of the buildings that Cassidy recognized from the night before, the stables and barracks of the Warden's garrison. Even farther, beyond the confines of the garrison, she could see the open fields that separated the compound from the outskirts of the Iron City, the network of its forest of buildings strangely softened by the sunlight, covering the gradual slope that ran down to the Long River.

Sweet Christ, where are we? Cassidy thought, ironically less certain then than she had ever been before. She knew where she had come from: Greenlea, New York. But she couldn't identify anything there in that deceptively pastoral place— because no place like that still existed in the real world, so primitive and so removed from civilization. The more familiar and detailed her memories of the real world became, the less possible that world in which she stood became.

With another automatic glance around them, Allen caught Cassidy's attention. Then he was looking at her, his expression expectant. Uncertain how she could possibly preamble her revelations, Cassidy opted to simply try to describe what had happened to her in the barracks the night before.

"Last night when they took us into that room to see the Warden and the captain," she began quietly and evenly, "I realized that the captain was someone I'd met before. She was one of the Troopers that Mike and I ran into down along the river-bottom pasture the night of the fire back in Double Creek."

"So that's why she recognized you," Rowena interjected. "What did she mean about her 'token'?"

Cassidy hesitated a moment. "I tried to get her to take me

with them that night," she admitted, still embarrassed by the memory of how close she had come to abandoning Rowena and their pact to stick together. "I asked her to take me to the Warden. She couldn't—not then; but she gave me a little ornament from her horse's mane and told me to present it at the garrison gate." Cassidy shrugged sheepishly. "It was in my jeans' pocket when the Woodsman stole our clothes."

But Rowena didn't seem upset by the implication of Cassidy's confession about the captain; if anything, she seemed amused by the memory of the Woodsman's theft. "So what was the deal with the Warden?" she asked. "Why did you pass out when you saw him?"

Glancing from the brunette's to Allen's face, Cassidy said, "I *know* him—but not from here. I know him from before, from my life before I ever came here."

Allen's expression remained impassive, a cipher; but Rowena's interest had definitely been piqued. Before the buxom woman could interrupt her, Cassidy continued, "Only that's impossible, because the man I know from before wouldn't even be able to function here, much less be a leader."

Allen and Rowena exchanged a significant look. Helplessly Cassidy realized that no matter how crazy or bizarre it might all sound, the only thing she had to offer them in proof were the facts that she had remembered. The words tumbled out then, rapidly and earnestly.

"When I recognized him, I remembered who *I* am—who I *really* am—and where I came from. My name is Cathy Delaney; I was his riding instructor. I taught him how to ride— that's how I know him. His name was—his name *is* Andy Greene. He was one of our special pupils in the riding therapy program we ran with Reiners Center. That's why he *can't* be here, he *can't* be normal, because—"

"Whoa—wait," Rowena interrupted her, reaching out to gently but firmly take hold of Cassidy's arm, as if by doing so she could rein in the accelerating flood of confusing words. "Wait a minute, Cassidy, back up; you're losing me." With a sidelong glance at Allen, who had not visibly reacted to Cassidy's revelations, Rowena went on. "You said that you know him, right? That he was a student of yours? Then why didn't he recognize you last night?"

Since she hadn't remained conscious long enough to have observed the Warden's reaction to her dead faint, the possibility that he hadn't even recognized her simply hadn't occurred to Cassidy. Once informed of it, the discrepancy momentarily stymied her. "I don't know," she admitted finally, shaking her head, "but I sure as hell recognize him—and he *can't* be the Warden of Horses, or the ruler of all of the eastern territories, or anything else because he's *autistic!*"

Both Allen and Rowena greeted that vehement disclosure with near-identical expressions of bafflement. "He's *what?*" Rowena asked warily.

"Autistic," Cassidy repeated, aware that her voice was beginning to rise precipitously but unwilling to temper her urgency. "It's a mental disorder, a kind of complete emotional withdrawal from—" She broke off, thinking with an almost hysterical edge of irony, *How the hell do you explain being totally divorced from reality to people in a world where being totally divorced from reality is normal?* "He's just very sick, mentally," she concluded emphatically. "He could never run this whole place—hell, he can't even speak!"

The sorrel-haired sheriff finally spoke, his deep voice calm and low. "Then how can the Warden be this same person that you know? He's been the Warden for years, and even though I've often disagreed with his ideas and his decisions he certainly isn't mute—or crazy."

Cassidy just hitched her shoulders, shrugging off Rowena's hand and shaking her head in helpless frustration. "I don't know," she said, "but he *is* Andy Greene—I'm positive of that."

"Maybe he's been cured of this disease thing," Rowena offered helpfully.

"You can't be cured of autism!" Cassidy snapped, more harshly than she had intended. An idea had been forming in the back of her mind ever since she had first regained consciousness back in that sunny bedroom; the more she thought about it, the more unattractively probable it seemed to become—probable and frightening.

Rowena made a little gesture unnervingly like Click's, a placating spreading of her palms. "Well, if the Warden is really Andy Greene, then he must have been cured," she said reasonably. "How else could he be here like this?"

The same way all of us are here like this, Cassidy thought grimly, reluctant to give voice to the grave but increasingly inevitable conclusion. "Maybe because he's not there anymore," she said dully.

But Rowena did not respond to the obvious implication of

Cassidy's statement. Instead for a few moments she just stared back across the lawn at the big brick house, where the climbing sun sparkled off the glass squares of the windowpanes and painted the masonry with a honeyed light. "Or maybe he is," she said slowly.

Cassidy was literally too baffled to speak; it fell to Allen to finally break the silence by asking the brunette the necessary question. "What are you talking about?"

Rowena turned to Cassidy, her hazel eyes bright with that kindred spark of discovery so familiar to Cassidy from their many secret discussions about their own world. In the stupefying enormity of her own rediscovered memory, Cassidy had nearly forgotten that Rowena shared with her the memory of that other life, even if not in the same detail, and that, unlike Allen, Rowena could draw upon it for explanations.

"You recognize the Warden, right?" she elaborated for Cassidy, ticking off the points on her fingers for emphasis. "You're positive he's Andy Greene; and you're positive that his autism thing couldn't be cured. So all I'm saying is that maybe everything is true: maybe he's both the Warden *and* he's Andy Greene."

Cassidy just shook her head, too confused even to be irritated by the glaring contradiction in Rowena's conclusion. "Rowena, that's impossible," she said. "No one can be in two places at the same time." And she didn't add that she had a far more plausible explanation for the situation.

But Rowena wasn't finished yet; the expression on her broad face was entirely calm and thoughtful. "Maybe not," she conceded readily. "But maybe a person can be in the same place at two different times."

Her headache was coming back with a vengeance; Rowena was seeing to that. *And I always thought that death would be a relatively painless state,* Cassidy mused. She shook her head again, more briskly, daring to antagonize the incipient throb just waiting inside her skull. "Rowena, what in the hell are you talking about?" she asked wearily.

But the light that sparkled in those hazel eyes had only intensified, as bright and incandescent as Cassidy had ever seen it. Rowena went on.

"Cassidy, listen: We both know that we didn't come from here, we came from somewhere else. We can *remember* it. But what if what we remember isn't some other *place*—what if it's some other *time*?"

Groping for comprehension, initially Cassidy's floundering mind found nothing. And she saw only her own bewilderment reflected in Allen's gold-ringed eyes. At a loss, all she could say was "Rowena, that's crazy."

Indefatigable, the brunette simply threw out her hands, encompassing in a single gesture the whole of the land that lay around them. "So? *This* is crazy, too. Are you saying my idea's any crazier than this whole place is?"

"I think you're both crazy," Allen muttered.

Biting down on her lower lip, Cassidy hesitated a moment, looking into the determined gleam that lit Rowena's eyes. "I think maybe there's another explanation for all this," she said slowly, "one where all these things really don't have to make sense." Conscious of both Allen's and Rowena's eyes upon her, Cassidy concluded, "I think maybe we're all dead."

But to Cassidy's surprise Rowena seemed entirely undismayed; she dismissed that grim theory with another bit of eccentric but inarguable logic. Again she made an all-encompassing gesture. "You think *this* is the afterlife?" she asked with an incredulous lift of her brows. "I don't know about you guys, but I was hoping for something with better food!"

Before Cassidy could form a rebuttal, Allen's head suddenly snapped up. He stared deliberately off across the wide expanse of lawn that stretched back toward the house. Following his gaze, Cassidy saw two Troopers briskly approaching them across the neatly shorn turf. The leather-clad man and woman strode along with an easy but purposeful gait, the fringes on their tunics fluttering.

Rowena saw the Troopers, too; but the brunette couldn't resist getting in the last word. "Besides," she hissed with obvious glee, "think about it: What use would *dead* people have for cigarette lighters or car keys?"

Cassidy had to bite her lip to suppress a spontaneous grin at Rowena's irreverent quip. Then she tried to school her expression into harmless neutrality as the Troopers approached. The man looked vaguely familiar to her, a stout fellow with a receding hairline; perhaps she had seen him at the garrison the night before. The woman was an unremarkable-looking brunette, with a stolid expression and her long hair neatly pinned up in a bun.

"The Warden would like to speak with you," the woman said.

Throwing Rowena a sharp warning glance that forbade her

to make any more wisecracks, Cassidy nodded politely at the
Trooper. "We'd be grateful for the chance," she said.

Actually when she thought about it, gratitude was pretty far
down on the list of emotions Cassidy was feeling as she,
Rowena, and Allen fell into step behind the Troopers and began to follow them back across the lawn. More than anything
else she felt apprehensive; but curiosity and suppressed anger
were running close seconds. The answers to the mystery of
that world had always seemed to dangle just out of her reach,
delivered grudgingly in such tiny bits and pieces as she had
struggled to learn the truth. For the first time she felt that there
was some hope of winning the struggle, even if the answers
would not be what she had hoped to find.

They did not reenter the Warden's house. The pair of Troopers instead led them around the side of the big two-story brick
building, where an intricately laid stone path followed the
outer walls of the structure and then climbed in a series of
broad steps up to an open-air garden deck. The deck was also
paved with stonework and surrounded by lush plantings of
flowers and shrubs and tall arbors hung with vines.

Their two escorts stood aside as Cassidy mounted the last
step, ushering them up onto the wide deck. Several tables with
chairs made of wood and wrought iron had been placed across
the paved expanse in such a way as to take advantage of the
friendly morning sunshine, but all of them were empty. As she
quickly scanned the area Cassidy saw several people standing
at the low stone parapet on the far side of the deck. Two of
them were Troopers, one the gray-templed man who had taken
them in from the gate to the barracks the night before. The
third person was Valerie, the Warden's captain, and the last
was the Warden himself.

As Cassidy, Rowena, and Allen crossed the garden deck
both Troopers looked up and watched their approach, but the
Warden and his captain remained facing the parapet, absorbed
in conversation. Unlike the encounter in the barracks, Cassidy
then could have described the young man's clothing with considerable precision; in fact, she found it impossible to keep her
eyes off him.

Much like the Trooper's distinctive garb, the clothes the
Warden wore were made of soft leather, fringed, incised, and
dyed. But his tunic and trousers were less ornamented than the
norm, the fringes plain and not festooned with any bead or
feather fetishes. The leather inseam of his pants, which tightly

followed the contours of his thighs and calves, was smooth and permanently darkened with the legacy of his office, which spoke of the years of sweat earned upon the back of a horse. Cassidy knew, because at home she had blue jeans very much like those pants.

But more mesmerizing to Cassidy than the familiarity of the Warden's clothing was her utter recall of his features. He *was* Andy Greene; seeing him this closely again Cassidy was unshakably certain of it. As she stared at him, Valerie glanced in their direction, and, automatically following the movement of that glance, the Warden turned and looked directly at Cassidy. And although there was life in those warm brown eyes—intelligence and emotion and light—there was absolutely no recognition.

Rowena was right, Cassidy thought, the finality of the realization wounding her with a pain beyond all logic. *He has no idea who I am.*

To add insult to an already smarting injury, Cassidy wasn't even the first person whom the Warden addressed when he spoke to them. He looked right past her and Rowena, turning instead to face Allen squarely.

"Justin tells me that there was an attack on Villagers near Pointed Rock," he said without preamble, "and that you alone survived it."

Allen shot a quick sidelong glance at the gray-templed Trooper, obviously the man the Warden had just named. "With the help of the Tinkers," Allen said, meeting the young man's gaze levelly, "and these two women, yes, I survived."

Cassidy was somewhat surprised by the acknowledgment from the sheriff, but the Warden barely glanced over at her and Rowena. He continued to study Allen's worn and solemn face. "They tell me that you're the sheriff of a village in William's Territory," he said then, his manner slightly less abrupt.

Allen nodded. "I come from Double Creek."

Quizzically the Warden cocked his head—*Andy*'s head, Cassidy thought stubbornly, watching with a weird sense of déjà vu as the sunlight struck golden highlights in the tousled mass of that soft hair. The encounter was fast becoming even more disorienting than she had expected, and when he spoke again she suddenly realized that she had never before even heard Andy Greene's voice.

"Then what were you doing riding with Villagers outside Pointed Rock?" he asked Allen.

Allen had several important advantages over Cassidy in dealing with the young man who stood before them. First and foremost, he was unfettered by the tangle of memories and their attendant contradictions that kept tripping up her perceptions. And even as a bona fide inhabitant of the Warden's world, Allen remained unimpressed by the man's titular position. Allen also did not have the added encumbrance of any sort of hidden agenda, as Cassidy and Rowena did. He wasn't trying to employ the Warden's help to get anywhere else; Allen didn't even believe there *was* anywhere else. And so the sheriff was free to respond with prompt veracity to the question.

"I was chasing them," he said simply, indicating Cassidy and Rowena with a nod.

For the first time the Warden gave both women a direct look. As those chocolate-brown eyes calmly scrutinized her, Cassidy was a little taken aback to notice the fine network of fatigue lines that bracketed them, incongruous etchings in that otherwise smooth tanned face. She found herself wondering just how much sleep the man was getting those days, with "troubles" wreaking havoc across his territories.

"Chasing them," the Warden repeated, slightly bemused; then in the pronouncement of those two words he somehow managed to make the smooth and nearly instantaneous transition from simple curiosity to logical conclusion. "You're the Horseman," he said to Cassidy.

It wasn't really a question, yet she found herself nodding anyway, forcefully struck by a single and painful thought. *Christ—how can you not remember me?*

The Warden's gaze lingered on her for a moment longer, then cut back to Allen. "You saw what happened out there then," he said. "You can describe it."

Again it was not really a question, and Allen chose to respond not with a nod but with a low grunt of assent. "I can describe what attacked me," he said, "but I couldn't begin to tell you what the hell they were."

Something stirred in those deep brown eyes then; Cassidy was incredulous when she recognized that something as a wry spark of irony. The Warden's lips thinned as he gave a little shake of his head. "I can tell you this, Sheriff Allen," he said ruefully. "At this point what the hell they might be concerns me far less than how the hell they might be stopped."

Turning back toward his captain, he made a small gesture to Valerie. "Call in as many of your field troops as possible," he told her, "so that all of them can hear what these people will have to say."

With a wordless nod of acknowledgment, Valerie turned to leave. Justin and the other Trooper fell in behind her as she crossed the deck to the steps on the far side. Then Cassidy, Rowena, and Allen stood alone on the paved court with the Warden, with only the pair of Troopers who had escorted them there waiting motionless on the far side of the deck.

Now that they had finally achieved their goal of finding the man, Cassidy felt amazingly at a loss as to how to proceed. She tried to regain the sharp edge of outrage that she had felt on the docks the night before, but the return of her memory had betrayed her purpose. She could hardly even look over at the Warden without gaping at him, because no matter what Rowena might have thought of Cassidy's theory of where they really were, seeing Andy Greene like that—animated and whole—was like seeing the resurrection of the dead. Shooting a quick glance over at Rowena and Allen, Cassidy furiously debated where she should begin. The monsters obviously were the Warden's main concern, but to Cassidy the creatures' existence paled in comparison to the other questions she had. But how could she begin to ask them; how could she even approach him with the bizarre explanation of what she suspected?

It turned out, as was so often the case with those fierce internal conflicts that Cassidy debated, the choice was suddenly taken out of her control by external forces. Giving them a rather distracted nod, the Warden said, "I'm afraid that now I must go, but I'll—"

"No, wait!" Cassidy cried, taking an abrupt step toward him.

Obviously unused to such impulsive commands, the young man simply stood staring at Cassidy with an expression of wide-eyed expectation on his face. From across the paved deck the two remaining Troopers had suddenly jerked to attention, ready to come to his aid as his slightest signal.

Looking up into those cripplingly familiar and yet totally alien eyes, Cassidy felt momentarily paralyzed by the cognizant directness of his gaze. When she could force her tongue to move, she blurted out hoarsely, "I have to talk to you."

Seemingly more puzzled than concerned, the Warden merely offered, "I know you do, but I want to wait for the rest of my people so they all can hear your story, and it'll be at least evening before Valerie can gather her field troops."

His understandable misinterpretation helped Cassidy to focus beyond the disorienting effect his mere presence was having on her. She felt the return of some of the indignation she had experienced down on the wharf. "No, not about that," she said quickly, still staring into his eyes, "about the baby."

At the steps the two Troopers shifted uneasily; but the young Warden briefly raised his hand, making only the slightest of gestures to restrain them. He looked levelly at Cassidy, his expression still puzzled but then also colored with concern.

"What baby?" he asked quietly.

At least he hadn't acted as if he didn't know what a baby was, Cassidy thought ironically. She knew that Rowena and Allen were uneasy about her choice to confront the Warden about the incident, but in recalling the experience Cassidy had rekindled in herself much of the same outrage that she had felt when she had seen the trashman's crude indifference to the tiny body. Even the Troopers' intervention wouldn't have been able to prevent her from going on then.

"Yesterday down at the docks," she said stiffly, "when our rafts were moored we saw a trashman dumping a baby out with the garbage."

A strange expression crossed the Warden's face. With Andy Greene there had never been any emotion to read on those smooth handsome features, and so for a moment Cassidy was at something of a loss as to just how to interpret it. But when the young man spoke, his tone was soft and concerned.

"Was the baby dead?" he asked her.

Only that gentle tone of voice kept his question from further infuriating Cassidy. "I think so," she admitted, adding "If it hadn't been, it was once he was finished with it. He smashed its skull against the pier."

The Warden shook his head, his mouth pulling down in a little grimace. "I've asked them not to do that," he said with obvious regret.

Unsure if his comment referred to the bashing of babies' skulls or merely to the dumping of dead babies into the river, Cassidy pushed on. "What kind of people could treat an infant that way, even if it was dead?" she demanded hotly. "What kind of people could treat any body that way?"

As she stood glaring at him, Cassidy was somewhat disarmed to see a deep and genuine pain in those warm brown eyes. Obviously the issue was of no small matter to the Warden. "It's always been especially difficult with babies," he murmured, so softly he might almost have been speaking to himself. "Even to care for the living ones—so often they just die."

He straightened himself, tossing back his head as if to push away an unhappy thought, and gave Cassidy that calm, direct look again. "I'll see to it that the incident you've described is investigated and that the man involved is dealt with, but please don't judge him or the others too harshly. The babies are a great disappointment to many." Then both his tone and his expression grew more intense as he went on.

"Please know that I appreciate what the three of you have done, traveling here to the city to bring us the information of what you have seen in the hills. I'm grateful for your help, and I wish to offer you my hospitality while you're here. In fact," he added, "I had been about to explain that even though I must leave now, I'll see to it that you're brought breakfast and anything else that you need."

As he had been speaking, Rowena had edged up beside Cassidy, to where she could then give her a sharp but surreptitious poke in the side with her elbow. Cassidy jumped slightly, but Rowena interrupted before Cassidy could respond with any further outbursts. "Thanks," the brunette said brightly to the Warden. "Breakfast sounds like a great idea."

Giving them all a pleasant if slightly distracted nod, the young man said, "You can eat out here if you wish, since the weather's fair. I'll have Bobby see to it."

Cassidy was about to take another step forward, words ready at her lips, when Rowena grabbed her by the shoulder and firmly restrained her. Even as Cassidy turned to glower at the interference, the Warden turned and began to stride away across the deck toward the two remaining Troopers.

"Why the hell did you stop me?" Cassidy hissed, frankly not caring whether the Warden was out of earshot. "We didn't even get a chance to—"

Ignoring Cassidy's baleful glare, Rowena interrupted. "And just what else were you going to tell him? 'Hi, your name is Andy Greene—and oh, by the way, have you noticed that you're dead?' "

Her posture still stiffened with irritation, Cassidy stood stubbornly as Allen turned and began walking across the deck toward one of the tables. Only when Rowena yanked forcibly on her arm did she reluctantly stumble after her. "I was going to tell him about the Memories," she insisted angrily.

"Yeah? Well, you can still tell him later," Rowena told her calmly, leading Cassidy toward the table. "First we'd better try to help him out and get on his good side, because I've got the feeling this guy's got enough troubles already without all the shit you're about to dump on him."

Cassidy made a rudely disparaging noise and tugged free of Rowena's hold, but she obediently followed the brunette's example and sat down at the table with Allen. Much as she hated to admit it, Rowena's approach did make sense. It was just that Cassidy had sustained herself for so long on the belief that finding the Warden would prove to be the solution to their problems. It was depressing to consider that their real problems might be just beginning.

Chapter 13 ◀▥

It took her several minutes of pointless sulking before Cassidy relented and spoke to Rowena again.

"I want to go check on my mare," she said.

But Rowena waved her down. "Later," she said, "after we eat."

Sighing, Cassidy sat back and surrendered to the soothing beauty of the Warden's garden deck. A pattern of sunlight and shadows splashed across the intricately laid stones of the deck's surface, and the sweet scent of the flowering vines and shrubs perfumed the cool air. Although the raised area was built right off the big brick house, very little of the building could be seen from the tables that were placed there. The heavily draped arbors and the surrounding trees acted like a screen to isolate the deck from even the rest of the gardens and lawn.

Given the time to ponder the move rationally, Cassidy could no longer be angry with Rowena for having stopped her from trying to confront the Warden further. The sudden return of her memory had given her an almost schizophrenic reaction to their presence there. In a way she had become two people: Cassidy, who was desperate to escape a frustrating world where she did not belong, and Cathy Delaney, who was terrified of finding out that there no longer was any world where she did belong. To either person the Warden's concerns about monsters seemed petty and remote. Yet Rowena had a point when she counseled caution. Even Click had warned Cassidy about making the wrong assumptions.

The thought of the Tinker leader brought a new kind of uneasiness to Cassidy's mind. She was still convinced that at least some of the Warden's Troopers knew Click; and all of them seemed to have treated him with a puzzling mixture of overt dislike and grudging respect. How was a Tinker linked to the Troopers and to the power that governed the Iron City?

Cassidy was still mulling over that puzzle when she saw a young woman approaching them, climbing the broad stone steps where the two remaining Troopers kept a desultory sort of watch over them. The woman was not another Trooper; at least she was dressed in a simple outfit of a sleeveless shirt and cut-off pants rather than the decorated leathers. And she was carrying, with the kind of casual adroitness that led Cassidy to believe the woman did it on a regular basis, a big tray that was heaped to capacity with food.

"You must be Bobby," Rowena greeted her cheerfully. There was nothing like food to perk up the brunette's spirits, Cassidy noted sourly.

Upon closer inspection Cassidy realized that the young woman in the cut-offs was really no more than a girl. She couldn't have been much more than sixteen, and her heart-shaped face was smooth and lightly tanned beneath a cropped-off shock of reddish-blond hair. "Bobby's the cook," the girl corrected with a toothy smile, bending to slip the generously laden tray onto their table. "I'm Mickey."

Rowena made quick introductions while Mickey deftly transferred plates and dishes from the tray to the table. Tantalizing aromas rose from every container, making Cassidy's mouth water. For the first time since waking she realized that she hadn't had anything to eat since lunch on the rafts the day before.

"Can you sit with us for a while?" Rowena asked as the girl whisked the tray aside.

The invitation surprised and vaguely irritated Cassidy; she resented Rowena enjoying herself. But Mickey responded with total aplomb. "Sure, if you want," she said easily, pulling up a chair.

From the other side of the deck at the stone stairs the two Troopers casually scanned the garden, seemingly disinterested in the quartet seated at the table. But Cassidy still thought of the man and woman as guards, and she wondered a bit uneasily just what Rowena had had in mind when she'd invited the blond girl to sit with them.

"You're the guy who got attacked by the monsters, huh?" Mickey asked Allen with a disarmingly ingenuous curiosity.

The bearded man had been plumbing the depths of a steaming mug of what smelled to be excellent coffee. The candid comment caused him to lower his cup abruptly while he studied the girl's guileless face over the edge of it. "Not exactly how I'd wish to be known," he said.

Undaunted by his terse response, Mickey looked around the table at all three of them. "I've heard you all have seen those things," she said.

While that was not precisely true in Rowena's case, Cassidy didn't see any need to quibble over details. She studied Mickey's friendly face with a new interest. If the girl was that talkative, perhaps she could answer questions as well as ask them.

"Yeah, we have," Cassidy said ruefully, "but we don't exactly consider that a stroke of good luck." Pausing for a calculated moment, Cassidy tried to keep both her expression and her tone as nonchalant as possible as she added, "No one else here has seen them yet?"

Mickey shrugged, her thin browned shoulders hitching beneath the flimsy shirt. "Maybe some of the field Troopers have by now," she said, "but no one here in the city. There're reports always coming in from the hills, though." Absently gnawing at a hangnail, Mickey fixed them all with an expectant look. "That's where you're all from, right?"

"Double Creek," Allen said shortly, ladling jam onto a piece of fresh bread the size of his fist.

"Well, out there's where it all started, isn't it?" Mickey said. "The troubles, I mean." Inspecting another finger, she nibbled at the edge of its nail before adding, "They say there's always been talk of monsters, but talk is all it ever was. Everyone thought it was just stories—stuff that crazy people talked about."

Cassidy's interest was definitely piqued by then. Perhaps she could salvage something from having been abandoned there by the Warden for the day after all. Not only was Mickey a talker, she also seemed to be a self-starter. Both Allen and Rowena had their mouths full of food then, so Cassidy took it upon herself to follow up on Mickey's comments.

"So exactly when did the real trouble with the monsters start?" she asked the blonde.

"Just this summer, I guess," Mickey said. "At least that's when the reports started coming in to the Warden from the hills."

"What has he done about it?" Cassidy prompted, figuring if she couldn't interrogate the man himself she would try to do it by proxy.

Mickey gave her an odd look, bemusement mixed with mild exasperation. "He sent out the Troopers, of course," she said, as if that would have been self-evident. And perhaps to a Horseman it should have been. Warily Cassidy backed off a bit.

"Do they have any idea where the monsters came from?" she said casually, as if the answer were really of little interest to her.

Rowena shot Cassidy a sharp look, but Mickey didn't seem to find anything suspicious about the question. "Not really," she replied, absently scanning the fingertips of her other hand. "And of course the Troopers haven't gotten much help from the Villagers—oops!" she added, with an apologetic glance in Allen's direction. But when the sheriff just grunted, the girl continued. "Valerie says Villagers would just as soon lynch Troopers as cooperate with them, even with all the trouble. She says that maybe now that the monsters have killed some people, the Villagers'll be a little more helpful."

That opinion was recounted with an ingenuous candor, but Cassidy could see the way Allen's body stiffened at the mention of the deaths outside of Pointed Rock. For a few seconds the big man's jaws stopped chewing, then he silently resumed eating. Mindful of the enmity between Villagers and Horsemen and of Allen's particularly painful memories, Cassidy decided it would be prudent to change the subject for the moment.

"Do you work here at the house, Mickey?"

"Yeah," the girl said with a grin. "But it really isn't much work. Mostly I help Bobby in the kitchen, and with the mess hall down in the Troopers' barracks. When I first came here I helped Sharon with the other house stuff, but I like the kitchen stuff better."

Deliberately nonchalant, Cassidy popped a piece of sliced apple into her mouth and asked, "How long have you been here?"

"You mean here at the Warden's house? About a year, I guess. Before that I was down in the city." Mickey flashed that toothy grin. "I like it a lot better here!"

While Cassidy considered the reply and just how to follow it up without appearing too nosy, Mickey confirmed Cassidy's growing presumption that the perky blond girl simply didn't have any sense of suspicion by spontaneously continuing on her own.

"Down there I was just hanging around by the docks, you

know? With some of the gangs." She shrugged with complete and effacing innocence. "Stealing stuff and trading what we stole for food—till the Troopers caught us. Boy, I thought I'd get exiled from the city for sure." She flashed a sunny smile. "But when the Troopers saw some of the stuff I had, they brought me up here. And when the Warden saw what I'd found, he let me stay here. He's a really nice guy."

Cassidy paused with a slice of smoked meat poised halfway to her mouth. Across the table from her, Rowena was trying valiantly not to choke on the food she had just swallowed. The two of them traded one swift significant look across the tableware. Forcing herself to take one careful, casual nip out of the piece of meat she held, Cassidy fought down the sudden surge of excitement she felt and made herself speak calmly.

"You said you had some stuff you'd found . . . Mickey, are you a Finder?"

The girl made a gesture of cheerful assent, spreading her gnawed fingertips. "Yeah, at least that's what the Warden told me. All I know is that I can find weird stuff—always could." Her slender shoulders hitched slightly, more a gesture of self-deprecation than one of puzzlement. "Everyone back in the streets just thought it was junk. Heck, if I'd known that the Warden saved the stuff, I would have come up here to his house on my own a long time ago!"

Taking another little bite of meat, Cassidy said, "When you found this stuff did you ever know what it was? Do you recognize any of it?"

Allen looked up then from the rapidly diminishing pile of food on the plate before him and finally shot Cassidy a warning look. But she pointedly ignored him, and Mickey seemed totally without mistrust.

"Naw, not really," the girl admitted blithely, resting her hands on the surface of the wooden table and loosely meshing her fingers together. "To me it's just a lot of odd stuff."

Cassidy swallowed, deliberately using the pause to diminish the impact of her next question. "Does the Warden know what the stuff is?"

Again Mickey just shrugged, a gesture with which she managed to convey both bemusement and a good-natured nonchalance. "I don't know," she said, "but he sure seems interested in it. He has all kinds of stuff that people like me have found—whole rooms full of it."

Again and less subtly, Allen shot Cassidy a warning look,

and again she chose to ignore it. She didn't even glance across
the table to Rowena, lest something in the brunette's expression compromise her own composure. Cassidy just looked at
Mickey, assuming an expression of the most innocent sort of
curiosity she could muster.

"Do you think we could have a look at this stuff the Warden
has?" she asked the girl.

"Sure, why not?" Mickey responded promptly. "Bobby said
the Warden told us to take care of you guys and to see that you
got anything you wanted."

Cassidy wanted to leap immediately to her feet and drag
Mickey back into the house; instead of a frustratingly wasted
day stretching out ahead of her, she had suddenly been handed
a chance to find out something significant about the Warden
and what he might know. But by some superhuman effort of
will she managed to continue sitting there at the table, picking
at the selection of food. Allen and Rowena both seemed to
have finally lost interest in eating, but Cassidy wasn't sure if
that was because they had been so studiously stuffing themselves earlier—or if because they, too, had begun to appreciate
the importance of what Mickey had told them.

The found things had been one of the first things Cassidy
had suspected as a link between that world and the real one.
When Click had given her the car key, the memories it had
provided convinced Cassidy that her theory about the found
things was correct, that they were things which had somehow
been carried there from her own world. Being able to remember who she was and where she had come from had not ne-
gated that theory; if anything, her new and enhanced memory
had only made her recognition of the found things more defin-
itive and complete.

Aaron, the old black stableman in Double Creek, had been
the first person to tell her about Finders; but by then Cassidy
had already met one. Kevin, the young would-be Horseman
who with her had ridden with Yolanda and Raphael, had been
a Finder—whether or not he'd realized he was. Kevin was responsible for two of the first really incongruous things Cassidy
had seen in that alien new world, Yolanda's sunglasses and her
cigarette lighter. Considering the hypothesis Cassidy and
Rowena had worked out regarding found things, a chance to
examine some of the items that the Warden had collected
might provide her with some further clues to the continuing
mystery of how Cathy Delaney, riding instructor from Green-

lea, New York, had become Cassidy, Horseman in the land of the dead.

For a good ten or fifteen minutes longer, they sat at the table on the Warden's pleasant deck. Once Cassidy had stopped priming her with loaded questions, Mickey had continued talking, but on less consequential topics, including what Cassidy could only categorize as household gossip. Besides Bobby the cook and Sharon, the woman who apparently oversaw the general running of the house, Mickey mentioned several other people who seemed to be residents of the big brick house. Cassidy listened with half an ear, her mind mulling over what she had already learned.

Despite her impatience to get on with her investigation, Cassidy was still capable of enjoying the peaceful garden. The morning sun had climbed to nearly midpoint in the cloudless sky, high enough to warm the deck's interlaid stones, and bees and other nectar-seeking insects droned hypnotically in the flowering vines and shrubs. With a little food in her belly and her mind completely occupied with the information Mickey had so freely dispensed, Cassidy had become so engrossed that she was caught by surprise when Allen, Rowena, and Mickey all got to their feet. They pushed in their chairs, the iron legs scraping dully on the paved surface.

"We can help you carry this stuff back to the house," Rowena offered, waving toward the litter of dishes on the table.

But Mickey dismissed her offer with a grin. "No hurry," she said, with a significant glance toward the pair of waiting Troopers who still stood on the far side of the deck. "They can bring it in later."

The young blonde led the way across the deck toward the house. As they passed the two Troopers on the wide steps, Mickey gave them both a friendly smile. Then she confided, in a loud stage whisper, "They'll finish up whatever's left over anyway!"

Cassidy wasn't too sure about the ranking or the chain of command among the Warden's Troopers, but obviously his household members were held to a pretty lenient set of rules, at least if Mickey was any indication.

At the side of the house the girl ushered them in through a pair of French doors that were set directly off the paving-stone walk. It was not the front of the house, but from the amount of wear on the wooden threshhold Cassidy suspected that it was the entrance that saw the most use. Immediately inside the doors they stepped into a large sunny room, rather sparsely furnished with several widely spaced couches and upholstered chairs. It looked like some kind of informal sitting room; although some of the furniture appeared fairly old, none of it looked very used, and its arrangement gave the impression that the various pieces had once been assembled for filling a much smaller room.

"This is just the front room," Mickey announced, leading them across the bare but polished wooden floor. "Nobody uses this room much."

"Just how many people live here?" Rowena asked curiously, temporarily relieving Cassidy from her role as inquisitor.

Mickey shrugged as she opened another door, preceding them into a short wide hallway. "It depends," she said. "The Warden and Becky both travel a lot, and Bobby sometimes lives down at the barracks." At the center of the hallway, which appeared to be some sort of foyer of the house's actual front entrance, Mickey paused at the foot of a broad wooden staircase. "About six or seven of us right now," she added over her shoulder as she started up the steps.

"Do any of them have the Memories?" Cassidy asked, in a manner calculated to be offhanded.

Rowena had been right behind Mickey and just ahead of Cassidy. When the brunette heard what Cassidy had asked, she almost stumbled and Cassidy nearly collided with her. Rowena gave Cassidy a look of wide-eyed surprise, but Cassidy ignored it. Behind them, Allen's steady advance kept both of the women moving along after Mickey.

"Becky," Mickey replied. She had reached the head of the staircase and could turn to look back down upon them to elaborate. "I guess maybe some of the others had the Memories once, too."

As all of them gained the upstairs hallway, Cassidy continued casually, "Are they all people that the Warden brought here because of what they could remember?"

"I guess so," Mickey said. She reached for the knob on the door of the first room off the hallway and turned it, swinging the door open and stepping across the threshhold into the room beyond. "You'd have to ask Becky about that," she said as she beckoned for them to enter.

"Where's Becky now?" Cassidy asked as she passed through the doorway. "Is she—" But the question died on her lips once she saw what was in the room before her.

From the layout of the house, whose interior was actually more spacious than the outside of the building would have suggested, logic would have made this a bedroom. Instead it looked like a chamber in some odd sort of museum. The entire room, which was easily as large as their generous-size downstairs bedroom, was filled with shelves and cabinets and glass-doored cases. And all of those storage spaces were filled or covered with one of the most bizarre collections of unrelated objects Cassidy could have imagined.

Speechless, Cassidy stepped farther into the room. Directly before her on a set of shelves small metallic items vied for space: bobby pins, keys, coins, paper clips. To her right stood a cabinet containing nothing but scraps of paper, most of them small pieces like business cards and ticket stubs. And to her left the surface of another display case was arranged with an even more eclectic mix of things, with items as wildly disparate as plastic audiocassette cases and wristwatches. There was even an area devoted entirely to a collage of foil-wrapped condoms, several in varying stages of deterioration.

"Well, here it is," Mickey announced cheerfully, spreading her arms to encompass the whole of the large but cluttered room. "Pretty odd, huh?"

Oh, no, not "odd," Cassidy thought, almost giddy with a surging rush of recognition as her fingers skimmed over the collection of metal baubles, *real—this is real stuff!*

Rowena was already moving from cabinet to cabinet, peering inside each with an expression somewhere between amazement and delight. Only Allen seemed unmoved by the wealth of found things. He still stood in the doorway, a vaguely uneasy look on his bearded face, as Cassidy and Rowena explored the contents of the room.

Genuinely overwhelmed and unable to conceal that fact, Cassidy tore her eyes away from the cabinet before her—which, she noticed with considerable amazement, contained among other things a caseless but otherwise undamaged audiocassette tape of the Beatles' *Abbey Road*—and gaped at Mickey. "Finders found all this stuff?" she asked incredulously.

"Sure, but this isn't all of it," the blond girl assured her blithely. "There're two more rooms like this up here, and I've heard there's even more stuff down in the basement." She shrugged as she added, "I guess some of the stuff is pretty old."

Rowena's head lifted from her stunned contemplation of skate keys and pawnshop tickets. "I can't believe this," she said to Cassidy. "You were right about the found stuff! I've never—"

Cassidy interrupted Rowena before she could blurt out something incriminating. "Yeah, it's really interesting, isn't it?" she said, giving Rowena a pointed look. "I can't believe how much stuff the Warden has collected."

But Mickey didn't seem to have noticed anything unusual about Rowena's excited comment; she just added helpfully, "Well, this stuff wasn't all collected just by this Warden. I guess all of them have saved stuff like this."

Cassidy's attention returned to Mickey. The girl's casual revelations seemed to just keep on dropping, like a string of bombs. Cassidy had never encountered quite so voluble a source of information in that world. And the fact that Cassidy finally remembered the real world only made the possibility of what Mickey might know about that one all the more enticing. The most difficult thing was deciding what to ask first; the second most difficult thing was trying to keep her excitement out of her voice.

"You said all the Wardens have collected this stuff," Cassidy said, giving an inclusive little wave. "Just how many—"

"Hey, Jeremy," Mickey said, unintentionally interrupting Cassidy to greet someone who had just appeared behind Allen at the door.

Cassidy looked past the bulk of the sheriff's body to see that a far more slightly built man stood in the hallway right outside of the room. His thinning hair and rather stooped posture gave him a somewhat doleful look, and his words were immediately apologetic.

"Bobby's looking for you, Mickey," he said, spreading his pale hands as if to ameliorate the message. "He says he needs you to help him in the barracks mess."

Mickey seemed to take the news with the same equanimity she applied to everything else. "Okay," she agreed readily, "thanks, Jeremy." She made a loopy little wave toward Cassidy and Rowena. "These are the people Justin brought in last night—you know, the ones who saw the monsters? Can you show them some more of the found stuff?"

"Sure," Jeremy said, running one hand back over his receding hairline in a gesture more self-effacing than primping.

"You can give them the grand tour." Mickey grinned at him as she slipped past him out of the room. She waved. "I'll see you guys later."

Before Cassidy had much time to become disappointed at losing Mickey, or even to wonder if she dared hope Jeremy would prove as helpful, the meek-looking little man surprised her with a question of his own.

"Did you really see the monsters?" Jeremy asked in a tone that bordered on both reverent and hopeful.

Was that all that any of those people cared about? Cassidy thought irritably. But she stifled her annoyance to answer him. "Allen and I did," she said. "That's part of what brought us here."

Jeremy's thin and sallow face brightened visibly with anticipation, but before he could ask more, Cassidy concluded, "But the real reason we've come is the Memories."

"Oh," he said, "then you're waiting to see Becky." His transparent expression was openly disappointed that there would be no further talk of monsters.

"Where is Becky now, Jeremy?" Cassidy asked, following up on the question she had been asking Mickey before she had been overwhelmed by the bounty of the found things. "Is she the one who knows the most about the Memories?"

Jeremy nodded vigorously, causing further disarray among the flyaway strands of his sparse hair. "She's out on a boat," he said, "because she's still the one who remembers the most." He hesitated a moment, his deferential voice falling even lower. "I used to remember stuff, but I don't really remember very much anymore."

Simultaneously, almost involuntarily, Cassidy and Rowena exchanged a brief but meaningful look. Cassidy was reluctant to ask the timid little man what both of the women had been thinking. "Do you mean that you used to remember more than you can now, Jeremy? Have you started to forget things?"

Jeremy straightened his stooped shoulders a bit, his voice lifting with pride. "When I first came here, I had the Memories," he declared. Then he shrugged. "But now I don't. They say that happens to everyone here eventually, so Becky says I shouldn't feel bad about it. Besides," he added with an echo of pride, "I work in the yard and the gardens. The Warden says I'm so good with plants, I could make a rock sprout roots and bloom!"

As Jeremy gestured for them to follow him from the room, Cassidy caught Rowena's eye again. She was disheartened to see that the brunette had obviously come to the same conclusion as she had. Both of them had long been troubled by the possibility that they might eventually lose their true memories

and become like everyone else in that world. Since Cassidy
had regained the near entirety of her past, she was especially
upset to discover the added evidence of the inexorable erosion
of memory in everyone else who had displayed the Memories.

We may have come all this way for nothing, Cassidy thought
glumly, *unless we can find a way to get out of here quickly.*

It was nearly a full minute later, not until Jeremy was politely ushering them into another museumlike upstairs room,
that Cassidy suddenly realized the assumption under which she
had just operated. *I'm still worried about losing my memory,*
she realized with bemused irony. *But if we're all really dead,
what the hell difference would it make?*

That was when Cassidy first discovered that she had, at least
subconsciously, bought into Rowena's bizarre theory of exactly
what that alien world might represent.

After Mickey had gone, Jeremy had proven to be an affable
if less loquacious host. He showed them two more upstairs
rooms full of the found things, most of them similar to what
they had seen in the first room. Some of the items, everything
from fountain pens to pocket watches, had appeared older, possibly even antique. But everything had been objects for which
there was no recognized use there, objects from another
place—or another time.

Jeremy also introduced them to several of the other people
who lived in the Warden's big brick house: Sharon, the apparent housekeeper; Bobby, the cook; and Laura, who wore
leather clothing similar to the Troopers' and seemed to divide
her time between the house and the garrison. Like Jeremy, they
seemed far more interested in Cassidy, Rowena, and Allen because of the fact that they'd survived a brush with the monsters
than for any possible Memories that they might have. Cassidy
was disappointed to find that none of them seemed to have any
intact Memory of their own, even though all had initially come
to the Warden's compound still carrying those elusive remnants
of their other life. All of her oblique attempts to solicit more
information from them were met with interruptions asking
questions about the monsters, or with suggestions to speak
with Becky when she returned.

Frustrated at the lack of progress and physically restless,
Cassidy finally announced that she was going out to check on
her horse. No one in the house made any objection, and no one
stopped her from just walking right out the door and across the

shorn lawn, toward the rolling expanse of pastureland that sloped down to the garrison's buildings. When she Called Dragonfly, the horse came cantering lazily out from among a group of the Troopers' horses that had been grazing along the same hillside.

Sliding to a halt, the mare buried her long aquiline head in Cassidy's shirt and pushed gently as she blew through her nostrils. Cassidy cradled the big face, embarrassingly happy just to touch the gray again. Lightly scratching the bases of the horse's ears, she slowly scanned the grassy sweep of land that led down to the tree line marking the rear of the barracks building. A few Troopers were visible striding across the courtyard there, but for the most part the garrison looked deserted.

Beyond the garrison on one side, back the way from which Cassidy had just come, lay the landscaped grounds of the Warden's handsome brick house. And to the other side, straggling down toward the Long River, rose the distant outskirts of the Iron City. Although the day was still fair and pleasantly breezy, and there on the hillside the sun was set like a clear yellow disc in the azure dome of the sky, the air over the city itself was smudged with a faint pall of greasy smoke that only seemed to intensify as it hung down over the warehouse district near the docks. Apparently even the afterlife wasn't free of air pollution.

Engrossed in thought, Cassidy continued to rub Dragonfly's head. It seemed that the more she remembered and found out, the less her concept of found things seemed to fit in with either her own or Rowena's weird theory. Cassidy was willing to concede to Rowena's point that dead people wouldn't need things like car keys or cigarette lighters, and heaven knew they certainly wouldn't need condoms. But if Rowena's outrageous idea had any validity, if they all had somehow become different versions of themselves trapped in some other frame of time, then how and why were all those random objects from their own time cropping up in that one? Car keys and cigarette lighters made little sense for people without cars or cigarettes, and why would you find condoms in a world without sex?

About the only thing that finally made more sense was why Yolanda had been so eager to bring Cassidy to the Warden. Presenting him with someone who had the Memories would have been a very smart career move for a would-be Trooper and her apprentices. And no matter whose theory, if any, held up about the *why* of the place, the simple *what* of it still seemed to Cassidy to be pretty much as she had originally proposed: The Memories were the only real source of new technology or diversity there. No wonder the Warden had collected the people with Memories as avidly as he had collected the oddities discovered by the Finders. Memories and found things were the only concrete link with the real world.

Looking down again past the garrison to where the distant shapes of the city's structures were arrayed in blocks of buildings leading down to the river, Cassidy reexamined the sense of determination that had driven her to come there. She had learned so much since she and Rowena had fled Double Creek, but she had always held fast to one tenet: She had always thought that if she could reach the Warden of Horses then all of her questions would somehow be answered.

Well, we didn't come here for nothing, she told herself stolidly. *Even if the Memories fade and the found things mean nothing, at least now I know who I am.* All that remained was to discover why she was there, and how she could again become Cathy Delaney.

Cassidy didn't realize how deep her reverie had grown until Dragonfly suddenly pulled her head up from Cassidy's chest and stared down across the grassy hillside. The mare whinnied at an approaching horse and rider, a pair whom Cassidy had not even noticed until the gray had moved, despite the fact that they were already halfway up the slope from the garrison, from the direction in which Cassidy had ostensibly been looking. The rider was a woman Trooper mounted on a dark bay horse, traveling at a brisk and businesslike jog, and yet Cassidy did not sense any alarm or particular urgency in their approach.

As the horse and rider drew up to them the gray mare nickered at the bay. It seemed ironic to Cassidy then that whatever clashes between expectation and reality she and Rowena may have suffered in coming to the Warden's city, Dragonfly probably was perfectly satisfied with the arrangement. As the bay horse halted a few yards from them, Cassidy studied his rider. The Trooper was a big and rather raw-boned–looking woman with a few streaks of gray in her dark auburn hair and a plain but amiable-looking face.

"Are you Cassidy?" the Trooper asked her.

"Yeah, that's me," she replied, still more curious than concerned about the Trooper's arrival on the calm sun-washed hillside.

The woman smiled then, a broad and loose expression that

sat familiarly on her generous mouth. "I figured as much," she said. "They told me that you were the one who was the Horseman, so I knew I'd find you out here." She jerked her chin toward the garrison. "You've got a visitor down at the gate."

Cassidy's brow furrowed slightly. "For me?" she said somewhat stupidly.

The Trooper just shrugged her broad but bony shoulders and gave Cassidy another smile. "That's what they told me," she said. "Come on, you might as well have a look."

As the Trooper swung the bay around, Cassidy quickly hopped up onto her mare's wide sun-warmed back. She let the gray follow the bay horse at an easy ground-covering lope, too preoccupied even to enjoy the smooth and pleasant ride through the knee-deep grass. By the time they had reached the garrison and were winding their way at a more sedate walk between the barracks and the stables, Cassidy thought she had figured out what sort of visitor she might have. After all, there were a limited number of people she knew in the Iron City.

The Trooper on the bay horse stopped by the edge of the stables and waved Cassidy on toward the gate. "There you go," she encouraged affably.

Riding on past her, Cassidy could see that although the wide iron gates stood open, a trio of Troopers kept watch there on foot, pacing casually back and forth across the aperture. Beyond them, standing alone with an air of relaxed patience on the dusty roadway outside the garrison, was an instantly recognizable figure. Tightening her calves around the mare's barrel, Cassidy urged the horse into a trot again, covering the remaining distance to the gate in mere seconds.

"Click!" she said excitedly, dropping down from the gray's back even before the horse could come to a complete halt.

None of the three Troopers—two men and a woman, all unfamiliar to her—made any move to impede her, but Cassidy nevertheless came to an automatic stop just inside the gate. She threw the guards an inquiring look, uncertain of what protocols she might be violating in her unseemly enthusiasm to see the Tinker leader again. Finally, because the Troopers seemed less inclined to stop her from going out than they might be to stop Click from coming in, and because it was just the simplest thing to do, she stepped right past the little contingent of Troopers and out onto the road beyond the gate.

To her own considerable amazement, she was so embarrassingly happy to see the tall dark-haired man again that she nearly went right up to him and threw her arms around him. Fortunately for her, that familiar expression of barely veiled irony that glinted at her from those umber-colored eyes enabled her to catch herself in time, and so instead she just stumbled to a halt in front of Click, beaming up at him with a helplessly sappy smile on her face.

"What are you doing here?" she asked him, too glad to see him to try to be more oblique about it.

"I've come to bring you and Rowena your things," he said placidly, gesturing toward the dusty roadbed at his feet.

For the first time Cassidy noticed that there was a canvas-wrapped bundle resting on the pavement beside him. From its size and shape she could have guessed its contents, but the continuing look of rather dumb perplexity on her face must have prompted Click to elaborate.

"Bonnie dried and packed your other clothing for you," he said with another little wave at the parcel, "and Mitz sent along the wicker baskets Rowena made on the river." The graying tips of his dark mustache twitched slightly upward. "As for the rest, well, we figured you've both certainly earned the bedrolls and tent by now."

Still too distracted by the unexpectedly powerful sense of relief she felt at seeing the man, Cassidy could only stare stupidly at Click and murmur some incoherent sound of thanks. It was only when she became aware that Dragonfly had followed her through the gate and had moved past them to graze calmly along the roadway that Cassidy glanced back over her shoulder. The guards still paced idly across the gate opening, affording her and Click only the slightest of notice.

"Are you all right, Cassidy?" Click asked her quietly, drawing her attention back to him again. He was regarding her with a particularly intent look and his dark eyes had suddenly gone completely sober. "I heard about what happened to you in the barracks last night."

Suddenly abashed, Cassidy felt the heat of a blush flood up her neck from her shirt collar and burn across her cheeks. She dropped her eyes. "That was nothing," she said hastily, "I just—"

Click didn't need to say anything to interrupt her; the shrewd directness of his gaze did that without words. So smoothly that she should have expected it, he reached out and gently but briefly touched her on the arm, forcing her to look up at him again. "I know that Horsemen hold their Warden in great regard," he said wryly, "but merely being brought into the sphere of his presence hasn't typically been known to cause immediate loss of consciousness."

Embarrassed, and angered by the transparency of that embarrassment, Cassidy straightened stiffly. "I didn't faint!" she insisted. "I was just . . . tired."

"Of course," Click agreed easily, which only irritated her more. She probably would have made some further retort had not the genuine concern in Click's eyes shone past the veneer of his ironic humor at her expense. Touching her arm again, he said casually, "Walk with me for a moment."

Cassidy reflexively glanced back toward the three Troopers in the gate. "Aren't you going to come inside?" she asked Click, not much caring if the guards heard her.

Click also gave the Troopers a look, but it was a look of a different sort from the one Cassidy had bestowed. Once again she found herself strangely aware of some tense if subtle undercurrent between the Warden's guards and the Tinker leader as Click calmly studied the three studiously indifferent faces.

"I think not," he said to Cassidy, guiding her gently by the arm and adding as they turned away, "I think these Troopers would rather see you outside their gates than see me within them."

Too puzzled to protest or question him further, Cassidy simply acquiesced, content for the moment to begin a slow stroll along the road at Click's side. She was still abashed by the effect his presence was having on her, but if she was honest with herself she would have had to admit that the feeling was not entirely unpleasant. In fact, much to her bemusement, she discovered that having regained her own real identity again had somehow given her a little better perspective on the reaction that Click could elicit from her. And so she walked slowly alongside the taller man, accepting his silent companionship as the grazing mare tagged along after them.

Cassidy had quickly grown so relaxed walking with Click that when he looked over at her and suddenly spoke, it almost startled her. "There was trouble last night," he said quietly, "down on the river."

She automatically came to a halt, but Click touched her elbow, urging her forward again. It took surprising concentration to be able to both look up into his face and to keep walking; despite the level surface of the roadway she nearly tripped over her own feet as she asked him in a hushed voice, "What do you mean, trouble? What kind of trouble?"

"The usual kind," Click responded dryly; but he was not merely being facetious. He inclined his dark head a little nearer to Cassidy as he went on. "Two barges sank and a man drowned. The harbormaster is saying that it was an accident, that the barges collided because one of them failed to yield the right of way." The tips of his mustache twitched. "But I know of few people who truly believe that."

Too stunned to speak, Cassidy could only think of one thing: the wild ride with the Tinkers' rafts down the lower rapids—and of the huge and silent creature that had risen beneath her own body as she had been carried on the current. And when she looked sideways into Click's face, she could see that he knew what she had been thinking about. But when he spoke again it was not about the incident on the rapids or about Wanda's sheared-off rudder shaft.

"And that isn't all," he said gravely. "This morning four people were found dead in an alley in the warehouse district, not two blocks from the docks."

"Dead?" she asked. "What happened to them?"

Click shot her a look of patent skepticism. "Gang problems, if you believe the report the Troopers made to your Warden," he said sourly. "And if you believe that then you would also have to believe that Allen fell victim to some disgruntled forest wildlife."

"*Monsters?*" Cassidy whispered in dismay. "Right here in the city?"

But Click merely arched one dark brow at Cassidy, as if he found her incredulity rather ironic. "Did you think the city would be exempt?" he asked her. "Actually I can hardly think of a better place for such creatures to prey."

"But—but they told us that no one here had ever seen monsters," Cassidy blurted out, her eyes still wide with disbelief.

Beside her, Click merely spread his hands. "And I doubt that anyone has seen them yet," he said, "unless the dead will come forth to speak."

They walked a bit farther without speaking, but then the silence was no longer a pleasant or comradely thing. Remembering Valerie's solemn morning conference with the Warden, she understood then just what had so urgently called the young man away. Would the Warden realize what Click found to be so self-evident? And if he did, would he reveal it publicly?

Rowena had certainly been right: The Warden had enough problems already without the weighty conundrum Cassidy had been about to drop on him.

Engrossed in thought, Cassidy almost just kept right on walking past Click when the Tinker finally did come to a halt. A few paces ahead of him, she turned to look back and was freshly surprised by the expression on that lean and familiar face. There was a soft glint in his deeply set eyes, one less of irony than of simple perceptiveness. And although she had no idea what he was going to say, somehow when he spoke she was not surprised by his words.

"So now that you have met your Warden, Cassidy," Click said softly, "have you found your answers?"

A familiar spark of alarm coursed through Cassidy's nerves then, and, not for the first time, she thought, *He can't know— can he?* Looking helplessly into those utterly calm eyes, she struggled to regain her equilibrium. But Click didn't seem to expect a reply.

"I think that perhaps the young man has proven to be a mixed gift," he continued quietly, "much like the key I gave you at the rafters' wharf." Click's tone was gentle, almost teasing, but those umber eyes were unblinking in their scrutiny, and for some reason Cassidy was absurdly grateful for the few feet of space that still separated them as he concluded, "Just what is it that he's made you remember?"

Cassidy stood frozen, staring at him in heart-thudding silence for a few moments before she realized Click had intended that question, as well, to be rhetorical. Then the little spark of humor brightened his eyes again and he gestured for her to begin walking with him back toward the distant gate.

Cassidy reached Click in two long strides, catching the hem of his leather vest and hanging on so that he had to stop again and turn to face her. When he looked down at her the expression on his face was more mildly quizzical than anything else. She had to force out the words before she lost her courage in the face of his calm bemusement.

"Why didn't you ever ask?" she said hoarsely, still clutching the edge of his vest. "You knew I had the Memories—why didn't you ever ask me before about what I remembered?"

But Click's expression remained essentially unchanged, the silvered wings of his mustache lifting only slightly to reveal a soft and fleeting smile. "I told you that I'm not concerned with the matters of Villagers or Horsemen," he said evenly.

But Cassidy suddenly found his equanimity infuriating; she jerked her hand back from his vest and snapped, "What the hell *do* you find of concern then?"

Click's gaze never wavered, and the very intensity of his calm control frightened Cassidy far more than any display of anger could have. "Your welfare," he said softly with a disarming candor. "This city has become an even more dangerous place, Cassidy; please remember what I have told you."

When he turned and began to walk away again, she fell into step beside him; but for most of the short journey back to the garrison's gate she could only keep an uneasy silence. And as she walked there was just one clear thought in her mind: Cassidy might still have harbored mistrust for Click, but Cathy Delaney was no longer able to.

Just before they drew within earshot of the three deliberately bored-looking Troopers who guarded the iron gate, she looked over at Click and said, "You'll be there tonight, won't you? When we have to talk to the Troopers about what we've seen?"

With a little dip of his shaggy head, Click indicated the garrison that lay before them. "No one here has requested that I come," he said. "And what use would I be to them?" he added, a shade less acerbically. "I saw nothing that night."

"You saw what the woods looked like," Cassidy countered promptly. "You saw what happened to Allen—hell, you saw as much as I did!"

To Cassidy's chagrin, when she had raised her voice one of the Troopers at the gate had glanced over at them. But Click seemed unperturbed by either her outburst or the Trooper's notice. He shrugged his shoulders. "If they ask for me, I'll come," he told her. "But I doubt that they'll ask."

"Oh, I wouldn't be too sure of that," Cassidy said. "They'll ask all right."

Bending smoothly to lift the canvas-wrapped bundle for her, Click offered her both the parcel and one of his secret little half-smiles. "If you have anything to say about it," he surmised wryly. "Either way, Cassidy, I will see you again. Just remember what I have told you."

And then without so much as a backward glance the Tinker turned and started striding briskly back up the road toward the city. Cassidy stood and watched him until he was no more than a tiny figure against the backdrop of the distant buildings before she Called her mare and reentered the garrison.

Chapter 14 ◀▥

By the time the Warden's captain had assembled the Troopers in the garrison's mess hall that night, news of the deaths in the harbor and warehouse district had spread across the city. The official word from the Troopers on patrol was still that the incidents were under investigation, but the general consensus at the house was that the "troubles" had come down out of the hills. The prevailing sentiment ranged from uneasy interest to concerned speculation, but no one yet seemed unduly alarmed. Then again, Cassidy thought, none of those people had witnessed the things that she had seen.

Cassidy was particularly concerned just what sort of tenor would be set for that night's meeting. The slaughter in the woods outside Pointed Rock was too horrible to be reduced to some sort of vicarious entertainment, and Cassidy stood poised to reveal events that were just as incredible, if considerably less gruesome. She was determined that their revelations be taken seriously. At least partially on account of that determination, Cassidy persisted at the garrison until Justin, the gray-templed Trooper, agreed to speak with her. And she was relieved when, after hearing her arguments, he agreed to send word to the Tinkers' enclave requesting Click's presence at the Troopers' briefing that night.

Cassidy suspected that Click might not be enthusiastic about the summons, but she also knew that he would come. His own sense of irony had led him to trap himself into that. Cassidy also suspected that Justin and the other Troopers would be even less enthusiastic to have the Tinker leader there, but to her way of thinking the mysterious antipathy between Click and the Troopers was one puzzle that would just have to be set aside until the more crucial matters had been dealt with.

That evening Cassidy, Rowena, and Allen shared a meal with Bobby, Mickey, Sharon, and Jeremy. The Warden had not returned to the house all day, and when Cassidy asked about Becky, Mickey merely shrugged as if to say that the woman's absence was not particularly unusual, either. Even though the food was delicious, Cassidy's anxiety kept her from truly appreciating any of it.

It was nearly an hour after sunset before one of the Troopers, the same stolid-looking woman with her hair in a bun who had found them in the Warden's garden that morning, came to the house to summon them again. Cassidy didn't even try to ask any questions of her; the woman clipped along at a brisk no-nonsense pace as she preceded them out the side door of the house and out across the shadowy slope of the darkened lawn.

The evening air was still warm and calm and a burgeoning chorus of insect sounds rose from the grass and bushes as they passed the edge of the grounds and continued along the wide paved path toward the garrison. Fireflies winked like tiny bursts of lightning over the black shadows of the tall grass. Away from the stench of the harbor and the smoke of the city, the air smelled faintly of horse manure and bruised grass, and the black sky was hung with tens of thousands of crystalline stars.

If this is the afterlife, Cassidy mused with a sidelong glance in Rowena's direction, *I guess things could be worse.*

The mess hall was a vast room in the long two-storied barracks building that Cassidy recognized from the night before. She had paid very little attention to the details of her surroundings then, but the interior of the barracks still looked familiar, with its bare wooden floors and white plastered walls. As they followed their guide into the mess hall itself, Cassidy's first thought was that she had never seen so many Troopers together in one place. The long wooden tables had been arrayed in rows leading from the front to the rear of the big room, and even though chairs had been placed only on the far side of each table, facing forward, there must have been at least sixty leather-clad men and women of all ages, races, and shapes seated there.

When they entered Cassidy could tell that the group had already been assembled for some time, and she sensed that considerable discussion had already taken place. Although no one spoke as they came in, arrangement, demeanor, and body language of the various Troopers all suggested that some debate, perhaps even argument, had already occurred in their absence. The Warden and the captain stood behind a smaller table that had been set at the front of the hall. Both of them were leaning forward slightly as if they had just fielded some particularly difficult exchange. She thought that the Warden, in fact, actually looked relieved to see them come into the room.

One of the most disconcerting effects of Cassidy's newly refurbished memory was that she was constantly being vividly reminded of something from her real life by the things in that world. The ranks of leather-clad Troopers seated at the mess hall's tables were not in themselves anything that was even remotely familiar to her, but if she closed her eyes for a moment the combined aromas of horses, leather, and lamp smoke could have convinced Cassidy that she was back home in the tack room on the farm. What a relief it would have been to have been able to transport herself so easily, merely to blink and transform herself back into Cathy Delaney again. But when she looked out across the rows of the Warden's Troopers she saw only a few familiar faces. She knew Justin, of course, and the black-haired woman who had been in the room with the Warden and Valerie the night before. She also recognized two of the Troopers from the gate, the amiable-looking woman who had summoned her from the pasture that afternoon and a couple of Troopers from up at the house. Finally, far in the back of the hall and sitting off to the side all by themselves, she caught sight of Click and Willie.

Buoyed by a little rush of relief at seeing the Tinkers there, it took Cassidy a moment to realize that Valerie was also looking in their direction. The captain's gaze, however, was decidedly chilly; in fact, the expression that she had been visiting upon Click could only have been described as furious. Willie shifted on his chair, looking distinctly uncomfortable there among the ranks of the Troopers. But Click looked not only calm but also faintly amused. He reminded Cassidy exactly of some long-lost heir seated unexpectedly among the alarmed distant relatives at the reading of a wealthy man's will. And just before Cassidy made herself look away, Click looked directly at her and actually winked.

Rowena had to poke Cassidy in the side before she realized that not only had the Warden been speaking, he had been speaking about them.

"These are the people who came down the river with the

Tinkers," he announced to the hall full of Troopers as he beckoned for Cassidy, Rowena, and Allen to come closer to his table. "They've come here to tell us what they saw out in the
hills."

Cassidy stayed close to both Rowena and Allen, feeling unexpectedly nervous once they were finally to have their forum.
She wasn't sure exactly what was expected of them; the three
were exchanging an uneasy glance when the Warden spoke
again.

"The Tinkers have already told us about the devastation they
found in the woods after the attack outside Pointed Rock." he
said quietly, coming out from behind his table to speak to them
face to face. The young man reached out spontaneously and
with a genuine concern in those chocolate-colored eyes to
touch Allen's arm. "They also told us about the gravity of your
injuries, Sheriff—why didn't you say something last night or
earlier today? They said that you nearly died out there."

Clearly nonplussed at being singled out for sympathy, Allen
shifted his feet; but he looked directly at the Warden as he replied gruffly, "What's past is past; I survived. The others out
there that night weren't as lucky."

Dropping his hand from the bearded man's arm, the Warden
nodded and said, "Then tell us what happened; tell us what
you saw."

In a low but steady voice Allen briefly and almost dispassionately recited the same details that he had so wrenchingly
revealed to Cassidy and Rowena only a few nights earlier outside the Tinker camp beside the Long River. If time had given
the big man some opportunity to distance himself from the personal horror of the account, then it had done nothing to blunt
his recollection of the details. Cassidy felt the hair rising on the
back of her neck and arms by the time the sheriff reached his
description of the malformed little creatures that had attacked
him.

"That's the last thing I remember," Allen concluded, "those
things swarming over me. I don't remember anything else that
happened until my fever broke in the Tinkers' camp."

The room, which had fallen utterly silent during Allen's
short but vivid narrative, erupted then into questions. At the
head table Valerie commanded the Troopers into some semblance of order again so that the Warden could speak. The
young man studied the sheriff with a calm directness for a moment before he spoke.

"Justin told me that you suffered wounds of a distinctive sort from this attack," the Warden said. "Four people were killed in the city last night, stabbed to death. Some have proposed that it was merely a gang matter." If his tone of voice did not betray his own opinion of that conclusion, then the cant of those graceful brows did. "After what we've heard here tonight, I think perhaps there's another explanation for what has happened."

Silently, with no further prompting and with no more reservation than he would have shown if someone had just asked to see his hand or his foot, Allen pulled the tail of his shirt free from the waistband of his pants. Holding the bottom of the shirt up with one hand, he used the other hand to tug his trousers down a few inches, as well. The lamplight in the mess hall was bright enough to clearly display both the extent and the unusual pattern of his scabbed-over wounds. For as many times as Cassidy had seen the scars, she was still affected by the appearance of that grim, mottled network of marks.

For several long moments no one in the hall stirred or spoke a word, although every eye was plainly upon the wounds that Allen had revealed. Then the Warden lifted his head and signaled one of the Troopers sitting at the second row of tables, beckoning the man to come forward. As the lank man unfolded himself from his chair and came to the front of the room, Cassidy thought he somehow looked familiar, although she wasn't certain where she might have seen him before.

The Warden was looking at the Trooper when he spoke, indicating with a gesture the bare pale expanse of marred skin that Allen had exposed for their inspection. "Are the wounds the same?" he asked tersely.

The tall man had dark thinning hair, pulled back with a leather thong into a ponytail at the nape of his neck. The combination of his high forehead and long chin gave him a particularly sober look, and as he silently studied Allen's side that sobriety appeared almost scholarly in its intensity. "I'm not sure," he finally admitted. "They're all pretty well torn up."

The Warden's eyes never wavered as he directed the Trooper, "Then check them again."

The tall man's head jerked up. "They've already been buried," he pointed out.

For just a second Cassidy thought that she saw in those deep brown eyes the same dead and unflinching focus that she had always seen in the perfect blankness of Andy Greene's expression. "Then dig them up again," the Warden said flatly.

To his credit, the Trooper's response held no detectable hesitation. "I'll see to it at once," he said.

Then the light of an almost morbidly dry wit kindled in those achingly familiar eyes. "The morning will be soon enough, Tag," the Warden said. "I doubt that they'll be going anywhere, and we're not quite finished here yet tonight."

Dismissed, the Trooper quickly returned to his chair while the Warden received and apparently ignored a pointed look from his captain. Instead he turned to Allen, who was replacing his clothing, and said, "Thank you, Sheriff."

If she had harbored any illusions that the dramatic testimony of both Allen's words and wounds had eliminated the need for any statement from her, Cassidy was quickly disabused of that notion when the Warden's gaze suddenly fixed upon her. "You were out there in the woods as well that night; what did you see?"

Cassidy had thought that she would be prepared to answer. Heaven knows she had thought about it often enough. But that was before she knew that her inquisitor was going to be Andy Greene, before she knew that she would find out who she really was. After a short but clumsy delay, during which she could hardly concentrate on anything beyond the incredible intelligence in that expectant young face, she began to blurt out what had happened that night after she and Rowena had fled from the Tinker camp. And although her experience may have lacked the personal tragedy of Allen's, there were at least two points at which she was certain that she had the Warden's and Valerie's complete and undivided attention. The first point was when she mentioned the foul stench of the carrion eaters; the other was when she described Allen's condition when she had found him.

Cassidy had barely finished her narration when Valerie took a step away from the front table and toward her, her dark eyes wide with an avid speculation. Before the Warden could speak, the captain was confronting Cassidy. "That night along the river, the night of the fire in your village when you saw those creatures—was that the first time you'd seen them?"

The Warden's eyes narrowed with a small frown of concentration as the young man scrutinized Cassidy's face. "Then you've seen these creatures before Pointed Rock?"

Cassidy could no longer think of any reason to dodge the

question they put to her. In fact, she had finally come to recognize that in order to win any cooperation from the Warden,
she was going to have to disclose everything she knew about
the creatures that so occupied his attention. And so she looked
up calmly and steadily into that frowning face and answered as
fully as she was able.

"Yes, I've seen them before that night—not the big ones
that look like dirty smoke, but the carrion eaters, and the ones
that live in the water."

Touching her on the arm as if to assert his right to address
her first, the Warden stared down intently into Cassidy's face.
"There are creatures in the water, as well?" he asked, his frown
deepening. "Where have you seen them in the water—and
where else have you seen the carrion eaters?"

When he looked at her with that sort of intensity, it seemed
as if his were the only face in the room. She could have easily
ignored the rows of Troopers, those men and women who sat
there with varying degrees of surprise and skepticism coloring
their expressions. She could have even forgotten that her old
friends Click and Willie were still sitting at the back of the
hall, hearing from her those things that she had never before
revealed. For the moment there was not even Andy Greene,
there was only the Warden of Horses.

And so Cassidy told him about the hanging things, the stinking monsters she had seen twice before in the forested hills.
"But until that night of the fire, I thought I had to have been
imagining them," she added, "because I was always the only
one who saw them."

An ironic little gleam flickered in the Warden's eyes then, so
much like Click's own understated humor that Cassidy was
momentarily disarmed by it. "I would say that you no longer
have to worry about that being the case, Cassidy," he said.
"Now, what about the creatures in the water?"

Cassidy hesitated for the space of a few heartbeats, poised
on the uncomfortable edge of further confession. She deliberately avoided looking toward the back of the hall where Click
and Willie sat. "That was the first kind of creature I saw," she
said quietly, "on the first night after I found myself here. And
it's the kind I've seen most recently, too."

Continuing puzzlement sat tentatively on the Warden's brow.
"Most recently?" he echoed. "Just when was the last time
you've seen these creatures?"

"Yesterday afternoon," Cassidy admitted, "on the rapids of the Long River."

As quickly and succinctly as possible, as if to put the task behind her, Cassidy told of her encounters with the water monsters. As she related what had happened on the lower rapids of the river, she knew that Click and Willie must have been the two most attentive people in the whole hall, but she could not risk looking up and meeting their eyes from across the room. In a way she felt that she had betrayed them by not telling the Tinkers everything before, especially since their people had been endangered by the incident. But she salved her guilt by telling herself that the conspiracy of silence had been two-sided, with the Tinkers seemingly choosing to ignore the clear physical evidence of something unknown being involved in the damage to Wanda's raft. Cassidy only hoped that her rationalization would hold up the next time she was alone with Click, because she did not want to have to meet those dark and perceptive eyes without the protection of at least some small measure of understanding.

When Cassidy finished speaking the Warden turned away from her, toward Valerie. "This is even more serious than we had feared," he said. Turning further, he fired off a brisk command to the attentive Tag. "Speak to the harbormaster tonight; I want all nonessential river traffic at the docks eliminated immediately."

To his considerable credit, the lanky Trooper resisted pointing out the obvious, which was that the edict would be met with protest and scorn. Tag merely nodded and rose to his feet, and this time when he made ready to leave the hall at once, the Warden did not detain him.

The Warden's attention had already returned to his captain, and while the two of them huddled in a tersely worded and almost inaudible conference only a few paces away, Cassidy took advantage of the opportunity to move a little farther away from the table at the head of the room. Rowena and Allen gravitated to her, keeping close but not speaking. They didn't have to worry about anyone noticing their subtle distancing; by that time the hall had erupted into a stir of movement as the Troopers gathered into small groups, the murmur of their combined voices filling the room. Many of the Troopers had already drifted out the doors before Cassidy looked toward the back corner and saw that Click and Willie were both gone.

"See what I mean about this guy already having enough trouble?" Rowena whispered loudly.

"And if what happened last night is any indication, I expect he's due for still more," the sheriff said, "even without you two and your crazy ideas."

It was a toss-up as to which of the two women would have been the first to provide a snappy comeback to Allen's dour assessment, had not they all been interrupted by the Warden's sudden return to their side. Since Cassidy had been standing with her back to him, she was particularly grateful that she hadn't had a chance to open her mouth for some blunt comment before the young man's quiet voice intervened.

"I want to thank you all again," he told them, "for your valuable help."

Unhampered by neither the distortion of memory nor the weight of past enmity, Rowena was far more capable than either Cassidy or Allen to deal with the Warden on a comfortable basis. She gave him a somewhat lopsided smile and quipped, "It looks to me like all we did is ruin everyone's evening."

The quip brought a brief but stunning smile to the young man's lips. "Well, Rowena, they say that truth corrupts the security of ignorance," he said, "and if that was the case here tonight, then I thank you for your corrupting influence." He gave Allen a companionable clap on the arm and added, "With your permission, Sheriff, I would like to have Becky take a look at those wounds when she returns tomorrow. She has a knowledge of injuries and healing." He glanced over to a Trooper near the door. "And now," he concluded, "I'll have you shown back up to the house."

Cassidy had turned to follow Rowena and Allen to the door when the Warden startled her by addressing her specifically. "If you could stay a bit longer, Cassidy?" His brows were tented inquiringly, but his expression revealed nothing else. "There's something further I'd like to discuss with you."

The lewd wink that Rowena threw her did little to ameliorate Cassidy's sudden feeling of apprehension. She watched with a certain glum sense of fatalism as the stoic Trooper led Allen and Rowena out the door, and the Warden turned back to Valerie for a few final terse directives. Then the young man was back at her side, echoing Click's words of only that afternoon with an almost eerie precision when he said, "Let's walk for a bit, Cassidy."

Seemingly without volition, Cassidy obediently followed him out one of the mess hall's side doors. Crossing its threshhold put them directly outside on the far side of the barracks building. The only light there seemed to be that which spilled from the open door; when the Warden closed that behind them, Cassidy blinked and almost stumbled on the bare, scuffed earth of the dirt sideyard. Then he was beside her again, walking closely enough that if she actually had tripped she would have bumped right into him.

For the first few minutes the Warden said nothing, but seemed content merely to walk as they traded the packed earth of the sideyard for the shadow-dappled grass of the meadow beyond the garrison. The evening was still warm enough that no dew had formed yet, and the grass smelled faintly of horses and dust. As her eyes adjusted to the darkness, Cassidy could make out the darker shapes of several horses in the distance on the hillside. After the brightness and close atmosphere of the crowded mess hall, the airy calm of the summer night was a welcome change. But Cassidy still felt on edge, wary of the Warden's casual request and frankly uncomfortable with finally being left alone with the man whom she could not hope to be able to integrate with the Andy Greene she so vividly remembered. When he finally did pause and turn to speak to her, it was almost a relief not to have to anticipate it any longer.

"Why didn't you tell me that you had the Memories?" he asked her, with no accusation in his even tone save that which her own paranoia might have conjured up.

Cassidy didn't even consider denying it, even though it then seemed to her almost laughably naive that at one time she and Rowena had been prepared to come there proclaiming it from the rooftops if they had needed to. Like all of her expectations, that one had suffered mightily from recent events. Instead of denial she merely grappled for the most beneficial way to present the truth. Temporizing while she cast about for some sense of his true reaction to the fact, Cassidy said, "Who told you that I did?"

His answer was predictable. "Valerie—among others," he said. "She never thought to mention it to me last night," he added, "although she did tell me how she met you."

Cassidy shrugged, even though she was uncertain how well the gesture translated in the near darkness of the pasture, and said with deliberate calm, "Rowena has them, too. That was why we originally wanted to come here. There just didn't seem to be any good time to discuss it, what with this other problem."

"That's what Valerie said," the Warden replied. It was impossible to gauge the expression on the young man's face, but his tone held no hint of reproach; if anything he sounded extremely attentive. "Do you remember how long you've been here, Cassidy?"

She thought she understood what he was getting at. She nodded before she realized that he probably couldn't see that, so then she simply said, "To the day."

There was no way he could have kept the eagerness from his voice. "So your Memories are still strong?" he asked.

He had given her the ideal opening; Cassidy knew she would never have a better opportunity to present the bizarre truth to the Warden. She was unexpectedly grateful for the cloak of darkness that, while masking his facial expressions from her, also protected her from the unsettling familiarity of that handsome young face as she made the decision to cross the line with him.

"Oh, my Memories are very strong," she said quietly. "In fact, the longer I've been here, the more I've been able to remember."

Cassidy didn't need to have been able to see his face to register the confusion that beset the Warden at her words. Before he could come back at her with a question, she asked him one of her own.

"What do you believe the Memories are, Warden?"

Relaxing fractionally, he looked at her in silence for a few moments before replying. Cassidy doubted that the pause was due to any lack of previous thought about the question; quite the contrary, everything she had been told about the man from the first time she had heard him mentioned had suggested to her that just the opposite was true. Cassidy suspected that he had spent a good part of his life there mulling over and even discussing that very subject. And when he did speak his voice was measured and thoughtful.

"I think the Memories are parts of another world—a time and place that no longer exists except in the minds of a very few, and then only fleetingly. The Memories are all that we have left of that world, Cassidy, and the only way we can hope to recapture all of the things that have been lost."

Although Cassidy was not surprised by either his perceptiveness or his articulateness, she still felt the shaky buzz of adrenaline kicking through her veins as she asked her next question.

"And all those things you've collected—the found things—what do you think they are?"

The hesitation was still there, but that time it was far briefer, and when the Warden spoke his tone was more decisive. "Relics of the old world," he said simply, "left behind the way the Memories linger in some people's minds. I'm afraid that's why we don't know what all of those things really are."

The only thing that did surprise Cassidy and gave her a tentative basis for some hope was how oddly similar the Warden's belief was to what she considered to be the possible version of the truth. In fact, in a way his belief had managed to fuse elements of both her own and Rowena's theories, giving credit to both another place and another time in his explanation of the inexplicable. Cassidy felt a disturbing sense of guilt at her intention to corrupt the security of his ignorance.

Somewhere on the hillside a horse nickered softly, a sound that Cassidy found reassuringly anchored in reality. She could still sense the Warden's puzzled expectation and she knew that if she hesitated for too long he would begin to question her further on the contradictory comment she had initially made about her Memories. Drawing in a deep breath, she tried to keep her voice steady and matter-of-fact as she went on.

"And what about the people here? Do you think that they all came from some other place and time, too?"

For the first time Cassidy wished for the benefit of some sort of illumination so that she could have seen exactly what expression was on that handsome young face, because at her words she saw the slim silhouette of his body stiffen in response. For a few moments the silence was so profound that it seemed to settle over him like a veil. His face could have revealed any of a number of strong emotions: shock, anger, fear, ridicule. And although Cassidy desperately wished to know which reaction her question had provoked, it was not until he finally spoke that she found, quite to her surprise, that the Warden's response was one of excitement.

"Is that what your Memories tell you, Cassidy?" he asked, his words spurred on with eagerness. "Because I've been told that there have been others, those in whom the Memories were the strongest, who believed at least initially that—"

With a fierceness she had not realized she possessed, Cassidy closed that one step which remained between them and grasped the Warden by both leather-clad shoulders. As much to her own amazement as to his own, she gave him a quick shake, cutting off the flow of his words as effectively as if she had clapped her hand over his mouth.

"It's not a *memory,*" she hissed harshly, "it's *real!* I *know* that I came from somewhere else—and I know *you* because you came from that same place."

The Warden could easily have dislodged her grip; in fact, Cassidy realized with a certain detached sense of irony, he could easily have flattened her with one shove. That was why she was surprised by his response to her outburst. His face, just inches from hers, remained hung in shadow, but his voice was calm and clear.

"You think that you've met me before?" he asked her curiously.

"I *know* you," Cassidy reiterated. "I've known you for almost two years." Forcing herself to unclench her fingers, to loosen the death grip she had assumed upon his tunic, she continued in a voice so steady that it was almost without inflection. "In the place that we both came from your name is Andy Greene, and I was your riding instructor. In that place you were ... different; you had a severe emotional problem that kept you completely withdrawn from other people. But you loved horses—you loved my horse." Cassidy's voice rose slightly, her fingers tightening again without volition on his shoulders. "The gray mare that I rode in here on is Dragonfly—the horse you learned how to ride on."

Cassidy might have expected skepticism or even outright denial; she wouldn't even have been surprised if the young man had just laughed right in her face. But instead the Warden stood there calmly, the dark shape of his face fixed as if to study hers, regarding her with complete equanimity as he considered what she had said. And of all possible responses, that kind of nonreaction was the one that stopped Cassidy cold.

Dropping her hands from his shoulders, Cassidy suddenly took a step backward from him again, shaking her head in dismay. "You really don't remember me, do you," she said softly, almost to herself. She looked directly into the dim outline of his face across that chasm of darkness which separated them. "Andy, when I first saw you I remembered *everything.*"

The Warden took a step forward, replacing himself exactly in front of her again. In the warmth of the night air an agreeable scent seemed to cling to him, the aura of leather and smoke and horses. This time it was he who took Cassidy by the shoulders, his slender hands landing gently upon the top seams of her shirt.

"Cassidy, I don't recognize you," he said, his voice as soft as his touch. "A fact that I find entirely regrettable, since it would seem that you have what is easily the most remarkable Memory I've ever found."

Normally to have received such an elegantly simple compliment from any man, even Andy Greene—*especially Andy Greene*, she goaded herself sharply—would have been enough to have mollified Cassidy completely. But in some perverse way the Warden's eloquent expression of conciliation only infuriated her. She jerked back, stepping out from under his hands and bluntly confronting him.

"It's *not* a memory!" she repeated tautly. "Not just an illusion. If anything *this* place is a fucking illusion—the place we came from is *real!*"

Tactfully keeping the distance that she had put between them, the Warden seemed to consider a different strategy, something perhaps a bit less incendiary than his simple honesty had been.

"You said that when you first saw me last night," he said, "you remembered everything. Do you mean that you remembered this other place where you think you've come from?"

"Where we both came from," she corrected him. "When I first got here I was sure it wasn't where I belonged, and I know I'm not the only one here to ever have that feeling. So I kept trying to remember things, and the more I remembered the more I understood why I didn't fit in."

"Cassidy, sometimes people just have trouble getting—"

" 'Adjusted,' " Cassidy shot back at him, "yeah, so I've heard. Well, I'm not about to adjust because whatever or wherever this place is, I want to go back home."

Circumventing her outburst, the Warden tried instead to redirect Cassidy back to his original question. "You've said that you know me from this other place where you've come from, yet how can that be? Cassidy, I've been here my entire life—and I honestly don't recognize you."

Shaking her head so vigorously that he could undoubtedly see the motion even in the darkness, Cassidy took one more defiant step back from the Warden. "I don't know—but that doesn't make it any less true, damn you!" Frustration and despair vied for dominance in the turmoil of her emotions. It was bad enough that he didn't believe her assertion; what was even worse for her was that she herself no longer knew just what to believe about the whole situation. Her original theory had been shot full of holes by the young man's mere presence there, whole and rational; and neither her own suspicion or Rowena's current theories were going to sound very plausible to him.

Making another attempt at placation, the Warden once again regained the ground he had lost when Cassidy had stepped back from him. She could see his hands rise in a reasoning gesture, although he did not repeat his mistake of trying to touch her. "Tomorrow I would like you to speak with Becky," he said. "I think she has shared much of your frustration here. Perhaps she'll be able to help you where I've failed." His voice dropped slightly, its tone filled with genuine regret. "Cassidy, I wish that I *could* recognize you. All my life I've searched for some link between my own life and the Memories, some way to tap into all of the lost things. I don't disregard what you've told me; in fact, if just seeing me has made it possible for you to remember anything at all, then even if I'm not anyone you really know, I've still been a part of something very important. I just wish I could do more."

At those soft and sincere words a sudden connection sparked in Cassidy's mind. When she had first revealed what she remembered and suspected and had discovered to Rowena, the brunette's response had been eerily similar to the Warden's. It had taken some prodding to retrieve and revive Rowena's fading memory; perhaps the same thing would work with the Warden, as well. Only with him, Cassidy realized that she had neither the luxury of time nor the eager willingness to believe that she had found in the village goatherd. If she hoped to jar loose any sense of recognition in Andy Greene, it would take more than just a suspicion or a scrap of cloth to do it; it would take . . .

No—you can't tell him that! she warned herself. But even as the cautionary thought ran through her mind, she realized that she would have to do it.

"Listen," she said quickly, her hand darting out to catch the fringed sleeve of his tunic, "you said you've been here your entire life, right? And you're the Warden of Horses. So when did you learn how to ride?"

There was a simple perplexity in his voice. "I don't know; when I was a child."

"You don't remember anyone teaching you?" she persisted.

"Someone who first let you get up on a horse? Someone who rode double with you so that you'd be allowed to ride outside of the school ring?"

"I don't think—" the Warden started, but Cassidy cut him off, plowing rapidly onward before she could think better of it and keep the shameful secret to herself.

"Do you remember the first time you galloped out on the trail?" she said, her voice tight with the emotion she did not want to admit. "I rode behind you, Andy; I had my arms around you. The mare was going flat out—it was just like flying. You were so excited; for a few minutes you were like anyone else—you could have been anyone else. And when I finally had to make you pull the mare in again and let her walk, you turned and looked back at me and you were smiling—for the first time in your life you were *smiling*—and then I—"

Cassidy broke off, uncertain if she could finish. *But I have to—* Her fingernails dug into the soft leather of his tunic's sleeve. "And then I kissed you, Andy," she whispered.

Again the expression on the young man's face could have revealed any number of reactions; in the darkness there was only his silence. Numb with shame and disappointment, Cassidy dropped his sleeve and took a step backward, her head hanging. Ironically one of the things that had been most deeply troubling her about this strangely normal Andy Greene was the nagging fear that he would remember the unforgivable exploitation of her impulsive act in that other world. But it appeared that she had debased herself for nothing. Not only did he not remember the incident, he simply could not even understand the reason for her shame.

As Cassidy swung away from his slim shadowy shape, the Warden did not attempt to approximate her movement. But he did break his disconcerting silence, his voice soft with puzzlement and concern.

"Cassidy, I swear to you that I've never seen you before Justin brought you to me in the barracks last night," he said. "I honestly don't know you."

"I know," Cassidy replied in a hoarse whisper, her back still turned to him, *"but I know you."*

Stymied by her insistence and plainly fighting his own frustration, the young man took a tentative step toward her again. The fringes of his leather tunic stirred softly in the darkness as he raised his arm in entreaty. "Please, Cassidy—speak with

Becky in the morning. Perhaps she'll be able to explain this. I'm only sorry that I can't."

Something in his tone made Cassidy turn back toward him. In the warm anonymity of the summer night everything about him—the shape of his body and the way it moved, the scent of his skin and leather, even the dim outline of that clean profile—was suddenly so painfully familiar and yet so hopelessly remote that she felt her whole chest ache with despair.

"Please, Cassidy," the Warden said softly, "don't give up."

That night in the Warden's house in the large airy bedroom that she shared with Rowena and Allen, Cassidy dreamed.

Surprisingly, given the wealth and intensity of the day's events, she did not dream about anything that had happened to her there. Instead she dreamed about totally mundane things from her past, the kind of things that would have happened to Cathy Delaney and not to Cassidy.

It was not until the very last moments before awaking that Andy Greene even entered the picture. And when he did he was the real Andy, not the calm and capable leather-clad stranger she had met there. When she tried to call out to him, to get his attention, just like the real Andy Greene he utterly failed to respond to her.

Chapter 15 ◀▥

When Rowena awakened Cassidy the next morning by insistently shaking her, the brunette was already dressed and the
big bedroom was flooded with sunlight.

"Come on, get up!"

"What the hell?" Cassidy slurred sleepily, rolling over in
bed.

"Maybe your theory about what happened to us is right after
all," Rowena complained good-naturedly, taking in Cassidy's
groggy reticence. "At least you sure sleep like the dead! Come
on, get up—Becky's back and something's going on."

"What's going on?" Cassidy yawned, slinging her legs over
the side of the bed. She levered herself upright and squinted
across the room. "And where's Allen?"

"He went out ages ago," Rowena said, flipping clothes at
Cassidy. "He's the one who told me Becky's back."

"What's the hurry?" Cassidy grumbled, fumbling with her
shirt. But Rowena merely thrust Cassidy's pants at her.

In the short time they'd been there in the Warden's house,
Cassidy had had the opportunity to familiarize herself fairly
well with the layout of the big brick building. Although there
were bedrooms on the second floor, many of them seemed to
be used for storage and most of the people who lived there
slept in the ground-floor rooms. Besides the foyer and the
little-used front sitting room, there was also a large kitchen
with an attached dining area on the first floor. But in fair
weather the raised stone deck seemed to receive the most use,
and that was the direction in which Rowena led Cassidy that
morning.

As they followed the inlaid stone walk alongside the house
Cassidy could hear the strident tones of an unfamiliar voice

raised in argument. Following Rowena up the broad stone
steps, she found several people milling about, including two
Troopers, but Cassidy did not see Allen. And the source of the
discord was a diminutive black woman, who appeared to have
literally backed one of the Troopers into a corner and was
soundly berating him for something.

Hesitating at the head of the steps, unwilling to walk blindly
into the disturbance, Cassidy had just begun to turn to Rowena
to counsel caution when from out of the corner of her eye she
caught sight of someone she did recognize. And for a few moments she was uncertain what to do because that person was
not someone she had expected to find there.

A young man in tight leather trousers and a loosely fitting
sleeveless gray shirt stood tentatively at the far edge of the
deck, frowning as his eyes swept over the empty tables. Then
his gaze met Cassidy's, and Kevin's frown disappeared.

Despite the apparent confusion and the ongoing tirade taking
place on the deck, there was not fated to be any repeat of the
comic little pas de deux that had occurred when Cassidy had
first seen Raphael outside the barracks. For within seconds of
making eye contact, Kevin reacted, and his actions were anything but evasive.

"Cassidy!" he called out to her with an eager wave. He immediately strode across the deck to where she stood and
clapped her enthusiastically on the arm. "So you really are
here!"

Acutely aware of Rowena's inquisitive stare, Cassidy blurted
out with total candor, "Kevin—I'm really glad to see you."

"Becky said there were some new people here," the odd-
eyed youth continued excitedly, "and that one of them was a
Horseman. So Yolanda was right about you—you do have the
Memories?"

More than she could have imagined, Cassidy thought, but
what she said, pulling Rowena up alongside her, was "And so
does Rowena; I met her in Double Creek."

Kevin greeted the brunette with an enthusiasm almost equal
to that he'd shown Cassidy. While the two of them sized each
other up, Cassidy was quickly scanning the activity on the
deck, particularly the continuing confrontation between the
black woman and the Trooper on the far side.

"What's going on here, Kevin?" Cassidy asked.

Kevin's head snapped around, his pale ponytail streaming in

the dappled sunlight. "Didn't you hear? There was trouble down by the river again last night."

Too alarmed to worry about being tactful, Cassidy gave him a sharp look, fixing on those two mismatched but guileless eyes. "What kind of trouble? Monsters?"

Kevin flinched back at the word, his reaction fleeting but quite perceptible. "I don't know," he said, seeming taken aback by her bluntness, "but I heard some more people were killed."

Totally focused on Kevin, Cassidy struggled to restrain the jolt of urgency that had suddenly banged through her. She reached out to touch the loose front of his shirt. "Who was it, Kevin? Where were they killed?"

But before Kevin could answer another voice intervened, deep, husky, and tartly querulous. "Down beyond the marsh bridge, in the Tinkers' enclave."

Cassidy looked up in surprise to see that the argumentative little woman who had been haranguing the Troopers had come across the deck and was standing right behind Kevin. The woman's short but rounded frame was dressed in Tinker-style clothing, loose pants and a bright magenta shirt, and her broad-featured face was capped with a crown of long dreadlock braids. Despite her size there had been nothing diminutive about her voice, and Kevin quickly stepped aside so that Cassidy could transfer her inquisition.

"Were any Tinkers killed?" Cassidy asked tersely. "Do you know what happened?"

The black woman shook her head—just once, like a dog snapping at an irritating fly. "I don't know what the hell is going on," she complained. "The Warden was here earlier, but he didn't stick around to answer questions." She seemed particularly annoyed by that fact. "He goes and asks me to look at some wounds on that sheriff from out in the hills, and then without so much as a howdy-do he hightails it out of here with a bunch of Troopers and takes the damned sheriff with him!"

"Allen went with them?" Rowena interjected, elbowing her way past Cassidy and up the last step onto the deck. "Where did they go?"

The woman's temper did not seemed to be improved one whit by all of the questions being fired at her. "Down to the enclave would be my guess," she said, adding testily, "Apparently that was more important than having me look at those wounds."

"Shit!" Cassidy growled. She spun around on the deck and

was about to hop down the steps when Rowena snagged her by the arm.

"Cassidy, you can't go down there by yourself," Rowena objected, hanging on. "What if it's—"

But Cassidy rounded on the brunette, unable to stifle her anger. "How dare he endanger Allen like that?" she fumed. She kept moving, dragging Rowena after her down the steps and onto the lawn. "He can take his Troopers anywhere he damn well pleases, but he doesn't have any right to—"

"Wait a minute!" the woman bellowed after them. "Are you Cassidy and Rowena? Where the hell are you going? I'm supposed to talk to you!"

"Later!" Cassidy flung over her shoulder. Even towing Rowena she had already managed to put a fair distance between them and the garden deck where the woman who could only have been Becky stood glaring after them with her fists planted on her hips. Calling Dragonfly as she strode across the turf, her boots swiping furiously through the lush grass, Cassidy barely slowed even as Rowena further entreated her.

"Cassidy, you can't just go tearing out of here without—"

Cassidy slowed just enough to turn back and look into Rowena's face. "Just stay here," she commanded, "and see what you can find out from that crazy nigger while I'm gone."

Rowena's expression ricocheted from concern to shock. "What—you mean Becky? Wait a minute—Cassidy, you don't even know where you're going!" she cried.

"I can take you," Kevin said quietly from right behind them. On his long legs the odd-eyed boy had been silently shadowing the progress of their erratic duel across the lawn. He came up beside Cassidy. "I know where the Tinkers' enclave is."

Cassidy came to an abrupt halt and swung around to confront Rowena directly. "I'll be all right," she said, her tone finally softening. "You heard what Becky said—the place will be crawling with Troopers." She touched Rowena's arm, simultaneously freeing herself from the brunette's grip. "Just go back and try to calm her down, huh? We need to talk to her later."

Rowena still looked unconvinced, but by then she had little choice. Dragonfly was approaching them at a lope across the sun-washed stretch of grass, her hoofbeats drumming on the sod. As the horse slid to a halt before them, Cassidy saw with amusement that there were still a few long blades of grass hanging from the mare's muzzle. *So much for breakfast,* she thought wryly.

When Cassidy hopped up onto the mare's back, Kevin followed with a practiced ease. Genuinely grateful for the young man's offer of help, Cassidy felt him settle in behind her. Then she looked down at Rowena and gave one final instruction.

"Go on, go back up to the house," she said. "See what you can find out from Becky. We'll be back as soon as we can."

Turning away from Rowena's disapproving scowl, Cassidy urged the mare into a canter. As the horse sped across the meadow toward the garrison, Cassidy's mind was filled with a churning mixture of emotion. People had been killed in the Tinkers' enclave—it had to have been monsters. Why else would the Warden have gone; why else would he have taken Allen? Almost sick with dread, Cassidy could not help thinking that she had somehow been responsible for leading the creatures to those people. *God, what if it was someone we know?* Familiar faces, friends from their journey to the city, danced tauntingly through her mind: Willie, Bonnie, Carlotta, Mitz, Old Paul ... And then the inevitable thought lanced in with knifelike sharpness to torment her: *What if it was Click?*

Without conscious volition Cassidy tightened her legs around the gray mare's barrel, and the big horse instantly picked up speed. Behind her, Kevin rode so neatly balanced that she was scarcely even aware of his presence as they cut across the barracks and the stables toward the road leading out of the garrison. The mare's hooves clattered on the pavement but her pace didn't slacken until they had reached the big iron gate.

The handful of Troopers keeping watch at the gate scrutinized the gray horse and her riders with overt suspicion, but Cassidy's previous assumption appeared to have been accurate. Their duty was to keep unwanted people out of the compound, not to prevent anyone from leaving it, and none of them moved to impede the mare. No one even said a word to Cassidy or Kevin as they passed, although their speed was still imprudent and she recognized several of the Troopers from last night's meeting in the barracks.

Out beyond the gate on the road to the city, Cassidy let the mare gallop full out. Her unshod hooves pounded dully on the gritty pavement, her big body rocking steadily between Cassidy's knees. She actually had to concentrate to be aware of Kevin's presence behind her on the horse's broad back because even at that rapid gait he didn't bump into her. However anxiety gnawed at her, Cassidy nevertheless attempted to reestablish some of their old spirit of camaraderie that the young man had displayed toward her earlier on the deck.

"How long have you and Rafe been here, Kevin?" she asked him.

Cassidy couldn't see anything of his expression, but Kevin's voice, coming nearly in her ear, was both earnest and reassuring. "A couple of weeks," he said. "We were lucky because we met some Troopers out on the trail, and they brought us right in to the garrison." He hesitated a moment and then added deferentially, "I know you went with the Riders to one of the villages, but how did you ever get here?"

"That's a long story, Kevin," she said, leaning farther over the mare's whipping mane. She gave him a brief and deliberately edited version. "Rowena and I left the village and joined up with some Tinkers. We came with them down the river to the city."

"Oh," Kevin said, suddenly beginning to comprehend Cassidy's concern. "Then you know some of the Tinkers." Suddenly he pointed. "Turn here; take this road."

As she swung the mare off the main road and onto a narrower dirt track, Cassidy realized that they were nearly at the outskirts of the city itself. She was just thinking that it was a good thing at least one of them knew where the hell they were going when Kevin startled her by touching her right between the shoulder blades, his palm gently massaging her back.

"Don't worry, Cassidy," he said softly, "we're almost there."

There was more, much more, that Cassidy would have liked to ask him, but it was not an opportune time. As they galloped along the dirt road, Cassidy saw that most of the land immediately outside the city was sloping meadow with very few trees. Down toward the river the terrain became more wooded, its surface thrown up in a series of hummocklike hills. And in the lowland between the city and the enclave's road lay a long shallow slough, marshy land that probably terminated in an estuary as it fed into the Long River.

Through the trees in the distance Cassidy could see the patchwork evidence of human habitation: the roofs of various buildings, little grids marked off by fences, the neatly cut shapes of lawns and gardens. Despite the warmth of the clear summer morning, a few random curls of smoke rose up from the cluster of structures, most of them small houses. An image suggested itself to Cassidy then, that of a peaceful little English village nestled along the riverbank, and she remembered how the Tinkers had spoken longingly of returning to their homes again.

Of course, that was before I brought those creatures here, Cassidy thought grimly.

Cassidy didn't need further directions from Kevin as they rode down the earthen road to the enclave. The mare automatically slowed to a jog as they entered the settlement. A few hundred feet beyond the first of the brick and timber houses three Troopers stood with their horses beside what had once been a wooden slat fence, studying the ground with a sober intensity. It was not difficult to reconstruct what must have happened. From the looks of the fence, the grass, and even the remains of the nearby trees, something very large and very heavy had simply rolled by the house, crushing everything in its path. As one of the Troopers glanced up at them, Cassidy looked beyond the trio and saw that the same trail of demolition had passed right through the yards of the adjacent houses, as well. Then a second Trooper looked up, and Cassidy saw that it was the woman who had led them down to the barracks from the Warden's house the night before. Cassidy brought the gray mare to a halt.

"Are you looking for your sheriff?" the Trooper asked her. At Cassidy's quick nod the woman pointed into the little cluster of houses. "They're down there, near the river."

Dragonfly's ears swiveled constantly as she stepped along across the litter of crushed vegetation and cut through the yard of another neat little house. It was not difficult to follow the path of destruction across the Tinkers' enclave. Cassidy was both puzzled and alarmed by the extent of the damage the farther they moved into the craftsmen's community. Not only fences and trees and gardens had been flattened; as they rode nearer to the river, she could see that some small outbuildings or sheds had also been demolished, and several of the sturdy-looking houses had broken windows, the shattered bits of glass glittering in the bruised grass like shards of fresh ice.

"What could have happened here?" Kevin murmured from behind Cassidy, his tone uneasy.

"Monsters," Cassidy said flatly.

Kevin's body stiffened so abruptly that his lower torso bumped into Cassidy's back. "M-monsters?" he stammered. "Monsters could do all this?"

Inwardly Cassidy cringed; she had forgotten the odd-eyed boy's skittishness. She was surprised and dismayed when Kevin suddenly twisted sideways behind her and nimbly slipped off over the mare's hip, dropping to the ground at the horse's side. She was certain she had frightened him with her unthinkingly blunt talk of monsters.

"Kevin, wait; I'm sure they're—"

But Kevin was not paying any attention to her, and by then she could see the reason for his sudden defection from the horse's back. Among the Troopers who were engaged in moving the shattered timbers of what had once been a grape arbor was Kevin's friend, Raphael.

As Cassidy rode on alone, a perfectly preserved little set piece of memory presented itself to her: the image of a bedraggled Kevin huddled in the back of the cliff overhang the night of the storm, terrified that he and his companions would be left in darkness. That night she had not been able to understand the primal fear that she had seen in those mismatched eyes, but since then she had come to realize what it was that had so badly frightened the boy. She had seen his monsters.

Among the questions that still bedeviled Cassidy, however, was why had she been seeing them—and had he?

The last few houses Cassidy passed had sustained far more damage. Chimneys were toppled, doors and windows torn from their frames, and wooden shingles ripped from the roofs and slung about like big playing cards across the trampled earth. Among the buildings that lay in the path of destruction several Troopers poked around, solemnly assessing the debris. The whole scene seemed weirdly familiar to Cassidy. Initially she assumed that was because of the devastation she had witnessed out in the woods outside Pointed Rock. But with her recovered memory of the real world, she realized then that there was another reason. The Tinkers' enclave looked as if a tornado had torn through it.

Cassidy didn't need any further directions from the Troopers to find Allen and the Warden. The trail of havoc that had been visited upon the little settlement was obvious enough, and as she followed that path she heard the sound of loudly arguing voices. Several of those voices were familiar to her. Dragonfly stepped daintily over the remains of what had once been some kind of a small brick building—a smokehouse, perhaps, Cassidy thought distractedly. The horse rounded the corner of a stoutly made but partially dismantled house and then sud-

denly there was nothing left between them and the river but a
torn-up stretch of rubble-strewn ground. In the middle of that
disrupted stretch of ground, amid the almost unrecognizable
detritus of what must once have been another house, two
groups of people were squared off into obviously opposing
factions. On one side stood the Warden and a handful of his
Troopers, and on the other side stood Allen and several Tinkers. To her relief Cassidy saw that one of those Tinkers was
Bonnie, and another was Click himself.

Cassidy was so happy to see that at least two of her friends
were unharmed that she rode right into the dispute, momentarily oblivious to the ongoing argument. Allen and the Tinkers
stood facing the river, and Click was having heated words with
the Warden as the gray mare approached. It was only when the
Warden glanced up and noticed Cassidy's arrival that the
change of expression on his face must have alerted the Tinker
leader. And all that Cassidy had been able to hear before Click
abruptly fell silent was the bitten-off end of his vehement declaration to the Warden.

"You can't afford to underestimate the importance of this!"
the dark-haired man hissed at the younger man. "Can't you see
the danger she—"

When Dragonfly halted a few paces from the dissenting factions, there was a moment of awkward silence, and Cassidy
wondered just what she had blundered into. As relieved as she
was to see Bonnie and Click, she didn't recognize the other
two Tinkers, a man and a woman, who were with them. And
for a brief but uncomfortable period of time none of the people
who stood there, either the ones she knew or the ones she had
never seen before, seemed inclined to enlighten her. Click was
finally the first to speak, although his response was not exactly
what Cassidy had expected.

"What are you doing down here, Cassidy?" Click asked her
flatly. "You should have stayed up at the compound."

Cassidy was less startled by his opinion than by his tone and
expression as he delivered it; both contained something that
she did not think she had ever heard the Tinker leader evince
before. Click was demonstrably angry. But before she had the
chance to consider whether his anger was directed at her per-
sonally, or was just the spillover from whatever disagreement
he'd been having with the Warden and his Troopers, another
calmer voice intervened.

"I'm glad you've come," the Warden said, taking a few

steps over the rucked-up ground toward Dragonfly. "I'd like you to have a look at what's happened here." He made an economic but all-encompassing gesture at the enclave. "Is this similar to what you saw outside Pointed Rock?"

Cassidy's eyes had been automatically pulled from Click to the Warden when he spoke; they then skipped over to Allen, as if to defer to the sheriff on that particular judgment. But when Allen spoke up, he did not excuse Cassidy.

"I didn't really see much after the attack," Allen reminded Cassidy. "I guess you and the Tinkers would have a better idea than I would of what it looked like out there."

Cassidy tried looking to Click again, but his deep brown eyes had gone strangely opaque. He was angry, all right, but was he angry at her, at the Warden, or just furious about what had happened? Reluctantly she glanced around at the ragged swath of destruction that had been leveled across the Tinkers' settlement. Maybe a tornado was not the best analogy after all; ground zero at a nuclear detonation came as easily to mind. When Cassidy's eyes met the Warden's again, she had to remind herself that he was still expecting an answer from her.

"It looks pretty much the same," she said. After a moment's hesitation she added, "But there was some stuff—slime or something—in the woods. And blood."

After a couple of years of having dealt with the perfect blankness of Andy Greene's face, Cassidy was still easily surprised by how clearly the Warden's expressions reflected his emotions. The young man's tanned and finely planed face tightened with a grim regret and his eyes cut away from hers to sweep down toward the river. "Yes, there was blood here, too," he said tightly. "Two people were killed."

"Two of our people," Bonnie reminded him tartly, speaking past Click's stony silence. The big blond woman had no problem interpreting the particular stricken look on Cassidy's face, and her voice softened slightly as she elaborated, "You hadn't met Charlie or Marv. They stayed in the enclave, kind of like caretakers for everyone else's houses when the rest of us were out trading." She scuffed one foot in the almost homogeneous rubble where they stood. "We're standing practically in the middle of what used to be their house."

The Warden took the last few steps up to the gray mare's shoulder, where he stood looking up directly into Cassidy's face. "I would appreciate it if you could take a look around,

Cassidy, with Allen and the others," he said. "And if you feel you could, if you would also look at the bodies?"

Remembering what she had found out in that shattered stretch of forest, Cassidy had to suppress a shudder. But seeing the familiar faces around her—the Warden's quiet expectation, Allen's stoic calm, even Click's taut reserve—she nodded almost without choice and slid down off her horse.

It took some time for Cassidy to traverse the whole course of the destruction. Several Troopers walked along ahead of her, moving debris when necessary, and Allen walked silently by her side. The big bearded man barely exchanged so much as a glance with Cassidy as she scanned the damage, yet she found his simple presence supportive and comforting. The Warden had been right about there being blood; it was splattered up the side of one of the partially collapsed houses. From its pattern Cassidy could deduce that the building's roof was where the two Tinkers' bodies had been found, although both had been removed to the ground below and covered with one of Willie's tarpaulins.

When one of the Troopers, a short muscular woman with a deliberately expressionless set to her face, pulled back the edge of the canvas, Cassidy felt the shock of recognition run through her. For although she had not known those two old men in life, the manner of their deaths seemed to intimately connect her to them. They both had been gray-haired, one slightly built and the other more stout, each dressed in the tattered remnants of their colorful Tinker garb. But their corpses were like the bodies outside Pointed Rock had been, senselessly brutalized, their features mangled almost beyond recognition.

As she abruptly turned away from the sight, Cassidy felt one of Allen's big callused hands land lightly upon her shoulder and squeeze it gently. *That could have been him out there that night,* she thought unwillingly, *if I hadn't been out in those woods.* Perhaps the sheriff was thinking the same thing.

When Cassidy and Allen returned to where Dragonfly stood waiting down by the river, she saw that Click and Bonnie were gone. The other Tinker man and woman still stood there, but at a slight distance, as if they were reluctantly awaiting something. It took Cassidy a moment to realize that they probably were waiting for the Warden to release the dead men's bodies to them.

Kevin had found his way back to Cassidy's mare. He stood

at the horse's shoulder, slowly stroking her long neck and warily eyeing the people around him. Cassidy wondered why the
pale-haired youth was not riding with the Troopers like Raphael was, or if the Warden suspected that Kevin knew anything
about the monsters. If Kevin actually did know anything, that
was; all Cassidy had to base her assumptions on was the fear
she had seen him display, and that could have been nothing
more than a particularly strong sense of superstition on his
part.

*Yeah, and it could have been a tornado that ripped through
here last night, too,* she told herself.

The Warden stood at the edge of the trail of rubble, conferring with four Troopers. Cassidy recognized one of them as
Tag, the morose-looking man from the meeting in the mess
hall, and another as Walt, the dark-haired bearded man who
had ridden with Valerie the night of the fire in Double Creek.
The Warden glanced over briefly at her and Allen, but continued his solemn conversation with the Troopers, and they were
too far away for Cassidy to be able to hear anything they discussed.

As Cassidy came up alongside the mare, she saw that Kevin
was watching Allen with a thinly veiled concern. "You're the
sheriff," the young man said, his tone as uneasy as his
demeanor.

Allen automatically grunted his assent; then he took a second closer look at Kevin and deduced, "You're a Horseman—
the one who was with that black bastard the night he stole our
foal."

Eager to avoid a confrontation between two of the only real
friends she might have in that world, Cassidy quickly intervened by pointing out, "Kevin is a Finder—that's why he
came to the Warden." Realizing only belatedly that neither
Kevin's talent nor his association with the Warden were likely
to curry any favor with Allen, she hastened to add, "And he
helped me when I first got here; he's my friend."

Allen just grunted again, a sound that lay somewhere between contempt and grudging tolerance.

Cassidy had been so occupied with mediating any incipient
ill-will between Allen and Kevin that she hadn't even noticed
the Warden's approach until he was almost up to them. Whatever the young man had been discussing with his Troopers, it
had done nothing to ease the grimness of his mood. He was
frowning and that painfully familiar face was marred by the

telltale hangovers of sleeplessness and fatigue. Cassidy wondered if he had slept at all the night before.

"Was it the same?" he asked them without preamble; there was no need to ask for clarification of what he meant.

Cassidy knew that he was addressing both her and Allen, but when a beat had passed and the big man said nothing, she was the one who replied for both of them. "I think so, at least as far as I can tell." She hesitated for a moment, then added, "The bodies—the people who were killed—that was the same."

The Warden shook his head, less in negation than in frustration. Then he looked directly at Cassidy, and for a few seconds there was a strange look in his eyes that she could not interpret. But before she could try to analyze what it had been, the look was gone and he merely appeared grimly weary again.

"I have to go into the city," he said, "but I'll have Marla or one of the others take you back to the house. Becky is undoubtedly waiting for you there." A hint of wry humor suddenly lit his face and then just as suddenly was gone, flickering and dying as fast as summer lightning. "And Becky is not a very patient woman."

"I showed Cassidy the way out here," Kevin said. "I can take them back."

Another ameliorating expression, that time the fleeting touch of an actual smile, crossed the Warden's face. To Cassidy's surprise, he reached out and gave Kevin a fond clap on the arm. "Fair enough, Kevin," he said. "Thank you." Then with a dismissive nod he turned and strode back toward his Troopers.

Several horses had come forward and stood shifting restlessly at the periphery of the swath of rubble. The Warden approached one of them, a powerful but refined-looking chestnut gelding who was the crisp color of freshly cut cedar, and hopped up onto the horse with a casual agility that belied his haggard appearance. Two of the Troopers, Tag and Walt, also mounted up and then all three of them rode off, retracing their route along the path of devastation that bisected the enclave.

Kevin gave Allen a swift little sidelong glance and offered, "I'll go get your horse for you." As the boy quickly headed off, Cassidy realized it wouldn't be too hard for Kevin to pick out the correct horse for the sheriff; there probably was only one mount in the whole area wearing tack.

Allen had been methodically scanning the area, as if he were monitoring the remaining Troopers' work as they continued poking through the debris from the attack. But as soon as Kevin was out of earshot, the sheriff's candid scrutiny was turned upon Cassidy. "Did you tell him last night?" he asked her.

The segue from what she had been thinking about was a little ragged, but Cassidy realized almost immediately to just what Allen was referring. She thought back to her frustrating encounter with the Warden in the dark pasture the night before. She nodded. "Yeah," she said, "I tried." *For all the good it did.*

The big man's shaggy head was cocked just slightly, his brows canted quizzically, and yet his words were not a question. "And he didn't believe you."

Cassidy shook her head, reluctant to admit even the obvious. "No," she said, "he didn't. He doesn't even remember me, much less believe me."

Allen had looked away again, his eyes traveling to the distant blood-splattered side of the half-ruined house where the two remaining Tinkers were carefully shrouding the bodies of their dead under the watchful eye of one of the Warden's Troopers. But when the sheriff spoke, what he said surprised Cassidy.

"Well, if this keeps up," he said, "he might have to believe you. Hell, if this keeps up, I might even have to believe you myself."

"Let's see you drop those pants."

In another place or time—another life—Becky's casual request, delivered in that deep no-nonsense voice, would have impressed Cassidy as wildly inappropriate, perhaps even comic. Especially considering that Allen, the subject of her request, was standing on the garden deck in full sight of several people. But for Allen it was an old routine, Cassidy reminded herself as she dutifully trampled down an entire set of newly remembered mores; a simple matter of pragmatism. Becky merely intended to examine his wounds.

Allen had already stripped off his shirt and passed it to Rowena to hold. Under the curious and attentive gaze of Becky's fellow housemates, Mickey, Jeremy, and Sharon, the sheriff unfastened his pants and opened his fly to the point where he could slide the garment down over his hips. And no one but Cassidy seemed impressed by the alacrity with which

Allen could shuck his pants; the rest of them were all concentrating on his injuries, not on the exposed expanse of skin of his side and thigh. Previous exposure to the big man's scars had finally rendered them less remarkable to Cassidy; she had forgotten how much interest and controversy the wounds could provoke. And she wished without success that she could equally forget the pleasingly solid masculinity of Allen's body.

"Holy shit," Becky remarked, squatting down beside Allen to get a closer look at his leg. She ran her slim dark hand along the scabbed-over marks that decorated his thigh like ghoulish tattoos. "It's hard to believe these were bites." She scanned his side, squinting as she straightened up, shaking her head. "They look more like cuts—incisions, almost. What the hell kind of teeth could make wounds that clean and sharp?"

What kind indeed, Cassidy thought morbidly, but she took the question to be rhetorical, and Allen did not comment.

"Well, it looks like whatever the Tinkers did for you, they saved your ass," Becky said with finality. "I don't think I could have done anything more. I'm sure you're still sore, but the wounds are really pretty well healed."

As Allen hitched up his pants again, Rowena handed him his shirt. Already Mickey, Jeremy, and Sharon were drifting away; they seemed to have lost all interest in Allen once Becky had made her pronouncement on the wounds, and Cassidy suspected all three of them had other duties. In a few moments only Becky remained with Cassidy, Allen, and Rowena on the deck.

One thing that Cassidy had noticed immediately about Becky was that she had no subtlety about her, and once the matter of Allen's wounds had been dispensed with, the little black woman proceeded with characteristic bluntness. Her deep-set eyes, dark and cannily bright, fixed upon Cassidy. "The Warden told me that you've still got a very strong sense of Memory," she said.

Feeling for some sense of exactly how the Warden had explained Cassidy to Becky, or just how much he had told her, Cassidy remained cautious. "Both Rowena and I have the Memories," she said evenly.

Either Cassidy's ambivalence was obvious or Becky was as perceptive as she was candid because she immediately came to the point. "I can see that living out in the hills has made you grow used to having to hide what you know," she said. "So let me tell you something about myself first, and then we'll talk about you."

Cassidy was aware of Rowena beside her, curious and focused, but she did not allow herself a glance in the brunette's direction. Instead she calmly studied the feisty woman with the rebellious hair and the bright clothing. "How did you know to come here?" she asked Becky.

Becky shrugged, casually spreading her hands. "I didn't," she said. "I just woke up one day not knowing where the hell I was—or even who the hell I was. Luckily, I wasn't too far south of the city, so the first people I ran into were Troopers instead of Villagers. They're the ones who brought me here."

Becky's remark about Villagers didn't seem intended as a deliberate slight and even though Cassidy winced, Allen never even blinked. In some ways the black woman's early experience there had been eerily similar to Cassidy's. Not only had she realized that she had forgotten almost everything that she felt she should know, she had also persisted in her belief that she belonged somewhere else and that things where she was were all somehow askew. Yet like Rowena, Becky's literal recall seemed absent, and she hadn't had anyone there like Cassidy to help rekindle her memory.

As Becky told her tale, Cassidy found herself wondering what her own position there might have been like had she originally fallen into more sympathetic hands. The Troopers who found her had taken Becky to the Warden, who had encouraged her to remember everything that she could. He had also given her access to all of the found things and had urged her to question the other people who had once had Memory and who still lived in his compound. The other thing the Warden had facilitated for Becky, since she had been found so close to the city, were trips into the surrounding countryside to search for anything that might seem familiar or jog her memory. In fact, she had just come back from a two-day boat trip along the southern coast of the Gray Sea, accompanied by two accommodating Tinkers.

"Did you find anything?" Cassidy asked, trying to quell the hope in her voice.

But Becky shook her dreadlocked head. "Naw, not really." Yet even as she spoke, a vague and thoughtful frown crossed her broad face. "But I think there might be something down there, if a person went far enough, or knew where to look . . ." Discarding that topic, Becky quickly backtracked to her origi-

nal narrative. "The other people here who once had Memory
all had the feeling that they didn't fit in with the other people
in this place," she continued, "although I was the only one
who still remembered when I had first gotten here. That seems
to be something the 'normal' people around here forget pretty
quickly. So I'm assuming that whatever happened to all of us
with Memory is unusual, although I'm damned if I've come up
with any explanations for it."

Cassidy finally exchanged a fleeting, almost involuntary
glance with Rowena, and Cassidy knew that the brunette was
probably thinking exactly the same thing she was: Becky
didn't realize how lucky she was not to share the theories the
two of them had come up with in that regard.

"So no one else here really still has the Memories?" Cassidy
asked then.

"Guess not," Becky said. "At least not like me—and certainly not like you two."

As Cassidy had listened to Becky she had felt an increasing
sense of despair. She realized there was no way Becky or any
of the other people at the Warden's house would believe something as fantastic as what she and Rowena had planned to
reveal. And no matter what the Warden had said about Becky
possibly being able to help her, Cassidy feared that the blunt
but likable woman would find their whole theory totally incredible. The only hope to which Cassidy could still cling was
that perhaps somehow Becky still remembered more than she
realized, and that, like Rowena, her memory could be
prompted by someone who remembered more. But even that
was scant comfort. All along Cassidy had been counting on the
Warden and his people to know more than she did; it was depressing to find that they in fact knew considerably less.

"Well, enough about me," Becky said, "let's talk about you
two." She made a dismissive wave toward Allen and continued, "I know he doesn't have the Memories, he just had the
misfortune of getting mixed up with both of you."

That brought a gruff grunt from Allen, but Cassidy could
tell that the big sheriff appreciated Becky's sense of fatalism,
a characteristic the two of them seemed to share. Still disappointed by the lack of recall of the people there, Cassidy decided to risk being blunt, as well.

"What did the Warden tell you about us?" she asked Becky.

Becky's momentary appraisal was unblinking. Her dark
eyes, button bright beneath the smoky plum-colored arch of

her brows, were disconcertingly direct. "He told me that not only do you two think that you come from somewhere else, but that you also have memories of where that was," she said. "And that you told him that he came from the same place because you remember him from there."

Becky's tone of voice during her recital was factual, not one of disbelief, but Cassidy was still uncertain of her true reaction. The black woman's typical expression of forthright candor had the unfortunate aspect of masking the subtleties of other emotional responses, at least to someone who did not know her very well. And so Cassidy was forced to ask her outright for her opinion of what she had been told.

"The Warden doesn't believe that's possible," Cassidy said evenly, "but do you?"

A smile, totally unexpected and surprisingly engaging for all its frankness, flashed across Becky's face. "Hell, I don't disbelieve anything," she declared. "That's why the Warden values what I think."

Equally surprising to Cassidy was the fact that she found herself smiling back at Becky, spontaneously and genuinely. She still wasn't sure if she trusted the woman, but she couldn't help but to like her. Throwing Rowena a little sidelong glance, Cassidy said, "Whether or not you believe it, I think Rowena and I remember a lot more than you do. Do you think we could go inside and look at some of that stuff the Warden's collected? That might be the easiest way to explain just what I mean."

Alone with Rowena in their bedroom that night, Cassidy dropped down onto her back on the bed, her arms flung up over her head. "Well, coming here certainly has solved all of our problems," she muttered sarcastically.

Rowena flopped down onto the other bed with a deliberately theatrical sigh. Over the combined rise of her breasts and belly, she peered at Cassidy's recumbent form. When she saw that her exaggerated reaction had not elicited a more good-humored response, she offered helpfully, "Maybe we should have tried to tell Becky more."

"What more could we have told her?" Cassidy said glumly. "Not being able to remember what a car is when you see a hubcap is one thing; but if you can't remember what a car is when someone *tells* you what a car is—what it looks like and how it's made and what it's for—then how much more could we tell her?" She made an abrupt gesture of frustrated dismissal. "And if she doesn't even remember what a car is, then why the hell tell her about Detroit?"

There was a moment of silence. Then from the other bed Rowena said quietly, "Cassidy, I don't remember Detroit, either."

Stricken by guilt, Cassidy whipped her head up and looked over at her friend. "God, I'm sorry, Rowena; I didn't mean—"

"No, you're right," the brunette interrupted with equanimity. "I remember a lot more than Becky does, but maybe just trying to tell her everything we remember isn't the best idea." She grinned. "She probably already thinks we're nuts!"

Dropping her head back down onto the bed, Cassidy exhaled a sigh of agreement. Their experience trying to explain the found things to Becky had been less than a stunning success. Cassidy and Rowena had learned that, with the simpler low-tech objects, if they explained what an item was for, Becky could understand it even if she didn't remember it. *Just like sunglasses and cigarette lighters,* Cassidy thought ironically; even though she had forgotten they had existed, once she had seen them she could easily figure out what they were for. But when they'd gotten to things like cassette tapes and hubcaps— well, even explanations did not seem to stimulate Becky's memory enough for her really to grasp the object's origin, no matter how much information Cassidy and Rowena gave her. Disappointed, they hadn't even tried to tackle most of the found things. *I wouldn't have touched those condoms with a ten-foot pole,* Cassidy told herself morosely.

Rowena interrupted Cassidy's reverie with a word of encouragement. "Maybe it'll just take more time," she suggested. "After all, Becky did understand some of it." The brunette rolled over onto her stomach so that she could face Cassidy across the space separating the two beds. "And let's face it: If you'd tried to explain things like stereo cassettes or motorcycles to me when you first met me, I don't think I would have been able to remember them, either."

Cassidy threw her a sharp look. "Rowena, when I first met you I didn't remember things like stereo cassettes or motorcycles myself," she reminded her. With another sigh she crossed her wrists over her forehead and stared up at the white plaster ceiling, where the multiplied shadows of the wall-mounted oil lamps glowed in concentric circles of yellow. "But maybe you're right about expecting too much," she said after a moment. "And at least Becky remembers dreams."

In one of the day's small successes, Cassidy had been gratified when she had cautiously broached the subject of dreams with the fiery little woman, and found that Becky's response had been almost identical to Rowena's. She remembered what dreams were, even if she didn't dream. *At least not that she remembers,* Cassidy reminded herself. She had gotten to the point where she refused to make any assumption about the people there.

"Yeah, she remembered dreams—but she didn't recognize what writing is," Rowena couldn't resist pointing out.

To Cassidy that was still one of the oddest phenomena in a decidedly odd world. When pressed, Becky described the writing on the ticket stubs and other bits of paper they showed her as "designs," as if it meant no more to her than the abstract patterns on a bright piece of Tinker cloth. How could the people there be so articulate and yet not use a written language? How could they use the concept of counting and numbers and yet not recognize those same numbers in their written form? Frustrated by far more than Rowena's last quip, Cassidy reached out and, without even looking, lobbed one of the bed pillows at the brunette.

Laughing, Rowena retreated over onto her back again. "Better watch out," she said. "If Allen walks in and finds us having a pillow fight he'll think we've really gone around the bend."

Cassidy felt her mood suddenly sober again. "Rowena," she said to the ceiling, "do you think it was unfair to bring Allen here with us?"

Rowena shrugged, an abbreviated gesture when performed in her supine position. "Cassidy, you saved his life," she said. "He was willing to come." She paused for a moment and when she resumed her voice had grown softer. "I don't think he's very comfortable here, though. I think he misses the village."

As little as Cassidy shared that feeling, she understood it. "Where is he tonight?" she asked Rowena. She had not seen the sheriff since she and Rowena had left the garden deck with Becky that morning. Neither Allen nor the Warden had appeared at the house all day.

"Mickey said he was down at the garrison all afternoon," Rowena said.

Cassidy's brows rose in surprise. "The garrison? I thought he hated Troopers."

Rowena performed another abbreviated shrug. "I guess maybe he feels more at home down there with the horses and stuff than he does around this house."

With the crazy people and all the odd junk, Cassidy's mind automatically supplied. Mildly stung for reasons she didn't even want to examine, Cassidy dropped her arms out perpendicular to her body and stretched. Although she understood Rowena's explanation, Allen's deliberate absence still depressed her. She had to admit that they had maneuvered the big bearded man there against his own preference, but she still wanted to be able to think of him as a willing comrade in their search for the truth. That he was more comfortable with his old enemies than with his new friends somehow seemed an ominous precedent to Cassidy.

Later, when she and Rowena had trimmed the lamps and crawled into bed, Cassidy found that she could not sleep. She lay awake for what seemed like hours, watching the faint mooncast shadows of the trees outside the windows creep across the pale walls. Allen had not returned to the bedroom but Rowena was sleeping soundly beside her, her breathing regular and softly nasal.

The Warden's big brick house was filled with silence, but Cassidy was unable to buy into it. Her mind kept playing and replaying the day's events, from the grisly devastation in the Tinkers' enclave to their disappointing session with Becky and the found things. When she closed her eyes the shifting shadows of the garden's trees were replaced by a series of more disturbing images: the rubble-strewn swath that had been cut through the Tinkers' settlement, the stony opacity of Click's dark eyes, the hopeful puzzlement on Becky's broad face.

Rolling over for at least the tenth time, Cassidy stared across the other bed and out the windows. Coming there was supposed to have brought the solution to their problems; instead all it seemed to have done was precipitate even more problems. And Cassidy couldn't shake the suspicion that their arrival in the Iron City was in some way connected with the way in which the "troubles" that had started in the hills had become more serious and widespread.

Frustrated, Cassidy flung back the covers on her side of the bed and sat up. She groped for her clothing and then dressed quickly in the moonlit room. With a final glance at Rowena's peacefully slumbering form, she slipped around the back of the beds and across the floor to the tall frames of the casement windows. The windows had been left slightly ajar, and the faint perfume of the garden's flowers filtered in from outside. When she pushed lightly the windows swung open soundlessly on their hinges.

Outside the house the shorn strip of lawn stretched toward the dim border of the flower beds, its nappy surface pebbled with dew. Cassidy stepped slowly and precisely, not for the sake of stealth but to minimize the likelihood of soaking her boots. Long shadows from the trees and shrubs lay across the grass, but the flood of moonlight was still intense enough to paint the entire garden with a weird and ghostly glow. The leaves and flowers, robbed of their color by the night, appeared intensely detailed in their shape and form, silvered in that odd light.

Inhaling the cool damp smells of earth and vegetation, Cassidy felt herself begin to relax slightly. In a world without Halcion, perhaps the oldest remedy for insomnia would work for her that night. She moved slowly along the edge of the flower bed, her eyes on the garden, making a conscious effort to blank from her mind the unproductive loop of worries that had been running through it.

She wasn't sure exactly what it had been that made her suddenly stop and look across the yard; the sleepy cry of a mourning dove, perhaps, or just the glimpse of some shadowy movement caught out of the corner of her eye. Whatever had interrupted her nocturnal stroll, she froze when she saw that she was not alone in the moonlit garden. Not fifty feet from her across the shadow-painted grass a solitary figure paced. It was the Warden.

The instant she realized that he hadn't seen her yet, Cassidy had to make a decision about what she would do. She could have just continued to walk forward and greeted the young man; after all, she had a perfectly legitimate if rather mundane reason for her own midnight stroll. Yet something held her back from such simple forthrightness with him, and it had less to do with her own purpose than it did with the Warden's own.

He paced with his hands locked behind his back, his head bent as if in deep thought. It was no wonder he had not noticed her; he moved mechanically, almost like a sleepwalker, totally lost to his surroundings. Stepping backward into the shadow of one of the garden's trees, Cassidy studied him with genuine concern. Didn't the man ever sleep?

Her first instinct then was to go to him, to offer him succor. Surprised and dismayed by how strongly her memories of Andy Greene affected her reactions there, Cassidy shied away from that automatic compassionate response and instead she thought of evasion. After all, what could she offer the Warden? About as much as he had been able to offer her, she thought ironically: nothing more than a sympathetic ear.

Turning soundlessly in the shadows, Cassidy prepared to retrace the trail of darkened patches that her footsteps had made in the silvery grass when a soft but imperative voice interrupted her impromptu flight.

"Cassidy? Wait a minute, please."

Cassidy felt inexplicably flustered, as if she'd been caught committing some misdemeanor. Would he think she had been spying on him? When she obediently turned she saw the Warden walking purposefully toward her from around the edge of the flower bed. But from what she could see of the expression on his face, he didn't look particularly upset to find her out in his garden in the middle of the night. If anything, he seemed puzzled and concerned about her presence there.

"Cassidy?" he repeated as he came up to her. "Is there something wrong?"

"No—uh, no, I just couldn't sleep," she stammered hastily. "I thought maybe if I got out and took a little walk . . ."

Her voice trailed off as she got a closer look at the young man's face. The Warden didn't just look concerned then, he looked downright haggard, his lush brown eyes bracketed by a growing skein of lines and ringed in deep shadow. "Are you all right?" she blurted out, turning his own question back on him.

He gave a sort of shrug, a casually dismissive gesture that seemed to serve as his answer. He continued studying her with a calm concern. "Did you have a bad dream?" he asked her. "A nightmare?"

Initially startled, it took Cassidy a few moments to realize that both Valerie and Becky could have told the Warden that she dreamed; and his query did not imply personal experience, only an informed interest in her well-being.

"No, I never even fell asleep," she admitted.

The expression on that weary face grew increasingly thoughtful then, although she detected a certain note of delicacy in his voice. "What is it like to dream?" he asked. She almost thought that he was being rhetorical until he added,

"When you dream, do you know that the images you see aren't real? When you awaken, do you still feel like the events were something that actually happened to you?"

Cassidy was momentarily stymied by the insightful complexity of his questions. Dreams had to be one of the most difficult things to explain to someone who did not experience them, more difficult even than sex. "Dreams have a reality of their own," she said cautiously, "while they're happening. But once you wake up you can separate what happened in a dream from your real life."

For a moment she thought the Warden was going to ask her more; he certainly looked as if he had more to ask. But he just shook his head, slowly and almost apologetically, and said, "I'm sorry if you're having trouble sleeping, Cassidy." There was an easy sincerity in his voice. "I'm sure you're still upset about what happened last night."

For a few moments—during which Cassidy could have sworn that her heart actually stopped beating—she thought that he was referring to their conversation after the meeting in the mess hall with the Troopers, and of her bizarre revelations and her shameful confession to him. But as the Warden went on she realized that her assumption had been wrong, and her heart resumed beating.

"Thankfully most of the Tinkers are still out trading, or the casualties could have been much worse," he continued. His head gave a little shake, an almost reflexive expression of frustration that sent an errant forelock of his soft brown hair spilling across his forehead. "They have a good reason for concern, and I understand their anger. It was all I could do to get them to allow the Troopers to assist them in recovering the bodies, and they continue to refuse to accept my protection." He caught himself then, the solemnity of that young face briefly replaced by ironic self-deprecation. "Not that my protection has meant much lately," he added.

"I'm not concerned with the matters of Horsemen," Click had told her. Cassidy remembered the way the Tinker leader had stood amid the devastation in his enclave, angrily squared off against the Warden, and she knew that their antagonism must stretch back far beyond the current crisis. What could have caused the rift between the Tinkers and the Horsemen, she wondered, and more specifically the rift between Click and the Troopers?

Cassidy was so engrossed in thought that when the Warden

moved again it startled her, even though his actions were quite casual. As he turned back toward the house he reached out and lightly laid one hand on her arm, deftly guiding her along with him as he began to walk.

"Becky told me that she was unable to be of much help to you," he said. He paused for a beat, and when he continued his voice contained a wry note of irony. "Actually what she told me was that you and Rowena remember far more than she ever did, and that you were the ones who should be helping her."

Uncertain whether he was being serious or just teasing her, Cassidy concentrated to keep from stumbling over her own feet as they walked along side by side over the wet grass. She wished that she could see his expression then, but she couldn't think of any casual way just to turn and look at his face. Her mind spun for something to say, but before she came up with anything the Warden spoke again.

"Becky said that you and Rowena recognize many of the found things that are stored here in the house. I wonder if you'd be willing to do something for me."

When the Warden stopped walking, Cassidy took the opportunity to turn and face him. His hand still rested on her arm. His gaze was unblinking yet curiously soft, and there was a sort of hopeful expectancy to it. In that moment she could not imagine anything he could have asked her for that she would even have considered refusing him.

"Sure," she replied immediately, "what is it?"

As the Warden looked down at her, his youthful face painted by the moonlight, his expression was thoughtful and grave. "There is an artisan in the city, a man named Gustav. While he has no Memory himself, he has proven very helpful to me in reproducing some of the found things and in interpreting the Memories of others." His fingers shifted slightly on her sleeve, the movement almost a casual caress. "If you and Rowena could help Becky select some of the found things that you recognize—things that might be of some use to us if Gustav could reproduce them—I would like you to take these things to his shop in the city and explain them to him."

Cassidy was acutely aware of the Warden's touch, the warmth of his fingers and the subtle scent of his leather clothing. It was an effort to remember that he had just said something that called for a reply. "Sure, we'd be glad to," she told him.

The young man moved slightly, shifting so that he was leaning in closer to her. "If there is anything you've seen among the found things that might have some connection to these creatures," he said with quiet intensity, "I would especially appreciate you concentrating on that."

Cassidy knew full well that none of the Warden's found things had any bearing whatsoever on the monsters, but somehow she didn't have the heart to mention that right then. So she just hesitated for an awkward moment and then said, "Okay, we can try to."

The Warden rewarded her tactfully edited response with a weary and fleeting smile. His hand lifted from her arm to gently clap her on the back. "Thank you, Cassidy," he said softly. "You and your friends have been very helpful to me, and I am grateful."

His simple gratitude impressed Cassidy, and once again she found herself wondering why both the Villagers and the Tinkers seemed to have such a low opinion of the man and his office. *Of course, they might all be less affected than I am by the fact that he's drop-dead gorgeous,* she admitted to herself with rueful candor. She had to scramble mentally to catch up when she realized that the Warden was speaking to her again.

"Of course, I have no illusions about where the allegiance of your sheriff lies," he said wryly. With his head cocked just so, the shadows flattered the clean planes of his face, temporarily erasing the lines of fatigue. "I gave Allen leave to go back to his village, even offered him an escort. I feel that I've kept him from his duties long enough." He shrugged, but his expression was more amused than puzzled. "He told me that he would prefer to stay, that he'd sworn an oath to assist you." The look that he gave Cassidy was frankly appraising, but she did not find it offensive. "I know these sheriffs and they are fiercely loyal to their territories. They also do not give their oath lightly. Obviously you have earned this man's respect." His head dipped in an abbreviated salute. "I guess I'd do well to earn yours, as well."

Speechless, Cassidy just stared up at the Warden until his mouth quirked in a brief smile. "And now I think we both should make another attempt at sleep," he said, gesturing toward the house. To her surprise Cassidy found that they'd been standing practically right outside the opened windows of her bedroom for the last part of their conversation, and she hadn't even noticed it.

Back inside the bedroom, Cassidy tugged off her damp boots and then started on her clothing. She had her back to the bed and so Rowena's sleepy voice startled her.

"Little moonlight stroll?" the brunette drawled.

"I couldn't sleep," Cassidy retorted, annoyed to find herself responding defensively to Rowena's quip. "I didn't know he'd be out there."

"Sure." Rowena yawned. But by the time Cassidy crawled beneath the covers, the brunette's breathing had stretched out into the slow rhythm of slumber again.

Unexpectedly, Cassidy did fall asleep then. She did not dream.

Chapter 16 ◀▥

"What the hell do you mean you're supposed to escort us?" Becky demanded irately. "I've been to Gustav's a dozen times—I'm hardly going to get lost!"

"It was the Warden's orders," the beefy Trooper assured her. The jowly man's horse stood squarely planted in front of the two-wheeled gig cart that Becky had been about to drive out the front gate of the compound.

Becky had immediately impressed Cassidy as a woman who had an extremely low threshhold for exasperation, and that initial impression was being borne out by the confrontation that Cassidy was witnessing from her own position astride Dragonfly. The morning's plans had seemed pretty simple to Cassidy, but she had already learned to take nothing for granted in that world.

"His orders?" Becky repeated querulously, holding in the driving reins on her bay cart horse. "For crying out loud, we're just going into the city—since when do we need an escort for that?"

"The Warden said that Bill and I should go with you," the big Trooper said doggedly, gesturing to the second mounted man who waited alongside the cart. Bill was another stoutly built fellow but he, too, looked decidedly unenthused about his assignment.

At breakfast that morning Becky had seemed quite eager when Cassidy had relayed to her the request the Warden had made the night before. The three women had spent a good hour or more selecting items from the found things for their trip to the artisan's shop. And Becky had definitely surprised and pleased Rowena by commandeering the horse-drawn cart for their errand. Apparently, like Rowena, the black woman

319

was not a very skilled rider. It wasn't until they had reached the garrison's gate that anything intervened to disrupt their plans.

"Maybe an escort's not such a bad idea," Cassidy said, partially out of sincerity and partially out of a desire to placate Becky. "After all, we are carrying some of the Warden's found things."

"Yeah, but it's not like we're heading out across the eastern territories with them," Becky groused, glaring balefully at the stolid Troopers. "All we're doing is going into the city—I've done that hundreds of times and I've never needed any damn escort!"

Although he was insistent, the big Trooper who was blocking the cart seemed sensitive to Becky's indignation. "Things are different now, Becky," he said, trying to reason with her. "There's a lot of unrest in the city."

"Is that so, Hugh?" Becky said testily. She gathered the cart horse's reins as if she were about to drive right through the Trooper and his mount. "Well, white boy, if you don't move that piece of dog feed you're straddling and let us get under way, I'll show you what real 'unrest' is!"

Nodding to Bill, the burly man swung his horse aside. Becky drove the cart through the gates, leaving the two Troopers to fall in behind her as the little procession started up the road to the city. Cassidy let the gray mare trot alongside the two men's horses as she offered, "Thanks; I think this probably is a good idea." And although the Troopers certainly did not need Cassidy's approval of their duty, they both looked grateful for the only cooperation they were likely to see from the trio of women.

The air was cooler that morning, the sky streaked with long feathers of cirrus clouds that attenuated the sun's brilliance and formed a kind of shifting latticework of light. The weather made Dragonfly frisky, but the trip to the city was a short one and Cassidy made her horse keep pace with the two Troopers. Hugh and Bill rode along as unobtrusively as possible, letting their horses jog about thirty feet behind the two-wheeled cart.

After they'd ridden for a few minutes in silence, Cassidy asked Hugh, "Why is there unrest in the city? I thought that nothing had happened there last night."

The blocky man gave her a sidelong look. "Monsters aren't the only trouble around here," he said.

Cassidy waited a moment for him to elaborate, but when he didn't she said, "Is it gang trouble then?"

Bill shot a look at Hugh then, almost as if he were warning the Trooper not to comment. Hugh grunted. "People are getting riled up" was all he would say. "The Warden'd do well to be cautious."

Considering the importance with which the Warden had seemed to have invested their visit to the artisan, Cassidy had been surprised when she'd found out that not only did he not intend to accompany them, but that according to Becky he might even be absent from the compound for the entire day. The peppery little black woman had not offered any further explanation, but she seemed characteristically irritated by the Warden's absence. Cassidy wasn't irritated, but she did feel puzzled and somewhat concerned. With the recent concentration of incidents in the immediate area, she couldn't understand why he felt any need to go afield.

At least there had been good news at breakfast, as well: No further incidents had been reported in the city overnight. Perhaps the lull in the attacks had allowed the Warden a chance to pursue some other business that the "troubles" had forced him to delay. Or maybe the absence of fresh local attacks only meant that the problem had moved back out into the hills, necessitating the investigation of some other recent but less well-publicized incidents. The only thing of which Cassidy felt confident was that the bizarre attacks were far from over; she just wished that she had the same insight into a solution to them.

A small band of Troopers approached them on the road, riding out from the city toward the garrison. Forced out of her musing and into the present, Cassidy was chagrined to find that both Hugh and Bill were eyeing her rather oddly. She realized that she had probably been riding along with a decidedly vacant look on her face. *Maybe they'll think I was summoning Memories,* she thought ruefully, giving them both a small smile.

The oncoming Troopers trotted past them with nods of acknowledgment, which Becky ignored but which Cassidy and the others returned. Several of the leather-clad riders looked familiar to Cassidy. She had seen enough of the Troopers by then to be able to recognize many of them on sight, although she knew very few by name. The band that passed them appeared to be a patrol squad returning from their tour of duty in the city. The mounted men and women's demeanor was alert yet tempered by their long night's work, and their horses jogged along in a businesslike manner and without enthusiasm.

As the Troopers moved on by, Cassidy caught Hugh's eye and ventured, "At least they should have had a pretty quiet night."

But the stocky man shook his head dolefully. "A lot of unrest," he reiterated tersely. "Gangs, fighting, even arson—nothing but trouble in the city these days."

Doubly glad for the Warden's insistence on sending the Troopers with them, Cassidy made a surreptitious assessment of the two men who rode beside her. Hugh may have appeared phlegmatic, but the big man rode with a taut poise that suggested to Cassidy that he knew how to handle himself in a scrape. And Bill, who was so laconic that he had yet to speak a word in her presence, carried the solid weight of a wrestler combined with the casual grace of a bodyguard. Becky may have discounted their need for any escort, but Cassidy was far less confident of moving alone through the unfamiliar city and she was grateful to have the Troopers accompany them.

Unlike the night when she and Rowena and Allen had traveled its deserted streets with Click, that morning the city was aswarm with activity. Even at its outskirts the paved thoroughfares were cluttered with foot and vehicular traffic, much of it rudely reckless in its course. Where had all of the people in the city come from? Cassidy wondered in renewed amazement. An entourage of scruffy-looking men and women of all ages, all dressed in dirty clothing, converged on the horse-drawn cart and then smoothly parted to glide around it, their temerity probably tempered by the sight of the Troopers that followed the vehicle. Other horse-drawn conveyances met them, passed them, or cut in from side streets as they continued deeper into the city. Most of the people who were not driving wagons or rigs were on foot, but there were a few mounted riders who were not Horsemen. Everyone seemed bound on some business, laden with bundles or bags of goods or driving loads of lumber, feed, or manufactured goods. And everyone, even the most disreputably dressed, seemed to be watching their fellows on the streets with wary suspicion.

Apparently there's no honor among thieves even in this world, Cassidy thought as she watched a gang of gaudily garbed adolescents dart from an alleyway and pelt up the street after a spring wagon piled with bolts of cloth. The youths' brazen attempts to snatch the rolls of fabric from the wagon were met with curses and a few well-lobbed chunks of broken brick from the driver. Amused in spite of herself, Cassidy held the gray mare back as Hugh and Bill urged their horses forward, instantly scattering the gang of would-be thieves. *We could be on the streets of almost any big city you could name,* she thought, remembering the metropolises of her own world. *All that's missing are the horns, sirens, and the gunfire.*

Becky seemed unconcerned about all the activity around her. The little woman sat calmly poised on the cart's seat, deftly maneuvering the bay horse around the various impediments that they encountered. Beside her Rowena was visibly as fascinated as was Cassidy by the city's ambience, and too curious to refrain from staring at the chaos around them. However, after the gang had chased after the spring wagon full of cloth, Hugh and Bill took up stations riding right alongside the cart, and Cassidy noted that Becky didn't protest.

Once they had turned off onto a narrower side street, the busy throng was considerably reduced. Cassidy noted that none of the streets or buildings in the city seemed to be marked in any way, but Becky seemed to know exactly where she was going. They passed an impressive collection of garbage, ostensibly piled into trash barrels but liberally overflowing those containers and spilling out across the pavement. The cart horse's hooves slipped in the exudate oozing from the mounds of rubbish, and the stench alone was enough to make Cassidy's eyes water. Then they were past the offensive mounds and Becky skillfully turned the little cart into a short alley between two small and rather shabby-looking wooden frame buildings.

While the black woman bent to grope under the cart seat for the sack in which they'd stowed the found things they'd chosen to bring along, Rowena stayed seated in place. The brunette exchanged a single significant look with Cassidy before both resumed warily scanning their surroundings.

"This is it?" Rowena said in disbelief. "This is where this Gustav guy works?"

Becky hefted the sack and clambered down out of the cart. She looked back up at Rowena with a sympathetic smile. "Doesn't look like much, huh? Believe it or not, this is actually one of the better sections of the old part of the city."

Hugh and Bill rode up alongside the cart, giving the immediate area of the alleyway a vigilant scrutiny. "She's right," Hugh agreed, leaning forward to offer Rowena a helping hand in stepping down from the cart. "The worst of the old part burned down in the big fire."

Cassidy reluctantly slid down off the security of Dragonfly's back. "And you wanted to come down here alone?" she asked Becky.

Shrugging dismissively, Becky cradled the sack against her chest. "Hell, I've done it lots of times," she said. "Never needed any escort."

"Well, you've got one now," Hugh reminded her, dropping down off his horse. He threw Bill a meaningful look. "Anything suspicious, don't hesitate," he instructed the big silent man.

Cassidy didn't even want to speculate just what that might mean. None of the Troopers she had seen regularly around the garrison or the city appeared to be armed; but Bill didn't look as if he needed a gun to make his point. She also didn't mind admitting to herself that she was relieved to find that Hugh obviously intended to accompany them into the artisan's building, and that Bill would be right outside, guarding their horses. She no longer needed Click to tell her that the Iron City could be a dangerous place.

As Becky opened the wooden door and they stepped across the threshhold, Cassidy's first thought was that the artisan's shop looked less like some craftsman's place of business and more like an old-fashioned pawnshop. The long narrow room was filled with an incredible amount of clutter, crowded onto shelves and display cases and hung from the walls. Some of the items were easily recognizable as various types of hardware and their appropriate fittings; but much of the rest of it defied description. A hasty scan of the overwhelming collection of objects revealed items as disparate as leather boots and a crude but identifiable fiddle. If Cassidy's suppositions about that world's system of barter were correct, then perhaps the artisan's store actually was a sort of pawnshop, just as every shop or manufacturer in the city probably was, trading their goods or services for whatever someone else could make or do.

"What a mess!" Rowena whispered to Cassidy. But Cassidy could see that the brunette was just as fascinated as she was. Becky and Hugh had marched straight on through to the back of the shop where the woman set her sack on a long but almost completely overfilled wooden counter. Cassidy and Rowena hung back, peering at the wealth of objects that spilled off every shelf and hung from every available inch of wall space.

Nothing that Cassidy saw there would have qualified as a found thing. Rather, all of the objects were things that had been created there, and they included some rather sophisticated glassware, jewelry, and leatherware in addition to the more mundane pieces of hardware. Of the latter there was a wide selection, everything from small kegs of nuts and bolts to big wrought-iron hinges and decorative gate pieces.

Cassidy had been bent over a counter, eyeing one of the larger specimens of ironwork, when the shop's proprietor came out from a back room and greeted Becky and Hugh. Gustav was nearly as much of a surprise as was his establishment. After seeing the bizarre conglomeration of hardware and traded goods, Cassidy realized she'd expected the artisan to be some beady-eyed and wizened little gnome of a man, like a cross between an eccentric inventor and an absentminded professor. But the man behind the cluttered wooden counter was anything but gnomelike. In his loose shirt and leather apron he reminded her more of a jeweler or a watchmaker. He was tall and lean but quite fit looking, with fine pale blond hair worn cropped off at ear length. And as for wizened, Cassidy doubted that Gustav was any older than she was.

When Rowena poked her with one elbow, Cassidy realized that Becky was introducing them to the artisan and she blurted out a quick hello. As she and Rowena approached the counter where Becky and Hugh stood, the tall blonde was eyeing them with a certain cautious speculation.

"The Warden told me about you," he said. He glanced at Becky and then at the sack on the counter before him. "What have you brought me this time?"

Fifteen minutes and the entire contents of the sack later, Cassidy could call the encounter only a mixed success. Of all of the found things that they had brought to show Gustav, the artisan had no primary recognition of any of them. Of course Cassidy had expected that; the Warden had told her that Gustav had no Memory. As she understood it, his talent lay in his interpretation of the Memories of others. But she was a little disappointed that the items they'd selected to show him had not gotten a more enthusiastic response.

By tacit agreement Cassidy and Rowena had not picked out any found thing that could have proven controversial in the explanation of its use. But the blond man's reaction to the audiocassette tape had been typical of the frustration they had faced in trying to reconcile that world with the one that Cassidy now so clearly remembered. Even when she explained that the cassette was a means of storing music for repeated playings, Gustav was plainly puzzled.

"There's no way this thing could make music," he said deprecatingly, flicking his forefinger over the exposed brown edge of audiotape. Trying to explain electromagnetic recording was out of the question, and Cassidy's description of a tape player only seemed to confuse the artisan further.

Some of the more simple objects, like a ballpoint pen and a little plastic box of TicTacs, were at least easier to explain, even if Gustav could see no advantage in trying to reproduce them. And Cassidy could see the blonde's point. The Warden was seeking some kind of information about the origin of the monsters and some way to combat the creatures; somehow the Bic pen and TicTacs didn't seem equal to either task.

The only thing they had brought along that seemed to interest Gustav was a slightly battered triple-A battery. The lanky artisan thoughtfully rolled the little cylinder between his fingers as Cassidy tried her best to explain the chemical composition and effects of the simple device. Not for the first time in the past few days she found herself wishing that she'd paid more attention to things like science and chemistry when she'd been in school.

"I've seen other devices like this," Gustav mused, once Cassidy's greatly oversimplified explanation had staggered to a halt, "devices for the generation of electricity." He shook his head, his fine hair shimmering. "But they didn't look anything like this. Wait, I'll show you."

He disappeared through the narrow doorway behind the counter and into the rear of his shop. Cassidy exchanged a quizzical look with Becky, but the black woman merely shrugged. "I have no idea what he's got back there. I still don't even have any idea what the hell you two were just talking about!"

When Gustav reappeared a minute later he was carrying a block-shaped wooden object that resembled nothing so much as an old-fashioned manual coffee grinder, right down to the curved metal handle adorning its top. He set it down on the counter with a clunk and a small puff of dust. "Someone made this," he said unnecessarily. He gave the metal handle a slight experimental turn. "I never understood how it worked, but I know it was supposed to generate electricity." He cranked the handle further and an eerie squealing noise rose from the box. He looked across at Cassidy. "I guess it does mechanically what your little device does chemically. The only problem with either one of them is why bother to generate electricity in the first place? It's nothing but an oddity."

Trying to stifle the rising tide of frustration she felt at those people's unwitting ignorance, Cassidy reached out and lightly brushed her fingertips over the dusty surface of the crude little generator. Had whoever created it just given up, dismissed by people like Gustav? "Yeah, why bother?" she murmured under her breath.

"Listen, if you want to leave all these things, I'd be glad to go over them again later," Gustav offered with a shrug. "Maybe I can find more things in the back room that are similar to them, or related in some way."

Cassidy threw Becky a sidelong glance. She wasn't sure who, if any of them, had the authority to decide the disposition of the Warden's property. But from the unconcerned expression on the smaller woman's face, Cassidy got the impression that found things had been left before in the artisan's care.

"Just remember," Becky warned Gustav, "if you take any of this stuff apart, you'd better be damned sure you can put it back together again!"

As the four of them turned to leave the shop, Cassidy saw Gustav repacking the found things in their sack. She had the unsettling feeling that the cloth bag was the only thing that stood between the safety of the Warden's found things and having them be irretrievably lost in the utter chaos of the artisan's shop.

Even before Hugh opened the front door and preceded them back out into the alley, Cassidy could hear something amiss outside. A loud voice, raised in some unintelligible argument, could be heard even from the doorway. Hugh's big shoulders stiffened and he nearly bounded out into the alley ahead of them.

Bill still sat astride his horse in the alleyway beside the shop, guarding Dragonfly, Hugh's horse, and the two-wheeled cart. But far from being deserted, the area around the entrance to the artisan's building now roiled with a dozen or more people, several of whom were noisily badgering the mounted Trooper.

A rather overweight young woman dressed in a gaudy mismatch of ragged clothing was shaking her plump fist at Bill, shouting "Your job is to protect *us*, damn you—not *them!*"

Cassidy quickly saw that most of the people who had gathered around the cart and horses had the disheveled look that she had already come to associate with the city's numerous gangs. She also saw that they all seemed angry and agitated. Bill did not appear particularly alarmed by the fracas, but his horse was stepping about in place, flaring its nostrils and rolling its eyes at the unruly throng.

"Here now—move along," Hugh said sternly, wading into the tumult.

"There they are!" someone shouted. It took Cassidy a moment to realize that the irate exclamation had been directed at her and Rowena and Becky. As her eyes darted over the milling people, looking for who had called out, Hugh raised his beefy arms up over his head.

"Move along!" he commanded the crowd. "Let's not have any trouble here."

A florid-faced man with thinning hair and clothes that looked like he'd stolen them from someone who had been a hundred pounds heavier and color-blind aggressively confronted the big Trooper. "Don't talk to us about trouble!" he exclaimed angrily, his bony forefinger stabbing the air. "It's people like these women who've brought nothing but trouble to this city!"

Cassidy, Rowena, and Becky remained in the artisan's doorway as Hugh tried to disperse the crowd. When it became apparent that the motley gang was not amenable to his brand of reason, Hugh turned back toward the three women and gestured sharply for them to head for the cart and horses. Cassidy hesitated to try pushing into the angry mob, but Becky was less intimidated. She stepped past Cassidy and started toward the cart. She had taken only a few strides when something soft and malodorous splattered with significant force against the front of her shirt.

From the blaze of indignation in the dark woman's eyes, Cassidy suspected that Becky would have been quite willing to try taking on the entire mob single-handedly. Luckily for all of them, Hugh managed to reach her before she could make the attempt. Using the sheer advantage of his size, the Trooper caught her around the waist and propelled Becky forward, clearing a path through the shouting mob as he pushed her along toward the cart. Cassidy and Rowena tried to follow then, but before they could even catch up, the crowd's aggression escalated.

Cassidy had not been paying much attention to Bill, being more immediately concerned with just forcing her way through the throng of shoving, dirty people. So she did not see exactly what precipitated the sudden surge of action in the crowd, a shift that led to several members of the mob rushing the mounted man. The first thing Cassidy knew, people were literally launching themselves at the silent Trooper, clawing at his leather-clad limbs and trying violently to pull him down off his prancing horse.

Hugh dropped his hold on Becky and spun around, far more quickly than Cassidy would have believed a man his size was capable of. The mob tore Bill from his horse's back. Once the Trooper was down on the pavement, they began pelting him with spilled garbage and pummeling him with their fists while the big man thrashed about like an enraged bear. By then Hugh had dived into the fray, swinging his arms from side to side, his elbows sweeping aside the intervening rioters like twin scythes cutting wheat.

The cart horse was pretty well trapped by the melee, but the gray mare and the two Troopers' horses had scrambled free of the worst of it. As she Called her horse, Cassidy grabbed Rowena by the sleeve and yanked the brunette backward after her to the relative sanctuary of the doorway of Gustav's shop. *Where the hell are the cops when you need them?* she thought just as a lobbed piece of rotted garbage sailed past her head and impacted with a liquid splat against the wooden door.

Spinning around, Cassidy tried to reenter the artisan's shop. She was shocked to find that the door had been barred in some way; even throwing all of her weight against it did nothing to loosen it in its frame. "Shit!" she exclaimed, right into Rowena's anxious face.

Rather than following Cassidy and Rowena back to the dubious safety of the shop's doorway once Hugh had been forced to leave her, Becky had pushed forward into the mob, swinging with impunity at the temporarily dazed people who had just taken one of Hugh's elbows in their chest or belly. She was shouting loudly, but whether her invectives were aimed at the crowd or at the two brawling Troopers who were supposed to have been protecting them, Cassidy couldn't be certain. Then one of the irate crowd tripped the loud little black woman and she went down, falling to the pavement nearly under the cart horse's feet.

What had begun as merely a noisy inconvenience and then escalated into a boisterous brawl had become something far more threatening. Although Becky didn't appear to be seriously injured, she had scraped the heels of her hands when she had fallen and the abrasions were bleeding. At least for the moment she seemed either too dazed or too smart to try to get up again. And the mob was successfully preventing Hugh from reaching the besieged Bill. While the burly Trooper swung and batted at his antagonists, trying to force his way through to his comrade, Cassidy realized to her dismay that the men and women who were pummeling Bill were no longer just using their fists and feet. Several members of the mob were wielding short clubs or truncheons, in spite of the fact that Bill no longer appeared capable of resisting them.

With a clatter of slipping hooves and a loud snort of disapproval, Dragonfly skidded to a halt at the entryway of the artisan's shop. The horse's coat was splattered with some foul and unrecognizable garbage, but her demeanor was spirited and downright combative. It would have been very tempting to Cassidy to have just hiked Rowena up on the horse, hopped astride with her, and then ridden the hell out of there. But Cassidy was nearly as outraged as she was frightened at what was happening, and she never seriously considered abandoning Becky or the Troopers to the mob.

Cassidy had no idea what the hell had happened to Gustav—if the man hadn't heard the loud riot that had erupted right outside of his shop he must have been stone deaf— although considering the mood in the city she suspected that he had deliberately withdrawn to avoid getting involved in the fracas. All she knew for certain was that they were unlikely to get any help from that quarter. And she and Rowena weren't going to remain safe in his doorway for much longer. Becky had crawled under the two-wheeled cart to escape the crowd, but Cassidy figured that once the mob had knocked Hugh down, too, they would go after the feisty black woman. And once that happened, the angry throng would have a pretty clear shot at all three objects of their derision.

"We've got to get back to the cart!" Cassidy shouted to Rowena. They both ducked back against the door frame just as one of Hugh's half-stunned victims staggered right into the side of the building practically at their feet.

Casting a quick look out over the brawling mass that lay between them and their objective, Rowena rolled her eyes. More people had poured into the street and alleyway, apparently attracted by the uproar. "You've got to be kidding!" Rowena said.

But Cassidy was grimly serious. "Come on," she insisted, "we'll ride through." After locking her hands to give the dubious brunette a leg up onto the mare, Cassidy followed her up onto the horse's back with an agility fueled by a liberal shot of adrenaline. Beneath them the big horse sidestepped eagerly, her unshod hooves scraping on the wet paving stones.

Up on Dragonfly's back Cassidy felt in control again, and her anger at the vicious mob was redoubled. From her vantage point on the horse she could see Hugh going down to his knees, his adversaries swarming over him like wolves pulling down a crippled deer. Bill's motionless body had been abandoned by the crowd, which was just seconds away from turning on the cart and Becky.

Cassidy didn't need to urge or direct the mare; the horse sprang forward of her own volition, plunging into the chaos of bodies with about as much heed as she would have utilized in plowing into a troublesome hedge of briars. The shouting people who grappled to get hold of Cassidy's or Rowena's legs were summarily shoved aside or knocked down by the lunging horse's big body. Even the mob's attempts to stop the gray by beating at her with their fists or cudgels seemed inconsequential to the mare; she sliced through the throng like a snowplow, sending shrieking people scurrying out of her way.

As they came up alongside the cart, Cassidy shouted at Rowena, "Jump down!"

Rowena, who had been clinging to Cassidy's waist for dear life, just gaped incredulously at her. But Cassidy realized what was happening around them. With Hugh down on the pavement, the crowd had noticed that she and Rowena were making a run for the cart. The next focus of the mob's wrath would likely be Becky. The black woman had gotten to her hands and knees in the sanctuary of the small space between the wheels of the cart; but the mob was already attacking the bay horse, trying to unhitch him by ripping at his harness. The horse was well trained, but the melee was something beyond the scope of his experience, and if he hadn't been so thoroughly boxed in by the crowd he probably would have bolted already.

"Jump down!" Cassidy repeated insistently, trying to pry

Rowena's arms free of her waist. "You've got to get Becky into the cart before these idiots get hold of us!"

Rowena dropped down onto the seat of the cart, but it was only a partially voluntary move on her part; Cassidy had given her a liberal assist. While the brunette scrambled over the seat and down onto the footboard to extend a hand to Becky, Cassidy let Dragonfly leap forward. The irate mob that had been grappling with the cart horse's harness was forced back, scattering away from the big mare's plunging forefeet.

"Stop them—they're getting away!" someone in the throng shouted.

We are? was Cassidy's bemused response; but when she glanced back over her shoulder she saw that not only had Becky managed to climb up into the cart, but she had also gathered the driving reins in her bloody hands and was urging the frightened cart horse forward into the mob.

Spinning the gray mare around, Cassidy cried out to Becky, "Wait! What about Hugh and Bill?"

But the dark-skinned woman grimly shook her head, her dreadlocks flying. She slapped the reins across the cart horse's rump and the gelding leapt forward, undeterred by the wall of grasping and pummeling hands that confronted him. "It's too late—we can't help them now!" Becky shouted as the cart lurched away across the uneven pavement of the alleyway.

As much as she hated to concede it, Cassidy knew that Becky was right. If they stopped and tried to retrieve the two downed Troopers from the midst of that chaos, the angry mob would tear them all apart. She didn't even know if Hugh and Bill were still alive. But the cold logic of Becky's response didn't make it any easier for Cassidy to leave those two big motionless leather-clad bodies behind as she let Dragonfly bound up the alley after the cart.

The route they had chosen had all the virtue of necessity. While the alley was not deserted, it was considerably less congested with the rowdy thugs than the street had been, and the cart had been parked facing into the alley to begin with. But even in the alley they encountered an obstacle course, dodging a fresh infusion of the noisy haranguers who launched themselves furiously at the cart and horses, and swerving around overfilled trash barrels and the random stacks of crates and sacks. All of the shouting seemed to have attracted half of the malcontents in the city, and even those too prudent to try to block the escaping horses still expressed themselves by flinging trash and dung after the cart. Several times during the short dash up the narrow debris-choked passage the cart horse slipped and nearly fell, his shod feet screeching on the pavement. But he always managed to catch his balance again, and despite the ominous flapping of several loose straps his harnessing held together.

As they neared the next intersecting street Cassidy heard the clatter of iron-shod hooves behind them. But when she glanced over her shoulder, heart pounding, she was relieved to find that it was only the two Troopers' riderless horses and that the bulk of the crowd had been left some distance behind. As they burst out onto the throughway, the other horses caught up with the cart. Cutting onto the street, Becky executed a turn so sharp that Cassidy thought for certain the two-wheeled cart would flip over. Thankfully that didn't happen. But as the two Troopers' horses came alongside him, the cart horse skidded sideways on the pavement. He was scrambling for his balance when both he and the right wheel of the gig cart collided forcefully with a wooden handcart that was being pushed down the center of the street. The handcart tilted sharply, sending its cargo spilling out onto the pavement in a brilliant explosion of light and sound.

As the bay cart horse righted himself, he slid to a halt amid a sea of broken glass that glittered like an icefield across the street. The overturned handcart had been packed with windowpanes. From the seat of the two-wheeled gig cart, Becky and Rowena looked down in wide-eyed dismay at the wreckage. But Cassidy's concern for the damage that they had caused was only momentary. Instead she looked past the toppled cart to the three men who had been accompanying the ill-fated cargo. They all were eyeing her with identical expressions of mixed surprise, recognition, and consternation; for not only were the men Tinkers, they were Click, Tad, and Teddy.

"What the hell is going on here?" the blacksmith demanded.

Cassidy could barely restrain the prancing gray mare. "A mob attacked us!" she explained hastily. "They're coming up this alley!"

Teddy still stood in slack-mouthed amazement at the three women's sudden and calamitous appearance in their midst, but Tad was muttering under his breath as he regarded the shattered remains of their cartful of window glass. Only Click seemed to comprehend the gravity of the situation immediately. A quick glance had assured the Tinker leader that the gig cart and its driving horse and passengers were all still reasonably intact, and that Cassidy and her mare, although smeared with garbage, were both uninjured. Another glance up the alley confirmed for both him and Cassidy that the mob was still following them and was only moments behind. But Cassidy saw no anger on that familiar face, only a grim concern.

"Go!" Click said emphatically, a swift wave of his hand encompassing all three women in that blunt order. "Back to the garrison—you can easily outdistance these fools if you keep to the main streets."

Becky had gathered her reins in a deathlike grip. The cart horse was skittering sideways, the wooden shafts groaning as the gelding's shod hooves crunched sharply on the broken glass. The two Troopers' horses milled anxiously around the handcart, only adding to the damage. It was all Cassidy could do to keep Dragonfly under control, but the biggest problem wasn't that the horse wanted to bolt away up the street—the problem was that she wanted to charge back down the alley after the angry mob.

"Go!" Click repeated, his voice even more vehement when he saw Becky's hesitation.

"Hugh and Bill," Cassidy said breathlessly, fighting for the mare's obedience, "the two Troopers who were with us—the mob attacked them and—"

A sudden indefinable change came over Click at Cassidy's words. It still was not anger that she saw on his face, yet something—an expression both dark and resolute—dropped over him like a mask. He swung toward his two companions, swiftly but calmly firing off orders at them.

"Tad, right the cart," he said. "Wait until I reach the crowd; then you and Teddy follow me down the alley."

Becky seemed aghast at Click's audacity. "You can't go back there!" she protested, still struggling to hold in the nervous cart horse. "They almost killed us!"

"We don't even know if Hugh and Bill are still alive," Rowena added. "We couldn't get anywhere near them."

"Oh, they're alive," Click assured them grimly. "Not even these fools would risk killing a Trooper. Now go—*quickly,* before they get here!"

But Cassidy just tightened her knees around the gray's wide barrel. "No," she told him obstinately, "I'm going with you."

"Don't be foolish," Click threw off over his shoulder, even as he strode away from her. "It's too dangerous for you."

To Cassidy's considerable amazement, the tall dark-haired man was confidently approaching Hugh's horse, an advance that the stout brown gelding was regarding with pricked ears and flaring nostrils. "You're the ones they're after," Click insisted without looking back, "now *go!*" With those emphatic words he nimbly hopped up onto the big gelding's back, and within seconds he had the snorting horse redirected toward the mouth of the alley.

Despite the command, Cassidy was at first too startled to move in either direction. She was so stunned at her discovery that for a few moments even the approaching threat of the noisy mob held no immediacy for her. Her mind seemed capable of processing only one thought: Click was a *Horseman.* But then the Tinker leader shouted again, shattering her immobility.

"*Go,* damn you!"

Becky finally released her fierce hold on the cart horse's reins; the gelding needed no additional urging to spring forward again up the street. A few curious pedestrians, probably drawn even on this relatively quiet back street to the sounds of the crash and subsequent argument, had to leap aside to avoid being summarily run down by the two-wheeled gig cart.

Cassidy could have forced the gray mare to follow, to turn away from the imminent confrontation in the alley and to flee with Rowena and Becky back to the garrison, but the knowledge of what Click was about to attempt wouldn't permit her to leave him. Click had already sent the brown gelding bounding up the narrow passageway, not even looking back to see if she had complied with his order. He rode poised over the big horse's withers as if he had ridden like that every day of his life. And as Cassidy released the mare to follow him, she saw Click raise one arm over his head and she saw the glint of steel in his hand.

Click was almost on top of the oncoming crowd, and Cassidy's mare was nearly shoulder to haunch with his gelding, when she was able to identify the object he was brandishing overhead. *He wasn't kidding about having another gun,* she thought with a certain detached sense of irony, even as the Tinker leader fired off several shots into the air. The sound of the gunfire, sharp and percussive, echoed off the walls of the surrounding buildings as Cassidy suddenly fathomed Click's intent. *He'll bring every Trooper within a half-mile radius running.*

Their horses were almost side by side then, an equine flying wedge that sent the unruly throng of people parting like a forked river, when Click glanced over to acknowledge Cassidy's presence. Surprisingly enough, he still didn't look exactly angry; if anything, for just a second Cassidy thought that she saw the old flash of that familiar humor in those umber eyes.

"The garrison is in the other direction," he pointed out, even as his horse swerved to avoid a toppled stack of crates. The mob in the alley drew back against the walls of the buildings to avoid being trampled.

Keeping pace with him, Cassidy responded, "Yeah? Well, I never did have a very good sense of direction."

As they reached the other end of the alleyway, Cassidy could see the remnants of the angry crowd, still milling around the prone bodies of the Troopers. People looked up at the clatter of approaching hoofbeats. The shots from Click's gun and the anticipation of the Troopers that the sound would inevitably bring seemed to be having a salutary effect on the rowdy mob, for the remaining people put up no real resistance. Cassidy didn't know if any of them recognized Click, or if it was merely the sight of the pistol in his hand; but even the ragged-looking scoundrels who had been bent over Hugh and Bill, rifling through their clothing in search of some booty, quickly pulled back when the Tinker leader dropped down off his horse.

For a moment Cassidy hesitated, remembering the violent fury that the crowd had demonstrated only minutes earlier. But she saw then that those same thugs were rapidly dispersing, slipping back into doorways or disappearing up the street and alley again. As she hopped down off Dragonfly her boots squished in the scattered garbage, a pungent reminder of the unpleasant encounter.

Click had already dropped into a squat beside Hugh, his fingers going to the pulse point on the motionless man's neck. "He's just been knocked out," he said. "I don't think he's been seriously injured, even if he looks a mess."

Cassidy heard the thin grinding sound of metal on paving stones and looked up to see Tad and Teddy trotting up the alley, pushing ahead of them the big wooden handcart with its iron-rimmed wheels. A few more of the scruffy people who had been lingering in the intersection slipped past the pair, scowling and muttering dark but unintelligible deprecations.

Teddy looked nervous but Tad indignantly lobbed a stray bit of broken bottle after them.

Teddy's guileless blue eyes were as wide as soup plates as he took in the downed and bloodied Troopers. "Are they all right?" he blurted out anxiously.

Click had already moved to Bill and was gently rolling the unconscious man over onto his back. He barely glanced up at his comrades. "They will be, Teddy," he reassured the strapping youth. "That one's just been coldcocked, but I think this man has suffered a broken arm, as well."

Looking down at where Click crouched beside the second Trooper, Cassidy was dismayed to see that Bill was still bleeding messily from a deep gash on his forehead. Blood had congealed beneath him in a dark pool that clung to his hair like a gelatinous cap when Click had turned him over. And from the unnatural position in which Bill's left arm was bent, Cassidy was certain that Click was right about the fracture.

Briskly and without hesitation, Click tugged his own shirt tail free of his trousers and began to tear the fabric with a sharp jerk. "Tad, you and Teddy load the other fellow into the cart," he said calmly, even as he ripped off a long strip of the material. "We need to see them both out of here as soon as possible." Without glancing up, he added, "Cassidy, I could use your help with this man."

With one last wary look around the alley and street, Cassidy dropped down onto her knees on the garbage-strewn pavement beside Click. With her assistance he quickly and deftly bound the wound on Bill's forehead. Then he began tearing another strip off the ragged hem of his shirt, instructing her, "Look around in all of this trash and see if you can find two boards about so long—preferably two that aren't soaked with sewage," he added dryly.

Even under normal circumstances Cassidy probably could have scrounged up two pieces of board in the alley; the siding of the dilapidated buildings was easily ripped free. Many of the angry mob had obviously done just that when they wanted weapons, for there were numerous slats and chunks of board amid the litter they had left behind. By the time she had selected two relatively clean pieces of the appropriate length she heard the clatter of hoofbeats and looked up to see the first patrol of Troopers arriving from up the street.

The patrol's arrival was so precipitous, and the expressions on the faces of the mounted men and women so furious, that for a few seconds Cassidy wondered if she and the Tinkers were going to be mistaken for part of the rabble that had caused the messy incident. But several things probably saved them from the Troopers' wholesale wrath. One thing was that Cassidy recognized the woman who was leading the patrol, and so hopefully the Trooper recognized Cassidy, as well. And the other thing was that she and Click had obviously come to Bill's aid.

The patrol's horses skidded to a halt on the slippery pavement. The woman in charge, a chunky and entirely humorless-looking redhead on a chestnut-and-white pied horse, took in the entire scene with one swift scan before she demanded, "What the hell is going on here? What happened to these men—and who fired a gun?"

Reaching to take the boards from her just as if they had not been interrupted, Click worked in silence, leaving it to Cassidy to placate the female Trooper.

"The Warden sent Becky and Rowena and me on an errand to this artisan's shop," she explained hastily. "These two Troopers were sent to accompany us." Cassidy almost said that Hugh and Bill had been sent to guard them, but she hesitated to imply that any of them might have expected trouble in the city. "When we came out of the shop, a mob had formed; when we tried to leave, they attacked us."

The redhead looked around sharply, quickly surveying the garbage-littered alley. "What became of this mob then?" she asked suspiciously.

"Hugh and Bill tried to fight them off, while the rest of us escaped," Cassidy said. Although that was precisely what had happened, recounting it somehow made it seem as if she and Becky and Rowena had been cowards to abandon the two Troopers. "Once we started to make a run for it, the crowd followed us up the alley."

The woman on the pied horse did not appear critical of Cassidy's actions; rather, she was looking past Cassidy and scrutinizing Click. The Tinker had been silently and skillfully working while Cassidy spoke, and he had already fashioned a quite satisfactory splint out of the two boards and the strips he had torn from his shirt, all while the conversation had been taking place around him.

"And you, Tinker," the red-haired Trooper said sharply, "just how did you get mixed up in all this?"

Click had just made some final adjustment to Bill's makeshift splint and was lithely rising to his feet. In all probability he would have answered the woman for himself had Cassidy given him the chance. But she spoke so quickly that he never had the opportunity to defend himself.

"We ran into them on the next street over, when we were running from the mob." Pausing just long enough to get her breath, Cassidy felt slightly flustered as she recalled the collision and realized that what she had just said was the literal truth. "When they found out that there were still two injured Troopers down in the mob, they insisted on coming back here for them," she finished emphatically.

The redhead had listened to Cassidy's hasty recitation with an expression of patent skepticism, a reaction that was hardly ameliorated by Click's continuing silence. "Who fired a gun?" the Trooper persisted.

"I don't know," Cassidy lied automatically, hoping even as the words left her mouth that wherever Click had stowed his pistol, it was out of sight for the moment. "Maybe someone in the mob," she added, but not very convincingly.

As the red-haired woman cast a disparaging look over Cassidy and the three Tinkers, another patrol came loping up the narrow street. Cassidy easily recognized the man who led it, for it was Tag, the mournfully long-faced Trooper who commanded the city's security. The second set of horses skidded to a halt on the debris-covered pavement, still excited from their run and snorting through their nostrils at the foul odors that assaulted them.

Tag took in the entire scene at the mouth of the alley with a practiced but weary eye. "What's happened here?" he asked with resignation, of no one in particular.

The redhead briefly and concisely repeated Cassidy's explanation to her superior. Whether or not he believed the story seemed of little consequence. Tag was obviously not a man given to quibbling over details, and regardless of the cause he could easily see that there were two injured Troopers and the likely aftermath of a small riot. With a few economic gestures and terse commands, he dispatched most of the Troopers from the two patrols to search the surrounding streets, alleys, and buildings for anyone whose demeanor or condition might implicate them as having been part of the mob. That done, he directed two of his men to relieve Click of Bill's care and to carry the unconscious man to the wooden handcart where Hugh already lay.

As the two Troopers lifted their injured comrade, Click stood back out of their way. Cassidy saw that both the redhead and Tag were looking at the Tinker leader, but their expressions had nothing in common. The woman looked as if she were contemplating charging the dark-haired man with some hanging offense and relishing the thought. Tag's face, on the other hand, bore a characteristically sober mien, and he was regarding Click with a long-suffering regret.

"The Warden will be grateful for your timely intervention," Tag said solemnly. "And of course your cart will be returned to your enclave as soon as possible."

As much as Cassidy had always been puzzled by the interaction between the Tinker leader and the Troopers, their current exchange seemed destined to baffle her only further. Click's lean face was set in an expression of sardonic irony; he made a mocking little half-bow toward Tag and said, "The Warden is welcome to its use."

Tag just stared at Click for a few moments longer, his long face growing progressively more morose. "You've exceeded your authority here, my friend," he said quietly then. "There's enough trouble in this city already—don't ask for more."

Then with a curt nod the Trooper signaled for his men to proceed with the wooden cart. With one final scornful look in the direction of the Tinkers, the red-haired woman marshaled the remaining mounted patrol members as an escort to the two-wheeled vehicle. Swinging his horse around, Tag beckoned clearly to Cassidy.

"Mount up, Cassidy," the Trooper said. "It would be a convenience to me to have you back at the compound before Becky has managed to mobilize the entire garrison to rescue you."

Hesitating, Cassidy glanced from the gray mare to Click. He still stood with an almost studied indifference beside the blood-stained pavement where Bill had lain. The strips that had been torn from his shirttail had given the garment a weirdly cropped look and had exposed several inches of his tanned torso beneath the loose hang of his leather vest.

"I'm sorry," she said to him, "about the broken glass, I mean."

To Cassidy's tremendous relief, she saw that whatever unnavigatable emotional terrain might lay between the Tinker and the Troopers, he was not angry with her. The graying tips of his mustache twitched and the old humor was back in his dark eyes as he replied, "Don't worry, Cassidy. Your stock with the Warden seems to be high—I'm sure he'll be willing to replace a mere cartful of window glass for your safe return."

Weighted by a strange reluctance to leave him, Cassidy nevertheless leapt up onto her horse and turned the mare into the street behind the Troopers with the cart. As she rode away she could hear Tag's horse jogging off in the opposite direction, following the patrol that he had dispatched to search the area. But when she looked back over her shoulder toward the front of the artisan's silent shop, the mouth of the alleyway was deserted, and of Click, Tad, and Teddy there was no sign.

Chapter 17 ◀▥

"Jeez!" Rowena hissed, hastily glancing around them as she and Cassidy stepped from the sunlit courtyard of the garrison's quadrangle into the relative obscurity of the shadows in the corridor that ran between the barracks and the stables. "We could have been *killed* this morning!"

"Yeah, that's what I like about my theory," Cassidy said. "If we're all dead already, all this could be a lot less dangerous than it looks."

Feeling neither the obligation nor the inclination to dignify Cassidy's response with any witty repartee, Rowena merely reached over and punched her in the arm. "I'm serious, you asshole!" she said.

But Cassidy, for all the glibness of her remark, felt decidedly serious, as well. The morning's events in the Iron City had imparted a certain obligatory gravity to their position there; and her sarcastic attempt at humor had been more of a response to the overwhelming frustration she felt than it had been due to any failure to grasp the consequences of what had happened. For the first time she felt she fully appreciated Click's initial warning about the city being a dangerous place. Before that morning Cassidy had thought of danger in terms of the baffling and hideous creatures that they called monsters; it had never occurred to her that her fellow human beings, inflamed by resentment and superstition, could be a more imminent and just as real threat.

When Cassidy had returned to the Warden's compound with the injured Troopers, she found that Tag's glum prediction about a rescue attempt had nearly come true. Becky and Rowena's somewhat dramatic arrival in the gig cart had caused quite a stir among the guards at the iron gate. And never one to suffer fools gladly, Becky had loudly and determinedly insisted on seeing Justin himself to demand that more Troopers be dispatched to the city to retrieve Hugh, Bill, and Cassidy. By the time Cassidy and the Troopers with the Tinkers' handcart had appeared, Justin doubtless had been fervently wishing that it had been he and not Valerie who had accompanied the Warden into the country for the day.

Not surprisingly, the safe return of Cassidy and their two battered guards had done little to pacify the black woman. Becky had been absolutely furious about what had happened to them in the city, and Justin hadn't proven a particularly tolerant target for her wrath. If it hadn't been that the woman was the closest thing to a medical expert in the compound, the mounting battle between Becky and the gray-templed Trooper could easily have escalated into more than just a loud shouting match. But once Hugh and Bill had been brought in, Becky grudgingly turned her attention toward their care. As she began to examine the Troopers, Cassidy had noticed that Becky hadn't even taken the time to treat her own abraded hands until she was forced to by the need to attend to the men's wounds.

Becky had impressed Cassidy with her skill and knowledge in dealing with the injuries that Hugh and Bill had sustained. She had dressed their minor wounds and deftly sewn up the lacerations on Bill's arm and forehead. She left Click's crude splint intact, explaining to the stoic Bill that she would have to wait a day or two for the swelling to subside before she could apply a more permanent cast. And she also pointed out to him that he had been unusually lucky to have been unconscious when Click had set the fracture.

With Becky occupied, Justin had turned his interrogation to Cassidy and Rowena. Cassidy had been relieved that the cynical red-haired female Trooper who had accompanied them from the city had been able to substantiate most of their story. She had also been relieved when Hugh and Bill reiterated their story about the mob's attack on them. By then the morning was gone and Cassidy and Rowena had accepted the offer of lunch from the Troopers' mess. As they had eaten, Cassidy felt grateful that the seemingly interminable questioning was over, at least until the Warden returned.

After lunch she and Rowena had been able to slip from the mess without anyone following them. Becky had already gone to see Hugh and Bill installed in the barracks, and Justin had ridden back into the city to confer with Tag about the dangerous fracas. No one else paid them much notice as they left. And alone in the nearly deserted compound, feeling more comfortable with every step they took away from the confines of the garrison, Cassidy finally slowed her pace and turned to face the woman who had become her best friend.

"I know you're serious," Cassidy said contritely. "It's just that this whole morning has been a nightmare. I'm starting to think it was a big mistake ever to come to this place."

Rowena made an encompassing gesture. "You mean 'this place' like *this* place?" she asked. "Or, 'this place' like this whole place in general—in which case I might remind you that neither of us seemed to have had much choice in the matter!"

The brunette's conciliatory humor had the desire effect, drawing from Cassidy an appreciative little snort of amusement before her demeanor once again resumed its sobriety. "Listen, Rowena," she said, "I don't think there's anyone here who can help us. In fact, I think the longer we stay here the worse things are going to get."

Rowena made a face. "You mean like getting stoned by the local idiots?" she asked drolly.

But that time Cassidy did not respond to the attempt at humor. "Among other things," she said. "Rowena, I think we should get out of here."

Cassidy's words then rendered Rowena immediately sober, as well. "But what about the Warden?" she asked, clearly torn between relief and consternation at Cassidy's proposal. "You *know* him, Cassidy—he was the key to you remembering everything else."

"Yeah, and he doesn't know me from a fence post," Cassidy replied. "I'm the one with all the Memories, not him. How can he help us?"

They had cut from the edge of the quadrangle to the rolling expanse of sun-washed pastureland that lay between the garrison and the Warden's house. Rowena came to a halt, glancing around them at the brilliant green stretch of grass that was empty save for a few distant grazing horses. And despite the absolute solitude that they enjoyed there, when she spoke her voice was pitched so softly that it was nearly a whisper.

"But what about the monsters?" she asked Cassidy. "The Warden's asked you for help."

Equally needlessly but just as automatically, Cassidy also quickly glanced around them before she spoke. There in the sunny serenity of the Warden's meadow it was difficult to give credence to anything as bizarre as monsters. But Cassidy's voice was also hushed and grave. "I think maybe he'd have less trouble with monsters if we got out of here," she said.

For a moment Rowena just stared quizzically at Cassidy, the expression on her broad face one of pure puzzlement. "You think they're following us?" she finally asked.

Cassidy nodded, relieved to finally have broached a subject that she had long mulled over in private. "Not us—me," she corrected quietly. "I think they've been following me the whole time, ever since I first found myself in this crazy place."

"But what about the other times before you even got here? Mickey told us that there's always been talk of monsters."

"Talk, yes—but never anything like this," Cassidy reminded her grimly. "No one before ever even proved they existed, much less got attacked or killed by them." She shook her head resolutely. "The worst part is, it seems that the more I've been able to remember, the worse their attacks have become. Much as I hate to admit it, that mob this morning might have a point. If the damned things are following me, then I'm endangering the whole city by staying here."

Rowena was silent for a minute or two, searching Cassidy's face with anxious concern. "Where would we go?" she said then at last, loyal but pragmatic.

Cassidy glanced back down the gentle slope toward the garrison, its long wooden buildings shimmering in the heat distortion of the midday sun. Then she met Rowena's eyes. "You remember what Becky said about going south? About how she thought that if she went far enough or knew where to look, she might find some clue to her past?"

Rowena nodded even as she was immediately pointing out, "But 'south' isn't a very specific goal, and Becky admitted she didn't even know what she should be looking for. Even if the Warden would let us go, how would we get there? Becky doesn't know how to ride a horse."

Shaking aside Rowena's host of reservations with a toss of her head, Cassidy just said, "We didn't know how to find the Warden when we left Double Creek, but we got here, didn't we?" She deliberately refrained from pointing out the hazards of their journey from the village. "He can't make us stay here, and Becky doesn't even have to come along if she doesn't want to."

Rowena was frowning; she scuffed one boot through the

grass, avoiding Cassidy's eyes. "What about Allen? And Click?"

Intentionally being obtuse, Cassidy cocked her head. "Click? What does he have to do with anything? We don't need the Tinkers' permission to go anywhere. And as for Allen, he'll probably be glad to go back to the village once we're gone."

Rowena looked up, silently assessing what lay behind Cassidy's blunt words. Something subtle in the brunette's expression suggested that she could easily have disputed all of Cassidy's curt assertions, but she didn't. She just gave a little shrug. "Okay," she said, "let's talk to Becky about it." Her hazel eyes were steady and without guile. "Then if you still want to go south, especially if what you say about the monsters is true, I think we should leave here as soon as we can."

As they hiked the rest of the way up to the Warden's house, with the high sun heating her back through the fabric of her Tinker-made shirt, Cassidy wondered why she didn't feel more relief and satisfaction at Rowena's loyal acquiescence to her proposal. She wasn't especially concerned about Becky's cooperation; much as she appreciated the tough little black woman's skills, she knew that the two of them were far more valuable to Becky than she was to them. It was the other part of Rowena's observation that Cassidy kept shying away from.

What about Allen? What about Click? The sheriff should return to his village, Cassidy thought decisively; he owed her and Rowena nothing more, and she still felt guilty for keeping him from his true responsibilities. They would just have to release Allen from his vow to help them, before they endangered his life again.

As for Click . . . The matter of the Tinker leader was proving a far more slippery decision. *He doesn't owe us anything more, either,* Cassidy told herself firmly; the Tinkers would be far better off if she left the city. Why then did the thought of leaving suddenly seem so painfully final? And why did the image of Click, with his conchaed vest and silvered mustache, keep returning to taunt her?

Don't kid yourself, Cassidy told herself with the necessary ferocity. *Once you're gone he won't miss you for long.*

She would be the only one who would remember.

Cassidy and Rowena didn't have long to wait before Becky came back from the garrison, and they didn't have any trouble telling when she had returned to the Warden's house. Time and further consideration had obviously not improved Becky's intransigent mood, and the prickly little woman arrived with a great deal of loudly grumbled curses and the dramatic slamming of doors. Cassidy and Rowena were in their bedroom taking an inventory of their meager personal possessions. They didn't even have to go out into the hallway to meet Becky because once she had stomped into the house, she seemed to have headed directly for their room.

"Damned tight-ass little twerp!" Becky announced, sweeping into the bedroom with an obstinate toss of her unruly black hair. "Who the hell does he think he is?"

Although there didn't seem to be much doubt as to whom Becky was referring, since there had really only been one person with whom she had been most recently locking horns, apparently Rowena felt it was best to be certain. "Justin?" she ventured, closing the door behind Becky.

Becky spun around, dropping her rump down on the edge of one of the beds. "He's trying to confine us to the compound!" she proclaimed indignantly. Her dark face was expressively contemptuous of the beleaguered Trooper. "Says it's for our own safety," she continued, and from the venom in her voice for a moment Cassidy actually thought Becky was going to spit on the floor. "What a load of horseshit—just wait until the Warden gets back!"

"Can Justin do that?" Cassidy asked her.

Becky's heated gaze shot to her, momentarily diverted from her tirade by the question. "You mean can he keep us from leaving the compound?" She snorted rudely. "He's in charge when the Warden and Valerie are gone, so I suppose he thinks he can," she said, adding significantly, "Maybe he thinks he can sprout wings and fly, too—but I'd like to see him try it!"

Exchanging a glance with Rowena, Cassidy went over and sat down on the edge of the opposite bed, facing Becky. "When will the Warden be back?" she said.

Still visibly irritated and preoccupied by that irritation, Becky hitched her shoulders in a rough shrug. "Justin says by tonight." Her dark eyes flashed. "And when he comes back I intend to have a few words with that crazy white boy about the way these damned Troopers have been treating us!"

Cautiously, Cassidy went on. "You don't think that the Warden will agree it's a good idea to restrict us to the compound?"

Becky stared at her hard, as if she thought Cassidy must have somehow misunderstood everything she'd said since she'd first come into the room. "What, you think we're prisoners here?" she asked incredulously. "The Warden's never tried to confine me anywhere; these shit-kicking Troopers are just overshooting their authority because he and Val aren't here."

He's never tried to confine you because there's never been a reason before, Cassidy thought grimly. *Until now you've never been in danger of being killed by the local witch-hunters.* But she didn't say that to Becky. Instead she just tried calmly to redirect the conversation toward her and Rowena's original objective.

"Then you don't think the Warden would object to you going out . . . exploring again? To see if you can find anything you remember?"

Becky may have been temporarily distracted by her outrage over Justin's edict, but she wasn't stupid. Her gaze narrowed sharply on Cassidy's face. "You mean go south along the coast again?" she asked. As Cassidy nodded, Becky studied her shrewdly. "You want to come along," she said.

"Rowena and I would like to see if there's anything there that either of us recognize," Cassidy said evenly.

But Becky's scrutiny only became keener. "You're not just talking about a little day trip, are you?" she said. "You're talking about really leaving here—really going south."

Cassidy exchanged a quick look with Rowena. She couldn't think of any reason to try to dissemble with Becky; since they were hoping for her help, it seemed foolish to be anything but straightforward with the feisty little woman. Cassidy nodded again. "Were you serious yesterday when you said you wanted to go south again?" she asked.

"Of course I was serious," Becky said. Lacking all subtlety herself, she had difficulty understanding circumspection when she saw it in others. "But I didn't mean right this minute!" She shook her dreadlocks, eyeing both Cassidy and Rowena with rueful candor. "This might not be the best time to go out traipsing around on our own, you know, with all those damned monsters out there. Much as I hate to agree with that asshole Justin, I think going out into the country right now might be kind of dangerous."

Although Cassidy deliberately avoided looking at Rowena, she could feel the brunette's eyes upon her as she again waged a quick internal debate on how much to reveal to Becky. Once more Cassidy decided to err on the side of honesty. "Actually,

I don't think it's going to be particularly safe here, either," she said.

Becky frowned. "You think we'd be safer from those things out in the middle of nowhere than we are here in the Warden's compound?"

Reluctantly but candidly, Cassidy replied, "I don't think we're going to be very safe from them in either place—or anywhere else, for that matter. Because I think the monsters have been following me."

Absently tossing back an errant braided swag of her long hair, Becky considered that assertion for a few moments. "But they've never attacked you," she finally pointed out.

Shaking her head, Cassidy said, "I know—and I don't know why they haven't because I've been seeing the damned things ever since I got here, and I'm positive that they've been following me the whole time."

"Then why do you want to go south?" Becky asked. "Just to get them out of the city?" Her expression suggested that she was patently skeptical of that altruistic notion.

"Not exactly," Cassidy admitted, "although I think they'll follow me if we go. You said yesterday that you felt if you went far enough south, or if you went to the right place, you might find something you recognized."

"That's just a theory," Becky reminded her. "And it sounds to me like you're a hell of a lot more sure about those creatures following you than I am about finding anything useful down there!"

Rowena finally spoke up. "We just don't feel like we're getting anywhere here, and if Cassidy is right about the monsters, then it's hardly fair to everyone else for us to stay. Even if you don't want to go along with us, Cassidy and I are going to leave."

Becky held up one hand in a restraining gesture. "Hey, I didn't say that I don't want to go," she said. "I'm just pointing out that going south isn't as simple as it sounds. It isn't like some leisurely little cruise down the river. Once you get more than a day or two's travel out of the city, there aren't any settlements, even along the seacoast. No one lives down there— it's all woods and swamp. Hell, I don't even know how you'd get down there unless you go by boat along the coastline."

"That's one of the reasons we were hoping you'd come along," Cassidy admitted, "at least to get us started. You've been down there at least part of the way."

Becky laughed, a short bray of sardonic humor. "Yeah, a two-day trip down and back. That hardly makes me the resident expert!" She shook her head, but her tone was genuinely helpful as she continued, "You need to talk to the Tinkers."

Cassidy and Rowena exchanged a quick look of surprise. "The Tinkers?" Cassidy echoed.

"Sure," Becky said. "Who do you think lent me the boat and took me down there when I wanted to go? We used Pete's boat and Alice came along. She knew a lot about the area because she's a herbalist, and some of the other Tinkers go down there all the time to dig clams and gather certain kinds of plants." Amused by Cassidy and Rowena's surprise, Becky concluded, "If we're going to head south, the Tinkers are the place to start." She paused a beat and then added, "Of course, I'm not sure if you could interest them in anything more than a day or two's trip, monsters or not. They don't consider themselves tour guides!"

But Cassidy just shook her head resolutely. "That's okay," she said. "If they'd just give us the boat and some supplies, it'd be a start anyway."

Bemused by Cassidy's calm determination, Becky said, "Yeah, you might be able to manage that; just tell them you'll take the monsters away with you."

Cassidy stood. "I'm going to go down to the Tinkers' enclave," she said, "and see what I can arrange."

From the bed, Becky cocked a dark brow at her. "The Troopers won't let you past the gate," she reminded Cassidy.

But Cassidy was unperturbed. "I'm not going out the gate," she said.

"Wait—I want to come along," Rowena interjected.

Cassidy shook her head. "No, this is going to take a little . . . creative riding. You just cover for me here if anyone asks about me."

Becky still looked faintly skeptical and Rowena looked outright concerned. "Maybe it would be easier to sneak out after dark," the brunette suggested.

Halfway to the bedroom door, Cassidy paused and looked back, her expression grimly amused. "Are you kidding?" she said. "Between the local gangs and the monsters, I'm not going anywhere around here after dark!" But she realized that Rowena's concern was genuine. "Don't worry," she added. "I'll be careful."

Although the Warden's house and grounds appeared relatively deserted, there was a normal amount of activity around the barracks and stables down at the garrison. Cassidy went around to the far side of the house, well beyond the tended lawn and gardens, before she Called Dragonfly. The horse came from the east side of the building, from the pasture between the house and the garrison. Cassidy just hoped that no one near there had noticed the mare's abrupt departure.

Before she mounted up, Cassidy spent a few minutes just checking the gray's legs and feet and finger-combing the snarls from her mane and tail. The little inspection was not only a Horseman's ritual, it also allowed Cassidy time enough to tell if she had attracted any suspicion before she actually tried to ride away from the compound. Only when she was reasonably certain that none of the Troopers had noted the mare's movement or the attention that she had paid to the horse did Cassidy hop up onto the mare's back.

The Tinkers' riverside enclave was southeast of the Warden's compound, directly west across the marsh from the city. But Cassidy rode due west from the house, moving at a casual jog-trot. She knew that the thick stone wall fronting the garrison circled around the compound, surrounding the Warden's pastures. The wall may have formed a marker, but it was no real barrier to anyone on horseback. Once she had ridden out of sight of the house, Cassidy abandoned the pretense of her leisurely pace and let the gray out into an easy gallop. When they reached the stone wall, the horse cleared it without even breaking stride.

Cassidy wasn't very familiar with the land west of the Warden's compound, but she knew she couldn't get lost if she just headed south and followed the river back east toward the city. What she was less sure of was whether there were other settlements or people living in the area. The meadowland that she crossed outside the wall was deserted, but she suspected that once she got closer to the river, she would begin to encounter the homes of the people who worked in the mills and other industries that they had seen from the rafts on the outskirts of the Iron City. She could have just gone straight on through to the pull path along the river's bank and ridden along that; she doubted that the sight of a Horseman would arouse any suspicion. But one thing kept her from taking that easy, obvious route. When she had first come to the city, no one had known who she was. Since then she had become far less confident that she was safe in her anonymity.

The afternoon was warm but pleasant and the sloping meadows and wooded hills leading down to the Long River were a patchwork of shades of green, alternating between sunshine and shadow. Under other circumstances, in better times, Cassidy would have enjoyed the simple beauty of the ride. But in her mind she could not keep from working over the many problems and questions that she faced.

"You need to talk to the Tinkers," Becky had said. Why did it always seem to come down to those itinerant craftsmen? Cassidy wondered fatalistically. Perhaps she would be given the chance to say good-bye to Click after all.

Click was the single person to whom her thoughts kept returning again and again. She did not want to stop and closely examine all of her feelings regarding the Tinkers' leader, and yet one aspect of his character kept insinuating itself into all of her efforts to make some sense of everything that had happened. Why had she never realized that Click was a Horseman? After all, not all Horsemen were Troopers—she was proof enough of that herself. She should have suspected it the day he rode with her along the pull path; perhaps she would have, had she not been so distracted by his nudity and his other revelations. What Cassidy found hardest to understand was how any Horseman could just turn his back on horses and lead the kind of life Click did among the Tinkers. And could that renunciation of his true calling have something to do with the barely veiled hostility that seemed to lie between Click and the Troopers?

When she was close enough to the river to be able to hear the sounds of the industries that had been built along its shores, Cassidy cut east, parallel to them. It was not difficult for one person on horseback to keep to the natural cover; in fact, Cassidy hardly thought about it, letting the mare pick her own path. Instead she tried to think about what she had proposed they do. Becky would come with them; of that she had no doubt. No matter what the dangers, the stubborn little black woman was just too doggedly curious to let the opportunity pass her by. But Cassidy didn't share Becky's automatic assumption that the Warden would give their trip his blessing. And it was not just a matter of their safety, as real as the hazards they would face were. Of necessity, the Warden had his own agenda concerning both Cassidy and the monsters. Cassidy could not delude herself into thinking that his interests necessarily approximated her own.

The gray mare began to move more slowly, picking her way through a stretch of young-growth woods along what appeared to be a footpath. Cassidy had to duck several times to avoid low-hanging branches. She had more or less lost track of exactly where they were, but from the length of time she had been riding she knew they must be getting close to the enclave. What part the Tinkers would play in her plans she could not be certain. But she was confident that she would at least be safe there with them and that they would never take the Warden's part against her. And while that didn't necessarily translate into helping her and Rowena and Becky leave the city, she was forced to admit that once again she would have to ask the Tinkers for aid to get where she wanted to go.

Entering the small community from the west, Cassidy was initially spared the sight of the destruction that the monster attack had wreaked upon the enclave only the day before. From her perspective the enclave looked much more like what it had first reminded Cassidy of: a neat and rustic old English village. Small but entirely individual-looking houses stood surrounded by tidy garden plots and numerous workshops and supply sheds. All that was missing, Cassidy thought ironically, were storks roosting on the chimneys. It wasn't until she was actually on the edge of the settlement that Cassidy noted the after-effects of the damage that had been done there. Despite the pleasantness of the afternoon, the yards and gardens were nearly empty, and the sounds of sawing and hammering came from across the enclave. Nearly everyone currently in residence there was apparently over on the eastern side, helping to clean up and repair the detritus of the attack.

As the mare clopped quietly along the brick footpath that wound through the enclave, a few Tinkers looked up from their tasks in yards and gardens to watch the horse and rider pass. Cassidy realized she probably presented a somewhat contradictory picture: a Horseman who was dressed in Tinker garb rather than a Trooper's leathers. But no one moved to stop her or even gave her more than a passing glance. Because of her association with the trading party that had come down the river, Cassidy suspected the people there may have realized who she was.

The settlement was small enough that it only took a few minutes to pass through to the southeastern end, the site of the worst damage. As she approached, Cassidy was relieved to recognize several of the Tinkers who were working there. She was also a little alarmed when she saw Bonnie, Carlotta, and Old Paul struggling to remove a damaged section of wooden fencing from its lodging point high in the branches of a big tree. The two women had hold of one end of the unwieldy wreckage and were trying to rock it free of the tree's limbs, while Old Paul clung to the opposite end of the fencing like some wizened child trapped on a seesaw run amok. All the while Bonnie's two little dogs scooted around the women's heels, yapping frantically.

After dropping down off the mare's back, Cassidy hurried across the scarred and furrowed sod of what had once been a yard and reached for the middle section of the crippled segment of fence. She probably could have done the most good by taking hold of it down on the end by Old Paul, but she didn't want to antagonize the prickly old man by making it seem as if she thought he needed rescuing—even though he did. With the added impetus Cassidy provided, Bonnie and Carlotta were able to wrest the other end of the section of fencing down out of the tree. She helped them settle it to the ground with a creaking thump.

"Told you not to rock it!" Old Paul wheezed at the two Tinker women. "Told you just to tip it and we could get it down!"

"Well, we just needed a little help with it," Bonnie said diplomatically, shooting Cassidy a grateful look. Her dogs darted around the grounded wreckage, barking with renewed enthusiasm.

"Yeah, it takes three of us to keep up with you,'" Carlotta told Old Paul, giving Cassidy a quick wink. Her teasing was so subtle that Cassidy doubted the old man caught it; she was sure of that when he spoke again.

"Well, let's not just sit here resting on our glories," Old Paul demanded. "Let's get this over onto the salvage pile!"

Several dozen yards away, in what must have once been the foundation of one of the destroyed houses, Cassidy could see a collection of damaged pieces of wreckage that still contained wood that could be salvaged for other projects. After getting a good grip on one of the long rails of the truncated section of fencing, Cassidy staggered along with Bonnie, Carlotta, and Old Paul as they carried it over to the pile. They dropped it with a clatter amid the broken timbers and segments of board siding.

Pausing briefly to catch her breath, Bonnie eyed Cassidy astutely. "Thanks for the assist," he said, "but I don't imagine

you snuck out of the Warden's compound and came all this
way just to help us clean up this mess."

Cassidy's first reaction was more one of embarrassment than
surprise. Although she had been caught off guard by Bonnie's
comment about sneaking out of the compound, she was also
more than a little chagrined to realize that it had never even
occurred to her that the Tinkers could have used help cleaning
up and repairing the damage to their enclave. Just because they
had refused the Warden's offer of the Troopers' help didn't
necessarily mean they would have done the same if she and
Rowena had offered.

Flushing, Cassidy tried to conceal her abashment by blurting
out the first question that popped into her head. "What makes
you think I had to sneak out?"

Old Paul made a dry barking sound that Cassidy recognized
as the old man's peculiar laugh. Both Bonnie and Carlotta hid
their amusement better.

"After what happened in the city this morning, the Troopers
would have to be crazy to have let you ride off alone," Bonnie
said. She gestured toward the brick path upon which Cassidy
had ridden into the enclave. "And you certainly came the long
way around if you rode from the compound."

Cassidy just shook her head, ruefully but doggedly. "No one
tried to stop me," she insisted with poorly portrayed innocence.

"No one saw you." Old Paul grunted.

Relenting, Cassidy spread her hands in acquiescence. "Okay,
I did sneak out," she admitted. "And I didn't come here just to
help you clean up." She let the implication remain that helping
out was at least a secondary consideration, still too embarrassed to reveal that she had never given it a moment's
thought. "I came here because Becky wants to go south again,
along the coast, and this time Rowena and I want to go with
her."

Old Paul made a disparaging sound, but both women gave
Cassidy's announcement their serious consideration. "So you
need a boat," Carlotta surmised.

Cassidy nodded. "Becky told us that two Tinkers from your
enclave helped her the last time."

"Pete and Alice," Bonnie confirmed. Then the big blond
woman paused, her scrutiny of Cassidy sharpening. "But I
don't think they could help you with what you're planning.
You're going to need a bigger boat."

Cassidy tried without much success to remain casual in the

face of the woman's obvious insight into what she, Rowena, and Becky were planning. She shrugged lightly. "Well, where can we get a bigger boat then?"

Carlotta was frowning but Bonnie said promptly, "The seamen at the docks, I suppose. But I doubt that any of them would be willing to give the three of you a civil word, much less one of their boats."

Then it was Cassidy's turn to frown. "You mean because we don't have anything to trade for it? I think Becky can—"

Old Paul cut bluntly in. "Because of the monsters!" he cackled. "Monsters have shut down the wharfs—half the city's looking to lynch the lot of you!"

Cassidy's frown deepened. "You mean that mob this morning? They were nothing but a bunch of cowardly riffraff."

"Well, even cowardly riffraff can kill you," Bonnie remarked. Her expression had sobered, her voice dropping in genuine concern. "Don't underestimate the sentiment against you and other people with Memories, Cassidy. This morning may just have been a poorly organized bunch of troublemakers, but there are a lot of people in the city—serious people, business people—who see you and others like you as the cause of all their recent troubles."

"Other people like the seamen," Cassidy surmised.

"Right or wrong, it's all the same in the end," Carlotta offered sympathetically. "The whole city is astir. The Troopers are just trying to protect you from a lot of very angry, very frightened people."

In that context, Cassidy could hardly argue. And the city's people were probably right about her being a threat to their well-being. The monsters were already proving that.

"Then you'd think they'd be glad to do everything they could to send us on our way!" she muttered unhappily.

That won her a grudging snort of appreciation from Old Paul, and a smile of understanding from both Bonnie and Carlotta.

"The seamen won't give you a boat," the buxom blonde said, "but I think I know someone who they will give one to." She gave a slyly lopsided smile. "And I think he'd be willing to help you and your friends again—at least if you asked him yourself."

Cassidy's brow furrowed in puzzlement, then an unbidden blush bloomed up from her neck to suffuse her cheeks. "Click," she said softly, dropping her eyes.

Bonnie's expression was self-satisfied. "You can ask him when he gets back."

"In the meantime you can help us," Old Paul chimed in.

"Back? Where is he?" Cassidy asked.

"In the city," Bonnie replied, "at the glaziers' with Teddy and Tad."

Replacing the cartload of glass we smashed for them this morning, Cassidy realized ruefully. Feeling the heat returning to her ears, she quickly asked, "When do you think they'll get back?"

"Soon," Bonnie said placidly. She gestured toward the remaining debris that was strewn across the ruined yards. "And Old Paul is right: We can work while you wait for him."

A few minutes later, grappling with the splintered end of a ruptured section of wooden beam while Bonnie and Old Paul argued over the disposition of the wreckage, Cassidy asked Carlotta hopefully, "Do you think Click can get us a boat?"

"He can if he wants to," the metalsmith said.

Cassidy felt the prodding stir of anxiety. "Why wouldn't he want to?" she said.

Carlotta was silent for a moment, regarding Cassidy with a certain fond assessment while she weighed her answer. "What you're planning on doing is a risky thing, Cassidy," she said. Seeing the automatic denial in Cassidy's eyes, she quickly continued. "Perhaps even more dangerous than staying here would be. Click knows what it's like in the south. I think he might be reluctant to be responsible for helping you go there."

Completely abandoning her planned retort—something to the effect that staying in the city with the monsters and the lynch mobs seemed to really be the risky thing—Cassidy instead latched onto Carlotta's remark. How could the Tinker know what it was like in the south, unless he had been there? She felt a small stab of hope and excitement. But before she could ask Carlotta anything further, Cassidy was rudely jerked forward by Bonnie's and Old Paul's combined efforts on the shattered segment of beam. As she and Carlotta lurched after them, staggering under the weight of the wooden timber, the opportunity for conversation had passed.

It was some time later when she was down on her hands and knees in the dirt when Cassidy heard the Tinkers hailing someone who was coming along the pathway. Old Paul had assigned her the humble task of searching through the pulverized earth for whatever scattered metal nails could be salvaged. She looked up from the ground to see Click, Tad, and Teddy guiding their handcart packed full of glass panes into the enclave.

Scrambling to her feet, Cassidy hastily dusted off her hands and the knees of her trousers. Dusty strings of hair hung across her face, and as she brushed the back of one hand over her perspiring forehead she realized she was merely smearing the dirt over her skin.

Bonnie had gone forward to meet the returning trio of men; Click's lanky frame contrasted sharply to her rotund figure as he bent slightly to hear her murmured words of explanation. The dark-haired man shot Cassidy a quick look, a mixture of amusement and concern, all the while nodding at whatever Bonnie was telling him.

For some reason Cassidy felt uncomfortable and vaguely anxious when Click approached the area where they had been working. He acknowledged Carlotta and Old Paul with a wordless nod of greeting, but his attention was clearly focused on Cassidy, and for the first time in a long time she found that calm and steady gaze unnerving. *I must look like hell!* she told herself, even as she realized that was not the real reason for her uneasiness. She had thought she had finally come to feel comfortable, even relaxed, around the Tinker leader. But the events of that morning and the potential implications of Carlotta's earlier remark had changed all of that.

"Cassidy," Click greeted her with an almost playful sort of mock gravity. "How kind of you to come down here to help us."

Cassidy knew that Click, in his customary way, was only teasing her, yet she made a deliberate decision to treat his comment as fact. She shook back her hair, heedless of the dust which rose from it. "I didn't come here just to help you clean up," she told him. "There's something I need your help with, too."

Acceding to the tone of simple candor that she had set, Click nodded and replied, "Bonnie told me you need a boat." One of his dark eyebrows tented slightly in a quirky arch. "A rather large boat, apparently."

Before Cassidy could elaborate, Click had turned back toward the handcart. He gestured to Tad and Teddy, calling out to them "Go on ahead to Ben's; Bonnie will help you unload."

The big blond woman threw Click an odd look, more of stern warning than of protest; but she accompanied the other two men without comment as they resumed pushing the cart along the brick path. Old Paul and Carlotta had returned to stacking broken sections of beams, seemingly having no further interest in either Cassidy or in their leader's business with her.

Turning back to Cassidy, Click surprised her with a wink. "We won't let you near the glass this time," he said. Before she could respond, he stepped forward and, casually guiding Cassidy with a hand cupped around the crook of her elbow, began to steer her away from the wreckage of the flattened house. "Come, walk with me a bit," he said evenly, "and we'll discuss this matter of your sudden need for a boat."

As they walked away from both the other Tinkers and the worst of the monsters' damage to the enclave, Cassidy again found it easy to relax with the man. Glancing sideways at Click, she noticed that he wasn't much cleaner than she was, and that fact was perversely reassuring. His tanned sinewy hands were stained and grimy around the nails and his clothing, particularly his boots and the lower legs of his pants, was powdered with dust from his walk back from the city. And the inseam and seat of his pants were imprinted with the faint rime of faded dirt and sweat from his ride on the back of Hugh's big gelding, the distinctive soiling like the subtle ghost of some larger secret.

Until then Cassidy had almost forgotten again that Click was a Horseman.

Shaken from her surreptitious appraisal by Click suddenly coming to a halt, Cassidy was further surprised when he used his casual hold on her arm to briskly pivot her around to face him.

"I don't believe that you fully understand the risks of what you are about to do," Click said quietly.

There was no urgency in that familiar voice, but his fingers had remained on Cassidy's arm, their firm hold reinforcing the understated conviction in his words. Deciding that it was neither the time nor the man for evasion, Cassidy simply replied, "Rowena and I have to leave the city."

Nodding, Click said, "I don't dispute that." She could feel the warmth of his flesh in the grip of his hand. "But going south is no better than staying here. If you want to leave by sea and go along the coast, then go north instead."

Puzzled, Cassidy met those deep-set eyes with an honest lack of guile. "But Becky wants to go south. She said—"

Resolutely shaking his head, Click managed to cut off her

words by the mere strength of his gaze. Twice before Cassidy had seen that unshakable resolve in the Tinker leader's dark eyes: on the night of the attack outside Pointed Rock when he had rousted her and Rowena from their tent, armed her with his gun, and sent them out into the darkened forest; and again the evening on the city docks when he had first argued against and then finally acceded to taking her to see the Warden. A chill slithered along Cassidy's spine.

For all of the power of his stare, Click's voice when he spoke was curiously soft. "Your Warden has set you to chasing a dream, Cassidy. The man you seek doesn't exist; his myth was ancient long before you came here."

Too baffled to try to pretend she knew what the hell Click was talking about, Cassidy just automatically fell back on the most basic tactic she knew: She admitted her ignorance and pleaded for information. "What man? What are you talking about?" she asked, her dirt-smudged brow furrowing in confusion.

Click studied her perplexed face for a long moment in utter silence. Apparently her genuine bewilderment was credible to him. "Then he isn't sending you south?" he asked her with a quiet intensity.

Only slightly less baffled by that question, Cassidy replied, "You mean the Warden? He doesn't even know we're planning to go—hell, we're trying to sneak away!"

Click's eyes dropped from Cassidy's face as abruptly as his hand dropped from her arm. His next words were nearly whispered in a soft murmur, leaving Cassidy to wonder if he was even directing them to her. "Then he hasn't told you about the Alchemist . . ."

Only further confused, Cassidy blurted, "Who the hell is 'the Alchemist'?"

Click's gaze lifted to her face again, but he tossed his dark head in one swift negating shake. His expression was stolid, yet there was ever something of his wry sense of irony in the narrowing of those compelling eyes. "For that you must ask your Warden," was all he would say.

Cassidy could have tried to pursue the subject; she realized that whoever this Alchemist was, he was obviously someone of significance. But there was something forbidding in Click's eyes that prevented her from asking him more—at least about that topic. So although she reluctantly abandoned that line of questioning, she had another.

"Carlotta said that you knew about the south," she said. She could see immediately that she had hit the mark; Click actually flinched. Hastily she pressed on. "When were you there? How far south have you gone?"

Click quickly recovered his composure enough to give her a sardonic little smile. "Carlotta has a flair for exaggeration," he said.

Cassidy didn't hesitate to press what small advantage she suspected she might hold over that maddeningly self-contained man. "You know that anything you could tell me would help us," she reminded him. "And if it's so dangerous, we're going to need all the help we can get."

To Cassidy's surprise, Click's tight little smile broadened into a self-mocking grin of genuine humor. He reached out and clapped her on the shoulder in a comradely fashion as he pointed out, "If past behavior is any indication, Cassidy, I suspect you'll be going south with or without my help."

About to push him further for whatever information he was hedging, Cassidy was poised on the verge of speech when she noticed that Click's attention was no longer on her face, but had shifted over her shoulder and that he was looking at something behind her. Turning her head, she saw four mounted figures approaching the enclave from the north. Troopers, she knew instantly; as they rapidly drew closer at a brisk trot, she recognized Raphael among them and Justin in their lead.

Cassidy's first automatic reaction was to step back from Click, to remove his hand from her shoulder and put some more seemly distance between them. Considering how Click and the Troopers seemed to feel about each other, she expected that the Tinker's first instinct would be to do exactly the same. But instead, as the riders approached, Click actually moved a step closer to her, throwing his arm over her shoulders and turning her to face the oncoming Troopers. Suddenly standing side by side with Click, Cassidy could hear the soft creak of his leather vest pressed between them.

As the Troopers drew in before them, Justin gave Click a stiff little nod, which the dark-haired man returned with a pleasant smile. The Warden's lieutenant reserved his most severe expression for Cassidy.

"I suspected we might find you here," Justin said to her. "You weren't supposed to leave the compound without an escort."

Acutely aware both of Click's unprecedented nearness and

of the conflicting impression it might give the Troopers, Cassidy strove for a completely innocent mien as she baldly lied, "No one told me that. I just came down here to help the Tinkers clean up some of this mess."

Looking up at Justin with what struck Cassidy as an almost taunting sort of nonchalance, Click thumped Cassidy heartily on the back and said, "Cassidy is like one of our own group; I find her loyalty commendable."

Justin's eyes narrowed and his lips compressed as he regarded the two self-proclaimed comrades for a moment in silence. When he spoke again it was to Click, his words weighted like dropped stones. "And if anyone would know about loyalty, Tinker, you would be the man."

Cassidy was certain it had been intended as an insult, even if a veiled one. But Click's reaction was another pleasant smile as he dropped his own volley. "And if anyone could attest to my loyalty, Justin, surely it would be you."

Justin's three companions seemed only slightly less baffled than did Cassidy, and she suspected that only the principals understood the full meaning of the little exchange. She also suspected that Click had somehow just managed subtly to best Justin; but there was still such a deep subtext to the Tinker's relationship with the Troopers that she didn't understand that it was impossible to be certain of that. Regardless of who had come out ahead in the verbal duel, Justin remained firmly fixed upon his original mission.

"Call your horse," he instructed Cassidy, "and we'll accompany you back to the compound."

Cassidy hadn't intended to resist but Click swiftly encouraged her compliance by giving her a little push forward with his arm. "Feel free to go, Cassidy," he said expansively. "As grateful as we are for your help, we can manage now without you."

Even as she Called the gray mare, Cassidy turned to look up into Click's lean and neutral face. The Tinker began to turn, casually giving her another pat on the back. But as soon as his back was to the Troopers and his head bent near hers, he whispered softly to Cassidy, "Remember, ask your Warden about the Alchemist. Then if you still want that boat, I will do what I can."

Both surprised and frustrated by the scraps of information that Click had revealed to her, Cassidy shot him a sharp look, almost tempted to risk speaking aloud. The expression on

Click's face was impassive, maddeningly bland. But Cassidy knew it was neither the time nor the place to try to confront him further about what he knew. And so when Dragonfly trotted obediently up to her, wisps of grass still protruding from the sides of her muzzle, Cassidy just hopped up onto the horse without a word and guided the gray to fall into line behind the quartet of Troopers.

They were nearly back to the Warden's compound before Cassidy realized that she had never asked Click the one question that had so occupied her thoughts earlier in the afternoon as she had ridden to the Tinkers' enclave. She had not asked him about being a Horseman.

Cassidy was determined to speak to the Warden when he got back that night. When she relayed what she had learned from the Tinkers to Rowena and Becky, both of them were encouraged by Click's offer, however conditional it had been. But not even Becky had ever heard of the mysterious Alchemist Click had mentioned.

"I've never even heard that name used," Becky complained after supper, once the three of them had regrouped in the privacy of the large bedroom. "And I thought the Warden told me *everything*. He sure never tried to keep me from going south—he urged me to go. That's why the Tinkers took me."

"Yeah, for a day's travel," Cassidy muttered, picking at a loose thread on the quilted bedspread. "Maybe the Warden knew you wouldn't get very far."

"What could be down there that's so dangerous?" Rowena mused.

"You mean what could be worse than what we've got around here?" Cassidy replied sourly, ticking off the points on her fingers. "Lynch mobs, monsters, and house arrest?"

"Why would Click think that the Warden was sending us to look for this Alchemist if he's never even mentioned him to us," Becky continued doggedly, "and if it's so dangerous to go south?"

"It seems to me," Cassidy said, "that a better question would be why hasn't the Warden told us about this guy, if he has anything to do with the Memories or the monsters?" That had been the question which had been eating at her ever since she had left the Tinkers' enclave. And that was why she had decided that the Warden would not get by her that night without an explanation, no matter how late he got back to the compound.

Hours after Rowena and Becky had given up and gone to bed, and the big brick house had fallen into silent darkness, Cassidy sat up in one of the upholstered chairs in the unused front room waiting for the Warden's return. She thought about everything that had happened that day, from the city people's violent revolt to Click's feckless heroism. She knew that they had to leave the Iron City and that Click's advice to the contrary, their best hope lay to the south.

Gradually the stars faded, blanketed by an incoming bank of clouds, and distant thunder grumbled in the darkness. Her last thought before she finally dozed off was the irony of how for so long she had thought that if she could just reach the Warden and if she could just remember who she was, she would be on her way to finding her way back home. Well, she had reached the Warden and she had remembered who she was, yet she had less idea than ever before of how the hell she'd gotten there and no real hope of ever returning to her own world, a world that now taunted her in excruciating detail.

Cassidy had been dreaming when the splash of light across her face rudely awakened her. The dream had been a frightening and frustrating affair, a replay of the morning's encounter with the angry mob in the alley, except that the faces of the crowd had been replaced by dark and oozing visages, like masks made of the filthy slimy surface of the hanging monsters. And so when she was abruptly jerked from the dream, for a few confused moments she imagined herself still squared off against a small army of the repugnant humanoids. She leapt out of the chair just as the front room's door swung open, admitting a disheveled-looking group of Troopers holding lanterns and murmuring to each other in muted voices as they accompanied their Warden back into his house. From the center of that group the young man caught sight of Cassidy.

"Cassidy," the Warden said, surprise sharpening his weary voice as he swung to face her. "What are you doing up this time of the night?"

At first Cassidy was too surprised to reply. She stared at the Warden's lantern-limned figure with overt dismay. His fringed leather tunic was torn and dirty and the lower portion of one of his trouser legs hung in tattered ribbons. "What—what the hell happened to you?" she blurted out.

At the Warden's side, Valerie automatically moved between him and Cassidy, as if her stunned query represented some kind of threatening criticism. Cassidy's eyes darted from one leather-clad form to another as she tried to make some sense of the ragged appearance they presented. The captain's clothing had fared nearly as badly, the sleeves and shoulders of her own leather shirt ripped and stained. Several of the other Troopers looked equally battered, as if they'd all suffered some sort of mauling.

"What happened?" Cassidy repeated, taking a step closer. But by then she was finally both awake enough and close enough that she really no longer required an answer to her question. For when she was able to get a better look at the Warden's and the Troopers' tunics she could see that the dark staining on them wasn't mud, it was blood.

"Monsters!" she whispered harshly. "What happened? Where are Allen and Kevin?"

The Warden took a reciprocal step forward toward her, reaching out briefly to touch Cassidy reassuringly on the arm. "It's all right, Cassidy," he said. "Allen and Kevin are still down at the garrison, looking after the horses. None of us was seriously hurt."

"Not hurt? You were attacked by monsters!" Cassidy repeated incredulously.

"It was just those little ones—the demons," Valerie elaborated flatly. The curly-haired woman still kept protectively close to the Warden. Cassidy could see that her exposed hands and forearms were covered with the same sort of shallow circular and semicircular marks that had covered Allen's side after the attack outside Pointed Rock. Far fewer of the bites dotted the patches of skin she had glimpsed on the Warden's chest and leg. The woman's valor was self-evident: When they had been attacked Valerie had obviously thrown herself between her Warden and the vicious creatures, much as she currently seemed to be trying to protect him from Cassidy's midnight interrogation.

" 'Just those little ones' nearly killed Allen," Cassidy reminded Valerie, still boldly blocking the Warden's path. "And this is the first time they've dared to attack Troopers—or the Warden."

"We're all right," the Warden reiterated calmly, although from the pointed glance he directed in Valerie's direction, his assurance seemed equally aimed at her.

Ignoring the Troopers, especially Valerie, Cassidy refocused her attention on the young man in his ragged leathers. "I have to talk to you," she said resolutely.

The Warden's hand again went to Cassidy's arm. "I know; I have to talk to you, too, Cassidy," he said, his voice raspy with fatigue. "Justin told us what happened this morning in the city. But it will have to be in the morning. We all need to rest now."

But Cassidy shook her head. "No, this is about something else; this can't wait. I need to talk to you *now*." As if to forestall any objection that Valerie might be on the verge of raising, she added, "Especially after what's happened to you."

Used if nothing else to the young man's unfailing politeness toward her, Cassidy was a little surprised at the Warden's continued refusal. "It'll have to wait, Cassidy," he repeated patiently. "I'm very tired right now, and I need to get cleaned up and get some sleep first."

The small group of Troopers clustered around the open doorway shifted restlessly. Several of them looked as ragged as the Warden and Valerie, and none of them appeared to hold much sympathy for Cassidy's sense of urgency.

"You can go, Val," the Warden told his captain, waving a dismissal. Seeing her hesitate, he dropped his hand from Cassidy's arm and turned toward Valerie to instruct her, "See to your Troop. And in the morning I want you to have Becky examine those wounds."

Reluctant to accept his dismissal, Valerie still equivocated; but finally, throwing Cassidy a look of overt warning, she turned to follow the rest of the Troopers from the house. Before they were even all across the threshhold, the Warden had already started across the dimly lit room toward the foyer and the staircase.

Hurrying after him, Cassidy reached out for the trailing fringes of one of his tattered sleeves. Her fingers closed on the torn leather. "Wait!" she commanded.

The young man came to a sudden halt, swinging around to face her again. "Cassidy," he snapped at her, "I've told you that whatever it is, it'll have to wait!"

She had never felt his anger directed at her before; the unfamiliar edge in his voice might have been intended to silence her, but instead it brought out the sharpness in her own. Looking up directly into those velvety brown eyes, she demanded, "Why the hell didn't you tell us about the Alchemist?"

Unwittingly but with deadly accuracy she had found the verbal missile with which to disarm the Troopers' young leader. Across that handsome, misleadingly familiar face there flashed a comet's tail spread of emotions: first surprise, then alarm, and finally grim anger. Halted a scant few paces from the foot of the staircase, he confronted her steadily, his voice a low rasp. "Where did you hear that name?" he asked. "Your Tinker?" He tossed his head, the tousled forelock of his chestnut hair swinging, and when he spoke again his voice sounded not only angry, it also sounded bitter. "Well, I doubt there's much I could add to his explanation."

"He didn't explain *anything*," Cassidy said. "He just told me to ask *you*."

Clearly that was a revelation that at least partially disarmed the Warden's anger, and although he still regarded Cassidy with an edgy mixture of skepticism and irritation, at least he held his tongue.

"He thought you had already told me about him," Cassidy hastened to explain, deliberately avoiding revealing the circumstances that had prompted Click to have drawn that erroneous conclusion. "But when he realized that I'd never even heard of this Alchemist, all he would tell me was that I should ask you." She hesitated a moment. "I know it's important; please tell me."

The Warden exhaled softly and raggedly, dragging his fingers back through his unruly hair in a spontaneous gesture that made him look so much like Andy Greene that Cassidy felt her throat unexpectedly tighten. Then the anger seemed to leach out of him, swiftly, like water draining from sand. And watching the old tolerance and patience return to those incredible eyes, Cassidy nearly choked on the bitter reality of her own situation there.

Damn it, this isn't fair! I know you—and we're like total strangers to each other here.

Although Cassidy knew for a fact that he was several years younger than she was, in that moment the Warden seemed almost ancient, his youth deeply bent under the weight of the ever-escalating problems confronting him. The lines that bracketed his eyes had been cut deeper, forming an etched frame for the smudged, bruiselike bags beneath them. Even those eyes, then calm again and the color of a Hershey's bar, were the eyes of an old man, heavy with unwanted experience.

"I'm sorry, Cassidy," he said. "I didn't mean to be sharp; I'm not angry with you."

Sympathy for him and alarm at what had happened that night helped to cool Cassidy's own rhetoric; but nothing could deflect the urgency of her query. She looked directly into that fatigue-lined face. "Then tell me who the Alchemist is; and what does he have to do with the Memories and the Slow World?"

The Warden tossed his head again, not in irritation that time but in helpless frustration. "I don't *know* who he is, Cassidy—I don't even know that he exists."

"But if we were to go south—"

Immediate concern flushed fresh life into that haggard face. "It's not safe to go south," he said quickly. "There's far too much danger."

"It seems to me there's danger everywhere these days," Cassidy said, not even needing to drop her eyes to the young man's fresh wounds and tattered clothing. "I doubt we could do much worse by going south."

Although that notion clearly disturbed the Warden, it was just as clear to Cassidy that he honestly was too weary to engage in any rational debate. Both of his hands came up, an automatic gesture of restraint and conciliation, to rest upon her shoulders. "Please, Cassidy; don't do anything rash," he said hoarsely. "Let's discuss this in the morning. I swear to you, I'll tell you everything that I know."

Cassidy found herself reluctantly persuaded by both his exhaustion and his promise. "Everything about the south and the Alchemist?" she persisted.

"About the Alchemist, the south—everything," he vowed, his face gray with fatigue. "Just give me a few hours' sleep."

"Okay," she relented, finally allowing him to pass. "I'll wait until morning; but then I want to know everything."

A few hours' sleep had probably been too much to hope for, Cassidy realized in retrospect as she was yanked back into consciousness by someone urgently prodding her shoulder.

After her fruitless confrontation with the Warden in the foyer, Cassidy had gone back to the bedroom she shared with Rowena. Despite her frustration and the sullen grumbling of the approaching thunderstorm, she had immediately fallen asleep, stretched out fully clothed on top of the bed. She would have been willing to swear that it could only have been ten minutes later when she was so rudely awakened by the persistent poking and shaking of someone's insistent hand.

"Cassidy? Cassidy, quick—wake up!"

The moment she recognized the intruding voice, Cassidy's eyes flew open. She found herself looking up directly into Kevin's mismatched eyes, his whole face rendered into an image of ghostly agitation by the halo of light from the oil lantern that he carried in his other hand. His fingers, which had been sharply prodding her, then closed around her forearm, tugging imperatively.

"What the hell . . . ?" she muttered groggily.

"Something's wrong with the Warden, Cassidy," the young man pleaded. "You've got to help!"

From the dimness of the other bed, Rowena had risen unsteadily, half propped on one elbow as she regarded the two of them in sleepy confusion. Cassidy blinked, stifling a yawn and trying to summon rational thought as Kevin nearly dragged her to her feet.

"What about Becky?" she protested, even as she staggered after him.

"She's the one who said to get *you!*" Kevin explained, pulling harder on her arm as they picked up speed across the floor.

Cassidy had no idea where the Warden's room was except that earlier that night when he had finally successfully evaded her inquisition he had gone upstairs. Then Kevin was urging her up the same staircase, his lantern swinging in jerky arcs as he prompted her up each step. On the second floor they passed several of the cluttered rooms filled with the found things before Kevin abruptly swerved in through an open door.

It was one of the smaller rooms, tucked up under one of the gables with a wide dormer window dominating the far wall. Through the dark glass Cassidy could see the flickering sputter of distant lightning dancing across the night sky. Inside the room with the yellow wash of lantern light she could see little of its furnishings but a few plain pieces of furniture. Becky was leaning over the wide, high-postered bed, wearing only a long, printed shirt that was misbuttoned, her long black hair falling in a tangle of dreadlocks around her lowered face. She barely even glanced up at them as Kevin herded Cassidy into the room.

Cassidy was entirely unprepared for the condition of the young man who lay on that bed. She had expected something more kinetic in the aftermath of the monsters' attack—a sud-

den fever, delirium, or even the unprecedented manifestation of
a nightmare. But nothing, not even a nightmare, could have
surprised her more than what she saw in that unremarkable little room.

The Warden lay supine amid a casual rumple of bedcovers,
his body as limp and still as deep sleep—or death. And so as
she pushed past Becky, Cassidy was relieved to note the slow
and shallow but healthily regular rise and fall of that bare and
bitten chest. In the quaver of the lantern light the curved marks
of the monster bites looked shadowy upon his skin, like the
mottling of dapples on a sleek horse's coat. Only as she leaned
closer, bending over that slackened body, did Cassidy truly understand the reason for Kevin's panic.

The Warden wasn't just sleeping; he wasn't even unconscious. Despite his lack of response his eyes were wide open;
not focusing, not tracking, but open, their stare unnervingly
blank.

Cassidy felt as if all of the blood had suddenly drained from
her head; in the ensuing shudder of dizziness she had to press
her knees against the side of the bed to keep from swaying.
For the man who lay before her was no longer the Warden of
Horses; in the perfection of that beautiful vacancy his expression had transformed him, utterly and shockingly, into Andy
Greene.

"What's wrong with him?" Rowena's voice came from the
doorway as she shuffled sleepily into the room.

Jolted by the brunette's question, Cassidy forced herself
back to the present. "I don't know yet," she admitted, looking
down into that slack and boyish face.

Rowena stared at the motionless body on the bed. "Christ—
what happened to him?" she asked as she noticed the bite
marks.

"Kevin said they were attacked by monsters outside the
city," Becky said.

"Is that why he . . . ?"

"I don't know," Cassidy repeated, interrupting Rowena. "I
saw him when they first got back, and he didn't seem to be seriously hurt."

From the foot of the bed Rowena looked down anxiously at
the Warden. "Is he . . . dreaming?" she asked hesitantly.

Cassidy shook her head. "No, I don't think so."

"His eyes are open," Rowena said in surprise.

Cassidy shot her a quick look before glancing over to Kevin's worried face. "How long has he been like this?"

But it was Becky who answered. "It's only been a couple of minutes since Kevin woke me; he said he'd just found him this way."

Kevin's long tanned fingers were locked around one of the rear bedposts, but his anxious gaze scarcely strayed from the Warden's blank face. "I'd just come up," he said softly. "I'd been down at the stables, taking care of—"

With the return of complete wakefulness, Cassidy remembered the Warden having said something earlier about Kevin and Allen being down at the stables with the horses; and for the moment she was less interested in Kevin's reason for coming up to the Warden's room than she was in the Warden's condition. "Has this ever happened before?" she interrupted him.

For a moment Kevin faltered, his hesitation both clumsy and obvious. Cassidy stared at him, surprised by his reluctance and the implication which that reluctance cast. "Maybe—a few times," Kevin finally said. "But never like this—never for this long."

Before an incredulous Cassidy could pounce upon the young Finder for a further explanation, a soft sound from the bed riveted her attention back to the Warden. Suddenly all eyes in the room were redirected at the nearly motionless man. Cassidy saw his pale full lips twitch slightly and then move, almost soundlessly. As she bent closer over his face, something—a murmured syllable or two—was pushed from that familiar mouth. But she had to put her ear nearly to his lips before she could understand the whispered words he repeated.

"Please help . . . Cathy. Help . . ."

Chapter 18 ←||||

Over the past several weeks Cassidy had noticed a curious phenomenon: Sometimes the effect of further shock upon an already confused and adrenaline-primed mind was the sudden creation of a brief window of unexpected insight. In just such a moment then, bent over the Warden of Horses, Cassidy recognized the rough contours of the opportunity with which she had been so surprisingly presented, and realized what she would have to do to maximize its usefulness.

Looking up she quickly scanned the concerned faces of the other three people in the room. "Leave us alone for a minute, huh?" she said.

Becky's eyes instantly narrowed suspiciously. "What is it?" she asked. "What did he just say?"

"It didn't make any sense," Cassidy said, which was not exactly a lie. "Just give me a few minutes alone with him—so I can concentrate," she added convincingly.

But Kevin still clung to the bedpost. "Is he going to be okay?"

As much as she wanted to question Kevin further about any previous similar episodes, Cassidy realized she couldn't afford to take the time to do it just then. She put all of the reassurance she could summon into her reply to his anxious question. "He's always come out of it before, hasn't he?" she reminded Kevin. "Those other times?"

Reluctantly Kevin's hands loosened their hold on the post. "Yeah—but those were never like this," he muttered uncertainly.

Becky took a step back from the bed but declared, "I'm going to go get Valerie."

"No! No, not yet," Cassidy hastily amended. The captain of

the Troopers was the last person she wanted in the room right then. Scrambling to improvise a plausible reason for her objection, she said, "I don't think she—"

But surprisingly it was Rowena who came, however unwittingly, to her rescue on that point. "Let's give Cassidy a few minutes alone with him first," she said to Becky and Kevin, "and see if she can't bring him out of this." The brunette's face was filled with sympathy. "After all, he is the Warden," she reminded them all. She didn't have to go on then because her inference was clear: The fewer people who saw him like this, the less embarrassment and explanation the young leader would face afterward. The strangest thing about it was that Cassidy couldn't be certain if Rowena was just playing along with her, or if she really did believe in preserving the Warden's dignity. And the worst thing about it was that Cassidy could understand and even agree with the sentiment.

The others silently slipped from the room then, Kevin with obvious reluctance and Becky with patent skepticism. Was the black woman too cynical to accept Rowena's explanation, or just too irritated at the Warden to care about his self-respect anymore? The third possibility, that Becky was every bit as desperate as was Cassidy to find out what the hell was happening, only occurred to her after the woman had left the room.

Shifting slightly so that the lamplight didn't stream directly into the Warden's eyes, Cassidy bent over him again. Tense with anticipation, she reached out across the rumpled terrain of the bedcovers and found one of his hands. Despite the pallor of his color and the nearly catatonic stillness of his body, his fingers felt warm and strong as she gently squeezed them. For the merest split second, so transient that it was almost nonexistent, Cassidy felt the room drop away from beneath her, as if her physical surroundings had simply vanished. But she blinked and everything was still there, and the weird feeling was gone.

"Oh, Andy!" Cassidy whispered, overcome with a dangerous mixture of hope and despair. No matter what process had caused the bizarre transformation to take place, that was who the young man had temporarily become. But there was one important difference with that Andy, that potential opportunity which Cassidy's stunned mind had abruptly seized when he had spoken her real name: Somehow he was Andy Greene in that world now, and he had a voice. And if he could speak, he might be able to answer her questions.

Lightly brushing back the errant forelock of his chestnut brown hair from his forehead, Cassidy leaned over that disorientingly familiar face with its baldly staring eyes. "Andy, it's me—Cathy."

A little jolt of hopeful surprise ran through Cassidy as those slender fingers briefly tightened on hers. She had to keep her voice pitched low, but her face was so close to his that she was certain its soft intensity carried to him as she said, "Andy, where are we?"

For a moment the young man was silent and unresponsive, and Cassidy feared that she had overestimated his capacity. But then he exhaled raggedly and whispered, "A big house."

For one awful instant it was like being returned to the grinding frustration of her first days there, trying to pry information out of the obtuse and unhelpful Yolanda and her cohorts. *Now tell me something I don't know!* she thought sardonically. But she bit back her impulse to be sarcastic and instead lightly laced her fingers with his. "Where is this house, Andy? Where is this place?"

For the first time his smooth face assumed an expression; his brow furrowed and he even frowned slightly as if in concentration. Even that modest emotion instantly erased the perfection of his incarnation as Andy Greene, but Cassidy couldn't allow that change to distract her. Quietly she urged him, "Where is this house, Andy? Where are we now?"

"Big long halls," the young man murmured, squinting. "Lights—all white." His frown deepened and his low voice spiked up with an edge of alarm. "Needs help!" he exclaimed.

No shit! Throttling back the impulse to grip his hand more tightly, Cassidy merely gave it a little shake. "I'm going to do everything I can to help you, Andy," she assured him softly. "But first I need to know—"

Cassidy abruptly broke off, instinctively pulling back as the Warden suddenly sat up in the bed. It was not part of his odd trance, she realized immediately; for although he looked about as rational as did any sleeper who'd been unexpectedly wakened from his slumber, from the awareness in his eyes she could see that he was, for all of his confusion, really conscious again. And he was once again the Warden of Horses and not Andy Greene.

"Cassidy," he said, blinking at her in honest surprise, "what's happened?"

Suddenly embarrassed, she dropped his hand and took a

half-step back from the bed. For the first time she was uncomfortably aware of his bare, bite-mottled torso, and it occurred to her that he was probably completely nude beneath the covers.

As the Warden leaned forward toward her, his initial confusion was rapidly replaced by a genuine concern and he eyed her almost sympathetically. "Is there something wrong?" he asked her. "Are you all right?"

The totally innocent misplacement of his sincere concern was so ironic that Cassidy almost laughed aloud. "*I'm* fine," she assured him. For a moment she just looked down into that sleepy, still weary face. "You really don't remember what just happened?" she finally asked him.

Frowning again, this time quite consciously, the Warden met her gaze, seeming to study her expression for some necessary clue. Then something passed over his face, a darkening moment of self-realization. His eyes dropped and he toyed briefly with the hem of the bedcovers. "I did it again, didn't I," he said. It was not a question.

Oddly enough, his display of discomfort helped to relieve Cassidy's own; that was the only thing which made it possible for her to move toward him again, leaning against the side of the bed to look down earnestly into his open and upturned face. "What just happened to you?" she asked him intently.

It was the first time she had ever seen the young man at such a loss for words. "I—I don't know," he was forced to admit.

"You looked like you were in some kind of trance," Cassidy told him. "Do you remember that?" But the Warden shook his head. Trying to encourage him, she offered, "Kevin said you've had . . . episodes like this before."

But again the Warden shook his tousled head. "No, it was never like this before," he said, an ironic echo of the young Finder's earlier assessment.

Trying a slightly different tack, Cassidy asked, "How long has this been going on then?"

She was surprised to see a smile, however wry and fleeting, briefly shape that voluble mouth. "Since the night you arrived here, actually," he replied with a certain asperity. "But it was nothing like this at first. It was just little . . . lapses—like little flashes of being *gone*." He frowned again, as if dredging deeply into thought. "At first I thought that maybe I was—"

"Dreaming," Cassidy supplied, her voice a near whisper.

She gazed at him with a new intensity. "Last night out in the garden—that's why you asked me about dreams, isn't it? You thought you had started to dream." Her eyes narrowed as her voice deepened. "Why didn't you tell me then?" she demanded.

The Warden's bared brown shoulders traced a self-effacing shrug. "I didn't know for sure."

Cassidy shook her head. "You still don't know for sure," she pointed out. "What happened to you tonight was no dream. Are you sure you don't remember anything about it?"

But the bafflement on that handsome young face appeared completely genuine. His slender hands spread helplessly. "No, almost nothing."

She continued to gaze steadily at him, trying to see past the disarming appeal of that sleep-washed face to gauge not only his veracity but also his possible motives for dissembling. She did not think the Warden had ever lied to her; but he certainly was guilty of conveniently withholding information when it seemed to suit his purposes. Yet once again his tanned and finely planed face appeared utterly open and ingenuous. Watching for a reaction, Cassidy told him, "Well, whatever happened you called me by my name—my *real* name."

The young man seemed more troubled than surprised by her revelation. "I know that you believe you know me from before," he said slowly, "and this started to happen to me only after you came here . . ." His teeth lightly worried at his full lower lip. "So you think this has something to do with the Slow World?"

Cassidy nodded emphatically. "It has to do with you and me—with the way we were before either of us came here."

The Warden's frown only deepened, etching his face with a whole new skein of unmerited lines. "But I don't have any Memories, Cassidy; I never have. And I honestly don't remember you."

Cassidy reached out to tap her knuckles against his temple, frustration lending an unintentional vigor to the gesture. "*In here* you do!" she said vehemently. "Somewhere in here you still remember everything! And I think those little 'lapses' you've been having have been your mind's way of experiencing those blocked memories again."

Equally frustrated, the Warden reached up and captured her wrist, holding it gently but firmly between his thumb and fingers. "I wish I could believe that, Cassidy," he said quietly, his eyes meeting and holding hers with an earnest intensity. "All my life I've tried to uncover the secret of the Memories, tried to prove that the myth of the Slow World was true. And now I would do anything I could to make some sense of what's been happening to me."

Cassidy stifled her first reaction, which was to pull away from his hold, and merely permitted it, stolidly meeting his gaze. "If you really want the answers, then let me go south," she said.

She had, Cassidy noted, scored a direct hit with that one. The young man leaned even farther forward on the bed, his grip automatically tightening on her wrist as he brought his face still closer to hers. His expression was grimly taut. "I can't permit that, Cassidy—not now. Can't you see? It's far too dangerous for you." Anticipating her protest, he tightened his fingers even more, hastily continuing "The monsters have already violated the city, and we were attacked just tonight, not more than a hundred paces from the shore of the sea. How could I allow you to travel into the southern wilderness under conditions like these?"

His hold on her wrist was almost painfully tight, yet Cassidy forced herself to maintain a steady calm. "In case you haven't noticed, I'm not exactly safe here, either," she said matter-of-factly. "And if I go south, the monsters will go with me—you know I brought them here," she added.

The Warden could not prevent himself from reacting to that statement. He tried to hide it from her, but Cassidy could see the way his pupils constricted as if he were involuntarily flinching away from a blow. "I'm responsible for your safety," he said doggedly, his voice so soft that he might almost have been speaking to himself. "I can't just let you go."

Wrenching her wrist from his grasp, Cassidy took a half-step back from the bed. "I'll take responsibility for myself," she said, "and you can't keep me here."

The single-mindedness of her argument had lulled Cassidy into such a state of diminished expectation that when the Warden suddenly moved he caught her completely off guard. As he swung his long legs out from beneath the bedcovers and lithely propelled himself to his feet, she nearly tripped over her own feet trying to step back out of his way. And for a few heart-stopping moments, confronted with the completeness of his nudity, all she could think was *Christ! He's gorgeous!* Only the young man's own utter lack of awareness of any sexual dynamic in his action, and the grim reminder of the pattern of the bite marks across that smooth flesh, made it possible for her to keep a telling blush from her face.

The Warden reached out in entreaty and took a startled Cassidy by both shoulders. Standing, he was once again taller than she was, able to look down into her eyes with a compelling earnestness. "Please, Cassidy—listen to me," he pleaded. "I understand why you want to go, but your safety is at stake. And if what you suspect about these—these lapses of mine is true, then we have to explore them further. Going south now would be a foolish risk at best—and a fatal mistake at worst. I don't know what kind of idea Click has given you about searching for the Alchemist, but he of all people should know that you would be making a dangerous journey for nothing."

Cassidy had a split second in which to come up with a convincing façade to cover just how little Click had actually told her. Instead she opted for the truth. "Click told me the Alchemist was just a myth," she admitted, grateful for the opportunity to keep her eyes safely riveted on the Warden's face. "He told me that searching for him would be like chasing a dream."

Exhaling deeply, he seemed to relax fractionally then, as if reassured by her little concession. "As far as I know he has told you the truth then," he said. "All I can tell you about this Alchemist is that there has always been talk about a mysterious man living in the southern swamps." He shrugged slightly, his marred shoulders rising and falling. "The stories say he knows the path to the Slow World." Anticipating and forestalling Cassidy's questions, he quickly added, "But the myth is ancient, and talk is all it's ever been. No one has ever found this Alchemist and there's never been any proof that he even exists."

Cassidy let her eyes drop to the Warden's forearms and then to his bare chest, where his flat coppery nipples rested like two tarnished coins against the irregularly incised pattern of the skin over his breasts. Jerking her gaze back up she blurted out, "You said that Click 'of all people' should know that going south to look for the Alchemist would be a dangerous waste of time." She paused for breath, blinking up into those Hershey-brown eyes. "Is that why Click once went south? To look for the Alchemist?"

The Warden's grimly earnest expression softened slightly, and, to Cassidy's astonishment, he lifted one hand to her forehead and spontaneously brushed back a misplaced swag of her untidy hair. "That matter is the Tinker's concern," he said quietly. "You'll have to ask him, Cassidy."

Yeah, and he'll just tell me to ask you! she thought in frustration. But, still surprised by the young man's gesture of casual affection—and nonplussed by her own dangerously willing reaction to it—she did not voice that thought. Rather she followed up on a sudden hunch. "*You* sent him," she guessed.

But the Warden shook his head. In the lantern light his tousled hair was limned with gold. "No, I would never have sent him on such a fool's errand, Cassidy. That was before my time; he served another Warden."

Cassidy's head buzzed with a sudden disorientation, nearly as overwhelming as it had been to discover Andy Greene in the Warden's body. She felt as if she had been climbing a long, particularly steep staircase only to discover suddenly that the next step was not where her foot expected to find it. "He—he served another Warden?" she stammered stupidly. Had Click been a *Trooper?*

But before the young man whose hand still rested so easily and familiarly upon her shoulder could reply—however maddeningly vague his answer might have been—they were interrupted by the sudden sound of voices loudly raised in argument in the corridor outside the bedroom. Cassidy found herself stiffening as she recognized the most insistent of the loud voices, for it belonged to Valerie, the captain of the Warden's Troopers.

Although Cassidy realized she'd gotten far more than her few minutes alone with the Warden, she was still irked that Becky would have summoned Valerie. As frustrating as their conversation had been thus far, Cassidy felt that she had just been on the verge of finally getting some important information from him, if not about the Alchemist then at least about Click. Now as the curly-haired captain strode into the bedroom, Cassidy saw all hope of further useful discussion vanish.

As Valerie quickly appraised the situation within the little room, she barely spared Cassidy a glance. Her attention was almost entirely upon her Warden; and if she wondered what Cassidy was doing in his room in the middle of the night, with his hands still upon her, Cassidy saw no sign of speculation in that elegantly spare face. Cassidy's presence there seemed as unremarkable to Valerie as did the Warden's nudity.

"There are fires raging in the city," Valerie told him without preamble. "Tag thinks the gangs must have set them. Several blocks in the warehouse distract are ablaze."

Dropping his hands from her shoulders, the Warden immediately turned away from Cassidy, his eyes on Valerie even as he automatically and efficiently reached for the fresh clothing folded at the foot of his bed. "How many squads do we have on patrol?" he shot at the captain as he tossed the tunic over his head and yanked it down.

"Five in that district," Valerie promptly reported. "The two regular squads, the two extra ones you ordered earlier, and Tag called up a squad from the harbor when the alarm went out."

Cassidy stepped back out of the way, a little astonished at how swiftly the Warden was slipping into his clothing. She could see Rowena, Becky, and Kevin peering in anxiously from the hallway, backed by a pair of sober-faced Troopers. From the way the Warden and Valerie were acting, Cassidy might just as well not even have existed.

"Call in five more," he ordered briskly. "Not from the other districts—call them out from the garrison," he added, hopping to tug on his boots. Then he was striding out the door with Valerie right at his heels.

Finally goaded into motion again by their precipitous departure, Cassidy scrambled around the bed and bolted into the hallway. "Wait!" she called out, rushing past Rowena and Becky and catching up with the Warden and his Troopers just as Kevin joined them on the staircase. "What about me?"

The Warden paused, giving her a sympathetic but implacable look. "Wait here, Cassidy," he said tersely. "We'll talk further when I return."

If you return! Cassidy thought. "I'm coming with you," she said.

The pair of Troopers and Valerie were thumping down the stairs ahead of them; only Kevin hesitated, hanging back to regard both Cassidy and the Warden with distress and alarm in his wide odd-colored eyes. "Don't be foolish, Cassidy," the Warden said, his tone softly urgent. "The gangs are rioting— don't deliver yourself right into their hands."

Cassidy seriously doubted that gangs had started the warehouse fires, but she didn't see much advantage in trying to point that out just then. Like the night that the barns had burned in Double Creek, the people there had obviously already chosen their explanation; even the proven existence of the monsters seemed unlikely to convince them that bizarre forces were gathering in the city. So instead of disputing the Warden's conclusion she just entreated him, "But I'm a Horseman and you're going to need every hand. I know I could help."

Something in the Warden's face softened, that haggard visage regaining a fleeting measure of its rightful youth. His mouth—*Andy's* mouth, so achingly familiar that it nearly made Cassidy's eyes burn with tears—quirked gently. "What I need is to know that you are safe, Cassidy," he said. "Please don't give me anything else to worry about—my plate is already full."

Before Cassidy could further plead her case, Valerie shouted from the foot of the staircase. "Tag just sent word," she called urgently. "Justin says another block is burning, this time in the merchants' district!"

When the Warden turned away from Cassidy that time he never looked back. Despite the tendered debt of his fatigue he was off, bounding down the steps two at a time, firing off orders to Valerie even as Kevin scurried at his heels to keep up with him. The gathering knot of somber-faced Troopers who had formed in the foyer of the big brick house parted around him, ultimately enveloping the Warden as they all streamed across the front room toward the doorway.

Desperate with frustration, Cassidy shot a glance back at Rowena and Becky, who still lingered helplessly in the hallway outside the Warden's abandoned bedroom. And when she looked back down the staircase it was empty, and nothing remained of the mass of Troopers and their Warden but the echo of bootsteps, muted voices and the faint smell of horses and leather.

For a long moment her sense of indignation at being thwarted once again was so strong that Cassidy felt frozen to the spot, her hands clenched into useless fists. Like some oft-jilted bride left waiting at the altar, she stood at the head of the deserted staircase, furiously looking down the empty sprawl of steps. *Damn him!* she thought; and it was that anger which finally broke the paralysis that seemed to have locked her muscles.

For the first time since she had come to the Iron City seeking the Warden, Cassidy found herself regaining a clear and singular sense of purpose. And in order to do so, she had to admit something that she had been doggedly reluctant to face: Neither finding the Warden nor even remembering her own past had given her the answers about how she had come to be there—much less how to get back. Then it became a matter of utter simplicity. The answers lay elsewhere, and if she was going to find them she was going to have to leave that place and move on again.

Fuck it! Cassidy thought, an expletive she did not usually indulge in. But it felt so good that she even spat it aloud: *"Fuck it!"* she exclaimed loudly. Then she started down the steps, so recklessly that she was leaping them in twos and threes in her headlong rush to reach the bottom.

She was already in their bedroom on the ground floor, crouched over their meager collection of belongings, when Rowena and Becky caught up to her. The buxom brunette skidded into the room and came to an abrupt halt, her hazel eyes widening in the pale lamplight.

"Cassidy—what are you going to do?" Rowena gasped.

Cassidy scarcely even glanced up at them as she finished tugging something free from the small pack she had assembled that afternoon. The metal barrel of the little pistol, the weapon Click had given her the night she and Rowena had fled the Tinkers' camp outside Pointed Rock, flashed briefly as she wedged it under the waistband of her pants against the small of her back and concealed it beneath the floppy overhang of her shirttail.

"We're going to get the hell out of here," she said shortly, reclosing the pack with a perfunctory yank to its straps.

"You're crazy," Becky pronounced from the doorway. "How are we going to get out of here now—those idiots in the city are rioting!"

Straightening as she rose to her full height, Cassidy gave both of her companions a grimly sardonic stare. "Yeah, and where do you suppose those idiots'll be headed once they get all of the Troopers in this place busy fighting those damned fires? Or are you looking forward to being the guest of honor at a lynching?"

As the other two women gaped at her with near-identical expressions of surprise and disbelief, Cassidy started back toward the door. Rowena had to lunge forward as Cassidy strode past her, just managing to snag Cassidy's shirt sleeve and forcing her to spin around. "Wait a minute—where are you going with a gun?" she demanded.

Cassidy didn't try to shake herself free but she fixed Rowena with a look of such single-minded impatience that the brunette almost loosed her grip. "I have to go down to the Tinkers' enclave," Cassidy explained tersely. "I just hope to hell Click was able to get us that boat."

Becky stepped forward then, positioning herself between Cassidy and the doorway. "What about us?" the little black woman said tartly. "Or are we supposed to stay here and hold off the mob while you sail away?"

Unstiffening a bit, Cassidy shook her head. The small pistol felt like a cold stone pressed against her spine, reminding her that none of it would be a simple matter. "Listen, the garrison's going to be jumping for a while yet," she said, "but then most of the Troopers will be gone into the city. When it calms down, take our stuff and sneak down to the stables. See if you can get that gig cart out of there without getting caught."

"What if we do get caught?" Rowena interrupted, somewhat irately. But at least she had released Cassidy's sleeve.

Cassidy smiled thinly. "What, you think the Troopers will shoot you?" she chided. "All they'll do if they catch you is send you back up here, and you'll just have to try again. At any rate," she added, "try to not get caught."

"And if we can get out with the gig cart," Becky persisted, "then what are we supposed to do? This is hardly the night for a little jog in the country."

As if in emphasis, a long deep growl of thunder interrupted, causing the windowpanes to rattle. But Cassidy was undeterred. "Once you get through the gates, just take the main road to the side road outside the city that goes to the enclave. I'll be at the quay with the boat." Cassidy didn't bother to add the obvious, which was that it was hardly likely to be that simple. What would have been an easy trip for the cart in daylight would be considerably more hazardous in the darkness, even without the fires and the rioting in the city.

"I don't like this," Rowena announced darkly, to no one in particular.

"Yeah, I don't like this, either," Cassidy agreed with utter sincerity. Then she turned back toward the door, threading her way between Becky and Rowena.

Cassidy was so preoccupied with what lay ahead that she nearly strode full tilt into the broad form of a man who was just entering from the hallway. As it was she was able to catch herself just in time to turn an outright collision into a clumsy bumping. She looked up in surprise and dismay into a familiarly sober face.

"Allen!" she exclaimed, trying to recover the moment. "What the hell are you doing here? You just about scared the shit out of me."

The big sheriff's canny eyes quickly scanned the dimly lit bedroom before coming back to rest on Cassidy's face. "The Warden sent me up here to the house," he said then. "Said to watch you—that you might be in danger." His russet mustache twitched slightly. "He didn't say that you'd be going anywhere," he added.

Cassidy looked up directly into that solemn and watchful face, into the gold-ringed eyes of the man who had in the past both hunted and protected her—perhaps even at the same time, she thought then. "We're leaving, Allen," she said. "Going south along the coast."

Of all the things the stolid sheriff might have said then, of all the ways duty and loyalty and even common sense might have pulled him, the direction he took with her simply surprised Cassidy. He stared down at her in silence for a few moments, unblinkingly thoughtful. And when he did speak, his voice was soft, almost wistful.

"Coming here hasn't worked out the way you'd hoped, has it, Cassidy?" he said. "Looking for answers in this city has been like having a wolf on a leash—it's been more likely to turn on you than to hunt for you."

His blunt Villagers' metaphor was corny but uncomfortably apt. And unwillingly Cassidy found herself doing the only thing she could with his implacable loyalty: She shamelessly traded upon it. "We need your help, Allen," she said quietly. "I swear to you, this is the last thing I'll ever ask of you; then honor or no honor, I want you to go back to your village while you still can."

For a moment Allen looked as if he might comment on her final advice to him. But after a beat of silent consideration, silence during which Cassidy could hear the distant sounds of thunder and shouts and the drumming of hoofbeats from down at the garrison, the shaggy-headed man merely asked her, "What is it you need me to do?"

Relieved and grateful, Cassidy quickly explained. "I'm riding to the Tinkers' enclave. Click was going to try to get us a boat. But Becky and Rowena won't be able to just ride out of here like I can. Once things calm down a little around the garrison, if you could just help them get the gig cart out of the stables and—"

One of Allen's big hands dropped onto Cassidy's shoulder, interrupting her. "I'll see them both down to the quay," he said with steady assurance.

It was far more than Cassidy could have hoped for; if Allen could drive the cart along the roads and down beyond the city to the quay, the two women's chances of getting clear without being detected by the Troopers or attacked by irate gang members had just increased exponentially. "You don't have to do that, Allen," she began. "If the Troopers—"

"I said I'll do it," Allen interrupted gruffly. "You just get that damned boat." And as Cassidy hesitated, looking up into those somber eyes for whatever motive must lie behind them, some small spark lit their ringed depths. "You forget, Cassidy," Allen reminded her wryly, "that I'm just an outland sheriff; I don't serve the Warden."

Without realizing she meant to do it, Cassidy popped forward on her toes and gave his big solid body a quick hug. Then she turned into the hallway and strode rapidly toward the darkened front sitting room.

Cassidy had figured that the side door, opening onto the brick walkway beside the garden deck, would be the most effectively screened from view of the garrison by its heavy plantings of trees and shrubs. Once she got clear of the house she could Call her mare and ride west, away from the compound, until it was safe to circle around and double back, just as she had done that afternoon. It would take more time but she knew the main road would still be aclatter with Troopers, and she would have far rather sacrificed some time than risked being stopped by any of the Warden's troops. She hadn't just been facetious when she'd reminded Rowena that the Troopers wouldn't harm them; but once caught, breaking free of their custody a second time might be well-nigh impossible. If they caught Cassidy, her chances of reaching Click, getting the boat, and leaving the city would be slight indeed.

Not for the first time Cassidy had been so preoccupied planning for the long haul that she had neatly overlooked the more immediate. Glancing back across the darkened sitting room, she deftly twisted the knob on the side door and slipped through, feeling with the toe of her boot for the shallow step down onto the brick sidewalk. She looked ahead again just in time to avoid walking directly into the stern face of one of the Warden's female Troopers.

Two Troopers, a man and a woman, were stationed just outside the side door of the house. That shouldn't have surprised Cassidy, she realized ruefully and belatedly, and whether they had been sent to prevent anyone else from getting into the house or to keep her and the others from getting out—or most likely both—was really a moot point.

"Going somewhere?" the female Trooper asked.

The woman had short graying hair and shoulders as broad as any man's; Cassidy recognized her from the briefing at the garrison a couple of nights earlier, even if she didn't know the woman's name. Looking directly at her with what she hoped was a convincing expression of sincere concern, Cassidy said, "My horse; I just wanted to be sure she was all right." She glanced over at the male Trooper, a swarthy-looking man with a narrow bar of black mustache defining his upper lip. "With all the fuss down at the garrison . . ." She trailed off meaningfully, spreading her hands in a gesture of appeal.

But neither Trooper was buying such appeals that night. Cassidy could imagine what their orders, and the orders of the other Troopers who were undoubtedly stationed at every door of the house, had been. After what had happened in the city that morning, she and the others hadn't even been permitted to leave the compound in broad daylight. With the city in turmoil, the Warden had certainly tightened his security net.

"Your horse is safe," the black-haired man said. "The ruckus is all in the city." He inclined his head back toward the still-open door of the house. "Why don't you just step back inside," he suggested.

Cassidy casually leaned slightly back, one hand reaching behind her as if to brace herself against the door frame. "Why don't you both just step inside ahead of me?" she said softly, bringing her hand back out in front of her body.

To their credit, neither Trooper flinched or even blinked an eye at the sudden appearance of Click's silver pistol in Cassidy's hand. She sincerely hoped that neither of the two of them was similarly armed. Unfortunately it was too damned dark in the side yard for her to have been able to tell in advance whether they had been carrying guns of their own. But when she gestured economically with the barrel of the pistol, they both moved silently and obediently through the doorway.

Securing the two Troopers consumed precious minutes, but Cassidy had no choice. And ironically she thought she might just have found a way to avoid the added danger of having to ride cross country to get to the enclave. She commanded the female Trooper to tear off strips from the decorative valances of the front room's drapery to bind her partner's wrists and ankles behind him. The woman impressed Cassidy as being the tougher of the two; she was certain the job would be done properly. Then she demanded the woman's leathers and swiftly exchanged clothing with her. When they had finished, Cassidy similarly bound the stoically silent woman. Reluctantly then, because she honestly did admire their grit and loyalty, she gagged the Troopers with more strips torn from the valances. She left them lying, trussed up like shoats, along the wall and pulled one of the room's large upholstered couches over far enough to conceal them from casual discovery.

Cassidy slipped out the door again and into the empty side yard. Overhead the sky was angry with dark roiling masses of dim charcoal-colored clouds. Faint explosions of lightning skipped over the thunderheads and the low grumble of thunder ground like the sound of distant machinery. The storm that had been threatening all night was nearly there.

Using the ornamental shrubbery and trees of the garden as cover, Cassidy made her way to the edge of the lawn. Down the hill from the house, bars of light spilled from the doors and windows of the garrison and stables buildings. She could still hear the faint exchange of voices and the occasional clatter of shod hooves over the paving stones of the quadrangle courtyard. Because of the clothing's relatively light color she felt vulnerably obvious in the Trooper's leather garb. It was also a mediocre fit, too loose through the shoulders and a little short in the legs. But if push came to shove, along the dark road to the city it would serve her a sight better than would her own familiar Tinker clothing.

Pausing at the periphery of the meadow, Cassidy turned to take one last look back at the Warden's big brick house. With an unexpected stab of melancholy she realized that it might be quite literally her last look at the place—and her last connection with the man who lived there.

Damn it, he's not *Andy,* she reminded herself brutally, *no matter what you thought you saw up there in that bedroom tonight.* Andy belonged to her world, and the only way she had any hope of ever seeing both him and that world again was to turn her back on the Warden and his entire household.

Swinging around, she began to jog over the uneven clumps of meadow grass, setting a course slightly to the north of the brightly lit garrison. The night air had taken on a chill, exacerbated by the rising wind; but the Trooper's leathers were serviceably warm. When she reached the crest of the first slope, Cassidy Called the gray mare.

Dragonfly came to her from the south, up the hillside from the vicinity of the garrison. In the moonless darkness the mare was barely visible until she reached Cassidy. Then the horse slid to a halt, snorting softly, her wide nostrils flaring. Excitement thrummed through the big gray like the resonance of a tuning fork. Cassidy stroked the sleek neck, which was curved in an arch of restless energy. As Cassidy vaulted up onto the mare's broad warm back, her thighs closed over the bunched muscles of the horse's forequarters. And strangely enough the gray's sense of eager anticipation helped to bolster Cassidy's own will, briefly charging her with a surge of almost giddy confidence.

Then again, this damned horse has never been afraid of anything! Cassidy's little inner voice reminded her acerbically as she let the mare bound forward across the slope.

Trooper's leathers or not, Cassidy was not quite ballsy enough to attempt riding in across the stableyard and right out the main gate. Instead she kept the mare on a tangential course for a while, cutting across the wide swath of the upland pasture until they had reached and cleared the stone boundary wall. From the vantage point of the meadowland above the main road Cassidy could see the weird orangish glow that hung over a wide segment of the Iron City. The fires were more widespread than she had expected from Valerie's last report at the foot of the Warden's staircase. Either more of the blazes had been set or the feckless combustability of the city's buildings was facilitating the rapid spread of the initial fires—or both.

Halting the mare for a moment just beyond the compound's wall, Cassidy tried to orient herself. Valerie had said that the first fires were set in the warehouse district, which was near the harbor, and then in the merchants' district, which was in the center of the city. But the pulsating glow that bled from the skyline seemed to stretch nearly from one end of the city to the other, its coruscating light streaming great tails of malignant-looking sooty smoke up into the stormy night sky. From that distance Cassidy could not yet smell the smoke; the prevailing wind was at her back, coming from the west. But she could hear an odd sound almost like the rumble of thunder mixed with the muted crackle like footsteps through dry leaves. The city's wooden structures must have been igniting like slivers of tinder in a high draft.

Urging Dragonfly forward again, Cassidy cut toward the main road. She hoped to be able to follow it to the outskirts of the city where she could pick up the side road that led to the enclave from the north. Once on the main track, she let the gray gallop full out, and the horse bounded forward eagerly in the darkness. Cassidy was no longer particularly concerned about encountering any Troopers on the road; any of them would probably be heading into the city, and seeing her in the leathers of their uniform and galloping in the same direction, they would undoubtedly conclude that she was bound on the same business as they were.

As Cassidy drew closer to the city, she began to smell the pungent stink of smoke despite the backwind. The orange glow had resolved into distinct walls of leaping flame, surging along the crest of the city's skyline like a giant campfire run amok, greedily burgeoning along the top of the buildings. She could hear the sounds of the fire more clearly then, too, the dull grumbling crackle replaced by a louder hollow roar and punctuated by sporadic explosions and crashing noises. Cassidy thought of the fire the night of the storm in Double Creek and an uneasy wave of déjà vu swept through her. Another fire, another thunderstorm gathering, another desperate escape . . .

Cassidy was relieved when she was able to cut off the main road and onto the narrower road that led to the enclave. She still would have to ride near the city and the fires, but at least for the moment she no longer had the unsettling sensation of riding directly into that garish hell. She hadn't encountered anyone, even Troopers, on the main road, and she felt she'd be even less likely to on the side road. The surface of that thoroughfare was rougher, however, prompting her to persuade the mare to temper her speed, but Dragonfly was still handily covering ground. *I just hope to hell Click talked those seamen into giving us a boat!* she thought as the gray raced along, nearly parallel to the funneling clouds of smoke that fumed up from the burning city.

That hope birthed another thought, one that Cassidy doggedly tried to shove aside. It was one thing to realize what she was leaving at the Warden's compound and to convince herself to accept that loss. It was quite another thing to feel her heart be jerked up short by the thought of leaving the Tinkers' leader. *You think it matters to him?* she told herself roughly.

But it was a form of self-defense that played poorly, and more than ever Click was on her mind as she sped toward the enclave.

Even with the conflagration in the city, the stormy sky reflected back so little light onto the roadway that Cassidy almost didn't see the first of the refugees until Dragonfly snorted and swerved to avoid them. The shadowy stream of dozens of ragged city dwellers, most of them staggering under the burden of as many sacks and bundles as they could carry, surprised Cassidy until she remembered that the city was filled with homeless gangs. Not only had the fires chased them from their usual warrens in the alleys and buildings of the warehouse district, they had also afforded them an unexpected opportunity to loot the burning buildings in the merchants' district on their way past. For anyone fleeing the western part of the city, the road to the Tinkers' enclave was the most direct route out of the Troopers' clutches.

The mare dodged around several more groups of the itinerant thieves, some of them lurching up out of the ditch and others scurrying along the roadway itself. A few of them shouted angry epithets at Cassidy as the horse sped past them. She wasn't worried about being recognized anymore; in her stolen leathers and mounted on the big gray, the thugs took her for a lone Trooper. As hostile as the city dwellers had become, she still felt a hell of a lot safer masquerading as a Trooper than she would have been at being recognized as Cassidy, the infamous woman who had brought the monsters to the Iron City.

In a few moments she had left the fleeing refugees behind and was nearing the enclave. The stink of smoke had grown stronger, the chilly air thick with its foul efflux. Instead of the river and the sea, all Cassidy could smell was the heavy stench of the burning buildings. For the first time she found herself wondering if the fires would threaten the enclave itself, in spite of the wide slough that separated it from the outskirts of the city. She felt a moment's shame at her plans to flee at a time when every pair of hands might become critical in the fight against the spread of the blazes, but she realized it would be safer for everyone once she left.

When Dragonfly shied again, Cassidy assumed there was more pedestrian traffic on the roadway, more people escaping the city ahead of the fires and the justice of the Troopers. Visibility was so poor she couldn't see anyone along the ditch or in the roadway. Then the mare dodged sideways again, so abruptly that Cassidy nearly lost her seat. At nearly the same moment she smelled something that made her thighs tighten around the horse's barrel in an automatic spasm of fear. It was a fetid odor, a rotting reek so overpowering that it made her gag. The last time she had smelled such a stench was in the woods outside Pointed Rock the night Allen and the other Villagers had been attacked. It was the foul smell of the hanging monsters.

Heedless of the rough road or the smoky gloom that obscured their path, Cassidy urged the mare forward with all of her will. Harmless carrion eaters or not, the wretched hanging creatures meant only one thing to Cassidy: They would not have been there if their other more deadly companions were not already marauding through the city.

The mare tried to respond to Cassidy's frantic urging, but her hindquarters suddenly dropped down in a helpless skid. Cassidy slipped down the horse's sloping back toward her tail; one of her boots actually touched down on the roadway before the mare was able to lurch to her feet again, pulling a desperately clinging Cassidy back up with her. As she squirmed back up onto the horse's back, she looked down with horror at the darkened surface of the road. It was coated with a gelatinous scum, the filthy slime that oozed and dripped from the hanging monsters.

Shuddering with revulsion, Cassidy pulled herself up over the horse's withers. The big body beneath her shuddered, as well, but not in loathing. The gray was suddenly as helpless as a cow on ice, skidding uncontrollably on the slickened surface. The horse was no longer trying to run, she was struggling merely to keep her footing. And when the mare began to go down again, Cassidy was forced to make one of the most reluctant decisions of her short but eventful tenure in that bizarre world: She had to leap down off the gray's back so that the horse could regain her balance, or the mare would have gone down completely.

As her boots hit the pavement, Cassidy felt as if she'd hopped down right in the middle of a swamp of rotting phlegm. She was not at quite the same disadvantage as the horse; for one thing, she had a lot less weight to support, distributed over a larger bearing surface, and her boots gave her a better purchase than did Dragonfly's hooves. But she still found herself reaching out automatically for the mare's shoulder to try to brace herself—and found that usually steady shoulder shooting out from beneath her hand as the horse skittered helplessly away. As alarmed and frightened as Cassidy was at that moment, some part of her was also supremely pissed off. What kind of place was this anyway? And what kind of end would it be to have slipped, fallen, and broken her neck in a pool of putrid monster spittle?

I would have made a hell of a Trooper! she thought grimly, forced to watch impotently as her mare scrabbled along sideways on her hocks and knees, like some giant crustacean fighting her way toward the side of the road. But the horse had the right idea; no matter how much slime there may have been in the ditch, once there was grass or earth beneath her feet again she'd be able to get some purchase. And so, wobbling like a drunk on ice skates, Cassidy tried to follow her.

Just when Cassidy was certain things couldn't get any more ridiculously loathsome, she felt her feet fly out from beneath her. She landed hard on her butt on the beslimed pavement near the edge of the roadway, sending up a spray of muck that splattered across her face. A hot flare of anger shot through her because she knew she hadn't just slipped—something had *pushed* her. Glaring up at the roiling smoke-shrouded sky, the granddaddy of all sexually explicit oaths ready at her lips, Cassidy turned her face directly into the foul and floating mass of one of the hanging monsters.

For one horrible moment it was exactly like being smothered in a stinking caul of rotting offal. Cassidy felt the bile rise in her throat as she threw up her arms to fend off the repulsive creature. But it was like punching into a decomposing corpse; her fists sunk right into the bulk of the fetid black thing and ropy streams of cold filthy slime poured down her arms. Gagging, Cassidy averted her face, trying to breathe; but the hanging monster was wrapped around her head like a putrid shroud.

She could only think of one thing to do, and it took nearly all of her remaining strength to do it. Pulling one fist free from the rotten pulsating mass, she groped blindly for the pistol that she hoped was still stuck under the waistband of her pants at the small of her back. It was not the need she had foreseen for the weapon when she had taken it with her, but her desperation was inspiring. As her fingers closed over the butt of the gun, she was dismayed to find that her fingers were too slippery with slime to be able to pull it free.

Having one of the hideous creatures practically draped over her head added a whole new meaning to claustrophobia;

Cassidy's lungs began to burn for want of air, and she was so panicked that some small and detached part of her mind was actually bemused to note that she didn't really even notice the awful smell anymore. She was so frantic for oxygen that she would have gladly inhaled a whole chestful of the creature's wretched smell just to be able to breathe again. Furiously trying to wipe her fingers on the back of her already befouled shirt, she took another desperate yank on the grip of the pistol.

Cassidy grunted as the gun pulled free. She nearly dropped the weapon as she fumbled to bring it up and poke its short barrel into the foul mass that lay draped over her shoulders like a fetid shawl. Blood was pounding in her ears and she swayed with dizziness as she made ready to pull the trigger. Then suddenly she was being slammed forward with such a rude jolt that the gun nearly flew from her hand, and she fell facedown onto the repulsive creature that had been enshrouding her.

Tiny little starbursts of light sparkled in the darkness which swam behind her eyelids. *What a shitty way to die!* Cassidy thought, even as she felt great slobbering gouts of the monster's slime soaking through her filthy leather clothing. But then abruptly—miraculously—the writhing gelid mass parted from around her and she was being dragged, rapidly and not particularly gently, backward on her butt across the slippery roadway.

Cassidy barely had time to even start to absorb what had happened when she saw the dripping bulk of another one of the wretched carrion eaters descending on her from out of the murky sky. She struggled to raise her arm again, the silver pistol still clutched in her slime-covered hand. But before she could squeeze off a shot at the creature, the strong hands that had pulled her back from the first monster's embrace tightened even further on her shoulders and a stunningly welcome voice froze her with a single command.

"*No!* Cassidy, don't try to shoot it!"

Click released his hold on her as he lunged past her, his raised arm dropping in a sharp swooping swath. The grotesquely everted carcass of the second bloated monstrosity was suddenly split from top to bottom like a gutted ox, and a deluge of dark reeking fluid spilled from its falling body as it splatted onto the roadway. Scrambling backward out of the way on her butt and heels, Cassidy gaped up at the Tinker in amazement. In his hand he held a butcher's knife as big as a scythe, its gleaming blade still dripping with the creature's foul ooze.

"If you shoot them, they explode," he explained, somewhat out of breath. Then with one deft movement he thrust the knife back through his belt and leaned closer to offer her a hand up.

Still too astonished to speak, Cassidy gratefully grasped his wet fingers and, slipping and sliding, allowed him to pull her to her feet. There was at least six inches of the monsters' slimy secretion fouling the roadside but Cassidy no longer cared; she would have swum a river of the damned stuff if she'd had to. A few yards away Dragonfly had regained her own footing and stood impatiently, snorting in disgust.

As soon as Click could see that she was able to stand unassisted, he released Cassidy's hand and quickly scanned the smoky night sky. "I suspect that little bit may have scared the rest of them off, at least for now," he said as he swiftly surveyed the glistening wet surface of the flooded road.

Cassidy was finally able to speak. "How did you—what are you *doing* out here?" she panted in amazement.

As Click turned back toward her, Cassidy could see that the Tinker was nearly as covered with the fetid slime as she was; his face was so spattered with it that his mustache appeared glued on, like some kind of cheap theatrical prop. "I was coming for you," he said calmly.

"Coming for me?" Cassidy repeated stupidly, as if his simple explanation defied belief. To her chagrin she realized that she had been gesturing with the pistol still clutched in her hand.

"The city is under siege," Click said, patient with her shock. "You can't stay here any longer." He gestured east, toward the harbor. "There's a boat waiting for you at the quay; I was coming to get you and Rowena."

Still struggling to regain her breath, Cassidy looked over Click's shoulder, farther up the roadway past where the gray mare stood restlessly pawing. There was something lying on the pocked pavement, about fifteen or twenty feet beyond the stretch of slime. She had to squint to bring the object into better focus, and even when she realized what it was, her first impulse was to burst out laughing. The object was a bicycle.

I need a knight in shining armor on a white steed, she thought giddily, *and what do I get? A slimy Tinker on a damned bicycle!* But there was no one else in that world she would rather have seen.

Click was holding out his hand to her again, his sticky brows tented quizzically at Cassidy's decidedly loopy-looking expression. "Where are Rowena and Becky?" he asked as she reached out and allowed him to lock his fingers around her wrist.

"Allen's bringing them in the gig cart," she said, still fighting down the urge to break down into totally inappropriate laughter. "But they had to wait to get out of the garrison."

"Well, we can't wait for them here," Click said decisively, tugging her through the slime toward the gray mare. "The center of the city is all ablaze; there'll be more thugs coming this way."

Fumbling to replace her pistol in the waistband of her pants, she stumbled obediently after him. "Are the fires driving everyone out?" she asked.

Click nodded but said nothing further until they had reached the sodden horse and he had seen Cassidy vault up onto her slime-streaked back. With a smooth and automatic grace he hopped up behind her, his long thighs gripping the mare's barrel right behind Cassidy's. Seemingly unmindful of the wet filth that soaked her hair and clothing, he fit his body against hers as the horse began to slog along parallel to the road, looking for a break in the treacherous patch of slime. Click did not speak until the gray had scrambled up out of the ditch and onto the rough pavement, and had broken into a rangy lope.

"It's not just the fires, Cassidy," he said then, his voice low and grave as the big mare rocked along. "The city's people are turning on the Troopers."

"What?" Cassidy gasped. "The Troopers didn't have anything to do with those fires!"

"Of course not," Click agreed, "but the Troopers represent the Warden's rule, and the people blame the Warden for the monsters being here."

Click paused and for a moment the only sounds were those of the ongoing riot in the city and the steady drumming of the mare's hooves on the rough pavement. Then his words, so quiet and yet so chilling, were spoken at Cassidy's ear.

"The people are rioting, Cassidy, because monsters have overrun the city."

Chapter 19 ◄ꟷ

As they galloped along the road toward the Tinkers' enclave, for a full minute or more Cassidy was just too stunned
and alarmed by what Click had told her to know how to react.
She had come to the Iron City seeking the answers to her past,
with the hope that the Warden of Horses would not only reveal
who she was and how she had gotten there, but that he would
also help her return to her rightful place in her own world.
Well, she had gotten her answers, all right—some of them at
least—just enough to make the whole situation even more im-
possibly bizarre than it had been before. But what she had not
bargained for was that not only was the Warden as ignorant of
that mythical Slow World as she was, he also was equally desperate to solve the mystery its existence represented. What neither of them in their naïveté had counted on was the massive
rent in the fabric of the Warden's society that would be created
by Cassidy's arrival and the hideous creatures that seemed to
have followed her in from the hills.

I found the Warden all right, Cassidy thought numbly.
*Found him like a prince. And now I'm leaving him with a full-
fledged coup d'état . . .*

Click's voice, sounding low and urgent from over her shoulder, finally yanked Cassidy back to the brutal realities of their
plight. "The marsh bridge is unsafe," he said. "Refugees
from the city are flooding the enclave." He paused for a beat
and then added with a touch of his old irony, "And I doubt that
they would be particularly happy to see you right about now.
We'll have to cross the marsh to get into the city and down to
the quay."

Cassidy guided Dragonfly off the edge of the roadway and
toward the grassy slope of land that led down to the slough di-

viding the enclave from the outskirts of the city. There was a footpath along the edge of the marsh; she tried to remember from her previous visits just how wide the path was and what kind of footing it would provide. But it was difficult for her to concentrate. The cold stinking slime that still covered her and Click from hair to boots was a graphic and distracting reminder of just how close to death she had already come once that night. And the growing smoke and light and din of the burning city was an equally compelling warning of what dangers they still faced.

And although Cassidy would not—*could not*—take the time or attention to analyze it, the man who rode behind her, his lean body warming the slickness that seemed to glue them together on the horse's back, was a powerful distraction of another sort. As unwarranted as Allen's sense of loyalty to her may have seemed to Cassidy, she still felt that she somehow understood what motivated the burly sheriff to ally himself with her. But Click's repeated interventions on her behalf, the last one above all the rest, defied her understanding. Click owed her nothing; why was he once again risking his life to help her?

But even as the big gray horse hunkered down on her haunches and slid the last few yards on the slippery grass down to the footpath, Cassidy's little inner voice taunted her with a whisper of the truth. *You know why he's doing it,* the little voice suggested.

But her rational self insisted, *No I don't!* It didn't make any sense.

The gray's hooves thumped rhythmically along the packed sod of the winding trail that led along the edge of the slough. To their right rose the shallow slope leading to the Tinkers' settlement; to their left, across the rippling darkness of the cattails and sedge grass, lay the western outskirts of the besieged city. Great clouds of sooty smoke fumed overhead, temporarily blotting out even the massing thunderheads of the imminent storm. Only the powerful stench of the slime that befouled them both was stronger than the pungent stink of the fires. The entire eastern sky, looking toward the Gray Sea and serrated by the black cutouts of the city's skyline, was awash in quivering flame. A constant confusion of distant shouting and the crackling and crashing of the burning buildings crowded out all other sound.

Cassidy tried to avoid looking across the marsh. She could

not shake the hideous feeling that she was the one responsible at least in part for the chaos that was destroying the Warden's city. By coming there she had brought more divisiveness, inflaming the already volatile population of gangs and agitators. And she was certain that she had brought the monsters.

Click's steady voice at her ear once again pulled her back from her foray into self-recrimination. "The marsh bridge is just ahead," he said. "We'd better cut across the marsh here. Even if the refugees don't recognize you, they've been stoning Troopers in the city."

Stoning Troopers? Cassidy was incredulous at the thought. As she turned the mare into the reeds she peered ahead into the smoky murk, trying to pick out the long arch of the narrow wooden bridge that ran from the enclave to the city across the marsh. Silhouetted against its skeletal frame she could see the dim outlines of some of the city's refugees, most of them rapidly hustling across. She could also see that many of them were heavily laden with whatever booty they'd been able to steal as they fled the city.

Thieving little pricks! she thought indignantly. As illogical as it may have been, for a moment she actually felt more anger toward the retreating rabble than she did toward their counterparts who had remained in the city to confront the Troopers.

Sensing Cassidy's outrage, Dragonfly snorted loudly. She plowed steadily through the chest-high reeds and sedge grass, her hoofs splashing and sucking in the soft muck of the marsh bottom. The horse's curved ears lay flattened against her poll and Cassidy could feel the powerful muscles between her thighs bunch tensely.

Click also felt the change that had come over the mare as they crossed the slough. Unlike Cassidy, the Tinker seemed to understand it. His arms came up around Cassidy's waist; the warmth of his body was stronger then, pleasant heat like a fire at her back.

"She can hear the Troopers' horses—the fighting," he said tersely. "The closer we come the more strongly it will pull her. Don't let her have her head; once we get into the city you must keep her directed toward the quay."

Cassidy was about to assure Click that she had absolutely no intention of giving the mare her head—as a self-styled warhorse, Dragonfly had gotten her in trouble more than once already—when a sudden gust of wind raced across the marsh, flattening the sedge grass ahead of it like an invisible streamroller. With only a few seconds' warning Cassidy was left clutching desperately with her legs around the horse's barrel and her fingers digging into the long silver mane as the racing wall of air slammed into them. Behind her Click bent forward, burying his face in her shoulder and tightening his arms around her waist to keep his seat on the mare's back. The gray staggered to a halt as the fierce gust whipped up fragments of vegetation and droplets of water, which pelted against them. Then, just as suddenly, the freak wind was gone.

"What the hell . . . ?" Cassidy gasped, straightening again.

For a few seconds Click was utterly silent. Then he rasped softly, "Over the marsh—beyond the bridge—look! They're coming from the river . . ."

Cassidy didn't even have to ask who "they" were, because as she peered forward over the mare's head into the eerily calm murkiness of the darkened slough, she saw something that she had hoped never to see again in that life. Pouring over the estuary, floating above the marsh grass like some kind of grotesque giant parade balloons, glided the greasy black coils of dozens of the huge smokelike monsters.

Click's thighs jerked against Cassidy's, his heels tightening on the gray mare's barrel. "Quickly, Cassidy—we must get out of the marsh!" he hissed. And without any conscious awareness of having signaled the horse, Cassidy discovered that Dragonfly was doing exactly as Click had commanded. The mare shot forward again through the marsh, with such alacrity that had Cassidy not still been clinging to the thick mane, she would surely have been unseated. As it was it took all of Cassidy's skill as a rider to stay astride as the horse plunged through the belly-deep water, tearing through the tangle of cattails and sending up a syrupy splash of water across their already drenched bodies.

Behind her Click clung to Cassidy, melded to her as tightly as she was melded to the steaming back of the gray mare. For a few brief nightmarish moments Cassidy's principal concern was that the horse not founder and fall under their combined weight and go down in the slurping muck of the marsh. But Dragonfly kept churning onward, the air roaring in her dilated nostrils. Fat brown cattails and the coarse heads of sedge grass slapped against Cassidy's wet leather-clad knees as the horse's powerful muscles bunched and surged beneath her.

She did not look back toward the bridge until they had almost reached the far bank of the slough. Then what she saw there made her wish she had kept her eyes on the marsh. The sounds that came from the bridge would doubtless have drawn her attention no matter what she wished. The undulating forms of the huge greasy rolls had dipped down along the length of the bridge, sending scores of screaming refugees plunging over the rails in terror. They landed in the shallow water and muck of the marsh with sickening thumps; but they were perhaps the lucky ones. As Cassidy watched in helpless horror one of the gigantic creatures dropped, almost casually, and partially obscured her view of part of the bridge for a few moments. And when it lifted again, corkscrewing upward with a speed and grace astonishing for something of its size, there was nothing left where it had touched down that was still recognizable as having ever been human.

"Don't look back!" Click commanded roughly at her ear. "Just go—*go!*"

By then Dragonfly had reached the edge of the slough and bounded up out of the reeds, mud flying from her legs and feet as she galloped toward the road that led into the city. With a certain numb sense of fatalism, Cassidy realized that the dreadful air monsters would probably take the same route into the city. But as the mare's hooves clattered onto the roadway and Cassidy looked overhead, she saw to her amazement that the roiling creatures were already gone, seemingly having vanished into the hellish clouds of smoke that hung over the entire area.

"Webb's boat will be moored at the quay off the millers' dock," Click said as they sped past the first buildings. "We'll have to—"

The Tinker's voice broke off simultaneous with the sudden jerk of the big horse's body beneath them. A loud percussive sound rolled across the thick and reeking air. At first Cassidy thought that it had been an explosion of some kind, perhaps something volatile that had been ignited by the fires. But when the noise sounded again a few seconds later she realized that it was too precise and too concentrated a sound for that. It sounded more like gunfire, she thought; or rather like a whole squad of guns firing at once: a twenty-one-gun salute.

As the mare clattered over the pavement her head swung in the direction from which the volleys of gunfire had come. Cassidy's own sense was that the sounds had come from their left, toward the merchants' district in the center of the city, which was also where the fires had been the most intense. She had not intended for that thought to have been transmitted to the horse in terms of a command and yet, abruptly and much to Cassidy's surprise, the mare feinted to the left, dodging an abandoned handcart as she left the main street and swerved down the gloomy canyon of a narrow side street.

Cassidy tried to redirect the horse, but Dragonfly barely hesitated. She was clattering over the paving stones at a full gallop again, heedless of Cassidy's influence. The side street was pinched and cluttered with the dim outlines of a seemingly endless series of unidentifiable objects. Irregular flashes of light from both the lightning and the nearby fires strobed in crazy stabs and shafts, illuminating nothing for more than a few seconds as they sped past. It was as if some drunken giant staggered above the buildings of the city, swinging a guttering lantern in an unsteady hand far over their heads.

"Where the hell are you going?" Click shouted in Cassidy's ear, his hands biting into her waist as the mare slid around a corner and cut a sharp ninety degrees onto another street.

Although she could not see Click's expression, Cassidy could read the tension and urgency in his hoarse tone. Where his body touched hers the muscles were coiled tautly. "I don't know!" she shouted back. "I'm not doing this!"

From over Cassidy's shoulder, Click murmured something that was barely audible to her.

"What?" she demanded, edgy and suddenly very afraid.

Click's tone was an incongruous mixture of bemusement and rue. "The shots we heard—it was the call to arms," he explained in a louder voice. "It seems your mare still fancies herself a warhorse."

Dragonfly made another precipitous turn, dashing into a narrow and trash-strewn alley. Cassidy no longer even had any idea in which direction they were traveling, much less where the hell they were going. She winced as the horse slipped between two wooden rain barrels; the gap was not as wide as the mare was, and the impact sent one of the barrels tumbling to the pavement. Suddenly from the darkness against the wall of the nearest building, two ragged filthy men leapt out into their path, throwing themselves at the gray as she scrambled to regain her balance.

Cassidy felt one of the thug's fingers clutch at the toe of her boot as his body hit the horse's shoulder. Cassidy kicked, but the man clung, nearly pulling her from the mare's back. Click's grip around her waist tightened, hauling her back up as the man was dragged alongside the horse. Then Click's hold on her shifted, and when he leaned over the horse's side Cassidy saw the glint of metal in his hand. Click brought his knife down on the thug's arm; shrieking loudly, the man loosed Cassidy and dropped away. The gray shot ahead again, her speed unimpeded.

Cassidy's heart was thudding as they burst out onto a wider street, a smoky thoroughfare that appeared to lead straight into the maw of hell. Several blocks ahead of them the burning buildings of the merchants' district formed a solid wall of flame. Fiercely commanding, Cassidy was finally able to bring the snorting and unwilling horse down to a trot.

"What were you talking about?" Cassidy panted, still struggling to contain her mare. "What's the call to arms?"

"The volley of shots the Troopers fired," Click said, "it's a signal to the other squads."

Beneath them Dragonfly finally bounced unwillingly to a halt, snorting loudly, her rolling eyes showing their whites in gleaming half-moons. "What does it mean?" Cassidy reiterated, an edge of both fear and irritation in her voice.

"It means their Warden is in danger," Click said grimly. "Considering the situation, it probably means that they are besieged."

At that moment the first fine drizzle began to fall, presaging the coming storm. But the cool moisture was not unwelcome. Even at that distance from the burning buildings Cassidy could feel the unnatural heat, flowing along the street like a draft of smoke. The sound of the fire was a low deep roar, like some disagreeable animal. Dragonfly kept sidestepping impatiently over the rough paving stones, her breath jetting into the mist from her dilated nostrils. Cassidy could not believe the horse's apparent eagerness to race into that inferno. But when Click spoke again she grew even more incredulous.

"Do you know how to reach the millers' dock from here, Cassidy?" the Tinker asked her. "If you cut over to the next side street and—"

"Wait a minute!" Cassidy exclaimed, her head whipping around. "Wait one fucking minute! Where the hell are *you* going?"

Click had already shifted on the prancing mare's back, pulling back far enough from Cassidy that he could have easily turned and dropped down onto the street. But he paused as she twisted around, glaring at him in the dim and intermittent light.

There was a strange expression on that dark lean face, one Cassidy was not sure she had ever seen there before. Click looked indecisive, torn.

"They need help," he said, as if that were not obvious enough.

"Fine! They need help!" Cassidy retorted, each word shooting from her mouth, hard and clipped. She abruptly released the mare then, perversely satisfied to have made Click have to scramble mightily just to keep his seat as the horse bounded forward again. "So we'll help them!" she shouted.

"Cassidy!" Click reproached her, still struggling to regain his balance once more. "You *must* get to that boat—you're needlessly risking your life here!"

"Yeah, unlike you!" Cassidy lashed back, tremendously if illogically pissed off that the Tinker would even think of heading into that fray alone and on foot. Then she leaned over the mare's whipping mane and urged the horse on even faster, heedless of whatever might lay ahead.

"Cassidy, this isn't your concern." Click tried to reason with her, even as he was forced to reach out again for her waist to steady himself as Dragonfly skidded on the wet pavement around an indistinct mound of debris that looked alarmingly like a pile of bodies.

"Yeah, but it's yours, isn't it?" Cassidy shot back at him. She deliberately avoided looking at the lightning-lit glimpses of the evidence of human carnage that they whizzed past. She felt an odd fury she had not even realized she possessed toward that man, fueled by all of her thudding fear and complicated by some inchoate longing. "Why didn't you tell me you were a Horseman?" she added furiously. "Why didn't you tell me you were a goddamned *Trooper?*"

Perhaps mercifully, the questions became rhetorical; Click was given no opportunity to answer them. For at that moment the mare cut another ninety-degree turn onto another cross street and brought them right to the edge of a milling mob. Dozens of men and women, most armed with clubs and cudgels and various sharp-edged metal weapons, blocked the entire width of the thoroughfare. The buildings on either side of them had not yet caught fire, but the leading edge of the blaze that was consuming the whole block was less than a hundred yards down the street, and even at that distance the heat was considerable. The wind was at their backs, bearing the worst of the smoke away, but the persistent cold drizzle was heavy with

the stink of ash. The crowd did not immediately notice Dragonfly and her riders; Cassidy could see that they were intent
upon other quarry.

Against the hellish backdrop of the inferno raging down either side of the street, a smoke-blackened and battered band of
Troopers were being held at bay by the mob. The besieged
Troopers had commandeered and overturned several large
empty freight wagons to form a sort of crude breastwork from
behind which, with the judicious use of their guns, they had
apparently been able to hold back the crowd of angry thugs.
But many of their horses appeared to have been crippled or
driven off, and the voracious progress of the fire advancing up
the block on both sides of the street would soon turn their refuge into a deathtrap.

From that distance and through the murky pall of smoke and
mist, Cassidy could not recognize any of the beleaguered
Troopers, but she did recognize several of the horses that still
milled anxiously behind their little fortress. One was a brown
mare, darkened by sweat and the rain to the color of fresh
black coffee; the other two were chestnuts, one a tall gelding
the color of cedar shavings and the other a blaze-faced mare.
The horses she recognized belonged to Valerie, the Warden,
and Kevin.

Thus far the mob's efforts seemed to have been focused on
taunting the besieged Troopers and trying to lob various mis-
siles at them and their remaining horses. The inexorably advancing fire would soon do the real work for them, either
incinerating the trapped squad or driving them from their sanctuary. Cassidy was still astonished to see such blatant violence
and hatred directed toward the city's symbols of authority and
order. Only the morning before Click had said that not even a
mob would dare to kill a Trooper, but the riot before them suggested that proscription no longer applied. And if the situation
held, the men and women behind the overturned wagons had
very little time left.

Cassidy could hardly hold Dragonfly in; the horse wheeled
in a circle, her hooves slipping on the wet pavement while she
snorted in agitation. They had finally begun to attract the notice of the people at the back of the mob, and Cassidy quickly
realized that they would soon have to take action, whether it
was the direct charge the mare seemed to favor or the timely
retreat that would have been logical and prudent. Outraged at

the scene she saw before her, Cassidy was rapidly becoming a convert to the mare's plan.

Then Cassidy heard Click's voice at her ear. "Do you still have your gun?" he asked her calmly.

As she turned her head, her eyes caught the glint of the strobing firelight on the long barrel of the pistol he held gripped in his own hand. "Yeah—I think so," she said, fumbling behind her, between the two of them, for the weapon still wedged at the small of her back.

Several people on the fringes of the mob had turned around and were advancing upon them, weapons raised. "Troopers!" one woman screamed loudly. "Get 'em!"

"Shoot them," Click said, his voice as soft and dark as soot. "Let your horse go through now, and then shoot as many of them as you can as we pass." Hefting his pistol, he added with an almost clinical detachment, "Go for their heads if you can—shoot them in the face."

Appalled, Cassidy had no chance to protest before the big mare lurched forward again, launching herself into the mob. The horse's momentum and a certain element of surprise carried them a good thirty or forty feet into the milling crowd, with the gray's plunging legs tripping and trampling several people, before anyone could really try to stop them. Then a shirtless hulk of a man with a gleaming bald head and sweat streaming down his maniacal face spun around and swung an iron bar at them. His blow caught Dragonfly flat across her chest, causing her to stagger. As Cassidy shouted angrily, he stumbled backward and prepared to swing again. But before he could bring the bar to bear a second time, Click leaned in over Cassidy's shoulder and coolly and dispassionately fired his gun. The upper portion of the bald man's head disappeared in a crimson spray of blood.

Other members of the mob began to round on them, trying to stop the mare's progress. Cassidy found that her initial paralyzing horror at shooting a fellow human being disappeared amazingly quickly in the face of the simple expedient of self-preservation. She was not a very good shot, especially from the pitching back of the plunging horse; but the mob presented a wealth of easy targets, and the zeal with which they wielded their own weapons made Cassidy completely willing to use her own. Even in the midst of that frightening melee some pragmatic part of her mind understood Click's brutal philosophy of attack. They were badly outnumbered and time was critical;

the more mortal and demoralizing the wounds they inflicted,
the better their chances were of making it through to the besieged Troopers alive. So she shot people in the face.

Someone in the crowd cracked Cassidy across the knee with
a wooden slat; it hurt like hell but would not, she thought with
a surprisingly clinical calm, be a crippling wound. She fired at
the offender without even looking back to see the effect of her
shot. Twice Click was nearly knocked or dragged off the horse
from behind her, but both times he used his pistol like a black-
jack, felling his assailants with economically lethal blows.
Christ! He fights like one of those fucking hoodlums! Cassidy
thought with dismay, before her total attention was drawn back
to the overriding importance of merely remaining whole and
keeping moving ahead. As the mare stumbled over the bodies
of several people on the pavement—thugs or Troopers,
Cassidy did not want to know—Click fired off several shots in
rapid succession, effectively pushing back the ragged edge of
the mob behind them. Then Dragonfly plunged out into the
open no man's land between the rioting crowd and the Troopers' crude wooden escarpment.

That much closer to the burning buildings, the combined
heat and smoke stung in Cassidy's lungs like a deep breath of
fire itself. For a moment she couldn't see a damned thing, although Dragonfly kept pushing forward. The shouting of the
mob behind them rose in a taunting crescendo when sparks
flew into the street as a large section of the wall of one of the
burning structures beyond the Troopers collapsed with a roar.
Glowing fragments of charred wood skittered across the
street's surface, almost like living things seeking escape. But
the gray did not stop until she could scramble to a halt behind
the Troopers' fortification.

"Cassidy! What on earth . . . ?"

One of the blackened and perspiring faces that looked up
at them from the dubious refuge of the blockade of overturned
freight wagons was the only face in that world that was truly
familiar to Cassidy, even if there he was called the Warden of
Horses rather than Andy Greene. And for a few seconds she
just looked down upon him with mingled feelings of relief and
despair. He was alive and whole, but he and his companions
were filthy and exhausted and crouched amid a cruel number
of the bodies of their fellow Troopers.

Through the glistening veil of drizzle, which steamed on the
heated pavement beyond their fortress, Cassidy could see a

contingent of equally filthy and weary faces: Valerie, Kevin, Tag, Rafe, and two more female Troopers. None of them appeared to be seriously injured, although Rafe had a shallow but messy gash on his forehead and blood mingled with the rain that streamed down his dark face. But there were at least another half-dozen bodies in the small refuge behind the wagons; Cassidy did not want to look closely enough to see who they were, because if they were not already dead, they were too seriously injured to move.

A stone whistled by Cassidy's head, startling her into motion again. Click vaulted down off the mare, dragging her by the arm after him. By the time her soggy boots hit the slippery pavement, Cassidy understood the reason for his urgency. Behind them the mob was regrouping, angrier than ever, and the two of them had been like sitting ducks up on the horse's back. Dragonfly squealed indignantly, more peeved than hurt as a fist-size rock lobbed from the crowd struck her on the rump. Then the horse skittered past them, behind the barrier of the wagons and toward the remaining Troopers' horses.

"Cassidy, what are you doing here?" the Warden said as she and Click dropped down beside him. "I told you to stay at the house—I left you *guards,* for the safety of your life!"

The young man's anger at her defection from his house struck Cassidy as particularly ironic, considering the deadly situation in which he and his own Troopers found themselves. But before she could make any comment to that effect, Click said gravely, "Your house has probably already been overrun, Warden. The roads leaving the city are filled with gangs of looters."

Before Cassidy could absorb the full impact of what Click's statement implied, the soot-smeared woman who was crouched at the Warden's side glared up at Click with a familiar glint in her eyes. "What are *you* doing here, Tinker?" Valerie demanded. Without missing a beat—indeed, seemingly without even so much as glancing sideways to aim her pistol—the captain deftly fired at a shouting woman from the mob who had just commenced a reckless dash toward their barricade. "We have more than enough riffraff in this city tonight as it is!" she concluded archly.

If not for the dire urgency of their predicament, Cassidy would have found the captain's taut indignation almost amusing. But there was no time for her to indulge in speculation then about either Click's or the captain's past, although the Tinker took a brief moment to offer his simple explanation.

"You fired the call to arms," he said, unruffled, his tone barely a notch above sarcasm in its civility. His head tipped slightly toward where the gray mare stood, pawing anxiously and rolling her eyes at the encroaching fire. "And like a good soldier, the horse answered your call."

"Enough!" the Warden said brusquely, cutting off the little verbal duel. "What's done is done." One of his slender hands, darkened with soot and blood, reached out and grasped the filthy sleeve over Cassidy's forearm. His mouth quirked briefly, reminding Cassidy that she still wore the stolen Trooper's leathers. "You came from the west then; what did you see of—"

A sudden communal outcry from the milling mob effectively interrupted his question. For a moment Cassidy thought that another section of one of the burning buildings was falling, for she felt an abrupt draft of heated air wash over their precarious refuge in the center of the street. But the moment she looked up, away from the Warden, she realized what the call of alarm had been about. Then her heart began to hammer mercilessly in her chest, and all previous concerns about their safety there seemed pitifully insignificant.

Racing up the glistening wet thoroughfare from behind the surging mob, coming directly toward them, roiled an ominous contingent of the greasy black air monsters. Cassidy couldn't even begin to estimate their numbers—how could she even tell where one creature left off and another one began, given the coiling sinuous nature of the things?—but the curling bulk of their huge gaseous bodies literally filled the sky above the street, effectively blocking the entire stormy night sky.

Oh my God! Cassidy thought, even as the mob's cries turned to screams of fear. The unruly gang began to scatter, pushing and shoving into each other and knocking others down without regard in their terrified haste to flee. But there was no route by which for them to escape; the burning buildings with which they'd cornered the Warden and his Troopers blocked one end of the street, and the undulating loops of the smokelike creatures filled the other end. Cassidy could only watch in mute horror as the bloated shapes of the floating monsters dropped down into the panicked mob, much as they had on the refugees on the marsh bridge.

Several of the creatures—or was it just one long coiling loop of a single creature?—covered the pavement not fifty feet from where the overturned freight wagons lay. A half-dozen or so of the fleeing crowd had been running toward the makeshift barrier, as if seeking refuge there; swiftly but almost leisurely a thick black coil of the monster's massive body flicked out and engulfed the thugs. When the coil retreated a moment later, the stretch of damp pavement was littered with unidentifiable scraps of human flesh and clothing.

The whole writhing opaque mass of greasy tubular forms began to lift then, slowly separating and sorting themselves out into distinct long coiling shapes again. On the street below the creatures, where only seconds earlier dozens of men and women of the city had fomented civil rebellion, there remained nothing more than a macerated sprawl of mutilated bodies, as homogeneous as some gruesome sort of sausage.

The fires at their back had steadily crept closer; even with the cold light rain Cassidy found the growing heat nearly intolerable. There was no way in which they could escape the hideous creatures that roiled directly over them. *Another fucking lousy way to die* ... Cassidy thought with a final irony as she tore her smarting eyes away from the lazy mesmerizing roll of the air monsters, seeking to look just one last time into the sardonic umber eyes of the man who had brought her that far. Automatically she found herself reaching out, unmindful of the Warden's fingers still gripping her forearm, to take Click's hand.

And in that moment the great rolling mass of creatures suddenly lifted, and, like the rushing gout of thick black smoke that belched from an oil fire, they whirled upward into the wet and murky sky. Cassidy watched in stunned amazement as, rising with a rapidity incredible for anything of their size and dimension, the unmeasurable expanse of deadly bowel-shaped things simply disappeared into the acrid pall of smoke and rain that hung over the city's streets. Within seconds they all were gone, indistinguishable from the thick smoke and the lightning and the boiling blackness of the storm's clouds.

A loud drum of thunder boomed directly overhead, startling Cassidy into beginning to breathe again. In the kinetic flash of lightning that followed, she saw the horses suddenly leap forward, bolting into the grisly breach created by the monsters of the air where once the mob had ruled. The animals scrambled without regard through the slippery detritus of their former tormenters, not pausing until they had reached the relative comfort on the other side of the carnage, where the air was still cool enough to breathe and the surrounding buildings had not yet caught fire. Then without warning Cassidy suddenly found herself following the horses, being unceremoniously dragged along by her arms between the Warden and Click. She was glad that it scarcely felt as if her boots touched the pavement.

When they finally slid to a halt, a good long block up the smoky street, Cassidy was panting and her heart was pounding against her ribs. As he released her hand Click gave her a quick but incisive appraisal. The best she could give him in return was a shaky nod.

The Warden was looking up into the stinging, weeping sky, turning a complete 360 degrees in frank wonder. "Incredible," he murmured as the soft rain pelted his upturned face. "What made them pass over us, do you think?" He suddenly looked directly at Cassidy. "The fires?"

"I don't know," she replied, suppressing a shudder. But that was not the absolute truth. She seriously doubted that the hideous creatures had any fear of fire. And she could not help but recall her first experience with the flying monsters that night of another fire along the river-bottom pasture outside Double Creek, when she had been certain she had felt them—or some part of them—actually pass *through* her without harming her.

Seemingly untroubled by such esoteric considerations, Valerie and her fellow Troopers were moving among the horses, briskly and efficiently checking them for injuries. "Trey's mare is too lame to ride," the captain reported promptly, "but the rest all seem sound enough to travel."

From the fleeting involuntary grimace that crossed the Warden's weary face, Cassidy surmised that Trey was one of those Troopers they had left behind, one of those Troopers who would no longer be needing his horse anyway. "We'll have to leave her," he said flatly. "If she's able to travel she'll find her way back to the garrison on her own."

Click's hand closed over Cassidy's arm. "We'll only be needing the horse we rode in on," he said. "Come on, Cassidy; with the speed at which these fires are spreading, we don't have much time."

The Warden's hand darted out, his fingers grasping the wet leather sleeve over Cassidy's other arm. "Where do you think you're taking her, Tinker?" he demanded.

Irritated by being argued over like some bone between two dogs, Cassidy was about to answer him herself when Click replied, "She has a boat waiting for her at the quay beyond the millers' dock and a pilot to see her safely out of this city."

The Warden seemed more honestly surprised than angry. "You're going south?" he asked her. "Cassidy, I thought we had an agreement?" His fingers tightened earnestly on her arm. "If you really want to go south I'll take you there myself—I swear it! But this is hardly the time to—"

Cassidy couldn't keep from laughing. She didn't mean any disrespect to the young man, but she couldn't help herself, and the sound was harsh and almost hysterical even to her own ears. "Can you honestly think of a *better* time?" she demanded, trying to wave inclusively at the multiple scenes of disaster around them. Since Click still held one of her arms and the Warden the other, the gesture was comically truncated, which in itself was nearly enough to start Cassidy laughing aloud again. "If the fires or the monsters don't kill me here, the damned mobs and gangs will lynch me!"

The Warden was doggedly shaking his head, about to protest, when a calmly pragmatic voice intervened. "No, she's right," Valerie said, taking the few strides over to them from where she had been standing beside the horses. "This is the time to leave the city, all right," she told the Warden. "For you as well as for her."

Finally dropping Cassidy's arm, the Warden abruptly turned on his captain. "Leave the city—when all is chaos?" he asked her incredulously. "Val, I have a responsibility, not only to my Troopers but also to—"

Relentlessly the curly-haired woman cut him off again. "If you stay you might very well be killed by one of those 'responsibilities,' " she said with utter calm. "You're of no use to your Troopers or this city if you're dead. Fall back—go south until all of this madness has burned itself out." She took another step closer to him, nearly tall enough to look him directly in the eye, and unflinchingly logical. "The city has seen rioting before," she reminded him, "and parts of it have burned to the ground. You can't change that by being here, and there's no point in dying over a few merchants' shops."

In the moment of surprised silence that followed the captain's blunt assessment, Cassidy was the first to speak. "Come south with us now," she said, quietly insistent. "If you care so much about my safety, then at least think as much of your own."

Valerie set her hands at her hips, her dark eyes completely grave. "He has me to see to his safety," she said flatly.

But the Warden shook his wet tousled head. "No, Val, I want you to ride back to the garrison. You must—"

"Send Tag and the others back," Valerie interrupted him implacably. "I travel with you."

The Warden's brows climbed, but to Cassidy's ear the sternness in his voice did not ring completely true. "You are my captain," he began, looking directly at Valerie.

"Yes, you made me your captain," she replied, her voice low and almost harsh. "Your life is my responsibility."

Cassidy had forgotten that Click still held her by her other arm until his hand then suddenly tightened its grip. "Perhaps you two would like to argue over this a little longer?" he said, tilting his head back toward the inferno of blazing buildings that they had barely left behind them. "I think we might have at least another two minutes before the fires reach us here . . . unless of course another mob of thugs finds us before then."

Click's point well taken, the Warden shook his head with rueful self-deprecation. "Once more you are correct, Tinker," he admitted. "All right then; let me discharge what's left of my squad and give them their duties. Then Valerie and I would be grateful to go with you to this boat."

As the Warden turned away from them and started toward the ragged remains of his squad of Troopers, the storm finally broke and the rain began to pour down in a cold torrent. Cassidy tugged Click around, pulling him across the slippery pavement and away from the disapproval of Valerie's dark eyes. After everything that had already happened that night she did not even bother to be any more circumspect, either in her words or in the way she locked her hands around his muscular upper arms and looked up directly into those ironic umber eyes.

"We have to go back for the others," she whispered urgently. "I'm not going to that boat—not without Rowena and Allen and Becky!"

To his credit, Click didn't dispute her insistence, he merely matter-of-factly pointed out the truth. "They could be anywhere between here and the garrison, Cassidy, or if the Troopers caught them, they may very well never even have left the compound."

But Cassidy's fingers only tightened, giving the Tinker's arms an exasperated little shake. "Yeah? Well, no matter where they are, they could be stuck fighting off the same kind of crazies who nearly killed us before those creatures made monster hash out of them! I'm *not* leaving them behind!"

Click paused before he responded, meeting her sharply expectant stare with unflinching calm. In that brief moment Cassidy was bemused to note that the pounding rain was collecting in the wet tangle of his dark hair and dripping like beads of sweat from the silvered tips of his mustache. And to her considerable chagrin she suddenly realized just how completely she had come to count on the Tinker leader not to let her down, no matter what she asked of him.

"You must go to that boat—immediately," Click said. "It's far too dangerous for you to try to go back for them." But before Cassidy could protest he had rotated his elbows, neatly reversing their positions. "I'll go back," he concluded.

Cassidy blinked, her eyes unexpectedly filling. *It's the rain,* she told herself; *just the goddamned rain.* "But I—I want—" she tried to begin.

But before she could get any more words out, Click had released one of her arms and was pulling her by the other, sweeping her along over the drenched pavement so swiftly that she hardly felt her boot soles touch the pavement. Then suddenly they were beside the gray mare, her big steaming body smelling of damp hair and sweat and burned wood, a low nicker rumbling from the horse's throat as she lowered her mud-streaked face to inspect Cassidy's tunic.

"I'll go back for them," Click repeated, his voice gruff and yet at the same time oddly soft, as if he knew that she needed his comfort as badly then as she needed his decisive declaration. He tugged her closer, putting the bulk of the horse's body between them and the Troopers who still stood huddled with their Warden on the rain-washed street. "Go to the boat, Cassidy; there's nothing more you can do now."

The rain was falling in earnest, pummeling down in chilling streams from the smoky sky. Blinking furiously, Cassidy shook her head even as she reluctantly acquiesced. "We'll wait for you at the dock," she said doggedly. "We'll keep the—"

"No!" The pads of Click's fingertips pressed against her lips, sealing them. He had moved so closely against her that when Cassidy looked up it was directly into those dark gleaming eyes, and the scent of him—wet hair and perspiration and woodsmoke, like the mare—filled her nostrils. "No, don't wait," he commanded. "Tell Webb to cast off at once. He knows where to take you."

But Cassidy tossed her head, obstinately shaking free of his fingers. "I won't go without them!" she insisted. "And what about my horse? If you take my horse she—"

That time Click did not need to use his hand to silence her; the look on his face alone did that. "You can't take the mare on the boat, Cassidy," he pointed out gently. Feeling her begin to try to pull back away from him, resisting both his logic and his hold upon her, Click simply closed his arms around Cassidy, drawing her body against his. With an inarticulate little groan of despair, she buried her face against the wet leather of his conchaed vest.

I can't leave her! Cassidy thought fiercely. *She's the only thing I have—the only real thing . . .*

"I'll bring her to you, Cassidy," Click was whispering thickly over the dripping crown of her head. "I'll bring them all to you—I swear it upon my blood." His fingers slipped down, deftly but insistently hooking under her chin, lifting her face to his again. "But you must go now—you must protect yourself." The whisper had become a murmur, persuasive and utterly true. "Much as I would will it, that's the one thing I cannot do by trying to keep you here with me."

And then before Cassidy could utter a sound, his mouth was covering hers. At first touch the wet skin of his lips felt cold from the rain; but that sensation lasted for only an instant. Then the soft moist flesh burned with the kind of heat that Cassidy had long thought had never been ignited in that strange world; and when his tongue probed urgently along the rim of her teeth she found herself automatically offering it entrance, shuddering as it found its mate in her own mouth.

Nothing in that crazy world—not even the monsters—could have shocked or amazed her more. And for a few delicious seconds, her cold and filthy body pressed against his in the chill drenching rain, Cassidy felt as if she had somehow managed to slip across some plane of existence and straddle both worlds, her own and that bizarre one, as the incendiary warmth of Click's avid mouth kindled through her very bones.

Then reluctantly, almost roughly, Click pulled back. Caught off balance, Cassidy had to reach for his arm again to keep from stumbling sideways on the wet pavement. She gaped up at him, for a few seconds struck totally speechless. And when she could finally speak, the first words she was able to blurt out seemed hopelessly inane.

"You—you *remember sex!*" she accused him. Then, with equal inanity, she added in indignation, "You saw me *naked!*"

That familiar ageless spark struck in Click's dark eyes. The tips of his dripping mustache lifted quirkily. "As you saw me," he reminded her wryly. "I would say that makes us even."

Then so swiftly and gracefully that he seemed almost a blur, Click vaulted up onto Dragonfly's back. Snorting, the big horse shifted impatiently, eager to be away. Click leaned down over the gray's steaming shoulder and said intently, "Remember— you must cast off at once. I swear that I'll bring them all to you." Then he wheeled the mare around and she sprang off, her hooves clattering loudly over the gleaming pavement.

Still astonished, Cassidy might have stood there for a long moment just watching Dragonfly and her dark rider speed away up the empty city street had not her other companions reacted to the Tinker's abrupt departure on Cassidy's mare.

"Where the hell does he think he's going?" Valerie demanded, striding across the water-sheened paving stones to where Cassidy stood silently in the downpour. The captain looked irritably in the direction in which Click had gone.

The Warden came up alongside Valerie. "Cassidy?" he inquired, his perplexity more gently cloaked than that of his captain.

Cassidy glanced back toward the remaining Troopers, who had already mounted up on their drenched horses. She answered the question, but she was not looking at the Warden or Valerie when she spoke. "He's going back for Rowena and Allen and Becky," she said. There was a pause, as if she might have been about to explain further, but that did not happen. Instead Cassidy suddenly shook back her soaking hair, sending a dirty spray of water flying out into the rainy air. "Come on," she said with an abrupt and impatient air, "we've got to get down to the millers' dock."

The Warden studied her for a moment longer, as if trying to satisfy himself of something. Cassidy did not think that he was able to, but then he turned away anyway and gave his Troopers their final instructions.

"Raphael," the Warden said, making an economic gesture, "follow the Tinker. Give him whatever protection and assistance he requires."

For just an instant Cassidy thought that Rafe was going to

object, but in the end the black youth just nodded obediently and spun his horse around as the Warden dispatched the rest of the Troopers.

"Tag, I want you, Annie, Kim, and Kevin to return to the garrison. Report to Justin what has happened here tonight."

"No!" Kevin cried, his chestnut mare skittering nervously beneath him at the vehement retort. "I'm going with you!"

Even given the gravity of their situation, Cassidy found herself mildly amused by just how independent the Warden's troops were turning out to be. She'd always thought that Rafe was more troublesome than Kevin, but the odd-eyed boy looked absolutely adamant. But more to Cassidy's surprise was the Warden's response to Kevin's refusal. Even though the Finder was not a Trooper, she had expected the Warden to exert his authority and command the boy to obey. Instead the Warden hesitated a moment, his expression ambivalent, seemingly both torn and touched by Kevin's loyalty.

"Kevin," he said quietly, his wet and filthy face upturned toward the long-haired boy, "please go with Tag—I want to know you're safe."

But Kevin obstinately shook his head, as if mimicking the motion of his impatient mare. "No, I'm coming with you."

The Warden exhaled softly. "It seems that rebellion is in the very air of this city tonight," he said ruefully, making a little beckoning gesture of acquiescence to Kevin.

As Tag and the two women Troopers turned and galloped off, the Warden and Valerie quickly mounted up on their own horses. Cassidy realized that she was still standing there somewhat stupidly in the middle of the smoky street in the pouring rain. Click and her mare were gone, and she had no idea what might lie ahead.

Of that nighttime ride through the streets of the burning city in the copious rain, Cassidy would later have very little clear memory. She vaguely remembered selecting one of the remaining Troopers' horses, a leggy tobiano gelding who reminded her reassuringly of the big piebald horse that Allen had ridden back in Double Creek, and then following the Warden, Valerie, and Kevin as they rode away from the scene of their besiegement and the monsters' carnage. But she had no idea what route they took, or even in which direction they were traveling most of the time. All she was consistently aware of was the cold wash of the rain, the thunder and lightning, and the strange sense of emptiness she felt at being separated from Dragonfly, an emptiness that even the warm bulk of the pinto's big body between her legs could not help alleviate.

Because of the extent of the fires' spread in the warehouse district, she was certain they had not been able to take the shortest route to the docks; that may have at least partially explained her feeling that the stormy ride seemed almost endless. Chilled and exhausted, Cassidy used the dimmest, most elemental sort of Horsemanship to keep herself astride the gelding as they dodged and weaved through the unfamiliar streets. Several times they were accosted by drenched and ragged pedestrians, lurching out from the storefronts and alleys. Most of the time they could just gallop on past, but once Valerie, cursing, had to fire her pistol several times to discourage a confrontation.

Even real physical sensations seemed to elude Cassidy. Although she was so wet and cold that her teeth sometimes chattered uncontrollably, she was not aware of feeling any particular discomfort. Fear and desperation had made the first part of that night's ordeal real to her; numbed then by what had followed, she no longer vibrated to adrenaline's persuasive pluckings along her nerves. She could not even allow herself to think about what had happened with Click back there in that rain-soaked street, for to remember what the Tinker had done was to negate everything she thought she knew about the world in which she still was trapped. And if she had to give up everything she thought she knew, she would never have been able to go on.

Lightning continued shooting through the heavy-bellied clouds, followed almost immediately by the coarse growl of thunder. The drenching downpour that cascaded endlessly from the turbulent sky seemed to carry with it the reek of smoke, turning the black efflux of the warehouse fires into a tangible greasy shower. The fringed leather clothing that Cassidy had stolen from the female Trooper clung to her skin like the clammy raw rabbit skins that she and Rowena had once tried to tan out in the woods, a virtual lifetime ago. But even the effect of the storm presented only a peripheral interest to Cassidy. All she could really think of then was reaching the safety of the boat and fleeing the chaos of the Iron City. To fail in that would have been to invalidate all of the sacrifices made just to bring her to that point.

Riding the pinto gelding was nothing like riding Dragonfly;

Cassidy kept forgetting that the horse was not bonded to her and that he required a certain amount of her conscious control to do anything more than just blindly follow his stablemates. He was a well-trained horse and nimble on his feet despite his growing fatigue. And for the most part just allowing him to follow the other horses was enough, for Cassidy herself was capable of little better. It wasn't until they'd actually reached the vast plank roadway that bridged the area between the warehouses and the harbor that Cassidy even recognized where they were. Forced to become more cognizant of her surroundings, she tried to orient herself on the wharf.

She had not been down to that part of the city since the night they'd first arrived and had docked their rafts amid the maze of piers. In the cloaking murk of the smoke and rain the harbor's rows of oil lamps did little to illuminate the wet and gleaming network of wooden jetties that jutted out over the black water. Luckily the fires had not spread down that far yet, although the smoke and the sounds of random fighting carried in the damp air. Most of the long quays looked deserted, the night's tumultuous events apparently dissuading any wharfmen or seamen who had not already been put off by the restrictions of the Warden's edict concerning unnecessary river traffic.

Riding in the lead, the Warden and Valerie were forced to slow their pace as the horses clopped out onto the wide wooden plankway. The surface of the worn timbers was slippery from the greasy rain and their mounts were nearing exhaustion. Cassidy leaned forward, urging her gelding up alongside Kevin's chestnut mare. The odd-eyed young man looked both edgy and weary, and Cassidy inadvertently startled him when she spoke.

"Do you know how much farther it is, Kevin?" she asked, practically having to shout because of the noise of the wind and thunder even though they were only a few feet apart.

Kevin shook his head, water flying from his long unfettered hair. "At least it's quiet down here," he said, obviously meaning "quiet" in a relative sense.

Cassidy blinked through the steady rain, trying to pick out the outline of the tall rectangular granaries that would identify the millers' area of the docks. Even without the fires or the rioters, the fury of the storm seemed especially intense down there by the river. Would the seaman, Webb, have waited for them no matter what? What if he had decided that the tides were rising too fast, or the sea was becoming too—?

Ahead of her and Kevin, both Valerie and the Warden halted their horses so abruptly that Cassidy's and Kevin's mounts nearly bumped into them. Shivering in the cold downpour, Cassidy began to stammer out, "W-what the hell are we . . . ?" But she broke off even without having been interrupted, for then she could see for herself the reason they had all come to such a sudden stop.

Perhaps a hundred feet ahead of them—which was effectively at the periphery of their vision, given the rain and smoke and poor lighting—the huge wooden planks of the wharf's main throughway were shuddering like logs rolling down the rapids in a river. Wood creaked and then shrieked, a strained and tearing sound, as the broad pathway began to undulate, rising and falling as if to the movements of some gigantic subterranean serpent. The undulations were progressive and they were traveling toward them, almost leisurely at first and then more rapidly, like the approach of—

Something powerful and sinuous and monstrous, something that could move through the dark water which lapped beneath the wharf's planks like a great black snake, something that could prowl silently through a distant river or snap the rudder assembly off a raft or rise beneath a swimmer's legs like a sleek and gleaming lover.

Valerie shouted something—curse or command, Cassidy was never quite sure—but by then there really was no choice left as to what they must do. In a few seconds the buckling eruption of the massive planking would reach the place where their horses stood. Wheeling the pinto around, Cassidy saw to her dismay that the same groaning upheaval of the wharf was fast approaching them from behind, as well. To their left was the solid wall of the front of a vast and darkened warehouse. All four horses cut sharply right, down the long wooden path of one of the harbor's numberless piers.

As her gelding skidded and scrabbled along the narrow plank platform, Cassidy realized that they were about to be trapped at the end of the pier, a prospect only minimally less daunting than that of having been summarily crushed back on the main wharf. Of all of her previous encounters with the monsters, the water creatures had always seemed the least threatening to her, but Cassidy was willing to change her opinion of them as she found herself being driven farther out over the harbor's foul black water.

The city harbor was set deeply enough into the mouth of the Long River that it was protected from the worst of the Gray Sea's storms. But the rain-pocked surface of the water seemed unusually turbulent along the docks that night, swollen with the runoff from the thunderstorm and whipped by its driving winds. As the four horses slid to a forced halt at the end of the wooden quay, Cassidy could clearly hear the slap and sucking of the water along the pilings, even above the din of the thunder and the eerie screeching of the ruptured planking. Whatever had driven them from the main wharf had pursued them down the pier, systematically buckling the surface of the quay, its thick planks snapping like matchsticks as the decking beneath them heaved up.

Out of the frying pan, into the fucking fire, Cassidy thought fatalistically as she felt the gelding's muscles bunching beneath her thighs as he gathered himself for the necessary leap off the end of the pier. Again it was not as if they had any real choice. But this time Cassidy was certain that whatever it was Valerie had shouted, it had been a curse. Flashing back to Butch and Sundance, she added one of her own as they went over the edge.

The pinto's weight and momentum carried them both nearly beneath the surface of the water before the horse came bobbing back up, swimming strongly. Cassidy desperately grasped his long bicolored mane as the buoyant drag of the water threatened to float her off from his back. To her immediate left, Kevin floated behind his mare, towing himself by her tail. Ahead of them the twin dark outlines of the heads and necks of the Warden's gelding and Valerie's mare rose like the prows of some odd kind of ship, followed by the heads and shoulders of their half-submerged riders. The river water felt amazingly warm compared to the chill rain, and for a few seconds Cassidy was actually more comfortable than she had been all night. But her feeling of well-being was short-lived. They were supposed to be at the millers' dock, where a seaman named Webb waited for them with a boat; instead they were down in unfamiliar waters, pursued by water monsters.

When she first saw the long, huge, dark shape rise up out of the water not a horse's length from her side, Cassidy supposed that she should have been terrified. God knows the pinto gelding was; his eyes rolling wildly, he began to thrash so desperately and inefficiently through the water that he nearly managed to overcome his body's natural buoyancy and began to sink. Maybe Cassidy was just too tired or too jaded by everything else that had already happened that night. Maybe she was driven beyond the capacity for fear. Or maybe—just maybe—she had just come to the conclusion that there were some things no longer worth fearing.

Whatever the reason, Cassidy did not panic as the big bullet-shaped head rose slowly and gracefully from the dark oily surface of the river. It was easily as long as the horse's body, with tiny nostrils like two fluttering pockmarks, a massive chitinous jaw, and two flat wide-set eyes that glittered like diamonds against the sandpaper surface of its dripping skin. The water churned around Cassidy's chest as all of the horses frantically thrashed to escape the incredible apparition that glided alongside them. But Cassidy only stared out across the few yards separating her from the creature, steadily and appraisingly, as if challenging it to end her life.

The two things that happened next occurred so simultaneously that a logical person might be forgiven for assuming they had a causal relationship. Several shots rang out over the water, high above them, loud and booming percussions unlike the fire of the small pistols that the Troopers carried. Even as her head snapped in the direction of that sound, from the corner of her eye Cassidy could see that the silently slithering water creature had instantly vanished. Then she could pick out the fitful wash of lantern light wavering over the heaving surface of the water and she heard someone shouting her name.

The guttering light came from several oil lanterns that were strung along the rigging of the boat approaching them across the dark and churning water. The shout had come from the man who was braced at the vessel's stern, fighting to hold the boom of its billowing sail against the slashing pressure of the driving rain. Although the boat was a good twenty-five feet in length and rigged with double sails, compared to the enormity of the water monster Cassidy's first impression was that it wasn't much of a boat. But she didn't allow that impression to lessen her enthusiasm for its propitious arrival.

Lantern light played over them, glinting off the frightened horses' eyes and sparkling in their exhausted riders' soaking hair. The seaman at the tiller banked the boat abruptly, slowing its rapid glide. His clothing, the simple off-white cotton garb of his profession, was plastered to his tall but muscular form by the wind and rain, and as he peered down over the edge of the vessel's railing Cassidy could see the flash of his white teeth against the darkened oval of his streaming face.

"The mooring fobs!" he shouted down at them. "Let go of the damned horses and grab the mooring fobs!"

Kevin was closest to the rocking boat. He released his mare's tail and reached for one of the short thick fobs of neatly shanked rope that hung at regular intervals along the boat's hull. Because of his exhaustion and the boat's pitching, it took him several tries to get one heel hooked up over the railing; but once he did he was able to lever his body up out of the water and onto the plunging deck. He lay there for a few seconds catching his breath, then he leaned over the side of the boat and reached for the Warden's hand.

Cassidy was the last one to be hauled aboard the boat. Her pinto gelding was still so spooky that she finally had to just abandon any attempt to urge him to swim closer to the rocking vessel. Fearlessly she slipped free of the horse's back and swam over to the side on her own, where Kevin and Valerie pulled her aboard.

"Hell of a storm," the man at the tiller said. "Hell of a night!" He showed his teeth again in an expression that was a raffish near-smirk. He had a wet woolen cap pulled down over one eyebrow at a rakish angle. If he was worried about the greasy turbulence of the river's surface or the way the gusting sheets of rain fiercely buffeted his sails, there was no indication of any concern in his demeanor then. Cassidy had already begun to wonder just what sort of seaman Click had procured for them.

"I take it you are Webb," the Warden said, still on his hands and knees on the slippery pitching deck. "We expected you to be moored at the millers' dock."

"Well, I expected to be moored there myself," Webb replied, scarcely even glancing aloft at the billowing canvas as he deftly let the boom come around. He ducked at exactly the correct moment to avoid it. "But then I expected the millers' dock to still be there, too. Those idiots are blowing up the entire wharf," he added, entirely without rancor, flashing another roguish grin. "Besides, I guess if I'd been there, I wouldn't be here now where you are, would I?"

Cassidy groped along the side of the boat's rail until she found a good handhold. Then she hauled herself shakily to her feet, swaying as the wind-driven rain pummeled her body.

"How did you know where to find us?" she asked the seaman, both surprised and grateful that he had.

The boat fought the change in direction then, coming around with all the wallowing petulence of a stubborn sow. But Webb seemed rooted to his tiller, his agile and experienced hands playing out the boom as the sail ballooned out afresh in its new position. "The horses," he said after a moment. "I heard them squawking."

To Cassidy's tremendous relief no one else offered the seaman any explanation for what had set the horses to "squawking." Let him think that they had just been upset by the wharf "blowing up" and by their unwanted dip in the stormy river.

"So I fired off a few shots from the cannon," Webb continued mildly, "so you'd know where I was."

Kevin was still obviously distressed by the thought of the animals that they had left behind in the water. He was crouched on the rain-lashed deck at the Warden's side, but Cassidy could see the dismay in those odd-colored eyes. "What about our horses?" he asked anxiously. "What'll happen to them now?"

Webb hooted, his enthusiastic laugh surprisingly raucous. "Why, they'll swim back to the bank, boy—they've got a hell of a lot more sense than we do!"

Throwing the amused seaman a withering look, Valerie leaned down slightly from her position braced against one of the rail's posts. "They'll just go back to the garrison, Kevin," she said. "They'll be safe there."

The Warden nodded reassuringly at Kevin. "They know where to go, Kevin. And Webb is undoubtedly right about one thing: They'll be far safer now that they've parted company with us."

Kevin looked only partially convinced. Perhaps, Cassidy thought, he was remembering some of the same things that she was at the moment: the burning city, the rioting mobs, the ruptured wharf, and the sleek giants that had met them in the river. And where was her own mare by then? she wondered. What would become of her, and Rowena and Allen and Becky . . . and Click?

Shivering violently, Cassidy fought to keep her footing as the boat's deck shuddered beneath her. The vessel had come about nearly a full 180 degrees by then, with the wind-driven deluge broadsiding her and making the hull dip and lurch.

"Hell of a night," Webb remarked again, although he still

did not sound particularly worried. If anything, to Cassidy's amazement she thought the tall seaman sounded almost happy with the adverse conditions. The dark wool cap on his head was shapeless from the rain, slapped down over his forehead like a bad toupee; and what little of his own hair was visible beneath it lay plastered against his cheeks and neck. He threw his quartet of unsteady passengers a cursory assessment and then announced in a bemused tone, "Didn't expect to be hauling the Warden about, either . . . wait until I see that son of a bitch Click again! He owes me a hell of a lot more than we agreed on for this!" Then he laughed again, loudly and exuberantly, his callused hands expertly playing out the tiller.

If you ever see that son of a bitch again, Cassidy thought morbidly. *If any of us ever do.*

Exactly as if he'd plucked the thought from her head, Webb gave an amused little grunt and added, "If I ever live to dock this boat again, that is—and if there's even a damned dock left to moor her at!"

Caught on that gloomy probability, Cassidy was slightly startled when she felt a wet but warm hand close over hers, the slender fingers locking with her own. She looked down to see the Warden kneeling at her side, bracing himself on the rolling deck, his other hand clutching one of Kevin's.

"Well, Cassidy," he said, "it looks like for better or worse we'll be going south. Perhaps that's what was meant to happen."

Glancing over to where Valerie still stood at the rail, stubbornly upright despite the boat's bucking motion, Cassidy could see the Iron City receding behind the captain's silhouette. Through the sluicing veil of pouring rain the fiery glow of the burning buildings seemed oddly muted, even harmless, like the glimpse of a crackling fireplace seen through a wet windowpane on a stormy night. Of the monsters and their dreadful carnage, from that distance nothing could be seen. And every drenching gust of wind that billowed out the boat's slapping canvas carried them farther out, into the Gray Sea and away from the disasters that they were leaving behind.

Somewhere out there Cassidy was leaving nearly everything in that world that had linked her to her own time. And then beside her, his fingers laced through hers, was the one person she was convinced could bridge the inestimable gap between that world and the one from which she'd come. For she had been right all along, just not in the way which she had first expected. The Warden of Horses was indeed the answer to it all.

A renegade blast of wind sent rain rattling against the walls of the boat's tiny cabin, startling Cassidy. But then she realized that Webb had actually started to hum, his tanned hands dancing over the tiller as he fecklessly turned his square-jawed face into the wind.

Cassidy probably would have despaired at what awaited them; but Cathy Delaney could not afford to.

She gently squeezed the Warden's fingers. "With all of the troubles you've had lately, you needed to get away for a while anyway, right?" she said. "And I hear the south is lovely this time of the year."

The Slow World
will conclude in
Book Three
The Alchemist of Time
from
Del Rey Books

Also by
KAREN RIPLEY
THE PERSISTENCE OF MEMORY

Cassidy's earliest recollection was of meeting the people who called her a Horseman, for her ability to communicate almost telepathically with her gray mare. But they could tell her nothing about her missing memory, nor did they care. Yet when the sight of common, everyday objects began to trigger a flood of partial memory, Cassidy knew that something was dreadfully wrong. Worse yet, the more she remembered, the more she was certain she had come from a different world—a realization that threatened not only her sanity, but her very life.

Book One of *The Slow World*

Published by Del Rey Books.
Available in your local bookstore.

Or call toll free 1-800-733-3000 to order by phone and use your major credit card. Or use this coupon to order by mail.

__THE PERSISTENCE OF MEMORY   345-38120-3 $4.99

Name _____

Address_____

City_____ State_____ Zip _____

Please send me the DEL REY I have checked above.

I am enclosing	$_____
plus	
Postage & handling*	$_____
Sales tax (where applicable)	$_____
Total amount enclosed	$_____

*Add $2 for the first book and 50¢ for each additional book.

Send check or money order (no cash or CODs) to:
Del Rey Mail Sales, 400 Hahn Road, Westminster, MD 21157.

Prices and numbers subject to change without notice.
Valid in the U.S. only.
All orders subject to availability.   RIPLEY